PERMUTED PRESS

NEEDS **YOU** TO HELP

SPREAD THE INFECTION

FOLLOW US!

 FACEBOOK.COM/PERMUTEDPRESS

 TWITTER.COM/PERMUTEDPRESS

REVIEW US!

WHEREVER YOU BUY OUR BOOKS, THEY CAN BE REVIEWED! **WE WANT TO KNOW WHAT YOU LIKE!**

GET INFECTED!

SIGN UP FOR OUR MAILING LIST AT **PERMUTEDPRESS.COM**

PERMUTED PRESS

EXCALIBUR

☘ THE CAMELOT WARS - BOOK I ☘

MICHAEL CLARY

A PERMUTED PRESS book

ISBN (Trade Paperback): 978-1-61868-501-8
ISBN (eBook): 978-1-61868-435-6

EXCALIBUR
The Camelot Wars Book One
© 2014 by Michael Clary
All Rights Reserved

Cover art by Dean Samed, Conzpiracy Digital Arts

PERMUTED
PRESS

❧ **MERLIN** ❧

It came as a surprise when it happened. It really shouldn't have, but it did. I had long ago cast the necessary spells that would alert me if anything of importance should disturb the dead forest of the forgotten island.

The intruder was a young boy, no more than ten years of age. Looking at him, no one in their right minds could ever have guessed what destiny had in store for his future. No one could have known that when he grew up, he would become a great warrior, and a leader of men. No one could have known that the boy would one day become . . . a king.

Not even me.

Give me a little credit though . . . it'd been centuries since the forces of evil stalked the darkness of the forests in search of innocent lives. Centuries I tell you, since the great king destroyed even the merest trace of their vile shadow. Well, we all know what happened to that great king. There are various tales, most of what you'll read (if so inclined to do the research) are fanciful myths. However, it's an undisputable fact that a king was chosen. He carried with him a magical sword pulled from a stone. He ruled all of Britain and created a time of peace and prosperity never before imagined. He defeated all enemies of the land, but his glory came with a price, the battles were terrible . . . eventually, our great king fell.

I mourned his passing for a century. Even though I knew that he would one day fall in battle, I loved him as a father loves his son. He was too great a man to not love and he in turn treated me as a father. He sought my advice, he made me welcome in his home . . . he . . . he . . . well, is it any wonder that I felt a man such as this should grace the earth for a second time? Is it any

7

wonder that in pain and sorrow, moments after his death I cast the most powerful spell ever cast?

What was the spell?

Let's just say I feared that the terrible evil the great king fought so valiantly against in his life would one day rise again, and if that day ever came to pass . . . the great king would be reborn.

I digress.

Let's go back to the island with the dead forest.

Roughly ten years ago; the guardian of the king's magical sword brought the weapon to this very spot. . It's the final resting place of the great blade and as steel pierced stone; an immense shockwave of magic killed all life on the island in a burst of flame.

The forest never re-grew.

I cannot say why for certain, it's certainly not the usual way of a forest after a fire. However, I often felt the long forgotten traces of magic, as if the sword were still crying out for its master despite being forced into a slumber of stone.

It's a lonely place.

Why the sword's guardian brought the blade here, is yet another mystery I cannot answer. I always felt that the sword belonged in Britain as did the great king. Was there some mistake? How could I know? What should I do?

I'll tell you what I did, I followed the sword. The future king would be drawn to it. There would be no better place to find him, but the years passed and no one came. The evil never flooded the land, and the great king never came forth.

Surely the future king had been reborn, but there would be no reason for him to come for the sword if the terrible evil could not take root.

I became comfortable in the belief that the land would never again need a king. Of course . . . I was wrong. I had underestimated the power of evil. I should have known she'd find a way. Morgana was always very clever.

Almost ten years after the sword came back to us, the boy followed.

Where he'd come from would forever be a mystery. He simply appeared, and from a distance I watched as he climbed the stone stairs. His eyes were drawn to the great sword. At the top of the sword's resting place, he stood in silence for a long and unendurable moment with respectful and wide eyes.

I held my breath in anticipation. Could he possibly be hearing the song of the great sword? I strained my hearing and the little magic I had left in an effort to listen. Perhaps I caught the briefest note, but could not be sure. The sword only sings for the future king.

The boy slowly approached the prison of stone. A part of me wanted to grab him and turn him away. Another part of me wanted to hug him close and console him, because if the sword claimed him, his life would be fraught with violence.

The boy was too young to shoulder the weight of the sword.

"Give him time," I prayed to the great weapon. "He's too young. I Merlin, the greatest wizard to ever to walk across the rolling hills of Britain, beseech thee . . . not yet."

The boy closed in upon the sword. His wide eyes took in the weathered, tarnished handle and the foot of rusted blade that stuck out from the rock.

I bit my lip and clenched my fists in fear of what would transpire in the next thirty seconds.

The small hand reached for the handle.

Suddenly, overheard the clouds turned dark on the once sunny day and thunder roared down over the rapidly darkening land. The small hand withdrew in fear. The boy fell away from the stone and landed on his backside.

As suddenly as the clouds turned, the sky once again cleared and the sunlight shone unto the sacred resting place.

The crisis was averted; the boy quickly got to his feet and ran down the steps.

What had happened?

Was the child rejected?

The answer came with the brutality of a knife wound. The sword was inside my head . . . speaking . . . and warning me.

I obey your wishes for the moment, wizard. But someday soon that boy will be mine and I shall slumber no more.

I had to speak to the child.

With a speed that would be shocking to most people, I moved through the dead forest until I stood directly in his path. I must have startled him, because he let out a gasp of surprise as he saw me for the first time.

"Hello, little sir." I beamed down at him. "Have you gotten lost?"

It took him awhile to answer, the poor child was terrified.

"I . . . I thought I heard someone calling me," the boy answered in a shaky voice.

"Well now, who would be calling you, way out here in this lonely place?" I asked.

"I heard a name," the boy answered

"And what name would that be?" I asked.

"Excalibur," the boy answered.

I swear my immortal heart stopped dead in my chest.

"And . . . what might your name be, little sir?" I asked in a trembling voice.

"I am Arthur," the boy answered.

I reached out my hand to the nearest tree in an effort to support myself. Luckily enough, I didn't fall. The poor child was scared enough.

I looked him up and down. He had blondish-red hair, light skin which had been reddened by the sun, a slim frame, and piercing grey eyes.

"The king is reborn," I mumbled. "Long live the king."

To say that the events of that day were shocking would be an understatement. I placed the boy immediately under my protection, and took him to the nearest town, a place called Mill Ridge.

I had friends in the town that knew my true identity. I would need their help. The boy must be trained. The boy must be taught to love, and above all, he must be hidden.

That's why the guardian chose this relatively unknown area of the Pacific Northwest in which to place the sword. Here the boy would be safe. Here he would have time to prepare.

But how much time?

Another mystery.

The sheriff of Mill Ridge began a search in an effort to find the boy's family. Nothing ever turned up. The boy was an orphan, and possessed no other memory beyond Excalibur.

He simply appeared.

Fortunately, the sheriff was one of the three people who shared my secret. The two others were a young couple that caught me doing a tiny bit of magic in the forest one day while they were out hiking.

The couple had been trying to conceive with unsuccessful results over the last two years. It broke their hearts. Coincidence rapidly became opportunity.

I introduced them to Arthur, and they fell instantly in love.

The boy's adoption went smoothly. Sheriff Tagger saw to that, and in a small town like Mill Ridge a sheriff's badge carries a lot of weight. I was glad that the boy had a family that loved him, but explaining his destiny to the new parents wasn't easy.

I became Grandpa Merl to the boy, and training began immediately.

At first, it was only me playing games with wooden swords in the backyard, but as time went by and skill began to develop, I provided instructors. The game stopped being fun. Arthur wasn't interested in learning the sword. He wanted to play sports like the other young boys in Mill Ridge.

Fortune struck when Arthur met Wayne. The two of them were the same age and became instantly close ... Wayne began to join in on Arthur's lessons. He wasn't especially gifted, but his being there made the rigorous lessons more bearable to Arthur.

Time went by quickly in those early days.

The forces of evil hadn't yet risen. Perhaps in this new age Morgana didn't have the power to become a threat. Perhaps the boy would live a normal life. I wished for that. Arthur's parents wished for that, and for a long time ... our wishes came true.

Arthur was a happy child with a ready smile. He was also a kind hearted young man, and he offered his friendship readily. I was proud of him. His parents were proud of him. He was a leader among the boys in his class. Well liked by everyone.

His skill with the sword developed dramatically.

I was constantly replacing instructors as he outgrew them. He was rapidly becoming a master of the blade. Wayne's talents never truly improved much, but he was a big lad, and that made him more suitable for other weapons.

By Arthur's senior year in high school, I could no longer find an instructor capable of teaching him something new. They'd come, they'd fight; they'd leave with their heads held low.

Arthur was finally prepared.

Morgana had not yet come, but that didn't mean Arthur's life lacked tragedy. In the middle of his senior year his father was killed in a hunting accident. Arthur was devastated.

For a time, his mother and I were unable to reach him. Wayne tried as well with only slightly better results. The cheerful boy that we all knew and loved was gone. In his place was a sullen and angry young man.

"Time will heal him," I told his grief stricken mother.

Time however, is no one's true friend. It moves too quickly during the happy days, and slows to a crawl when times are difficult. It took over two years for Arthur to find his way back to us . . . it also took the aid of a young woman.

She was a pretty young thing and a delightful person. She made Arthur smile. She made him laugh, and before anyone knew it, they were head over heels in love. Arthur had finally come back to us.

I had reservations when they got married, but seeing his smiling face erased them from my mind. His young bride wasn't meant for him. There was another. Where she was, I had no idea . . . but she was out there . . . somewhere.

Or was she?

If Morgana never came . . . Arthur's life would be his own. He'd never need to learn his true identity.

I cried when the baby came.

I cried because Arthur was so very, very happy. He loved his family in an almost impossible way, and he was loved just as greatly in return.

Time once again became our friend. The happy days came so often they became a blur. Arthur worked with Wayne at a garage in the town square, and together they fixed anything from farm equipment to vehicles. They made good money. Wayne got married, and eventually fathered two children, himself.

Life was good . . . no, life was perfect. At least it was until tragedy struck Arthur's life once more. His wife and seven year old child were both killed in an automobile accident.

Arthur never recovered.

A part of him died with the death of his family.

Time once again slowed to a crawl. When the red fog appeared in Britain I was so devastated I missed all the signs. When Britain became unresponsive. . . I had an idea.

Other countries fell afterwards. One after another. The red fog would appear, and life would disappear.

When the red fog began to appear in America, I reluctantly said my goodbyes to my adopted family and set out for answers. If Morgana was the cause, there was much to prepare for. Arthur must be made ready.

❧ ARTHUR ❧

The world didn't end with a giant bang, and a great war. That's not what happened at all. It ended with a deep intake of air and a long, slow exhalation. I didn't really give a shit.

A red fog appeared over England. It was strange . . . a fog that dense, and in that color had never been seen before. Things got weirder still when the entire country abruptly ended any and all forms of communication.

That was only the beginning. The fog began to appear in other countries as well. They also fell off the grid. America sent planes out. The planes never returned. Eventually, the red fog appeared in the United States. It began in Washington, but quickly spread throughout all the fifty states.

Communications went down immediately. Cars stopped functioning. Computers died. Phones were beyond repair. Technology ended. It was crazy. It was insane, and no one could understand it. Panic set in when the guns and rifles stopped working.

After a month, the fog dissipated.

Mill Ridge had been transported back to the dark ages. Something in the red fog must have caused it . . . but what? ? Was it an attack of some kind? Was it a natural phenomenon? No one had a clue. We were effectively cut off from the rest of the world. Not that it bothered us much. We were a small town. We didn't need the technology. We knew how to live off the land.

So, while the fog wreaked havoc throughout the world, the citizens of Mill Ridge simply shrugged their shoulders, and went back to work. We didn't need the computers or the phones. All of us would miss the cars and trucks, but we could make do. We had horses.

I lived in a small cabin on the edge of town. It wasn't much, but it was more than I needed. In truth, not much about my life changed after the fog came and went. I spent my days fishing, and I spent my nights playing deputy. Yup, things were pretty much the same for me.

Until the stranger came into town.

Of course, I had no idea there was a ruckus up in the town square. I had had myself a rough night or cards and booze. Therefore, I was taking things easy that morning, and fishing off the pier in the backyard.

My Stetson was pulled down low to keep the morning sun out of my eyes. I couldn't see much, but I could feel a tug if a fish decided to bite, and I could hear the trotting of a horse making its way up my neglected driveway.

I slurped up the remains of my thick coffee when I heard footsteps on the wood of the pier behind me, but I didn't get up.

"Arthur," Martin said. "How ya feeling?"

"I've had better days," I replied. "What brings you down here so early in the morning?"

"A man came into town," Martin said. "He's saying crazy things. The sheriff took him down to the station, but people are getting worried. He wants you to come in."

I stared into my empty cup wishing I had just a bit more left to drink before answering. I hated my new job. Being a deputy, and dealing with all the drunks and crazies, was about the lowest form of usefulness as far as I was concerned. Still, a job was a job, and it was nice of the sheriff to take me on. No much use for a mechanic after the red fog came.

"I'm not scheduled to clock in until sunset," I grumbled.

It wasn't like this was the first stranger to come strolling into town. We got a few of them a month. Wanderers that came a wandering, it wasn't necessarily a bad thing either. They often brought news from the thousands of small towns scattered across the country.

"Sheriff Tagger said you'd say that," Martin laughed. "He also said to drag your lazy ass in regardless."

I gave a deep sigh and lovingly looked out at the lake before pulling up my hat and getting out of my lawn chair.

"Go on ahead without me," I said. "It'll take me a bit to walk to the station."

"I can give you a ride," Martin laughed. "Just hop on the back."

It was well known that I hated horses almost as much as they hated me. Martin was enjoying the moment tremendously.

"Aren't you a sweetheart?" I replied. "But I think I'll walk."

"Suit yourself," Martin said as we walked to his horse. "Don't take too long though. The sheriff will get pissed if you're not there soon."

"Just tell him I'm on my way," I said. "I'll get there when I get there."

I waved as Martin trotted off, and then I headed back to the cabin. I opened the front door and called out to Lance.

"Hey buddy," I said. "I'm going into town. You wanna come?"

The cabin was dark inside. I could see nothing, but I thought I caught a flurry of movement when I opened the door.

"No thank you," Lance answered. "I don't think I can right now."

"You wanna give it a try tomorrow?" I asked.

"Maybe . . . but, will it be okay if I don't?" Lance asked.

"Of course," I answered. "You take as much time as you need."

I closed the door as gently as possible. Lance had problems. The poor kid was an orphan, and his meds ran out a long time ago. I'm not exactly sure why he latched onto me, but I wasn't complaining. He was a good kid, and he kept my place as clean as a whistle.

I took a short cut through the woods instead of using the dirt road, but it still took me about forty-five minutes before I made it to the station. Sheriff Tagger was livid, and a crowd of about one hundred people had gathered by the front doors.

"Arthur," Stanley Shunter asked as I pushed through the crowd. "What's going on?"

"No clue," I answered. "I just got here."

"Hi, Arthur," Sarah Windsbane said.

I smiled in returned.

"I heard that this guy was talking about the fog coming back," Stanley said. "What's it going to take away this time?"

"I'll see what's going on, Stanley," I said.

"Hello Arthur," Michelle Barlow called out as I walked by. "When are you going to come visit me?"

"Very soon," I answered.

"Why in the hell are you going to visit Michelle Barlow?" Sarah demanded.

"Just being neighborly," I replied.

"Arthur," Jennifer Rains called out. "My daddy made some shine. You wanna come over tonight and have a sip?"

Then I was inside the station. Martin was laughing. The sheriff was ranting and raving.

"I brought you down to help calm people," Sheriff Tagger said. "Instead, we now have three young ladies screaming at each other."

"Yeah, Arthur," Martin said. "Why can't you keep it in your pants for once?"

"Shut your mouth, Martin," Sheriff Tagger growled. "But he's right, Arthur. This is getting ridiculous. I get about five different women a week stopping by here and looking for you. You're a good looking young man, but you need to slow down, son."

"Yes, Boss," I said. It was my standard reply for whenever he got on my case. The sheriff was a great guy, but sometimes he got just a bit fatherly with me.

"Blah, you didn't hear a word I said," He grumbled.

"You should repeat it, Boss," Martin added.

"I told you to shut your mouth," Sheriff Tagger snarled.

Looking around the room, I saw the two other deputies in the department, Betsy and Bedder. Both of them looked a little worried. That in itself was unusual. Betsy and Bedder were normally pretty cool customers.

"So?" I asked. "Why am I here?"

"This guy just wandered into town at sunup screaming out about the fog coming back," Sheriff Tagger answered. "He seemed a bit crazed, so I brought him down to the station. He was also starting to gather a crowd. Which is why I wanted everyone here, the possibility of the fog coming back could cause a panic."

"Where was he when you found him?" I asked.

"He was right in the middle of town square," Sheriff Tagger answered. "If he's unbalanced, let's try and give him what help we can, but if there's another fog coming . . . well, I'm open to suggestions on that."

"So how do you want to handle this?" Martin asked.

"I want the three of you to man the station," The sheriff answered. "Arthur and I will go talk to this guy and see what there is to see."

It was strange that the sheriff wanted me to accompany him. This wasn't my normal type of job. I was better off dealing with the drunks and trouble makers.

The man was waiting for us in our small interrogation room. He was in his early fifties by my guesstimate. His hair was brown and messy, and his clothes were torn and covered in mud. I also noticed a few blood stains on the leg of his pants. The sheriff nudged me until I started talking.

"Hello, Sir," I said as I sat opposite him at the table. "Looks like you've had a rough few days. We'd like to help you out."

"You can't help me," the man said. "I've already lost everything. I'm here to help you?"

"Okay," I said. "We appreciate that. Now, how exactly can you help us?"

"The fog," the man said. "Beware the fog."

"The fog's already been through here, sir," I replied. "It's been all over the world, but it's gone now. No need to worry."

"Not the red fog," the man said. "The red fog merely shuts off the lights. No, not the red fog at all . . . beware the green fog. They come in the green fog."

"Who comes in the green fog?" I asked.

"Soldiers."

"Soldiers?" I asked. "As in the military? Sir, our military was destroyed with the red fog. Nobody knows why exactly, but most people believe there was some sort of catastrophic accident."

"No, son," the man said. "Not our military, and there was no catastrophic accident. The military was killed. They were wiped out, and now I know why."

"Because of the green fog?" I asked.

"Because of what comes with the green fog," the man answered.

"Where did you see this green fog?" I asked.

"A town with no name," The man answered. "It was six days ride from here on horseback. I was staying there. I'm a salesman. At dusk a pale green fog drifted in. It moved throughout the small town as if it were searching for someone. There were about four hundred people living there, and they were getting nervous. The fog was unnatural. It flowed inside their clapboard homes, it sought them out. Around midnight, the soldiers came . . ."

The man had a coughing fit. Sheriff Tagger handed him a glass of water, and the stranger gulped it greedily. Looking him over, I realized that he looked rather sickly and dehydrated.

"Sir," I said. "Can't I get you something to eat? Would you like some more water?"

"No," the stranger said. "You need to listen. The soldiers came, and they fell upon the people. They slashed man, woman, and child. They showed no

17

mercy. I grabbed my son, and I ran. We had an old horse. The horse was terrified, but she carried us all the way to Bisping."

Alarm bells went off inside my head. Bisping was the next town over. The farmers here did a lot of trading with them. It was only two days away on horseback.

"Why'd you leave Bisping," I asked. "Did something happen there?"

"I tried to warn them," the man said. "They wouldn't listen. They had strong men, men that could fight. They had fought off troublemakers before. If trouble came, they were ready. The fog drifted in a few days later. I wanted to run, but my boy was sick . . ."

The man began to cry.

I waited for him to gain control.

"I'm sorry," the man said. "I'm so sorry, but he was all I had left in this world."

"What happened to your boy?"

"I was hoping the town was as strong as they said they were," the man answered. "I looked out the window of my boy's hospital room at midnight. Shortly after, I heard the screams. I couldn't see much in the fog . . . but I heard the screams. The men of Bisping fought as hard as they could, but they never stood a chance."

"Bisping has been attacked," I stated dumbly. "Were they any survivors?"

"Just me," the stranger answered. "I tried to protect my boy. There were too many of them. They laughed as they cut him. My God, I can still hear him scream. He called for me. He called for me, and I couldn't save him."

"I'm sorry for your loss," I said.

"Jack Winters left for Bisping four days ago to trade some horses," Sheriff Tagger said. "He hasn't returned yet."

"He's dead," the stranger announced. "If he was in Bisping, he's surely dead."

"How many of them were there?" I asked.

"More than a hundred," the man answered. "It's hard to say. The fog was thick."

"Bisping is as big a town as Mill Ridge," I told Sheriff Tagger. "They should have been able to fight off a hundred raiders."

"You think we're dealing with raiders?" Sheriff Tagger asked.

"I would think so," I answered. "Both Bisping and Mill Ridge has had to deal with them before. Never that many of them mind you, but my guess is that they're raiders . . ."

"These were no simple raiders!" The stranger shouted. "They wore armor. They spoke with an accent. They came with the fog. They wielded swords and daggers. They fought like no other men I've ever seen. They're a part of what happened to the world and, they're making their way across the land searching for someone, and killing all that stands in their way. What's even worse . . . they claim the bodies of those they've slain. I saw it with my own eyes. Great wagons filled with the corpses."

"Arthur," Sheriff Tagger said. "Can I speak to you outside?"

I walked out the door with my boss, and closed it gently behind me.

"It makes sense," Sheriff Tagger said immediately.

"What does?" I asked.

"Imagine and army of soldiers trained with swords and things like that. The military wouldn't be able to stand against them. Not with their guns and other weapons failing."

"Yeah," I said. "But this guy said there was only a hundred or so of them. They'd need an army a lot bigger than that."

"What if they have one?" Sheriff Tagger asked. "What if this is only a scouting party; and a larger force is somewhere behind them? What if they have soldiers scattered across the globe?"

I had no answer for him.

Instead, we made plans. A force of a hundred was something we couldn't ignore. We needed to prepare. Hopefully, the stranger was crazy, and nothing would come of his ramblings . . . but we couldn't take chances.

I went to my buddy Wayne's house.

His wife is the local blacksmith. She works all day long at the forge in the barn behind their house. At first she pounded metal for fun, but as her skills grew, she started making an income big enough to rival that of her husband before the fog.

Wayne was waiting for me on the front porch as I walked up the drive. I could hear the clanking sounds of metal on metal coming from the forge all the way to the porch. He was smiling, but it wasn't sincere. The news of an attack was spreading.

"How bad is it?" Wayne asked.

"Might be something," I answered. "Then again, it might be nothing."

"We've dealt with raiders before," Wayne said. "I've got a scar on my back to prove it."

"We haven't dealt with this many before," I said. "If this guy has his head screwed on straight, there's about a hundred, give or take. They're also trained."

"What do you mean trained?" Wayne asked.

"They know how to fight with swords and shit," I answered.

Wayne sipped his lemonade, and pondered what I just told him. Finally, he stood up and walked to the edge of the porch.

"We need to fight dirty," He said.

"Come again?" I asked.

"We'll take less damages that way," Wayne added. "Mill Ridge isn't exactly filled with skilled swordsman. Sure, I can swing a sword, and you can swing a sword—I remember our lessons but I'm by no means skilled at it. If these boys know how to fight, and fight in a group, our only chance of survival would be to trick them, and fight dirty."

"Any ideas?"

"Not so much," Wayne answered. "But I can probably come up with a decent idea or two."

"I bet you can," I said. "Now tell me, is your wife still making weapons and if so, how many of the townspeople would you say are armed?"

"Tell ya the truth," Wayne said. "I'm not sure, but I know we've been sitting pretty damn pretty for the six months or so. Hell, she even has orders from other towns."

"Good," I said. "Let's go talk to your wife."

We went around the house. The barn was big, red, and picturesque. Wendy was happy to see me when I walked through the doors. Scattered about were their two kids, a boy and a girl. Both of them were at work learning mama's trade.

I had a brief flash of memory; my son running into my arms after I came home from work, and my wife looking on lovingly.

I pushed the memory away almost as quickly as it had come.

Wendy hugged me. She was a beautiful woman. Her red hair drifted in tendrils around her dirt smudged face. I loved her like a sister.

"Tell me you aren't here to bust me for Wayne's stash of shine," She said.

"I'll bust you for marrying this scumbag instead of me," I answered.

"Deputy," Wayne grumbled from behind me. "Keep in mind all the sharp objects in this barn. I wouldn't want you to have an accident."

We all laughed, but Wayne was a big, big man. He stood about 6'5" , and he was over three hundred pounds of stocky muscle. The great black beard on his face, and his slicked back hair made him seem even more menacing, but I knew him well. He was a gentle, jovial man for the most part, but an absolute bear when angered. Fortunately, he wasn't angered very often.

"So what brings you to my forge, Arthur?" Wendy asked.

"I'm wondering how many of the folks around here have weapons?"

"Does this have to do with the raiders?" Wendy asked.

"Yes, Ma'am," I answered. "I'm hoping most of the folks that can wield a weapon, possess a weapon."

"So there's going to be an attack?"

"Well," I said. "We don't know that for sure. Better safe than sorry is my line of thinking."

"I hear you," Wendy said. "Well, we're all in luck. After that last bunch of raiders came through, half the town started ordering weapons."

"What types of weapons?"

"Mostly swords," Wendy answered like it wasn't the slightest bit odd. "Occasionally, a dagger or a spear, I just moved into making axes. I'm almost finished with two of them, but those are for Wayne."

"People have been buying swords?" I asked.

I was expecting daggers, and knives. I wasn't expecting the people to be buying swords. That could make my job thumping drunks over the head and dragging them to the jail infinitely more dangerous.

"Yes, swords," Wendy said.

With that, she went to a table and picked up a one-handed sword. It was relatively long, but it was also light.

"Nice," I said.

"You truly have no appreciation for a beautiful weapon," Wendy said. "Those blades are works of art."

"I have a Buck 110 that my daddy gave me before he died," I said.

"You really don't get it," Wendy grumbled.

"Nope," I answered. "Not really. My Granddad made Wayne and I practice with swords when we were younger . . . but honestly, who needs a sword?"

"We're living in an age where technology and modern weapons have been wiped out," Wayne said. "These weapons are the best ways in which we can defend ourselves."

"I hear ya," I answered. "But I'd prefer not to stab anyone."

"Says the only guy that carries a sawed-off bat," Wendy laughed. "You need to step up your game. Hell, I don't think I know of anyone that carries anything less than a twelve-inch blade nowadays."

"You're probably right," I answered. "But I had one major fight in my life, and three people died as a result. I'd rather thump someone over the head any day of the week versus pull a blade and possibly kill them."

"Well," Wendy said. "Take this just in case. I'm worried that you'll show up to a sword fight with a piece of wood."

She handed me a wooden-handled dagger with a wickedly curved blade, in a brown leather sheath, which would fit sideways on my belt.

"I'll call it a backup weapon," I laughed.

"Hopefully, you won't need it," Wayne added. "Now let's get to planning."

I listened to Wayne go over and over his plan for the next hour. It was simplistic. He wanted to create an easy target for the raiders, and when they came in to attack, the easy target would pull weapons while the rest of the town's fighters came in from behind.

I listened with half an ear. I really didn't believe an attack was going to come, and my hangover was getting the better of me. Sure, there were definitely raiders out there in the forests, but I seriously doubted there were enough of them to warrant an attack on a town this size.

Two days later, a green fog rolled in.

It came from the forests, and infiltrated the town. Locked doors weren't enough to stop it. The fog found its way inside of every home, and behind every locked door. The townspeople were frightened. The fog seemed to have a mind of its own, and just like the stranger said, it seemed to be searching for someone.

The Mayor and Sheriff Tagger met with us that evening, and Wayne and the sheriff outlined the plan to the man. Mayor Brunner argued and threw a fit, but finally agreed after he somehow convinced himself that he came up with the plan all on his own without any input from the rest of us. After that, we had a town meeting, and explained the plan to the townspeople. If an attack was coming, we'd be ready.

For three evenings, we held a fake party and dance under a large gazebo hastily erected in the front of the town square park. Half the town pretended to be living it up. The rest of us waited on the rooftops along the main road into town.

No attack ever came.

On the third evening, just as it started to drizzle, Sheriff Tagger sent me home from my rooftop vigil on a hardware store for being drunk.

"Son," Sheriff Tagger said. "Get your ass off this roof. Go home and sleep it off."

"Sounds good to me," I answered.

I had enough of boogey-man stories about soldiers that came out of the fog. I took everything as serious as I could, but after three days of nothing . . . well, if I was wrong, there were still people on the rooftops keeping a lookout. Let them deal with it. Unfortunately, the fake party in the town square park decided to stop pretending, and kick-started into a real barn burner. That was fine by me. I wouldn't have to listen to the farmers complain the next day about teenagers breaking into their barns in the middle of the night, and throwing parties.

"Arthur!" Ellie Smith shouted as I stumbled from the front door of the hardware store. "Are you headed home?"

"Looks that way," I responded.

"You need some company?" Ellie asked.

"Damnit, girl," The sheriff interjected before I could respond. "You let that boy get some sleep. You can jump on him some other night."

Laughter erupted from all the occupied rooftops.

I blew Ellie a kiss, and cut through the forest on my way back to my cabin.

I was dead-tired. Staying up all night waiting for something to happen had taken its toll on me. All I wanted was one more drink, and a long sleep. I barely registered that the fog was denser in the forest, until it truly became hard to see.

At this point, I believed the green fog was nothing more than some sort of natural occurrence. When the red fog came, its destructiveness was immediate. The green fog just sort of hung around. Perhaps some plants were giving off a weird pollen that was turning the fog a pale green color.

I had no idea . . . but I certainly didn't believe an attack was coming. So, I walked through the forest. I walked past the broken rock wall covered in moss that surrounded Mill Ridge, and I went home.

A funny thing about that three foot tall, broken up rock wall, the people that live in Mill Ridge swear it appeared in the middle of the night a day before my mother adopted me. I'm not sure if the story is true or not, but the people here took it as a good omen, and named it the Stronghold Wall.

The fog was even denser when I reached my cabin. I could feel its chilly dampness on my cheeks and hands. The drizzle had also intensified a bit. It wasn't anything serious yet, probably not even enough to break up the party in the park.

Green tendrils of fog reached out across my property as if they had a mind of their own. They touched a tree here. They touched a boulder there. I watched it for about twenty minutes, and then I headed towards the dock.

The lake had a layer of fog upon it, but it wasn't as dense as it was around my cabin. In fact, it was sort of pretty in a horror film kind of way. The fog hung low over the water. The gentle waves lapped against the pebble shoreline.

I heard voices.

Immediately, I looked behind me. I only saw the fog, my yard, my cabin, and tree's. I looked out towards the water. The fog was drifting across the lake, and I still saw nothing. I heard nothing unusual.

I walked to the edge of the dock, and listened to my canoe bump against the wood. I must have imagined the voices. There was nothing unusual on my property. So, I turned back to my cabin . . .

Laughter.

The sound sent chills up my spine. It wasn't normal laughter. It was sinister, a sound that would come from an evil man right before he tortured his victim. I spun back towards the water. My hand grabbed instinctively for the tire thumper on my belt.

"Arthur," Lance called from inside the house. "Get away from the water."

"Is somebody out there?" I asked.

"Yes," Lance answered.

A breeze moved across the lake, and stirred the fog over the water. My clothes were wet and I was shivering, but I didn't know if the shivering was from the wet clothes or the laughter.

I saw something.

I couldn't tell what it was at first, just a small shape moving through the lake about sixty feet from the dock. The green fog moved back in before I could make out any details.

I heard more laughter, this time; the laughter was followed by voices.

"Look at him," a voice said. "A sitting duck is what he is."

"That can't be him," another voice added. "Too much fear in his eyes."

The breeze stirred the fog again. I saw the same shape, but it was much closer. The breeze came on even stronger, and I saw that instead of just one shape in the water, there were dozens, and all of them were headed towards me.

I pulled out my tire thumper.

"Arthur!" Lance shouted. "Run!"

I wasn't about to run. What would I even be running from? Voices? Shapes in the water? The breeze stirred the fog over the water once more. The moving shapes were only around thirty-five feet away, and they were becoming larger.

No, not larger. They were emerging from the water, and the closer they came, the better I could see them.

Soldiers.

There were soldiers in the lake, and not dozens like I'd initially thought. There were at least a hundred of them, probably even more. The moving shapes were their heads as they moved through the water towards me. Some of them wore helmets. Strange metal helmets that exposed the face, but came down to protect the nose. Others had no helmets and their long hair was plastered against their faces.

All of them had swords.

From twenty-five feet away I could see they were in waist deep water. They wore medieval chainmail under black tunics with a white drawing of a dagger piercing a heart. From twenty feet away, I could make out the details of their faces.

They had silver, dead-looking eyes. Their skin was a sickly white. Some of them had grisly cuts that festered and seeped. One of them had a head wound so terrible; it seemed as if his entire skull was held together with metal bands. None of them looked good, and more were coming. I could see their heads coming out of the water.

At fifteen feet away from the dock, the soldiers began to spread out and surround me. They held their tongues, but all of them were staring at me hungrily. Some of them were even beckoning me to them. Most of them were smiling.

I ran.

I ran as fast as I could to the cabin. I ran so fast, I lost my Stetson. The soldiers' laughter taunted me from behind, but I didn't care. I knew I had to get away from the lake before they came out of the water. The fog impaired my vision. I slammed a shoulder against a tree so hard, it spun me around and dropped me on my ass. My tire thumper flew from my hand.

As I crawled back to my feet, I got a good look towards the lake. The soldiers were crawling up the dock, and walking across the small pebble shoreline, but they weren't pursuing me. Instead, they began forming a loose circle around my property.

The rain fell harder.

I saw a final shape emerge from the lake. A white horse came forth, and atop the animal was an immense man covered in black armor. The horse turned in a circle, growled, snorted, and reared up.

Then, both man and horse both turned their heads towards me. I found my feet just as the knight drew his sword, and I ran for all I was worth. I ran into things, I even tripped over an exposed root, but I didn't stop.

I leaped past the steps on my porch, and the front door opened for me. I dove inside the cabin as if the knight were hot on my heels.

"Lance," I said. "Light a lamp. I can't see a thing."

"No," Lance said. "They'll be able to see inside the cabin."

I saw Lance's outline looking out the window. Then he noticed I was watching him, and turned his large eyes on me for just a moment before vanishing into the shadows.

"What did you see?" I asked.

"They're just standing there," Lance answered.

"Where's the knight?"

"I don't see him anymore," Lance answered. "Why are they after you?"

"No clue," I replied. "But we need to get out of here."

"They have us surrounded," Lance said.

"There's a pretty large open space by the lake," I said. "When the knight came out of the water, the soldiers backed off and gave him a lot of room."

"You want to head towards the lake?" Lance asked.

"It's our only chance," I replied.

"Arthur," Lance said calmly. "They didn't swim across the lake. They walked across the bottom. Who knows if any of them are still under the water? Think of another plan."

"I don't have another plan, Lance," I snapped. "All I know is, we're surrounded, and nobody knows we're in trouble."

I saw movement by another window but by the time I looked, Lance had vanished. I looked around the dark living room in an attempt to find him. I was terrified, and his desire to remain hidden at all times was frustrating me.

"Stop trying to find me," Lance said.

The kid was a master at remaining hidden, and that thought gave me an idea.

"Listen," I said. "You can escape. You're too good at hiding. Plus, you know the forest. You can sneak out, and get help."

"I'm not leaving you," Lance said. "I know what you're trying to do. You're trying to save me, and you know I'll never make it back with help before they attack. Already, they're out there lighting fires. They probably want to burn us out."

"Lance, please," I said. "Even if you don't make it back in time for me, at the very least, you can warn the town."

Nothing, no response . . . hopefully, he was thinking about it.

"Fine," Lance finally said. "I'll find the sheriff. He's probably asleep by now. He normally heads to bed after you call it a night. I'll go to his window, but you need to hide Arthur. You need to stay safe."

"I'll wait them out as long as I can," I answered. "I'm sure they'll start some sort of communication before they light the cabin. I can probably stall them."

"Good," Lance said. "I'll go out through an upstairs window. It's by an old tree with a long branch. It's the one I normally use when I go out at night."

That was news to me. I had no idea he ever left the house.

"Lead the way," I said despite having a million questions.

His outline ran up the stairs, and that was all I saw in the darkness. I went to follow him, just in case he needed any help. As soon as I was in front of the front door, it happened.

The door exploded.

I was trapped beneath the ruble of the door and parts of the wall. Stars were dancing in my vision. I kept blinking my eyes in an effort to make them disappear, but that only caused my forehead to wrinkle, and the wrinkles created a pathway for the blood flowing from my scalp, straight into my eyes.

I blinked some more. I rubbed, and wiped. I had flashes of the great knight standing in the doorway. I saw dust, and broken pieces of the wall. I pushed against the pieces of wood on top of me. It took way too long, but I freed myself.

I looked around the room. The knight was standing in the doorway. He was bigger than Wayne, at least seven feet tall. He had to lower his head to walk into the room. Finally, the stars in my vision began to clear, and me with my ass still on the ground, I shoved away from him.

He laughed at my efforts.

"The future king," the knight said in an unearthly, deep voice.

His armor was rusted and scratched. His massive helmet had horns that rose eight inches above his head. He took a thundering step, and then held his sword before him. The blade was menacing, and looked wickedly sharp.

"I'm no king," I said. "Look fellah, I think you folks have the wrong idea. This town is full of peaceful people. We don't want any trouble."

The knight froze.

"Damn you," the knight said. "I want my revenge. I want a real fight. I begged her to wait... you are nothing. A coward, the Arthur of old would have already engaged me in glorious battle. Do you truly not remember?"

"I'm sorry, buddy," I answered. "I don't know what you're talking about."

"How unfortunate," the knight replied. "But my orders were very clear."

He swung the sword at me. I barely dodged out of the way. Instead of cleaving me in half, the sword buried itself into the floor. I scrambled to my feet. My head was still dizzy, but I managed to run up the stairs.

I heard the crunch and crack of the floorboards, as the knight began to follow. I would have thought that so much armor would slow him down, but he was fast. Way, way too fast. I ducked into the nearest bedroom, and slammed the door behind me.

I had some solid doors on my house. They would break, but it'd take more than a few light hits and a stiff shoulder. The massive knight collided against the door with a lot more than that. The loud sound echoed around the house, but aside from a small crack... the door held. Fortunately for me, I took a few steps back, because his next course of action was to ram his sword through the door, causing the tip of the blade to slightly poke my stomach.

That was enough for me.

I ran.

The cabin had three bedrooms. One was for Lance. One was for me, and the final one was a guest bedroom that nobody ever used. I was in the guest bedroom, and the adjoining bathroom connected with Lance's bedroom.

I ran through Lance's bedroom and back into the hallway just as the knight broke through the door. I ran right behind him, back down the stairs, and out the front of the house into the rainy night. I skidded to a halt when I saw that the soldiers outside the house had moved in closer, and tightened their circle.

I was trapped. I had nowhere to go. The net had been cast around me.

The dead-looking soldiers were waving their blades back and forth in a threatening manner, but they weren't advancing on me. From the house I heard the sound of heavy footsteps, and I turned to see the gigantic knight walk through the rubble of my front door.

I wiped at the blood on my forehead, and I wondered if Lance had made it out of the house. Then, I laughed. Here I was struggling to stay alive, but in the end, what did it matter? What did I have to live for? Yes, I cared about the people of Mill Ridge, but in all honesty . . . my life ended five years ago with the car crash that stole my wife and child from me.

I stood up.

"Do your very worst," I said. "And watch me laugh."

The knight advanced on me, and then . . . my entire world lit up.

The soldiers behind me flew thirty feet in the air. I heard them scream. The night was filled with fire and light. The fog was being chased away. The soldiers were scattered and running around in an effort to escape what appeared to be large fireballs.

There was a figure at the edge of my property. I couldn't make him out clearly, but the fireballs were coming from him. He was attacking the soldiers, and as a result, he was saving my life.

I felt a boot crash against my spine, and I fell back to the ground. In the chaos, I stupidly forgot about the large knight trying to kill me. Well, he reminded me that he was still there rather painfully.

"A weakened wizard will not be enough to save you from me," The knight said.

I twisted out of his way in the nick of time, and watched as he buried half his sword in the soft ground inches away from my head.

In a flash, I rolled away from him, but he was right behind me. The sword kept swinging as he advanced. Again I tripped and fell. Again I twisted away from his lethal attacks. I had nothing in which to defend myself with, my tire thumper was gone, and all I had was the . . . dagger.

I pulled it free from the sheath on my belt. I stepped inside his next swing, and attempted to bury it his chest. It was another stupid move on my part, his armor blocked my stabbing attempt, and he wrapped his metal encased hand around my neck.

With one hand, he lifted my in the air. The other hand drew back his sword. I closed my eyes and prepared myself for the stab . . . but it never came. I felt a searing heat against my bare skin, and both of us were thrown off of our feet.

I rolled and rolled across the wet ground in case I was on fire, then I stood up and prepared to run. What I saw before me, held me in my tracks.

The knight had also found his feet, but he was no longer interested in me. He was facing off against . . . an old man?

At least that's what the man appeared to be as he stood between me and the knight. He wore jeans and a light jacket. He had a white beard that hung down to his chest. He seemed somewhat frail, and I would have laughed at him standing there facing off against such a menacing threat, but the man had just saved my life.

"Do you truly think you still have the power to stop me?" The knight hissed in his deep and scary voice.

"Let's find out," the old man replied.

I watched as he made a rapid series of gestures with one of his hands, that made the ground erupt as tree roots and soil wrapped around the knight's legs, causing his sword fell to the ground, and trapping him at the same time. The old man then approached me, grabbed me by my arm, and brought his face close to mine.

"Arthur!" Grandpa Merl shouted. "Run!"

I didn't run. Geez, I couldn't even speak. My grandpa didn't waste a moment. Dragging me by the arm he led me through the forest of fireballs currently landscaping my front yard. Occasionally, a soldier would charge him, and Grandpa Merl would whip out a hand in a slapping motion, and the soldier would be knocked off his feet before he got anywhere near us.

"Arthur," Grandpa Merl said. "Please listen, I'm using up the remainder of my magic. I'm weakening. I can only hold Sir Francis back a little bit longer. I need you to run. I need you to run through the forest, and cross Stronghold Wall. You'll be safe once you cross the wall. They can't follow you there. Do you understand?"

I heard the words, but I certainly didn't understand.

"That big fucker's name is Sir Francis?" I asked.

My grandpa shook the sin right out of me. I blinked rapidly, and looked directly into his sea green eyes.

"He is the Black Knight!" Grandpa Merl shouted. "And he's here to kill you before you can reclaim your birthright. Now, run!"

He shoved me away from him towards the forest, right as a group of soldiers rushed towards us. The battle was engaged, but I was still weaponless. I wanted to help, but it didn't really seem as if my grandpa needed any help.

Soldiers were flying everywhere, fireballs were shooting out of his hands, and the ground between us became a wall of flame.

I didn't know what to do. I was the deputy. I couldn't leave my grandpa, but I had no idea how to help him. I tried to walk around the flame, but the fire seemed to follow me. It kept me away from him and at a distance from the battle.

I heard a low snort, and an angry animal bellow beyond the flames. I knew the source before I ever saw him, but I still about jumped out of my skin when I saw the Black Knight astride his scary white horse.

"There will be no escape!" the knight shouted as his angry horse paced back and forth before the flames separating us. "Already, the wizard weakens and attempts to flee as my men attack him."

"Unless you're fireproof, I already escaped, ya dumbass," I replied.

In the history of bad ideas . . . yeah, that one was up there. Knight and horse froze at my insult. Then I saw Sir Francis dig in his heels, the horse bucked up, charged through the flames, and the big knight was again swinging his damn sword at me.

I ducked, rolled, and took off into the trees. He followed behind me, but he couldn't get close enough to swing. There were too many trees, and I was running a hectic pattern through the forest. Fortunately, I was on my home turf. I knew the area's that were the densest.

I was running, and running. I was ducking, and diving through bushes, and under low branches. I was running out of breath, when I noticed . . . I was no longer being followed. I had lost my pursuer in the forest. Well, it was about damn time. That son of a bitch almost killed me multiple times.

My dagger was in my hand. Had I been clutching it this entire time? I couldn't remember. I placed it back in the leather sheath behind my back. I thought about having a sword made, wondered how long it'd been since I last practiced, and began cursing the loss of firearms.

I made my way through the forest. It wasn't very easy, the fog was still thick, fortunately the rain had lessened. I was still drenched and miserable, but at least . . . at least what? At least I was alive. At least I escaped?

I could warn the town, but were they even interested in the town? Were they only after me? Why were they after me? I had too many questions. I also had guilt. I left my poor grandpa. I left him there. I was the deputy. It should have been me protecting him, not the other way around.

So, I was feeling pretty low when I finally broke into the small clearing before Stronghold Wall. The clearing was only about fifty feet, and I was halfway across when I realized my mistake.

I was out in the open.

I quickly glanced to my left, nothing. I glanced to my right, and saw the white horse and black-clad rider move into the clearing. It was an eerie sight. I ran towards the wall. Two steps into my run, I heard the loud sound of horse sprinting towards me.

I looked over, and I saw the Black Knight bearing down on me. I ran harder. If I could at least cross the low wall, it might give him pause. If not, there were more trees I could run through again and hopefully lose him.

Ten feet away from the wall, I tripped in the wet grass, and fell on my face.

The horse jumped over me, came to an abrupt halt, and spun around. Sir Francis was twirling his sword as he closed the distance.

"Why even try?" The Black Knight asked as he came up in front of me. "Do you truly not remember me?"

"Look buddy," I answered. "If I slept with your wife, I can promise you she never told me she was married."

Sir Francis laughed.

I could almost make out his eyes in the slits of his helmet. They seemed as silver and dead as those of his men.

I was about to make my move, but the damn horse with its angry noises wouldn't stay still. It seemed to almost sense my intended actions. Up close, I saw that its hooves were bleeding; when it snorted a blood mist flew from its nostrils. The horse was as undead as its rider.

I didn't know what to do.

A rock came out of the tree line, and smacked right into the side of the knight's head. Sir Francis turned angrily at the distraction, and I was gone.

I ran as hard as I could. I ran for all I was worth. I was tired. I was cold . . . but damned if I didn't find the tiniest bit of energy.

I dove over Stronghold Wall.

I didn't get up as quickly as I would have liked. My legs were exhausted. I tried running towards the densest part of the forest. I felt hands upon me. I was captured. I fought against them . . . but my strength was gone.

"Relax . . . relax, Arthur," Wayne said quietly. "We're here, Lance brought us . . . What in the hell is that?"

Wayne had gotten his first look at my pursuer. I laughed a tiny bit, but the sight of a huge medieval knight on a wildly bucking horse quickly chased away any feelings of relief.

The knight charged.

His horse turned at the last moment, and raced along the wall. It was low enough, why didn't they just jump over it? Sir Francis answered my question when he swung his sword over the wall, and connected with an invisible barrier. Waves of blue energy reverberated through the sky from the impact.

"What did you do to the wall?" Wayne asked.

"I didn't do anything," I answered. "Grandpa Merl told me to cross the wall . . . so, I crossed the wall."

"Your grandpa's here?" Wayne asked.

"I think he's dead," I answered. "There were too many soldiers; I couldn't get to him because of the fire."

Wayne probably had another thousand questions, but the brush behind us was disturbed, and both of us turned around. The Sheriff Tagger came out of the bushes with Martin, Betsy, and Bedder. Following distantly behind them, came our own personal pain in the ass Mayor Brunner.

"This had better be good," Mayor Brunner complained. "I don't like that creepy kid sneaking around my town in the dead of night banging on people's windows?"

"Mine was the only window he knocked on," Sheriff Tagger added.

"Regardless," Mayor Brunner said. "I still don't appreciate him sneaking around the . . . *What in Sam Hill is that?*"

The Mayor finally saw the Black Knight. The rest of us had been staring at him for awhile. We watched as he raced his horse back and forth along the wall, slashing for a weak spot in the hopes of finding a way to cross over.

"Who threw the rock?" I asked.

"What rock?" Wayne asked.

"He was about to kill me, and someone beaned him in the head with a rock."

"Must have been, Lance," Wayne answered. "He was ahead of me the entire way here. That kid can really move when he wants to. At least, I think it was Lance . . . I never really got a good look at him."

"It was me," Lance said from some dark place I couldn't quite pin down.

"Good job, buddy," I said.

"Damn straight, good job," Wayne added.

"Well," I said changing the subject. "You folks wanna take this big bastard down?"

"Let's circle him, and start swinging," Wayne said after pulling two medium sized axes out of the sheaths on his broad back.

"That sound okay to you, Boss?" I asked Sheriff Tagger.

The sheriff held up a hand as if he were asking for patience. He wasn't watching the Black Knight like the rest of us. Something else had caught his attention . . . something at the far edge of the clearing.

"What do you see?" I asked.

"There are people hiding in the tree line over there," Sheriff Tagger answered.

"He came with soldiers," I said. "Probably over a hundred of them . . . they must have caught up with us."

"In other words," Mayor Brunner added. "It's a trap. You idiots go chasing after that maniac on the horse, and the rest of his men come out and grab you. Arthur, what the hell did you step in this time?"

"Me?" I asked. "What're you talking about? I don't know these fuckers."

"One of us needs to go out there and talk to them," Mayor Brunner added. "Sheriff, why don't you go see what they want."

"They don't much seem like the chatty type, Mr. Mayor," Sheriff Tagger replied. "We might want to get the rest of the town down here in case things go south."

"We don't have time for that bullshit," Mayor Brunner snapped. "I want these damn raiders away from our town before they go around scaring the citizens."

The Mayor walked closer to Stronghold Wall. I jumped forward and grabbed his shoulder, he slapped my hand away, told me not to touch him, and put a foot upon the wall.

"I'm in charge here," The Mayor called out. "State your business, and be on your way."

The knight and his crazy-ass horse froze.

Then they slowly approached the Mayor. The horse's face was about a foot away from Brunner when they finally came to a stop.

"You are in charge of nothing," Sir Francis said in that scary unnatural voice of his. "Bring me the future king."

"I can assure you," Mayor Brunner said. "I lead these people. I'm the Mayor of this town. There are no kings around these parts."

"Shut your mouth!" Sir Francis shouted. "Arthur, do you hide behind this fat weakling? Come and face me."

"Listen, friend," Mayor Brunner continued. "This doesn't need to get nasty. Whatever you have going on with Arthur, you can handle through me."

"Mr. Mayor," Sheriff Tagger said. "Step away from the wall."

The mayor hesitated for a moment, cursed under his breath, and stomped over to stand right in front of me. The second he turned away, the Black Knight spun his horse around and galloped to the middle of the clearing.

"What kind of play are you making?" Mayor Brunner asked me.

"Huh?" I replied.

"He called you the future king," Mayor Brunner said angrily. "Are you after my position as mayor? Is this some weird sort of power play?"

"Mr. Mayor," Sheriff Tagger said tiredly. "Let's all calm down for a second. Arthur isn't interested in taking your position . . ."

"You think I don't see what's going on?" Mayor Brunner asked. "A group of raiders show up, and Arthur's the only one that can stop them. Yes, let's make Arthur a hero. Let's give him the town. He's a damn leg-breaker, who's slept with half the women in Mill Ridge. He also isn't very well liked. Good luck unseating me in an election."

I was speechless. I mean, I knew the mayor was an asshole, but this was ridiculous.

"Mayor," I said. "I don't know what he's talking about. I don't want to be a hero. I certainly don't want your position. I don't what's going on. I was attacked."

"Of course you were," Mayor Brunner said sarcastically. "Well, if you and your friends think I'm beaten, well, you've got another thing coming. You think you can make deals? You've never seen me in action."

With that, Mayor Brunner marched right back over to Stronghold Wall . . . crawled over, and stormed out to the middle of the field.

A bunch of us made a move to grab him, but it happened too quickly. We never thought he'd be stupid enough to cross the wall. We were all taken by surprise.

Martin tried to follow him.

"Stay right where you are, Deputy." Sheriff Tagger said. "This wall is offering a sort of protection, and you aren't about to leave it for that asshole. He made his bed, let's just hope things work out for the best."

When the Mayor was twenty feet away from the wall, Sir Francis charged . . . the distance between them was covered in an instant. The knight's sword was scary sharp, it flashed out in an arc, and a spray of crimson flew from the Mayor's neck.

Another step and Mayor Brunner fell to his knees, his head separating from his body, and rolling off in the wet grass.

"What the fuck?" Wayne shouted.

Betsy screamed.

Sir Francis circled back, stabbed at the severed head, brought it up with the tip of his sword, galloped over to us, and launched the damn thing over the wall.

Betsy screamed again as the head landed at her feet.

From the tree line came the sounds of cheering men. Sir Francis held his bloody sword in the air and his cheering men came forth. They were loud, very, very loud, and they were enjoying themselves as they pounded the flats of their blades against their shields, and taunted us.

Sheriff Tagger hadn't moved, and he hadn't reacted to the violent display which had just occurred.

"Boss," Martin said, while putting a hand on the old man's shoulder. "You okay?"

"Nope," Sheriff Tagger answered slowly. "I think we're in a mess of trouble, and for the life of me, I can't seem to find a way out of it."

❧ MERLIN ❧

The look of shock when I snuck up behind Arthur's party was amusing. Not a single one of them knew I was there ... except for the boy. He was different. He seemed to be aware of my presence the moment I entered Arthur's vicinity.

I could sense him tracking me as I silently made my way through the trees. I called out to him quietly, and told him who I was in order to keep him from throwing rocks at me. He didn't answer, but seemed to be okay with my approach.

The walk winded me. I had used too much power defending Arthur at his cabin. I was tired, and old. On top of that, becoming invisible in order to escape the soldiers seemed to have used up the last of my magical reserves.

I was powerless.

I didn't appreciate the feeling. For centuries I clung to the last vestiges of my power. How sad that, on the day things came full circle, I was forced to use them up. I needed to be careful, Arthur needed me, and I would serve no purpose dead.

I stepped into the clearing just as the sheriff finished saying something about "being in a mess of trouble."

"There is almost always a light at the end of the tunnel," I announced scaring the hell out of all of them.

When the group calmed down, Arthur attempted to speak with me, but I waved him off, and approached Stronghold Wall.

The Black Knight came forward to meet me.

"Old wizard," Sir Francis hissed. "How long do you think this wall will hold me back?"

"Long enough," I answered calmly.

"Hah," Sir Francis laughed. "Even now the Dark Queen has been alerted. Her armies march to this very town in a force this world hasn't seen in centuries."

"As my grandson told you earlier," I said. "Do your worst, and watch me laugh."

With those final words, I turned calmly around, put my arms around Arthur and the sheriff, and guided them away from Stronghold Wall.

"They won't be crossing that barrier anytime soon," I told the sheriff. "However, we need to act, and we need to act fast because no wall is truly impenetrable."

"Is it truly upon us?" The sheriff asked.

"I'm afraid so," I answered.

Quickly, we walked through the forest, and made our way to the Sheriff's Station. Arthur tried to ask questions as the sheriff and I talked quietly. I told him to be patient. The others tried to ask questions as well, and the sheriff told them to wait until we were out of the rain.

Inside the station, the lanterns were lit, and the small party was bathed in light. The sheriff leaned against the nearest desk, and sighed heavily. He looked tired. He also looked much older than when I had seen him last.

"Alright," Arthur grumbled. "Somebody needs to tell me what's going on. I've got an army of somewhat-dead looking Monty Python rejects trying to kill me, my grandpa shows up throwing fire like he's from Harry Potter movie, and the mayor's dead. I'm not sure what the two of you were whispering . . . but I'm done, and you need to start talking."

"I apologize for that," I answered. "Sheriff Tagger and I were having a disagreement."

"About what?" Arthur asked.

"About how best to explain what's happening," I answered.

"Give it to us straight," Arthur said. "If we have any questions, we'll be sure to interrupt."

"Perhaps I should give you some background first," I said.

"I'm gonna walk right out this damn door if you stall any longer," Arthur growled.

"Very well," I said. "You are Arthur Pendragon. You are the once and future king. The legends were real, distorted with a bunch of nonsense, but real. In the end, King Arthur existed. He fought and defeated many enemies until the time of his death. His greatest enemy of all . . ."

Arthur was laughing.

"Arthur?" I asked.

He kept laughing.

"Arthur?"

He kept laughing. The others joined in as well, but not as heartily as Arthur. I looked towards Sheriff Tagger. He shook his head at me, and raised his arms in a "what did you expect" sort of gesture.

"Arthur," I said. "Arthur, I need you to pay attention."

The laughter continued. It was downright rude.

"Arthur!" I shouted. "This world is about to burn!"

The laughter stopped immediately. Arthur came to my side and gently touched my shoulder.

"It's okay Grandpa Merl," Arthur said calmly. "It's been a stressful time for everyone. Let's go find you a quiet place to sit down and rest. Bedder, can you go fetch the doctor?"

The damn boy thought I was insane.

"No," I said as Arthur gently but firmly guided me towards the door. "You need to listen. Time is of the essence."

Wayne joined Arthur on my other side. I tried to resist, but the boys were strong. Finally, Sheriff Tagger decided to join the party.

"He's telling the truth," Sheriff Tagger said quietly.

Arthur and Wayne stopped and released me.

"Boss?" Arthur asked. "You okay?"

"Not really," Sheriff Tagger answered. "But I haven't lost my marbles, and neither has your granddaddy. I've known who you were since the day you arrived. I've known about that damn sword even longer. I protected you. I tried to guide you. I kept you on when anyone else would have fired you a long time ago. I did this because of who you are, and who you are meant to become."

"King Arthur?" Arthur asked.

"Yes," Sheriff Tagger answered.

"How's that even possible?" Wayne asked when Arthur could think of nothing further to say.

"Magic," I answered.

"Magic isn't real," Wayne said.

"Not anymore," I answered. "I sealed it in a spell, and locked it behind a sword."

"I don't understand," Wayne said.

"Of course you don't," I said. "Be patient with me, and I'll sum everything up for you. The knights of Camelot battled for years against the forces of their greatest enemy, a Dark Queen of tremendous skill and power. I finally defeated this sorceress just as Arthur defeated her son in the bloodiest battle Camelot had ever known."

"I've seen this in movies," Wayne said.

"Of course you have," I replied. "Perhaps you've even read about it in books?"

"Doubtful," Wayne said. "Anyway, Arthur and the sorceress's son end up killing each other, but before Arthur dies, he has one of his men throw his sword Excalibur into a lake . . . and then a chick reaches up and catches the sword."

"I couldn't have said it better myself," I chuckled. "Regardless, there are things you haven't seen in movies. Spells I cast unbeknownst to anyone but me. Spells that tied Arthur's soul to that of the Dark Queen. Because, having fought her, I knew her power. I knew her strength. I feared she would find a way to cheat death. I feared she would come back. So, I cast a spell to ensure that if she ever returned, so would Arthur and the knights that fought so valiantly by his side. As Sir Bedivere threw Excalibur into the lake, I unleashed my spell."

"I have two questions," Wayne announced.

"Fire away," I replied.

"First question . . . what does this have to do with magic not being real anymore?"

"I had to power the spell," I answered. "It was the biggest spell I ever created. It needed a lot of power. I used the majority of the magic on this planet as fuel."

"So the magic has been used up?" Wayne asked.

"No," I answered. "It still exists. Excalibur is once again waiting for a king. The spell was attached to the sword. When steel pierced rock, the spell was triggered, and Arthur was reborn . . . but magic is still being held back. Only when the sword is free will the land once again be filled with magic."

"Second question . . . what's your name?"

"Technically, that's three questions," I answered. "And I am Merlin."

"I figured that's where you were going with all this mumbo jumbo," Wayne said.

"You've always been a very clever man, Sir Gawain," I answered.

"Oh, cool," Wayne replied sarcastically. "I get to play as well. I was afraid you were going to leave me out, but why can't I be Lancelot or somebody more popular?"

"You wouldn't want to be Lancelot," I answered solemnly.

"Okay," Sheriff Tagger interrupted. "That's enough, Wayne. Whether or not you wanna be a smartass is irrelevant. Because everything he's told you is true. This entire world will burn if the Dark Queen isn't stopped. I know it sucks, but there you have it. The two of you, plus a whole bunch of others have a destiny."

Arthur didn't believe a single word of what we were saying. I could see it on his face. He was also unusually quiet as he looked from one of us to another.

"Does this Dark Queen have a name?" Wayne asked.

"She has many names," I answered. "Some know her as Morguase. Others know her as Morgan Le Fay. Most commonly, she is called Morgana."

"Did she cause the fog?" Betsy asked from the back of the room.

"Yes, Madam," I answered. "Just as I have retained a small measure of magic, so apparently has Morgana. The red fog disabled modern technology. Computers, electricity, different forms of communication, firearms; you name it, she stopped it all."

"Why?" Betsy asked.

"She brought the entire world back to the Middle Ages," I answered. "A time of constant warfare, the type of which she is very familiar . . . in other words, the world would have beaten her forces with modern weapons. So, she took those weapons away."

"And then came the green fog," Wayne said.

"The green fog surrounds her armies," I said. "When the green fog came, it was already too late. The modern militaries outnumbered her forces, but they were weaponless and inexperienced in how to defend themselves against the weapons of her era. I tried to locate her before that happened, but I couldn't find her. Perhaps, she is somehow still incorporeal."

"In cor . . . what?" Wayne asked.

"Incorporeal," I answered. "That means there's a possibility that she doesn't yet have a body. I destroyed the body she was born with. She wasn't reborn . . . so, she must have come back in spirit form."

The front door of the station opened.

"Is it time," Arthur's mother asked. "Have you already told him?"

"We're trying to, Dellia," I answered.

The spirited woman moved with a strength and confidence. Quickly she crossed the room, and stood before a confused Arthur.

"I'm so sorry, Arthur," Dellia said. "We were hoping today would never come to pass. Even when the red fog came, and Merlin went out to investigate . . . I was . . . I was . . . oh Arthur, I'm so sorry."

"Mom . . . do you realize how all of this sounds?" Arthur asked.

Dellia turned on me without answering him.

"Merlin," She said. "You should have waited for me."

"He was rather impatient, my dear," I answered. "And time is of the essence. He must travel the road of his destiny."

"He's my son," Dellia countered. "I could have lessened the impact."

"I don't think it really matters," Sheriff Tagger interrupted. "The cat's already out of the bag."

"Well," Dellia pouted. "That's easy for you to say. You two assholes bring Arthur's entire world crashing down upon his ears without the slightest bit of concern for how he feels, and you now want to move forward, and put my son in harm's way. I won't have it. I won't have any of it."

"We need to act fast," I said. "He needs the sword, and he needs to unleash the magic."

"That damn sword is a cursed son of a bitch," Dellia grumbled. "I don't want him anywhere near it. I told you that a long time ago, Merlin."

"Dellia, be reasonable we've had this argument before," I countered. "Arthur needs his blade. The blade is his salvation. I'll teach him how to use and control it, because without it, he'll never survive, and if the king falls . . . Morgana will win."

"Hey fellas," Martin called from the back of the room.

"If my son is destined to be king," Dellia said. "Then he should be kept safe. Why don't you go and claim the sword."

"You know very well that the sword will not obey me," I said.

"Hello," Martin called again from the back of the room.

"What I know is that this entire town is currently under attack," Dellia said. "And you want to send my son out beyond the borders of Stronghold Wall. Does that make sense to you? You built a wall to protect him, and now you want him to leave that protection."

"The protection won't last forever," I said. "That is none other than the Black Knight that beats upon our doors. He will get through, and when he does, I want Arthur to be ready."

"The armor is rust free and ready," Sheriff Tagger said. "I've gone down to the cellars myself, and dusted them off. The swords and shields need a good cleaning, but if any aren't up to snuff, Wayne's wife is an excellent blacksmith."

"Let's not change the subject quite yet," Dellia said.

"Dellia, we can argue later," Sheriff Tagger said. "Right now, we're under attack. We need to move."

"Oh horseshit," Dellia grumbled.

"Arthur must be sent on his way before the sun rises," I said. "He has his best chance of getting past the enemy that way."

"Hey fellas!" Martin interrupted once again at a much louder volume.

"Yes, Martin," Sheriff Tagger asked gruffly. "What is it?"

"Arthur's gone," Martin said.

"Gone?" I asked. "What do you mean gone?"

"Amelia Brent came walking by, and he left with her," Martin said.

"Wow?" Wayne exclaimed. "Amelia Brent? Now that's an attractive woman. I didn't know Arthur was hooking up with her."

"Amelia Brent is married," Betsy added.

"A married woman?" Dellia asked in shock.

I heard a dark laugh come from the man named Bedder. It was a laugh I recognized. I approached the sitting man, and for the first time realized he had a prosthetic hand covered by a black glove.

"I'm sorry I didn't recognize you," I said. "It's been a long time, and we were never very close in the old days."

"You know me?" Bedder asked.

"I've already mentioned you," I answered. "You are Sir Bedivere, the knight who returned Excalibur to the Lady of the Lake."

Bedder reflected for a moment before speaking.

"I've had the strangest dreams ever since the red fog came," Bedder said. "Dreams of a different life . . . I never understood them until this very moment. I believe every word you're saying, but I'm not sure Arthur is the man you want him to be."

"Arthur will come into his own," I replied. "Have no worries about that."

"Of course he will," Dellia added.

"If we can find him," Sheriff Tagger exclaimed.

"I know where to root him out," Wayne added.

"See to it then, young man," I said.

I caught a glimpse of movement outside the window.

"I'll be back as soon as I can," Wayne said as he headed for the door.

"The rain seems to have let up," I said as I watched the hulking man depart. "I think I'll go for a walk, and reacquaint myself with the area. I suggest we all meet up at Dellia's farm when Arthur is found."

I didn't wait for a response. I had another matter to attend to. A secret matter of which none would approve . . . not even myself, but a promise made is a promise kept.

"Follow me, young sir," I whispered as soon as the door closed behind me. "I assume you have questions, and you can assume I have answers."

Another glimpse of movement informed me that I was being followed. A part of me wanted to turn him away. Unfortunately, another part of me knew the anguish that would overcome his life if I didn't act.

The potion became cold inside my cloak. It was ready, having been made a long time ago; it was therefore untouched by my loss of power.

I entered the park behind the Sheriff's Station, and found a comfortable bench next to a clump of trees, and I waited for the child to speak. It took him over thirty minutes to summon the courage.

"Who am I?" He asked from behind the trees.

"You are Lancelot of the Lake, reborn."

"Then I am a traitor," Lance said.

"Does this belief come from a movie or a story?" I asked.

"Both," Lance answered.

"Well, rest assured you are misinformed," I said. "Lancelot never stole his king's wife . . . such an idea is an outrage. Still, Lancelot considered himself a failure even when no others found blame in him."

"What do you mean?" Lance asked.

"I'll answer that question with a question," I said. "Tell me, son, what ails you? Why do you hide all the time?"

A moment of silence.

"I have a social anxiety disorder," Lance finally answered. "It's a pretty bad one. I used to have medicine to help me . . . but the medicine ran out a long time ago."

"The Lancelot of old suffered the same disability," I said. "He was older when he became afflicted with the malady. At first, he would never remove his armor. Eventually, he refused to even lift the visor of his helmet in the

44

company of others. As the years went by, he could no longer remain in the casual company of others. He lived as a hermit in the forests surrounding Camelot, only venturing away from his seclusion in times of battle."

"What happened to him?" Lance asked.

"The malady grew even worse," I answered. "Eventually, Lancelot could no longer fight. He wanted to, but the sickness refused to allow him. Lancelot hated himself for his weakness. Arthur understood, even as he lay dying he never once found fault in his favorite friend."

I allowed another moment of silence as my words sank in.

"Continue please," Lance's voice whispered from behind the trees.

"Lancelot died shortly after," I said. "I believe he simply lost the will to live. He hated himself that much. I was with him when he passed. He kept going on and on about how he failed his friend and king. No amount of words would console him. Finally, I told him of the secret spell I had cast. I told him how Arthur and his knights would be reborn if Morgana found a way to cheat death."

"So, I have been also been reborn," Lance whispered. "But why? I'm as useless as I was before. I can't help Arthur. I can't fight. I can't do anything."

"What if you could?" I asked.

"What do you mean?" Lance asked.

"What if you could help Arthur?" I asked. "What if I could work around this social anxiety disorder? What if I knew a way for you to overcome your disability, and help Arthur?"

"Tell me," Lance whispered urgently.

"Think hard on this, Lance," I said. "What I offer is a promise filled with regret, a promise to a dying knight that hated himself. You see, Lancelot begged me to help him. He begged me for a cure. If he was reborn, he was determined to change his fate. Unfortunately, I had no cure for him. Magic doesn't work like that. Then again . . . perhaps if I . . ."

"Tell me more," Lance whispered urgently.

"Well," I said. "I came up with something rather interesting. I came up with a way for a reborn knight to hide in plain sight, a way for him to work around the anxiety that afflicted him. I explained my idea to Lancelot. He agreed, and with three drops of his blood, I created a potion. A potion both powerful and terrible, because if you choose to drink it . . . your life will never be the same. You will be cursed, a demon-child of the forest, that is only your true self during the hours of sunset and sunrise."

"It will change me?" Lance asked.

"Yes," I answered. "And there is no cure; the potion has aged over centuries. It has a strength to it now that would be impossible to overcome. If I hadn't made a promise to Lancelot on his deathbed, I would never have even told you about it. Even now I shudder at the thought of you taking it. I never expected you to be so young."

"Would you take it?" Lance asked.

"No," I answered.

"Will I be able to help Arthur if I take it?" Lance asked.

"Yes," I answered. "You will have a freedom you've never known before."

"Let me see the potion," Lance whispered.

I withdrew the small bottle from my pocket, and placed it on the bench beside me. The glass was icy to the touch, and frost had begun to gather on the sides. The yellow liquid inside churned against its glass prison.

The time had come.

✤ **WAYNE** ✤

The idea was ridiculous. I wasn't buying a word of it . . . but then, Arthur's mother showed up. That had me wondering. She wasn't a woman easily fooled, and she was as much my mother as she was Arthur's. I never really got along with my mother. She wasn't good for anything but drinking, which meant I spent most of my time at Arthur's house when we were kids.

Grandpa Merl was always around, especially on the weekends. I remember the swordplay lessons very well. I never really got the hang of it, but Arthur excelled. That didn't mean he enjoyed it though. He used to hate it. He wanted to play football and basketball with everyone else, but Grandpa Merl insisted he fine tune his natural talents with a blade.

They were good days. I never thought there was any kind of destiny involved, or I would have paid better attention to what we were being taught, especially when he imported all those foreign instructors into town.

The lessons stopped before we graduated high school. Perhaps they should have continued. Whatever . . . obviously Dellia, Grandpa Merl, and Sheriff Tagger believed we were a bunch of legendary knights reborn, but that didn't mean I was buying into it . . . chances were, they were all crazy.

Then again, to the best of my knowledge . . . crazy wasn't exactly contagious.

That weirdo Bedder believed them. That was kind of odd. The dreams he mentioned . . . I had those as well. Doesn't everyone?

There were alarm bells ringing in my head. As reluctant as I was to believe them, I didn't see any point in taking chances. If they wanted Arthur to go off after some sword, well, I was inclined to help them send him off . . . just in case.

I stopped by Amelia's house. The lanterns were burning inside, and I could see her husband pacing by the window. Amelia was going to have a lot to answer for when she finally got home. Chances were pretty good that her husband was going to come looking for Arthur as well. That wasn't anything new.

My next stop was a small trailer park past all the houses near the town square. Arthur kept a small trailer there just in case he was too drunk to make it home. There were a lot of lanterns burning in a lot of homes. Word was spreading about the attack. It wouldn't be too long before everybody ended up in front of the Sheriff's Station asking questions. Sheriff Tagger better not go with the King Arthur and his medieval knights story, or he was going to get laughed out of town.

There was a lantern burning softly in Arthur's trailer. I could see its glow through the drapes. Fortunately for him, and a few of his girlfriends, I was the only male that knew about this place. Unfortunately for him, we lived in a small town, and sooner or later everyone was going to find out.

I knocked gently on the door.

Nobody answered, but I heard giggling, and let myself in. I saw shapes moving under the covers, but they hadn't yet noticed me, so I quietly lit another lantern and brought it closer to the bed.

They still didn't notice me, so I loudly cleared my throat. The giggling stopped abruptly, and two female heads popped out of the covers with wide eyes. Amelia had brought a friend with her. She was married as well.

"Alright ladies," I said. "I need to have a word with Arthur. So why don't the two of you get dressed, and get lost."

"We were just getting started," Amelia whined.

"Ladies," I said. "I know both your husbands. Take a hike, or I'll bring both of them down here."

I could hear Arthur laughing under the covers as the women gathered their clothes and belongings and left the trailer.

"Arthur," I said. "We need you. Grandpa Merl and your mama want you to track down some sword."

Arthur finally sat up.

"You're kidding me, right?" He asked.

"I wish I was," I answered.

Arthur sighed heavily, and reached over for the bottle of moonshine on the shelf next to the bed. I snatched it away before he could get his hands around it.

"What the hell?" Arthur asked.

"You'll need to be sober for this one, buddy," I answered.

"Are you touched in the head?" Arthur asked. "Those freaks almost killed me earlier. No way in hell, am I leaving this town."

"Look buddy," I said as I sat on the edge of the bed. "You're my pal, my best friend. I've stood by you through the worst of it, and there have been a lot of bad things."

"Oh boy," Arthur grumbled. "Are we about to have a serious talk?"

It was my turn to sigh heavily.

"It's like this," I said. "I'm not sure I believe them. All of it sounds pretty crazy to me, but I have a wife and kids. Look . . . I don't ask you for much, but I need you to do this for me. I know times have been tough for you. I know you can be pretty cold sometimes, but I believe you care about me. I truly do. Maybe I'm an idiot, but I believe it."

Arthur's face had gone blank. I couldn't tell if he was upset, or just wishing I'd leave him alone.

"Anything else?" Arthur asked.

"There's a medieval army at our gates," I added. "And they seem to want to kill you very badly."

"Yup," Arthur said. "I noticed that."

"So what do you think?" I asked.

"I think I'll go track down that damn sword," Arthur replied.

"It's probably a wild goose chase," I said. "But under the circumstances . . . why not check it out?"

"It's not," Arthur said.

"It's not what?" I asked.

"It's not a wild goose chase," Arthur said. "I saw it once when I was a kid."

"You did?" I asked.

"Yup," Arthur answered.

"Do you think you can find it again?" I asked.

"Yup," Arthur answered.

"Are you sure?" I asked. "It's been a long time since either of us were kids."

"I'm sure," Arthur answered. "It's been calling for me ever since the red fog."

I tried to get more information out of the man, but Arthur can be extremely frustrating when there's something he doesn't want to talk about. In the end, I gave up and together we walked to his mama's house.

Despite the late hour, news had apparently traveled even further while Arthur and I had our chat. People were coming out of their homes, and talking to their neighbors. Some of them were already walking in the direction of the Sheriff's Station.

Arthur and I did our best to avoid everyone by walking through backyards, and staying away from the active streets. Occasionally we'd still get a few questions shouted at us, but Arthur just motioned that he couldn't hear what they were shouting, and we hurried on our merry way.

The entire gang was waiting for us on Dellia's front porch. I scanned around for Lance, but I couldn't find him hiding behind any of the trees around the property. There was a chance he'd already made it into Dellia's house, but the windows were all closed.

"So what's the plan?" Arthur asked.

"Follow us into the barn," Grandpa Merl answered.

The group of us walked behind the house to the barn, and the open fields beyond. Dellia took a lot of pleasure in her barn, and to be honest, it was just a slight bit prettier than mine. The red and white structure was two stories tall, with a hay loft on top. Arthur and I were never allowed to play near it when we were growing up. In fact, we weren't even allowed inside the damn thing unless Dellia or her late husband was with us.

Dellia unlocked and threw open the large doors. She shuffled inside, and started lighting lanterns. The immense room was bathed in a golden light, and only then did she motion the rest of us inside.

Once we were all in, Sheriff Tagger closed the doors behind us. The room we were in smelled of hay, and horses. It wasn't an unpleasant smell, and under different circumstances I would have spent a few minutes with the three horses in the stalls at the back of the barn. I rather enjoyed horses, and owned a couple of them myself.

"Is Goliath ready?" Grandpa Merl asked.

"Yes," Sheriff Tagger answered. "He's been waiting in the forest since we first heard about the green fog."

"He's none too happy about it either," Dellia remarked.

I inwardly cringed. Goliath was the reason Arthur hated horses. He belonged to Arthur's late wife. She raised him up, and trained him herself. A wedding present from Grandpa Merl, Goliath was some sort of Friesian mix. He was a mighty black stallion that loved his mama greatly, and after her death, the great beast grew depressed and withdrawn, eventually he lay down upon the grass and even refused to eat. Maybe he knew she died. Maybe he was just missing her presence. Regardless, a week or so after the horse gave up on life; Arthur went down to the paddock behind his cabin to see what he could do for poor Goliath.

It was a huge mistake.

Arthur tried for hours to get the horse to stand. He tempted him with sweets. He yelled at him. He pulled on his head. He brought out a saddle. Nothing he did seemed to reach the horse. His lack of success wasn't a big shock considering Arthur wasn't in the best emotional state himself, so soon after losing his wife and child. Regretfully for him, in a moment of frustration, Arthur slapped the horse on the ass.

The reaction was immediate. The horse jumped to its feet, spun around and kicked Arthur right into the air. Dazed, and lacking any breath in his lungs, Arthur climbed back to his feet just in time to see the horse charging at him like a bull. Arthur ran for his life, but before he could climb the fence and escape Goliath managed to leave a rather large bite wound on his rear end.

Since that fateful day, Arthur has avoided horses at all costs, Goliath on the other hand found a new reason to live . . . terrorizing Arthur, and anyone else foolish enough to come near him. The only people immune to his psychotic temper tantrums were Dellia and Grandpa Merl. So it was Dellia that took him in when Arthur tried to sell him off.

"What does Goliath have to do with any of this?" Arthur asked.

"You'll need a mount," Grandpa Merl answered.

"I can walk," Arthur said.

"No you can't," Grandpa Merl said. "The distance is too great, and the enemy is upon us. You'll be run down and killed. Goliath is your only chance."

"I can use another horse," Arthur argued. "It doesn't need to be Goliath."

"Goliath is strong," Grandpa Merl snapped. "I picked him to be the perfect mount for you. He is the greatest horse in the world. No other horses can match his power. He will protect you when you need it most."

"He's crazy, and he hates me," Arthur snapped back.

"He's strong willed," Grandpa Merl said in a calmer voice. "Trust me, Arthur. Goliath is the right horse for you. He's a horse fit for a king."

"This is fucking ridiculous," Arthur muttered. "I'm gonna get myself killed out there."

"Arthur," Dellia said approaching her son and putting a hand on his shoulder. "Trust us. Goliath will protect you."

She said her words in gentle way. She said her words with an outpouring of love. Arthur said nothing in return. He rarely argued with his mother and if he did, he never did it in front of people . . . but he didn't look happy.

"What tunnel are you talking about?" I asked as quickly as possible.

In answer, Grandpa Merl moved across the room to a framed picture on the wall between some stalls. It was a photograph of Arthur and his father. Both of them were grinning from ear to ear as they rested their favorite rifles across their arms. Grandpa Merl moved the picture to the side, and uncovered a square hole in the wall. He reached his hand into the hole, twisted something, and a rumbling sound could be heard throughout the barn.

The three horses became agitated by the noise, and made grumbling sounds of frustration. Grandpa Merl took up a lantern from the wall, walked towards them, and entered an open stall on the right side. The rest of us followed him, and were shocked to discover a secret doorway had opened in the back of the stall.

I grabbed a lantern as well, and the group of us descended down a long flight of stone stairs into darkness.

"Did you know this was here?" I asked Arthur.

"Not a clue," He answered.

"Only Merlin, Dellia, Arthur's father, and I knew about this one, boys," Sheriff Tagger chuckled. "It's one of the best kept secrets in all of Mill Ridge."

"For good reason," Grandpa Merl added. "There are secrets in this chamber that aren't meant to be revealed until the correct moment."

"It's also the only pathway to the sword," Arthur said. "Isn't it?"

"How did you know that, son?" Dellia asked.

"The sword has been calling him," Grandpa Merl answered instead.

"No," Dellia said. "Arthur, is that true?"

"I guess so," Arthur grumbled.

"Where is this sword?" I asked.

"A long distance from here," Grandpa Merl answered.

"So it's in the forest?" I asked.

"Yes," Grandpa Merl answered.

"Then why hasn't anyone found it?" I asked.

"The forest is enchanted," Grandpa Merl answered. "Only those who start out on the intended path will discover Excalibur. Otherwise, the forest will turn against them, and never reveal its secrets. It wasn't easy mind you, not with my dwindling supply of magic . . . but hiding the sword and protecting this town with Stronghold Wall were rather necessary."

"If Morgana's army knew the sword's location, they'd surround the area, and prevent Arthur from claiming his birthright," Sheriff Tagger said. "They'd also succeed in preventing Merlin from reclaiming his power, and I have a feeling we're going to need that power sooner rather than later."

The stairway went on forever. To our left side was a rock wall. To our right side, was a darkness so complete our lanterns couldn't penetrate its inky blackness. Nothing but open air, and I couldn't judge how high we were, but the echoes of our voices led me to believe that a fall would be fatal.

After long moments, we reached the bottom. We gathered together on a stone floor, and Grandpa Merl went around the vast rectangular room lighting sconces on the walls. The room was bathed in a golden light. I heard someone gasp, and I understood their reaction completely.

We were in a large treasure room. Everywhere I looked I saw gold and silver, gems and coins, weapons of various types, armor . . . and in the very center of the room was a large circular wooden table.

"Wow," Martin said.

"Welcome to the war room," Grandpa Merl replied. "We've been preparing for this day a very long time."

"This looks like a treasure room to me," Betsy said.

"I needed the Mill Ridge to prosper," Grandpa Merl said. "The safest thing for Arthur was to keep him happy in a town no one had ever heard of."

"Well," Sheriff Tagger grumbled. "We kept him safe for as long as possible . . . but we knew they'd come for him eventually."

"You knew all this would happen?" Arthur asked.

"We knew there was a possibility of it happening from the minute you came into our lives," Dellia answered.

"We hoped for the best, but prepared for the worst," Grandpa Merl added.

"None of you ever bothered to tell me," Arthur said. "Why?"

"Morgana shouldn't have power," Grandpa Merl answered. "With the exception of the small amounts I kept for myself, I used all the magic to create the spell that brought everyone back. What can a powerless sorceress do to the world? Nothing, she would be insignificant, and there was no sign of her . . . not even a hint of her activities. I searched and searched . . . but nothing. There was no reason to tell you. You could have lived your life without ever being aware of who you truly are."

"How did Morgana get her magic?" Arthur asked.

"I doubt we'll ever know," Grandpa Merl answered. "That's why I left. I went to see for myself if the red fog was truly a sign of her return. Perhaps her soul retained some magic as I retained some magic. That's just a guess of course . . . she works with a darker magic than I have ever used. My knowledge of her abilities is a tad limited."

"But you were able to beat her before?" I asked.

"Yes," Grandpa Merl answered. "I was able to beat her."

"So what's next?" Arthur asked.

✤ ARTHUR ✤

Wow, I was having a great evening. That damn sword . . . I saw it briefly one time in my entire life, and I was never able to forget it. I had dreams about the damn thing, and in those dreams . . . it called to me.

That freakin sword wanted me. It wanted me to pull it from the rock . . . to release it from its prison. There was something scary about that sword. Excalibur wasn't supposed to be scary . . . at least not to the good guys. Regardless, I pushed those dreams out of my mind the second I woke up in the morning. They were just one of those odd memories that you retain from childhood. They can't affect you in anyway once you grow up . . . right?

I guess not.

The treasure room was incredible. It's no wonder my family never had any financial difficulties. Now that I think about it, neither did anyone else in Mill Ridge. Everyone made money. I guess that should have struck me as a bit odd, but nobody really tends to think about the down side of things when everything is turning up roses.

After another brief question and answer session, I had all I needed to know. I didn't doubt any of it. Oh sure . . . I tried to blow it all off in the beginning, but the minute my mother walked into the Sheriff's Station, I knew. I didn't want to admit it to myself, but I knew.

Then I saw Amelia and her friend, and I figured I'd take one last shot of avoiding everything that was coming my way. It probably would have worked out a lot longer for me if Wayne hadn't come. Damn Wayne, I couldn't say no to him. He's been like a brother to me, and he . . . well . . . damn, what does it matter. The man asked me to help, and I'm going to help. I owed it to him after all the crap he helped me through over the years.

"So what's next?" I asked after Grandpa Merl told Wayne that he had beaten Morgana in the past.

Everyone looked at me, and I knew exactly what they were thinking. I was the worst person in the world to put their faith in. If I hadn't let them down in the past, they simply hadn't known me long enough. With the exception of Grandpa Merl, and my mother . . . everyone looked very nervous.

"I'll show you the tunnel," Grandpa Merl answered.

He led me to the far side of the room, and twisted a sconce on the wall. Then, he pushed against a nearby rock, and a section of the wall swung open.

"All you have to do is follow the tunnel," Grandpa Merl said. "At the end of the tunnel, you will find another sconce. Twist it just like this one, and the wall will swing open."

I looked back at the others, back at the doubt in their faces.

"Are you sure it has to be me?" I asked.

"I am," Grandpa Merl answered. "Only you can pull the sword."

"Nobody wants to put their faith in me," I whispered. "I'm a screw-up."

"Arthur . . . my sweet boy," Grandpa Merl whispered back. "There is so much more to you. I wish I could make you understand what you are capable of. I truly do, but trust me . . . I would have faith in no one else but you."

I loved my grandpa. I loved him for those words, and I loved him for all the kind things he'd said to me in the past. He and my mother never gave up on me. No matter how many times I disappointed them . . . they always believed in me.

"Okay," I said. "What happens when I leave the tunnel?"

"Follow the trail," Grandpa Merl answered. "The forest will guide you. The trail will be easy to spot. Eventually you will come to a small wooden bridge and beyond that a great lake. Blow the horn on the pier, and a boat will come. Pay the Ferryman a piece of gold, and he will take you across the lake to the next leg of your journey."

"This sounds very *Clash of the Titans*," I said as he handed me a piece of gold.

"The wooden bridge marks the boundary of an area no mortal should ever cross." Grandpa Merl said. "The land is haunted; and the spirits that dwell there will know who you are. Do not fear them, but give them no opportunity to harm you."

"What about the soldiers that are after me?" I asked.

"At the end of the second leg of your journey you will find a smaller lake. Once there you must find the boat, and take it to the island. This is Excalibur's domain. Once you're on the water, Morgana's forces cannot follow you."

"So I'm only safe in Excalibur's domain?" I asked.

"Yes," Grandpa Merl answered. "While the enemy cannot follow the trail, they can certainly follow you. Hopefully, you can slip by them quietly . . . but that seems rather unlikely. Even now they are spreading out around the perimeter of Stronghold Wall."

"You're gonna get me killed," I grumbled.

"Have you forgotten what a skilled swordsman you are?" Grandpa Merl asked. "You are hardly defenseless, and let's not forget about Goliath. He'll do his part to keep you safe."

"I'm sure he will," I said.

"Be brave, Arthur," Grandpa Merl said. "Help will arrive when help is needed."

"Whatever that means," I said.

I said my goodbye's to everyone as quickly as possible. I didn't like the way they looked at me. It seemed that while everyone was having less and less difficulty believing in magic, they still refused to believe in me.

My mother handed me a change of clothes, and everyone but Betsy turned around while I put them on. In the pile of fabric, was a pair of fatigues, a grey long-sleeved shirt, hiking boots, and a flannel shirt.

Sheriff Tagger handed me a one-handed sword and a belt which I buckled around my waist. The sword was an unfamiliar weight against my hip. I drew it out, and gave it a few practice swings. It was a good sword, but I was grossly out of practice. Finally, I attached the dagger Wendy had given me to the back of the belt. Standing there in modern clothes with a medieval sword and dagger on my belt made me feel like an idiot. Grandpa Merl capped it all off with a green Jedi robe complete with sleeves and a hood.

"This will keep you dry," Grandpa Merl smiled as he helped me put it on. "It will also provide you with a bit of camouflage if you need it."

"I feel like an asshole," I said to a few snickers.

"Times are a changing, brother," Wayne said with a worried smile, and a quick hug. "You be careful out there, and don't get in trouble with any wild forest girls without me there to bail you out."

"I believe in you," My mama said while giving me a long hug. "I believe in you."

A few more hugs, some pats on the back, a burning torch in my hand, and I was off down the tunnel with Grandpa Merl in front of me. It was dark, and smelled of the earth, but the torch provided more than enough light for me to find my way.

My grandpa waited until we were out of earshot from the others and motioned for me to stop.

"This is as far as I'll go," Grandpa Merl announced. "This journey isn't meant for me but heed my parting words very carefully. Excalibur has grown dark, and angry. Do not use this sword. Do not draw blood with this sword no matter how great the temptation. It isn't safe. Do you understand?"

"Not really," I answered. "Why am I risking my life for a sword I can't even use?"

"You'll wield Excalibur soon enough," Grandpa Merl said. "I only want to prepare you so that the sword doesn't end up wielding you, and that takes time."

"Okay," I said.

"I mean it Arthur," Grandpa Merl said. "Don't use the sword. Touch it as little as possible."

"I hear you," I answered.

"Do you?" Grandpa Merl asked.

"Yes," I answered.

Grandpa Merl seemed somewhat satisfied, gave me a parting hug, and made his way back to the others in the dark, while I continued down the tunnel in the opposite direction. There were other torches along the wall. I lit them as I passed. I didn't need them at the moment, but I was worried that the torch I was carrying might go out, and leave me trying to feel my way through the dark until I found an exit.

The walls and ceiling of the tunnel were made of rock just like the treasure room, only the air here was damp and chilly. I was glad to have the cloak.

I took my time in the tunnel. I had the strangest feeling of being watched, and I was worried something was going to jump out at me. Perhaps the soldiers or even worse, the Black Knight found a way inside. With the torch held high in my right hand, I noticed that my left hand was resting on the hilt of my sword.

It took about an hour or so to make my way down the long and winding tunnel. Occasionally, I found swords and shields mounted on the walls. At the end, I found a red banner with a white circle in the center. Inside the circle was a red dragon. The banner looked familiar to me, but I couldn't place it.

I twisted the sconce on the rock wall, and waited as the door swung slowly open. I ground out my torch on the stone floor, and stepped out into the grey sky of the early morning. I moved slowly and carefully out of the tunnel, searching for the enemy. When I was finally confident I was alone in the small clearing, I searched for the trail.

It was right in front of me.

I could have sworn it wasn't there a second before, but it was as plain as day to me now. The stone wall closed behind me, blending perfectly into the rocky hillside. I had a brief moment of panic as I realized that I didn't know how to get back into the tunnel if things went badly.

Like most kids in Mill Ridge, I spent a lot of time in the forest when I was younger. So it was a bit unsettling to realize that I was in an unfamiliar area. Spotting the sun creeping up into the sky, I crawled to the top of the hill, and tried to orient myself.

Far, far away I faintly saw the tops of buildings, and chimney smoke in the sky. That was impossible. I was seeing Mill Ridge, but Mill Ridge was more than a day's hike through some seriously dense forest away from me.

I was only in the tunnel for an hour.

I was really beginning to hate magic.

There was no going back. My fate was decided. My eyes drifted back to the trail in the woods. I missed it on my first pass. On the second pass I located it immediately, a single path through the massive wall of green trees and dense vegetation.

Down the hill I went. I was breathing heavily. My nerves were getting the better of me. I didn't know what I was afraid of, but it had to do with stepping onto the trail. Despite my uneasiness however, I was soon standing in front of the path as if my legs had a mind of their own, and my heart was thundering inside my chest as if it were giving the lecture of a lifetime to my legs for being so stupid. I wanted to turn back. If I couldn't get inside the stupid tunnel, then I would do the long hike and try my best to sneak past all the soldiers.

Instead, I stepped forward onto the trail.

I felt a cold chill run across my body as I entered the forest. Looking behind me, I realized that the entrance was no longer there. The forest was forcing me to continue. It wasn't a pleasant feeling to be forced along a trail in a dark and unfamiliar forest.

I went forward.

The ground was soft. The branches and leaves were wet. The trees were tall and thick enough to blot out the sun. I was home. This was my kind of forest. Grandpa Merl made sure I knew how to make my way in environments just like this. He had been teaching me ever since I could walk.

I picked up the pace.

I heard the early morning song of birds. That was a good thing. If there were soldiers in these woods, the birds wouldn't be singing so loudly. The sound of their music relaxed me, and I set off at a slow jog. I had no idea how long this trip was going to take, and I also wanted to put as much distance between myself and the Black Knight as possible.

For two hours I traveled at a steady pace, and the trail was easy to follow. The forest rose up in green curtains on the sides, but the ground I treaded upon was a dark rich brown. Every now and then I would look behind me only to find that the trail had vanished.

After around four hours in the forest, the birds stopped chirping. I didn't notice it at first; I was concentrating on controlling my breathing. Years of drinking had robbed me of my endurance, and I trying in vain to keep up a good pace.

I stopped in my tracks when I finally noticed the lack of ambient noise, and listened intently. It was hard to hear anything over my labored breaths. Then ... I heard a noise in the distance. Something was moving through the forest, and that something was getting closer.

I crouched down immediately, pulled my hood over my head, and left the trail.

Hiding in the bushes, my heart started to race. Whatever I heard was headed my way, and it wasn't an animal. Well, there were probably horses, but what I was hearing were the marching sounds of many, many feet.

Eventually, I heard the strangely accented speech of the previous evening, and I knew I was in trouble. The enemy was in the forest. They were making too much noise to be hunting for me specifically, so that meant they were probably joining up with the Black Knight's forces outside of Mill Ridge.

When they were close enough, I put my skills to the test. It'd been a long time, but I still remembered all the tricks associated with remaining quiet in the forest. I stayed clear of the path, though it seemed to follow me every time I looked for it. Quietly, I moved closer and closer to the enemy. In no time at all I could hear their voices clearly, though I still couldn't see them in the dense vegetation.

"Do you think Sir Francis truly found him?"

"I do indeed. Sir Francis isn't one to make mistakes. If he sent out the call to arms, you can bet the fox is cornered."

"More like the dragon is cornered."

"He's hardly a dragon without his fangs."

"I fought him once."

"Yeah? And my daughter's a princess."

"No, it's true . . . but it wasn't much of a contest. He ran me through and damn near cut me in half. That's how I lost my life."

"Truly?"

"His blade claimed many lives that day. I'm nothing special, and I don't claim to be."

"Well, Excalibur won't be claiming anymore lives if Sir Francis has anything to say about it. He's focused our entire might on this little town."

It sounded like three different voices, but I couldn't be sure. I also worried about the amount of soldiers headed towards my town. Mill Ridge had close to twenty five hundred people living there. By most comparisons, it was a pretty solid amount of available fighters . . . but there was no way we could handle a gigantic army attacking us.

I moved just a bit closer, and poked my head around a tree. I saw two soldiers. They had that sickly pale skin, and soggy hair. Around their feet was the pale green fog, but it wasn't nearly as dense as it had been the night before, probably because there were just two of them.

Then I noticed the green fog flowing around me, only it wasn't coming from the soldiers. It was coming from behind me. I turned quickly, and saw the rusty blade of a sword swinging at my neck. I ducked immediately and rolled out of the way. The blade buried itself into the tree behind me.

"I've found us a snoop, boys!" The soldier shouted as he struggled to pull his blade free from the tree.

I found my feet quickly, and tried to run only to be surrounded before I could gain any momentum. They had done this before. They knew how to trap their prey . . . and they enjoyed the game greatly.

The two newcomers had already drawn their swords. Even rusted and worn, the edges looked sharp and deadly. I was cornered by experienced killers. Their silver eyes glistened in the sunlight. The fog gathered at our feet.

It was an experience I had never had before. These were men from a different age somehow brought forth into modern times. They had no respect for life, and that was truly terrifying. To be confronted by someone so eager to do you harm . . . well, there's no words to describe how vulnerable that can make you feel. I dealt with drunks on a regular basis, but most of them had no desire to take my life. They only wanted to smack me around, and go back to drinking, maybe even brag about it the next day. These soldiers were different. They wanted me to feel pain. They wanted me to suffer, and eventually they wanted me to scream.

I drew my sword.

"Whoa, lads," A soldier laughed. "Be careful, this one fancies himself a fighter."

"Let's see how good he is," Another soldier giggled menacingly.

The third soldier came towards me slowly. He lifted his blade until it was pointing at my heart. I turned my sword towards him, but I concentrated my attention on the others. That would be the perfect attack. He distracts me, and the other two finish me off.

The soldier approaching me, feinted a swing and a charge. I pretended to take the bait, and jerked my sword around clumsily. He laughed, and gained an incredible measure of confidence. I now knew which of them was going to attack. Yet, a part of me wondered at their stupidity.

The soldier came closer still, and I kept my eyes on the others. They were smiling. When he was close enough, he charged and swung his sword in a clumsy motion. I dropped my blade, stepped inside the arc of his swing, and chipped a large section of bone off his shin with an upwards sweep of my own.

It was a dirty move on my part. Attacking the hands and shins was often frowned upon by the many instructors Grandpa Merl had me study under . . . but it worked. Blood flowed past the soldiers leather boot, and he started to scream. I stabbed him through the heart right before he fell to the ground. I then pulled the hood off my head, and waited for the remaining two to attack.

They didn't attack.

"It's him," A soldier cried out. "It can't be."

"The king himself," The other answered.

"But that's not Excalibur," The first soldier said. "Let's take him."

"Try it," I replied.

My bluff didn't work. They weren't impressed. Instead of running off into the forest, they spread out a little bit more and advanced towards me. My blade went from one to the other, I was nervous . . . nope, I was terrified. My fist attacker was a clumsy idiot. I didn't know the skill set of the other two, probably it wasn't great . . . but there were still two of them versus one of me.

The first soldier charged.

He tried a stab at my stomach. Our blades collided as I blocked, and spun his sword out of the way before elbowing him in the nose. He fell back as the blood spurted, and his eyes filled with tears.

I didn't have the time to finish him off. Instead, I twisted immediately to the final soldier. I brought my sword up to block his downward swing. I tried to smack his blade to the side in order to attack, but he didn't fall for it. Instead of losing control of his weapon, he stepped backwards. That simple action meant he had skill

We faced one another with our blades pointed at each other's throats. One of us would step forward, and the other would step back. We were in a dance, and memories began to flood through my head. I thought of all the things I could do, but that was no good. Thinking things out wasn't the way to win; I needed my body to react without thought.

I was tired of the game. I charged him. He reacted with a swing, but I ducked and gave an upwards slice from his hip to his shoulder. We came apart, and he smiled at me. Then he noticed the slice across his tunic, and the broken pieces of his chain mail.

I saw fear in his eyes.

The killer had turned into the victim. He had training, he had experience, but it was nothing compared to mine. My confidence grew. In the corner of my eye, I saw the soldier with the broken nose rise to his feet, and wipe the blood away from his mouth with a chain-mailed sleeve.

He would soon be back in the fight, so I charged my current opponent once again in an effort to end things before Mr. Broken nose came after me. This time I didn't go for the chain-mail protecting his chest and shoulders. I went for his arm, and I cut his wrist before we pulled away from each other.

The blood began to gush.

"Dirty bastard," The soldier sneered.

This time he charged at me with a wild thrust. I spun his sword high in the air with a block, and then brought my own blade down hard on the inside of his thigh.

He fell instantly, both hands grabbing at his leg in a vain attempt to stop the flow of blood. He was out of the fight, and barely clinging to life.

I spun again.

Mr. Broken nose was back in business. Our swords collided with the fierce sound of grinding edges. He pushed. I pushed . . . then I side-stepped. The idiot fell forward, and dropped his weapon. I buried my blade in the back of head before he found his feet once again.

"Ah, ya bastard," The soldier bleeding out from his wrist shouted as I yanked my sword from his friend's head. "You've killed me again. I hope the Dark Queen and the rest of her Death Reapers take your soul. It's what you deserve."

I didn't reply. I only watched as he grew weaker and weaker. I was cleaning my blade when his head dropped to the earth. I had no sympathy. None of them deserved it. Death Reapers? The name fit them well. Such violent men could not be pitied . . . no . . . they must be destroyed.

Sounds in the forest.

More Death Reapers.

I could hear them calling out. They were probably searching for the men I had just killed. Good luck finding them in this dense forest. I could build an Aztec temple in these woods, and they'd never find it unless I gave them a map.

I wasn't worried. No, that's not true. I was very worried, but I was nevertheless confident that they'd never see me. I'd only need to be more careful on my journey.

Movement to my right.

The Death Reaper I'd been watching bleed to death wasn't quite dead, and apparently he'd heard his friends calling out for him as well.

He began to screaming something about how he had found the king.

I danced in place for a brief moment as I decided on whether to run, or finish him off. I decided to run, the damage was already done. I was about to have some unwanted company.

I hauled ass through the forest, realized I had no idea where I was going, and stopped. I scanned for the trail. In a moment, it appeared on my left. I heard movement all around me.

I headed along the trail as fast as I could. I was doing fine for about five minutes when suddenly I went weak in the legs. I slowed down to a fast walk as an overwhelming fatigue settled in throughout my body. Three minutes after that I was on my knee's dry heaving in the most epic adrenaline dump I've ever experienced.

I wasn't used to all the physical activity, and I certainly wasn't used to life and death battles. Too much adrenaline had been pumping in my system.

My body was worn out. I wanted nothing more than to lie down and have a nap.

There were shouts coming from all over the forest. Geez, how many Death Reapers were out there? Did it matter? One of them was too much for me to handle at the moment.

I picked myself up, and started walking. I needed distance. It wasn't easy, but I forced myself to move. I was the one the Death Reapers were after. If they knew the future king was in the forest . . . how bad would things get? Would they believe their dying comrade?

Did it matter? Even if they didn't believe I was alone in the forest with them, they were kinda obligated to find the person responsible for killing their friends.

I tried a slow jog, but that only resulted in more dry heaves. Things weren't looking to good for me. I barely had a head start, and I was losing that rapidly.

I rolled off the trail into the brush the second I heard the sounds of men running through the forest. If I wasn't going to be able to outrun them, I better be able to hide from them. It certainly wasn't the most glamorous way to handle things, but this wasn't a movie. If I was found; I was as good as dead.

I stayed as still as possible as Death Reapers searched the forest all around me. They moved in groups of three, and called out to one another. As soon one group would pass, and before I could relax the tiniest bit, it seemed like another group came out of nowhere to take their place. The brief snatches of conversation I was able to hear as they passed by me was rather disheartening.

"You really think he saw the king?"

"Well, somebody cut him up good and proper."

"Best we not take chances. Sir Francis would have all our heads on a pike if we let Arthur slip on by us."

"Well, let's hope we find the culprit soon. I don't fancy walking in these woods any more than I need to."

"Aye, not when there's a town full of women in our near future."

"I see tracks."

I was in a full panic. Perhaps that was a good thing, because I had strength in my limbs once again. It may have been a fleeting strength, but I planned on using it for as long as possible.

The Death Reaper that saw the tracks was standing less than five feet away from my hiding place. I couldn't draw my sword. The noise and the movement would have given me away. Instead, I drew my dagger.

"Where do you see tracks?"

"Right here, in the mud."

"I see them . . . where's the bastard headed?"

"Into the forest."

"That's no good. This forest seems haunted."

"Don't say that, like it or not, we're already in it."

Another Death Reaper moved even closer, and began scanning the forest beyond my position. Could I deal with another three of them? I didn't know. I felt like I could . . . but I had no way of knowing. If I got into a fight, and the exhaustion came back . . . I was a dead man.

The Death Reaper took a step forward into the brush I was hiding in. He almost stepped on my finger. I couldn't move; he'd see me for sure. Another step and he'd trip over me.

I stabbed my dagger through his foot.

He screamed for all he was worth, and I leaped from the brush thrusting my dagger into his throat. The two other Death Reapers, cursed in shock. I threw the dagger at the closest one. He blocked it with his sword, but it still gave me enough time to draw my own sword.

I went after the man as quickly as I could. He blocked for all he was worth. He wasn't the greatest swordsman, but he was decent enough to keep me from killing him immediately.

His friend came rushing up behind me. I was now fighting two of them at the same time. After seeing what I did to the last Death Reapers that underestimated me, they weren't taking any chances.

I had trained for this and more . . . but that was a long, long time ago. I've said it once, I've said it twice. I was out of practice, and out of shape. The exhaustion was already creeping back into my limbs.

I took a cut on my arm. It was deep, and the blood was flowing, but it wasn't incapacitating. I fought for all I was worth, but my opponents realized what was happening. I was losing, and I was too tired for any tricks that might save the day. They were both smiling at me as they circled and lunged just enough to weaken me even further.

I stumbled, and fell.

"Well," One of them said. "He's not quite the same king he used to be."

"Can you imagine our reward," The other added.

"Let's bring back his head, and collect it."

The thundering sound of hooves on dirt made both of them turn away from me and look into the forest. A great behemoth of a horse was charging towards them. At first they seemed unimpressed. Then they heard the angry growls, and realized that the horse meant to attack them.

I saw my dagger lying just a couple feet away from me. In a wild lunge that was probably completely unimpressive to see, I scooped it up, and stabbed the nearest Death Reaper in the groin. He screamed loudly, and distracted his buddy just enough to give the horse an opportunity to ram into him.

The groin cut Death Reaper continued to scream, and roll around in a widening pool of blood. I found my feet, and unsteadily made my way towards the Death Reaper that had been rammed by the horse. He cursed, found his feet as well, and rose to face me.

It was a huge mistake. The giant black horse was right behind him. I knew the horse well, and turning your back on that particular horse was a major mistake. The horse kicked the Death Reaper towards me, and I stabbed out sloppily in reaction. The end result had my sword buried in the man's chest all the way to the hilt.

I didn't breathe a sigh of relief.

Instead, I panicked a wee bit more.

Before me stood Goliath, the biggest, meanest horse in the whole damned world. I had forgotten about him. He wasn't outside the tunnel. I never saw him as I ran down the trail. Somehow he had found me.

I was in trouble.

My sword had been wrenched from my hand when the Death Reaper fell to the ground. I looked over at it. I looked back at Goliath. He watched my movements carefully. He sensed my intentions, gave a low horse growl, and scratched at the ground.

"Oh, fuck you," I said in a moment of complete despair.

Almost in response, the horse made a series of gruff noises that sounded suspiciously like laughter . . . but he didn't charge.

Mr. Groin injury bled out, and stopped screaming. That was a relief, his screams were going to give away my . . . too late. Nearby Death Reapers began calling out for their fallen amigos. I could hear them crunching through the forest around me, as they zeroed in on our position.

The horse still hadn't attacked me. I took a few steps to my side, and the horse matched my movements. I took a few more steps; he matched my movements once again.

"We gotta go, horse," I said.

The horse looked at me as if I were an idiot.

The Death Reapers were almost on top of us. The horse wasn't attacking, but it wasn't leaving me either.

I didn't have a clue.

A few more shouts on either side of me and just like I figured, three more Death Reapers burst through the tree line. I screamed like a little girl, I moved my dagger into my good hand, and jerked my head from side to side trying to keep both Goliath, and the Death Reapers in sight.

"Well, well, well," A Death Reaper exclaimed as he took in his fallen comrades, and then settled his gaze upon me. "It does indeed appear to be the future king. What do you say boys?"

Goliath slowly began to advance towards them. Was he protecting me? No way. The soldiers were ignoring him. No doubt they had a lot of experience with horses, and therefore remained unconcerned. That was the problem. All their probable experience counted against them, because I can guarantee they never met a horse like Goliath.

The soldiers were going to cut him down. Sure, he would probably get one or two of them, but a cut is a cut and a stab is a stab. He was going to get injured, or more likely killed.

"Goliath," I whispered.

A part of me still cared about him. I hated him, but he was my wife's horse. I couldn't let him get hurt.

Goliath jerked his head in my direction at the sound of his name, and my decision was made. I ran towards him, and jumped on his bare back. The horse's eyes widened as I grabbed a hold of his mane. Then he roared out an ear-splitting horse roar, and spun around. The Death Reapers reached out for me, and Goliath kicked them so hard I almost fell off his back in the aftershock.

One, two, three kicks . . . the Death Reapers were sprawled on the ground. Goliath bucked up, and they screamed out in terror just as five more groups of Death Reapers burst forward from the brush.

Before they could make sense of the scene, Goliath was already charging through them, and heading down the trail. The power and speed of the animal was amazing. I lowered my head, and wrapped my arms around his muscular neck as he gained speed. I held on as tightly as I could. Every now and then, my body would slip and slide to one side. I had very little experience with horses, and I'd never tried to ride one without a saddle before.

He ran, and ran, and ran. My arms were threatening to give out. I could no longer hear the screaming Death Reapers behind me. How far we had travelled, I had no idea. I was only concerned about staying on the horse. It wasn't easy.

We entered a clearing after what seemed like hours. The horse spun wickedly and unceremoniously threw me to the ground.

"What the fuck?" I shouted.

Then I looked around. There was a backpack, and a saddle and whatever that thing that goes in the horse's mouth is called . . . maybe a bridle? I had no idea, and putting a saddle on Goliath wasn't going to be my idea of fun.

I checked out the backpack.

Inside I saw some food items, a fire striker bar, a canteen of water, and a bottle of whiskey. I have never claimed to be an intelligent man, therefore I chugged some of the whiskey. The burn in my throat felt great after all I'd been through. The side pockets of the backpack were all empty except for my father's Buck 110. I slipped the knife into my pocket. A brief memory of my dad using it to whittle a piece of wood hopped into my mind, and I pushed it aside violently.

I looked at Goliath.

The angry bastard was staring back at me.

I picked up the saddle. Goliath scratched at the ground and made low angry noises. Damn, that horse scared the crap out of me. I chugged some more whiskey for some liquid courage. I held the saddle out before me, Goliath didn't move.

I slowly walked to his side. Eventually the Death Reapers were going to catch up to me. They knew the direction I headed in. They could find me. I needed to create as much distance as possible, and for that I needed Goliath.

I gently place the saddle over Goliaths back. He didn't try to kill me. I took that as a sign of encouragement. I then put his bridle thingie or whatever you want to call it on him. He still didn't try to kill me. Perhaps my luck was turning around. I attached the backpack to his saddle. All was still in the clear.

I grabbed the saddle horn thing, put my foot in the stirrup, and hoisted myself on top of him. He shifted a few steps, made a low moan, reached his big horse head to the side, bit down on my leg, and yanked me off his back.

I'm not sure what hurt worse, the fall or the bite. I was cursing him, and rubbing my ankle when I heard the sound of horses. They weren't hauling-ass, but they were moving as quickly through the forest as possible.

Goliath began making series of weird noises ... first at them, and then at me.

"I loathe you, horse," I said angrily as he looked at me.

Apparently, the horse wanted to leave the area, but the fucker had just bitten me. I wasn't in a hurry to get back on top of him. His weird noises became louder and louder.

I was in yet another predicament.

I should have stayed in bed ... for about a month.

The horses and riders broke into the clearing. There were a bunch of them. A quick count told me there were fifteen at least, and the very second the Death Reapers charged into the clearing, I was moving.

I damn near dove onto Goliaths back. I got my feet into the stirrups quickly, and he turned around to face our adversaries. They were charging right for us. Goliath bucked up, spun, and ran.

If I thought he was too fast before, I was grossly mistaken. The horse was impressive. From a dead stop, he had me hanging on for dear life. Regardless, the Death Reapers were gaining on us as he picked up speed.

After a few moments, I chanced a quick look behind me and was dismayed to see that one of them was already upon us, and about to swing his sword. I yanked the reins in his direction, and Goliath slapped into the smaller horse. The result was the smaller horse stumbling and falling to the ground in a tumble that took out two other horses and riders.

I didn't have a weapon to defend myself. All I had was my dagger and Buck knife. I dug my heels into Goliath's flanks. He answered with a low noise, which was probably horse language for, "fuck off."

Before I knew it, before I went into an absolute panic, we gained the much needed distance. The smaller horses couldn't match his pace. Goliath was screaming out in triumph. I even started to relax a bit and let out a quick triumphant laugh.

Then, the trail curved. Goliath had to slow down to make the turn, after that was another curve, followed by more curves. The curves slowed Goliath down, but the horses pursuing us were smaller and more agile. The riders atop of them were more experienced. They were gaining on us once again.

I cursed aloud. I couldn't believe my rotten luck. The second I thought I was in the clear, I wasn't. Things kept popping up just to ruin my already shitty day.

More and more curves appeared before us. Goliath was grumbling out a sound of frustration. I looked over my shoulder. The Death Reapers were right behind us. They had their rusty swords out. Some of them were pointed in my direction, others were held up high in the air, waiting for an opportunity to strike.

I dug my heels into Goliaths side.

Nothing... Goliath was moving as fast as he could move through the winding trail.

Somehow, over the pounding noise of hooves on dirt, I heard the distinct sound of a blade cutting through the air. I ducked out of instinct, and the movement saved my life.

A Death Reaper was to the left of me. His horse was frothing at the mouth. I tried to use Goliath to ram them into a tumble, but the rider saw it coming, and with a quick movement of his own, jerked his horse out of the way. As a result, it was Goliath that stumbled along the path, and came to a sudden stop.

He bucked up as the Death Reapers flowed around us. As soon as his front legs hit the ground, his back legs reared up and kicked out. He hit an enemy horse square on the ribs so hard it looked like he killed the poor animal.

It wasn't enough.

A sword came down towards my head. I reached up and managed to grab the hand holding the blade, and the two of us fought back and forth for control of the sword. Meanwhile, our horses slammed their sides against one another as if they had a stake in this morbid game as well.

Goliath was the bigger horse by far. The smaller animal, despite being fierce, drew the short end of the stick. After a short struggle, I ended up with possession of the sword.

I stabbed at the Death Reaper's neck the moment I claimed his weapon. Goliath spun into the whirlwind of horse flesh. We were surrounded by moving bodies. A sword would swing out, I did my best to block it, but things were difficult with Goliath twirling about.

One block, two blocks, and a swing of my own. I brought another rider down, but just as I did, a horse slammed against Goliath, and big burly arms wrapped around my neck. I tried to twist my sword around, but it was knocked out of my hand by another Death Reaper.

"A good chase," the Death Reaper that grabbed a hold of me laughed, while another placed a sword against my throat. "You almost got away."

I couldn't have replied even if I'd wanted to. The arms around my neck were choking the life out of me. My hands went to those arms, and I pulled against them for all I was worth. The Death Reaper didn't let up. I couldn't even twist my chin to the side for a breath of air.

Goliath was screaming and trying to twirl as stars appeared before my vision, and I began to black out. Then I saw the most curious thing. The forest above our heads came to life, and detached.

Blood was flying everywhere as the piece of forest went from horse to horse . . . cutting the Death Reapers? Five of them were down before any of them could scream. The arms around my neck went abruptly limp. I gasped in a great gulp of air, and looked behind me. The owner of the big arms was missing his head, and massive amounts of blood were gushing from the fatal wound.

A shape was moving amongst the now screaming Death Reapers. Yet, I couldn't see their attacker. Occasionally, I caught a glimpse of movement, but then it was gone.

Goliath was suddenly free, and he ran full speed ahead. A curve right before us on the trail removed the images of horror from my eyes almost immediately . . . but I still heard the screams. Those I heard very, very well.

"What the hell?" I shouted to no one in particular. "What the hell was that?"

Goliath ran on and on. Way too abruptly, the screams we were hearing ended. Goliath seemed as freaked out as I was. He didn't want to slow down; part of me didn't want him to slow down either. However, he was going to hurt himself. A horse can't run forever.

I pulled on the reins in an effort to stop him. Goliath jerked his head back down, and poured on more speed. His entire body was wet. His breathing was labored. I put my hand on his cheek, and whispered in his ear.

"She loved you, ya know. She loved you completely and totally. Don't do this. Don't die on me. Don't run yourself out."

Well, I don't know if it was my words that calmed him or not. . . but the horse finally began to slow down. I'm guessing it was the tone of my voice. Perhaps it had a calming effect on him. In an environment of violence and death, Goliath might not like me, but at least he knew me.

"There ya go," I continued to whisper. "That's a good boy. We're gonna be okay. I'll take care of you."

I hopped off his back to walk beside him. We had a weird moment, walking there on that strange trail in the middle of a dark and dense forest. He looked right at me, and I swear I could see the pain of loss in his big brown eyes . . . and maybe, just maybe he could see the same thing in my eyes.

Goliath was mine at that very moment. He was mine, and I would protect him with my life. Some people might find it silly to protect a horse, but those people probably haven't been through what I've been through. I knew what the loss of my wife and son had done to me. I knew I was closed off, and very people could get in.

So what?

Things were safer that way.

Stupid horse.

I put my hand on his wet mane, and walked beside him whispering calming words, in an even calmer voice. It was working, his breathing was easier . . . heck, even I was calming down.

I don't know. I'm guessing we walked that way for perhaps an hour before we came to a small stream. Goliath began to drink greedily. I went for the whisky.

I listened to the sounds of the forest all around me as I chugged from the bottle. I didn't hear the Death Reapers. Yet, I also didn't hear the sounds of the forest either. I was on as much of an alert as I could muster while developing a great feeling buzz in my head.

A flock of birds flew out of a tree across the stream, and a part of the forest again detached itself. What appeared to be a pile of branches and leaves landed before me in front of a large rock, and promptly vanished.

I drew my dagger.

What hope did I have against some forest demon?

"Arthur, relax . . . it's just me."

"Lance?" I asked of the familiar voice.

❧ LANCE ❧

Merlin walked away after placing the small bottle of yellow liquid upon the bench. I watched him leave for a bit, and then I turned back to the bottle. The yellow liquid inside was moving as if it were angry.

The all too familiar pressure in my chest built up at the thought of leaving the security of the trees. I forced myself to calm down. I had to. I couldn't miss my chance. I steadied my nerves, which took forever, and though my heart dropped into my stomach, I entered the tiny clearing around the bench.

I could barely breathe. I was absolutely weak in the knees. Why couldn't the old man have left the stupid bottle closer to me? He knew where I was. I couldn't fool him. He always knew. That's what made me nervous about him. He alone could find me wherever I hid. The others couldn't . . . or more likely, they never bothered.

I couldn't hear anyone. I couldn't see anyone. My body had broken out in a cold sweat, but I forced myself to take another step. Arthur was in danger, and my condition was getting worse. Eventually I wouldn't even allow myself to be near other people. I knew that, already the temptation to be alone was overwhelming.

I ran towards the bench, snapped up the bottle, and ran back to the trees. It took ten minutes for me to get my breathing under control and slow my rapidly beating pulse. The bottle was too cold to hold onto for any length of time. I set it down beside me on the grass.

The yellow liquid was still moving. If anything it seemed agitated by my touch. I thought about what Merlin had said. I thought about everything. I had no doubt Arthur was the legendary King Arthur. There was something about him. People were attracted to him no matter how hard he tried to push them away. He was a king reborn.

I was worried about drinking the potion.

What if it was bad? What if I didn't like what it did to me? Then again, I wasn't really happy with my current condition.

I had nothing to lose.

I grabbed the bottle, pulled out the small cork stopper, and drank the contents. I expected a burn. I expected a horrible taste. Nothing. It tasted like cold water. As the last drop hit my tongue, I really began to panic . . . but nothing happened.

I waited and waited. I looked at my hands, and arms. I looked at my feet and legs . . . nothing. There was no change. The fear vanished, and I felt deflated. It was too good to be true. I was destined to get worse and worse until I was nothing more than a hermit living alone in the forest.

I cried. At first, it wasn't much. My eyes welled up, and a few tears rolled down my cheeks. I wiped them away angrily, sat on the grass, leaned back against a tree, and then it really hit me. I cried like a baby. I hated it.

Even worse, I was terrified that the sounds I was making would attract a worried person to my location. I got myself under control. It wasn't easy, for the briefest moment I thought I had a future. For the briefest moment there was a light at the end of the tunnel. I should have known better.

There are no happy endings in this world.

I think I fell asleep.

I must have, because when I awoke the sun was coming up. Big deal. I was out of the game. The major players would move on without me. I couldn't leave the park. Not with the sun up. The sun meant people. There weren't enough places for me to hide outside the park.

Fortunately when I alerted the others about the attack, the streets were pretty much empty . . . but even so, it was difficult enough to cross some of the roads.

I was stuck in the park.

Just thinking about leaving was causing me to shake. I'd have to stay here until the streets were empty, and that might not even happen at all with all those evil soldiers out there surrounding the town. Sheriff Tagger would probably put lookouts everywhere while everyone slept, and if I could manage to leave the park . . . where would I go?

Arthur's cabin was outside of Stronghold Wall. It was the only place I felt safe. Arthur never bothered me. Arthur never pushed me. He accepted my problems and let me be.

Arthur was the best friend I ever had, and I was failing him. I wanted to run and find him. I wanted to be by his side; instead . . . I started crying again. I couldn't leave the park. I tried. I tried as hard as I could possibly try. I stood up, and forced myself to the edge of the trees again.

I was shaking terribly, but I forced myself to take a step into the open.

I couldn't breathe.

My throat closed up.

I ran back to the trees. The panic inside me had taken over. Normally, when something like this happened, I hid under a bed for a few hours. I couldn't do that in the park. I couldn't do that anywhere anymore.

I wanted to walk to a more secluded area. I wanted to be far away from the bench in case anyone came into the park. I couldn't do it. Not in my current state. All I could do was burrow beneath the nearest bush.

That's where I was when I remembered Merlin's words. He said something about me being me during the hours of sunset and sunrise. Hadn't the sun been up for at least an hour? I had no way of knowing; surely the sky was changing from grey to blue?

I felt a tingling sensation on the back of my neck.

My first thought was ants. I must be on top of an anthill, but I felt nothing on my neck when I rubbed it with my hand. The strange tingling crept down my arms and back, and then flowed back up my front side, ending at the top of my head.

Something was happening to me.

I laughed. The potion took a bit of time to work, but something was happening to me. Merlin helped me after all. I would be able to help Arthur. I would be beneficial. Already, I could feel the panic in my chest melting away as a new confidence swelled inside of me.

For some reason, about that time I also remembered Merlin's other words. He said something about me being a demon-child of the forest. Why would he call me a demon-child? I laughed at the idea . . . then my hands and feet began to bubble.

My laughter turned to screams.

Somewhere in the back of my mind, I was worried about attracting people with all the noise I was making, but I couldn't stop myself. The bones and tendons in my hands and feet were popping, tearing, and breaking. It hurt terribly.

My toes and fingers were stretching out. The noise was horrible. It was also loud. I could hear the noise despite all the hollering I was doing. I fought to remove my shoes as my toes curled painfully inside them. It was a struggle to use my hands with all the damage being done to them but I managed, and had a brief moment of peace as my toes were able to stretch out.

I was lying under the bush breathing deeply, in an attempt to refrain from passing out, when the real pain kicked in. It traveled from my feet and arms all throughout my body. I really screamed when that happened. As if all my previous noise was just a warm up.

Then it was over.

I crawled out from under the bush. People had to have heard me. I needed to leave the area, but I was too tired. The second I was away from the bush, I rolled over onto my back, and stared up at the sky through drowsy eyes.

Another tingling sensation spread all throughout my body, and I panicked. I didn't want to go through that pain again. I tried to roll over to my stomach, but I had somehow used too much energy, and shot off the ground some ten feet in the air.

I smacked into the nearest tree, fell back down, and landed easily on my hands and feet. Wait . . . I had no hands. I couldn't see them. I couldn't see my arms either. All I could see was the dirt, fallen leaves, and small plants all around me.

I crawled into the clearing, and gasped at the newfound speed. Once there, I tried to see my feet. They were gone as well. I removed my clothes. I saw brief flashes of skin, and then nothing . . .

I had vanished.

Or had I?

I could feel everything. Correction, I think my body was more sensitive that it had ever been. I put my hand out in front of my face, and waved it around. I could see brief glimpses of movement. I wasn't invisible.

What was I?

I put my arm against a tree. I felt a tiny tingling, saw another glimpse of something, and then nothing. I touched my arm. It was rough like the tree bark it was resting upon.

I understood.

My body was camouflaging itself. My skin took on the texture and colors of whatever it was in front of. The camouflage was perfect. Only movement could give me away.

I laughed out loud.

I even spun in a circle, I was so happy.

This of course, was a very bad idea. Apparently, my strength had also increased. I spun until I lost control, and fell on my butt many feet away.

Noises in the park.

Closing in on me.

I jumped in fright.

Straight up in the air I went. Probably fifteen or twenty feet . . . I grabbed a hold of the nearest branch on my way down. It was a big, thick branch, but my elongated fingers wrapped around it with ease.

I hung from the branch with one hand.

There was no strain whatsoever on my arm. Hanging there was easy, pulling myself up and wrapping my toes around the branch was even easier. I waited for what seemed an eternity. Eventually, they came.

Five men and two women. I'd seen a couple of them in town before things got too bad for me. They probably heard the sounds of a child in pain, and came out to see if they could help.

They couldn't see me in the high branches above their heads.

I had very little anxiety . . . perhaps just a slight worry. It wasn't much. So, I felt that it was okay to test things a bit.

I jumped down to a lower branch on another tree. I made very little noise, and they didn't hear me. I watched them easily, and listened to their conversation. They were looking for a scared, possibly wounded, child.

I dropped lower.

They continued their search.

I dropped to the ground, and backed up to a thick tree. They still didn't hear me. I could hear me . . . but, they couldn't. I made a noise with my throat. All of them turned in my direction, but they couldn't locate me. I was standing right before them, and they couldn't locate me.

I jumped maybe twenty feet in the air, and grabbed a branch.

And then I started laughing.

Merlin had saved me.

I jumped easily to another tree, and then another. From tree to tree I flew. Distance was nothing to me. I hesitated at the edge of the park, but just for a moment. Then I was across the street, and over the roof of a store.

I hit a field at a fast run.

I could really move, and I wasn't even trying. Through the overgrown field I ran. I was practically a ghost. I couldn't stop smiling. Nope. I seriously couldn't stop smiling.

Before I knew it I was in Dellia's front yard, and running up her driveway. Everyone was standing on her front porch . . . everyone except Arthur.

Was I too late?

I had to find him.

I leapt to the front of the porch, right above everyone's heads. They had no idea I was even there. I listened to them as they talked about Arthur finding Excalibur, but in what direction did he go?

Wayne started talking about a tunnel inside the barn. That was all I needed. I had to find the tunnel. Instantly, I was off the porch, and moving towards the barn. I sneaked inside through an upper window, and dropped to the floor below.

The horses could sense me. I made them nervous. So, I started speaking to them in a soothing voice while I searched for the tunnel. I couldn't find anything. I was getting frustrated.

Then I heard a soft cough from behind me.

I jumped instantly to an upper level.

"No need to worry, young Lancelot," Merlin said. "I'm only here to help you on your way."

"Can you see me?" I asked.

"Not really," Merlin answered. "But I'm aware of your presence. After all, I made the potion. Now, if I may . . ."

Merlin moved a picture on the wall, grabbed a lantern, and entered a secret doorway in a stall. I followed him, and down we went. I felt a little uneasy about walking so close to someone, but the feeling faded rapidly, and Merlin never once tried to locate my exact position. Instead, he talked on and on about how I needed to use my new abilities to protect Arthur.

I was amazed when I saw all the treasure, weapons, and armor.

We hadn't quite reached the bottom of the stairs when everything came into view, and I couldn't wait . . . Merlin walked too slowly. I leapt over his head and landed on a pile of coins.

"Ah," Merlin said as he looked right at me. "Be careful how you conduct yourself young Lancelot. You may be silent when you wish to be, but mistakes in judgment can give away your position."

I stepped off the pile of coins, and he laughed out loud.

"Youth will not be wasted on you, young man," Merlin said. "Perhaps I was wrong. Perhaps you'll enjoy your new found freedom."

"I'm enjoying it already," I laughed as I hopped around the room.

"Truly excellent, but gather closely for but a brief moment," Merlin said.

"I'm here," I announced when I got close to him.

"Of course you are," Merlin laughed. "Listen my young friend. My heart sings at your joy, but joy is not what I need from you this moment. The world has gone dark and grey. It has become filled with an evil we will all be fighting valiantly. The road ahead of you is no place for a child . . . but you are no ordinary child. Even before the potion, you didn't think, talk or act like a child."

"My parents used to tell me I was very smart," I said. "The doctors tested me and stuff."

"Truly, you are," Merlin agreed. "Combine that with an ancient soul, and those poor doctors probably had no idea what to make of you. Still, despite all that, I wish you weren't so very young. There are things no child should ever see or be asked to do."

"People will try to kill me," I said. "Won't they?"

"Yes," Merlin said. "If you follow Arthur, the forces of Morgana will try to kill you. What might be just as bad . . . you will also try and kill them."

"Can't I just wound them?" I asked. "Capture them? Tie them up?"

"No, young Lancelot," Merlin said sadly as he walked over to a chest and opened it. "When the time comes for violence . . . kill them all. Show no mercy. Have no regret."

He produced two long and slim knives from the chest. Their dark wooden handles were almost as long as the straight, one-sided blades that glinted fire in the dimly lit room. There was no guard between the blade and the handles, but it didn't matter. They fit my long hands perfectly.

I twirled them around to get a feel for them. They were perfect. I'd always wanted a knife. I'd never asked for one, but I'd always wanted one. Every boy should have a knife when he hits a certain age.

"They're beautiful," I said.

"They're deadly," Merlin answered. "The blades are keen enough to bite into the bone with a casual flick of the wrist, and don't get too attached to looking at them. Anything you touch for any length of time will pick up your camouflaging abilities before you know it."

"You mean they'll change, like me?" I asked.

"Only visually," Merlin answered, and pulled out a bundle of black clothes from the trunk. "Now take these as well, and remember . . . during the hours of sunrise and sunset, you will be a normal boy."

"I understand," I said as I watched the twin blades slowly begin to vanish.

"Also, these clothes have hidden pockets all throughout," Merlin added. "Inside them you will find various types of spikes, and throwing weapons that will allow you to strike from a distance."

"Wow," I said thinking I'd hit the mother lode.

"Now follow me if you're ready," Merlin said.

I'll admit it, I was nervous. What was about to start? It didn't seem like it was going to be a fun adventure. No, it didn't seem like that at all. I was worried about what I'd have to do. But despite my worries, Arthur needed me.

"Follow the tunnel, and the trail beyond," Merlin said after showing me how to open the door. "Move quickly, and you should have no trouble catching up with Arthur."

"Okay," I said. "I won't let you down. I won't let Arthur down."

"I'm already beaming with pride, young man," Merlin said. "And remember . . . when the time comes, strike hard, strike fast, and leave no survivors."

With those words, I was off and moving down the tunnel as fast as I could. Then I remembered I was carrying a bundle of clothes. So I stopped, put them on, and continued on my way. I liked the clothes. They were soft, and baggy. Sort of like a ninja outfit. In fact, there was even had a ninja-like mask to go over my head. There were no shoes though, not that I needed shoes with my new feet and toes.

I could also see very well in the darkness of the tunnel. I had night-vision. Things were just getting better and better for me.

At the end of the tunnel, I found the door, opened it, froze for a moment, found the trail, and bam, I was off like a rocket.

At first, I ran along the trail, and then I saw a branch, jumped up, grabbed it, and started moving through the trees. If it was possible, I believe I could move even faster through the trees. I could also move silently. Not even the birds took flight when I moved by them.

I loved it.

My smile came back to me. I never used to smile like this. Sure, sometimes I'd fake a smile for my mom . . . but that seemed a long time ago.

I missed my mom.

She was a sweet lady. She was also very pretty, and kind. Before the red fog, when I started having problems, I'd hide in a closet. My teachers couldn't understand me . . . but my mom could. My mom always understood me.

There were tears in my eyes, but I was still smiling. My mom would be proud of me. I found a way to beat my problem. I found a way to be beneficial, instead of becoming another problem.

She'd also be happy that Arthur found me.

Arthur took care of me. Arthur was good to me. I wish Arthur had been my father. My dad was mean to me. He was embarrassed by me. I think I'm the reason why he left. I never even heard them argue before I started having problems.

I wouldn't however want Arthur to date my mom. Nope. No thanks. I'd seen way too many girls pounding on our cabin door demanding to see him. They were always angry, sometimes they were even crying.

My mom probably wouldn't approve of all the girls Arthur dated.

On and on I went. I felt like Tarzan moving through the jungle, but I doubted he could move like I could. No one could move like me. I was too fast. I was an arrow shooting off in the distance.

More laughter. I couldn't help myself. For the first time in a very long time I was happy. I was unafraid, and I was happy.

Once or twice I almost lost the trail. I needed to pay more attention. I didn't want to get lost. How far ahead was Arthur? I should have asked. Whatever, I knew I could catch up to him. He was only human. I was so much more.

I saw his tracks on the trail. Then I saw his tracks leave the trail.

I dropped to the ground.

"Did you hear that?" A voice asked.

"I heard something," another voice answered.

I wasn't alone in the forest. I froze. I was right between the trail and the tree line. I hadn't been paying attention. I was too high up in the trees to see that there were soldiers everywhere. Merlin had warned me about these kinds of mistakes.

Quietly, I stepped into the tree's right as the soldiers zeroed in on my position. There were three of them, but other groups were moving in.

My hands went to the long knives on my back.

I wasn't afraid. I was incredibly calm. If anything, it was my calm that worried me. I should have been terrified. They were a mere two feet away from me.

"Well something was here," a soldier announced.

"You've got that right," another soldier answered. "Take a look at those tracks."

"What could have made tracks like that?"

"Nothing I want to follow. Those aren't human tracks. Those are something different. These woods have a demon in them, of that I have no doubt."

"The tracks lead into the forest."

"Right where we lost some of our own."

"You think the king has a demon ally?"

"It would explain why he's so hard to kill."

One of the soldiers stepped closer to me as he attempted to peer into the forest. His face was about two inches from mine as he leaned forward.

"You're a fool if you think I'm going to chase after whatever left those tracks."

"There's something wrong with these trees. . ." the soldier in front of me started to say before I slit his neck in a scissor cut with both of my knives.

He had gotten too close.

His eyes went wide after I cut him. He tried to gurgle out more words, but my attack went through his vocal cords, and probably nicked his spine as well. It was a wonder his head was still attached.

Both his hands went to his throat. He stumbled backwards, lost his balance and was dead before he hit the ground.

His friends went into a full on panic mode, and began shouting for help. I was on them immediately. I sliced, and they bled tremendously. In no time at all, three dead men were littering the ground.

I leaped to the nearest branch, just as another group of three moved in. I heard shouts coming from all around the forest now. How many of them were out here? I climbed up, and up. I climbed until I broke free of the forest, and took a look around at my surroundings.

In a clearing about a mile away was a great army, and they were slowly marching towards Mill Ridge.

I climbed back down. There were about forty men standing over the corpses of the soldiers I had killed.

"That's the second time," a soldier shouted. "There must be others, and they're in the forests. They hide behind the trees waiting to attack. Don't go poking around all alone like an idiot without expecting to get cut."

"It wasn't human, Sir," another soldier said. "I saw it run off right as we arrived."

"Then what was it?"

"A demon that changed its shape," the soldier said. "I've never seen anything like it before."

The soldiers began to shift around uncontrollably.

"Well, whatever it is, it's none of our concern. Our quarry today is human, and when we find him we can leave these woods once and for all. So, let's move on. There's a slight chance that the king himself is in these woods, and I doubt any of you can truly image the rewards if we're the ones who capture him, so stick together, and let's re-group with the main search party."

They knew Arthur was in the woods.

They weren't positive it was him, but they were pursuing him anyway. I moved off rapidly. I followed the trail from the trees, and eventually came upon another large group of soldiers. This group was bigger than the one I had just left. There were about seventy of them by my count. Some of them were in full armor. A smaller group of them had horses.

I hopped from tree to tree in order to get the lay of the land.

There were dead and wounded soldiers lying all over the trail. One of them was next to the tree line. Arthur must have used the same tactic I had and attacked from the trees. That would explain why the one soldier said something about my attack being the second time.

I watched them, and I waited.

Eventually the party of forty arrived on the scene. Their leader consulted with a man in full armor. The story of the demon in the forest began to spread amongst all of them. I laughed as each man upon hearing the tale took a few steps away from the tree line. I enjoyed their fear.

After a bit, a few more groups joined the large group I was watching. Words were exchanged, and I thought I understood the situation. These soldiers weren't sure of what they were up against, so the leader sent out men in all directions in an attempt to find out.

"No more waiting," the leader suddenly announced. "No more rumors of a forest demon. Enough of you cowards have seen the king . . . now let's go take his head."

Yep, they wanted to stay put and take a stand at this location just in case there were more enemies in the area ready to sneak up behind them and attack when they weren't prepared. Now, with the exception of a possible forest demon, they were certain there was only one man in the woods.

A group of fifteen riders and horses were assembled, and sent out to follow a trail of horse tracks which apparently marked the direction Arthur had taken. Arthur was riding a horse? I almost laughed out loud. Well, I guess if he really needed to get away in a hurry he might take a horse, but things would certainly have to be pretty bad for that to happen.

The riders moved off down the trail, and the men left behind followed slowly behind them. I followed the horses, they weren't exactly moving fast but they were moving much faster than the soldiers on foot.

Sometime during my pursuit of the horses, I realized why they were going so slowly. The riders couldn't see the trail. Nope, they couldn't see even the barest outlines of the trail. They were following the tracks.

Magic . . . it's weird.

On and on we went. For the most part, we followed a straight line with occasional slight turns to the right. I was getting a bit frustrated at their slow pace.

Just as I was about to move ahead of them, the soldiers came to a brief stop, pointed at the ground, exchanged a few words, and then picked up their pace. I matched their slight increase in speed easily.

Without warning, the soldiers broke into a clearing.

I saw Arthur for the first time. He jumped onto Goliath's back. The great beast of a horse rose up angrily . . . and the chase was on.

I followed closely, it still wasn't hard to keep up with them, but they were moving fast enough to make me indecisive. I wasn't sure how to help. I had the spikes inside the pockets of my clothes, but I wasn't confident of my aim. I didn't want to hit one of their horses, or even Arthur by mistake.

I freaked out a bit as a rider got close enough to Arthur to harm him, but Goliath remedied the situation immediately by knocking the smaller horse to the ground with a mighty slam. The tumbling horse took out two other riders, and with a burst of speed Goliath shot away from the soldiers.

As the distance between Arthur and his pursuers grew, I hung back with the soldiers in order to keep an eye on them. It was a good thing I did. After just a brief moment of triumph, the trail developed some seriously abrupt turns and the enemy began catching up to him.

I'm no expert on horsemanship, but the horses of the soldiers seemed better able to navigate the twists and turns than Goliath. Perhaps it was because they were smaller, or perhaps it was because Arthur was so crappy with horses. Whichever answer worked . . . Arthur was in trouble.

I shouted out right as Arthur ducked a swing at his head.

Arthur almost died.

I'm failing him.

I can't fail the king.

I sped up, passing by the soldier's, and as I passed them by, I threw out some spikes from my pockets. I hit four soldiers, and they immediately fell from their horses. The spikes weren't big enough to kill them, so they must have been poisoned.

The group of horses came to an abrupt stop. At the front of the line, Arthur was immediately surrounded, and after a violent struggle, a particularly large soldier had an arm around his neck.

Arthur was being choked.

Without thought, I leapt from the sanctuary of the forest, and dropped into their midst. As I fell, my blades came free. I landed on the nearest horse, and I sliced. Without waiting to see the damage I had inflicted, I immediately moved to another horse. I sliced and stabbed, but it wasn't as violent as one might expect. Instead, my actions had a certain poetry of destruction.

I was a painter. The canvas was a forest, and I was painting it red. Eventually, the soldiers began to panic. The demon was upon them, but that didn't help them any. I twirled and slashed. I found the edges of their chain mail, and plunged my wicked blades. Their blood was upon me, but it soon began to vanish beneath the power of the potion Merlin gave me.

I was invincible.

I was a demon.

Arthur was able to get away.

I saved my friend. I saved him, but the look on his face spoke volumes. He was frightened. Of me? That wouldn't do at all. I needed to catch up to him. I needed him to understand . . . but first, I needed to finish my masterpiece.

The painting continued.

I let one soldier escape. Let the stories of a forest demon continue. Let the enemy tremble in fear . . . and never let it be said that I didn't appreciate a good joke.

I stood among the dead. I wasn't even breathing heavily. One soldier was still twitching. I walked over to him, and with a brief flick of my knife, I opened his neck.

I did my job.

I protected Arthur.

I did as Merlin asked me.

Then why was I now trembling? Why were there now tears in my eyes? I knew the answer. I didn't like it, but I knew the answer.

I was a boy.

I was a boy, and boys shouldn't have to do the things I had been doing. I was changing. I had killed . . . I had never killed anything before.

I stared at the carnage for a long while. Red on green. Blood on leaves. I did this. I caused this. Was I horrible? Was I the villain?

No.

I didn't want this fight. Arthur didn't want this fight. The people who lived in Mill Ridge didn't want this fight. All of us were the victims. We were the ones under attack. I shouldn't feel bad because I suddenly had the ability to fight back.

But the looks on their faces.

They didn't die well. They died in fear and pain. Their faces were horrible to look at. I averted my gaze and walked away from them. I was finally beginning to breathe heavily. What have I done? I saved the king. I saved my friend.

The thoughts in my mind were chaotic. Was I the bad guy or was I the hero. Did good guys kill bad guys? Merlin told me to kill them all. I was listening to Merlin. I wanted to go home. I wanted to go back to my room and hide. Hiding was what I was good at, and then I remembered . . . I no longer had a home.

The fog had taken away everything that ever mattered to me. The Queen made the fog, the soldiers worked for the Queen. My mother. My beautiful mother, her perfect, pale skin . . . her eyelids fluttering as she died in my arms. She gave me everything, and took nothing for herself. All the food . . . she gave me all the food . . . why didn't she take anything for herself? She was so skinny.

I was crying.

I hadn't thought about that moment in a very long time. If Arthur hadn't found me in the forest . . . I'd be dead as well. I let the tears fall as I walked down the trail. I felt the fabric of my cloth mask grow damp, and I felt my face twist and contort in rage.

Morgana caused the loss of all that I held dear. Now her forces sought to kill my truest friend. I no longer felt bad. My heart was no longer held in a grip of remorse over what I had done. Whatever spark of humanity I felt for taking so many lives was gone in an instant.

I wanted to kill them all.

I ran down the trail. I felt the tears dry around my eyes as I took to the trees. I moved just as quickly as before. I needed to find Arthur. I didn't want him to feel alone. I never wanted to feel alone again.

I moved faster and faster. From one tree to another I moved. I enjoyed the freedom. Not only the freedom of moving so quickly through the forest . . . I also enjoyed the freedom from guilt.

It didn't take long even though they traveled a long distance, to find Arthur. He was drinking from a bottle of whiskey, and Goliath was drinking from stream. I borrowed the same branch being used by a small flock of birds that took flight when they felt my weight.

Arthur was startled by the commotion.

I didn't want my friend to experience any fear. I needed to let him know that I was there, so I dropped to the ground in front of a large rock.

Arthur drew his dagger. He no longer had a sword.

"Arthur, relax . . . it's just me," I said.

"Lance?" He asked.

"It's Lancelot now," I said.

"Are you in front of that rock?" Arthur asked.

"Yes," I answered.

"Why can't I see you?" Arthur asked.

"I took a potion from Merlin," I answered.

"Was it you that killed all those Death Reapers?" Arthur asked.

"Death Reapers?" I asked in turn.

"That's what they're called," Arthur answered.

"Yes, I killed them," I said. "My job is to protect you. I plan on doing that."

"You're not hiding anymore," Arthur said.

"I'm still hiding," I said. "I'm just hiding in plain sight. Merlin freed me."

"Wow," Arthur said. I could tell the liquor was getting to him.

"We should leave," I said. "There is a large group of over a hundred Death Reapers tracking you down this very instant."

"How far away are they?" Arthur asked nervously.

"Three hours behind us . . . maybe more," I answered.

He relaxed visibly at that bit of information.

"I need to take it slow," Arthur said. "Goliath needs to rest."

"That shouldn't be a problem," I answered.

We allowed time for Goliath to drink his fill from the stream, and then Arthur set off down the path while I kept up with him in the tree line. I asked him what catastrophic events led to him riding Goliath, and he in turn questioned me about the potion Merlin had given me.

He wasn't uncomfortable to be around me. He knew I had killed a large group of Death Reapers, and he still accepted me. He was curious, but I could tell he wasn't bothered by me. Arthur was my truest friend. He accepted me as I was, I almost started bawling again.

He told me what Merlin had told him about following the trail, and where it would lead. I told him all about how the Death Reapers were unable to see the trail, and instead relied upon following our tracks.

An hour later, Arthur figured Goliath had had enough of a rest, and attempted to climb onto the horses back. Goliath however, had other ideas. As soon as Arthur was halfway up, the great horse turned his massive head, grabbed Arthur by the arm, and threw him on the ground.

At first I was shocked.

Arthur looked pissed.

Goliath simply continued walking along the trail.

Arthur started cursing.

I started laughing, and I couldn't stop.

"You think that's funny?" Arthur asked. "It's not the first time he's done that to me today. That stupid horse has an attitude problem."

I was still laughing.

Arthur threw a stick in my general direction, and I was off like a rocket. From tree to tree I moved like an immense spider until I was directly above him on a wobbly branch full of dead leaves. Arthur heard me move, but he had no idea where I had gone to.

I bounced on the branch, sending a cascade of leaves on top of his head.

"Aren't you clever," Arthur laughed while taking a swig of whiskey.

"I certainly have my moments," I laughed.

With one look behind him, Arthur brushed off his cloak, and continued down the path. I stayed in the trees, and followed his progress. Occasionally, I would climb high, and look to see how far the Death Reapers were behind us. I couldn't see them, but I knew they were there. I could sense it. They gave me a very uneasy feeling.

"Why do the Death Reapers look so gross?" I asked.

"No clue," Arthur answered.

"They look almost . . . dead," I said.

"Well, they aren't dead," Arthur replied. "Because they talk, they scream, and they die. Dead things don't do any of that."

"Maybe they've been resurrected from the past somehow," I said.

"Any things possible nowadays," Arthur said. "But something about them seems a bit modern. I'm not sure why that is, but I don't think they're from the past . . . at least not their bodies."

"Arthur," I said. "I saw the main lot in the distance while I was in a tree. It's a huge army. If you combine that with the possibility of other groups headed towards Mill Ridge . . . how can one sword defeat so many?"

"I'll file that one under not my problem," Arthur answered. "I said I'd go get the sword, and that's all I'm about to do. I have no interest in being a king, unless my job consists only of drinking and whoring."

I started laughing.

Arthur stopped, looked up in my direction, and frowned.

"I shouldn't have said that in front of you," Arthur said. "I apologize, sometimes I forget your age."

I was still laughing.

"Stop laughing," Arthur said. "It wasn't funny, it was rude."

I laughed even harder.

Arthur looked up again. He had a slight grin that he was attempting to repress.

"What?" Arthur asked.

"You meant it," I answered. "That's what's so funny. You meant it."

"I did not," Arthur said.

"Yes you did," I said.

"No I didn't," Arthur said. "I made a bad joke in front of the wrong company."

"Why don't you want to help them?" I asked when I had calmed down.

"I don't like them very much," Arthur answered. "And they aren't too fond of me. It's also the responsibility of being a king. I have no idea how to be a king, and to be perfectly honest . . . I'm no hero. I'm about as far from being a hero as a person can get."

"I think you're right about most of the town not being fond of you," I agreed. "Except for the women, they seem to love you."

Arthur laughed.

"But don't you think Merlin would help you be a good king?" I asked. "Isn't that sort of his job?"

"It's not easy to carve rotten wood," Arthur answered. "I've disappointed just about everyone in my life. It's kind of my thing. I screw up too much. Besides, I doubt anyone would accept me as a king anyway . . . not with my track record."

"I would," I said.

Arthur stopped and looked in my direction. He tried to say something, stopped, tried again, stopped, and smiled at me.

"You're a good friend, Lance," Arthur finally said.

He made my day. I was glad he couldn't see me. I was smiling from ear to ear, and blushing like a little kid.

Goliath who was walking ahead of us stopped at a little wooden bridge spanning a small stream.

"It's just a little bridge," Arthur laughed as he grabbed the horse's reins and attempted to pull him along, but the horse would budge. "Are you kidding me ya big sissy?"

Goliath began making strange noises.

"What's wrong with him?" I asked.

"No idea," Arthur answered. "He doesn't like the bridge."

"Maybe it's not the bridge," I said after I climbed higher and looked around a bit. "There's a weird old house about half a mile away in front of a vast lake. The trail leads right to the lake."

"Looks like we're in the right place," Arthur said. "If we can put that lake between us and the Death Reapers, I'll certainly sleep better tonight."

Arthur made his way across the bridge. As soon as he was across, Goliath began to make all sorts of angry noises. Arthur shivered, and looked around.

"What's wrong?" I asked.

"I don't know," Arthur answered. "This place feels weird."

He stepped off the trail, which was easy enough, the land here was more open, and filled with knee high grass mixed with small clumps of trees. After walking a bit, Arthur knelt down, and began to pull the grass from the ground.

I leapt over the stream and joined him in the grass. He had no idea I was standing behind him, until I spoke, and he jumped.

"What did you find?" I asked.

"We're standing in a graveyard," Arthur answered.

I looked around in a panic. He was right. I myself was standing directly upon an old tombstone lying flat in the earth. The area made me nervous. I didn't like being there. I'd much rather have gone back to the still-complaining Goliath.

"These woods are a haunted place," Arthur said.

"Huh?" I asked.

"That's what my grandpa told me," Arthur said. "These woods are a haunted place."

"Should we be here?" I asked.

"No," Arthur answered. "We shouldn't be here, but Grandpa Merl said it was safe."

Part of me wanted to go back up into the trees. Another part didn't want to leave Arthur's side. The shadows were closing in around us as the sun suddenly began to lower from the sky. When did that happen?

"It's getting darker," Arthur said as if he had also just noticed it for the first time.

"What do we do?" I asked, feeling the tingling of my power all along my back.

"Let's get on that boat," Arthur said. "It can't be any worse than staying out here in an old graveyard."

"What about Goliath?" I asked.

"He'll come or we'll leave him here," Arthur said as he walked off towards the trail.

Goliath complained loudly, but in the end, he crossed the bridge in a thundering of hooves and ran up to Arthur as if Arthur would protect him from whatever was making him nervous.

"Arthur," I said. "I'm having problems."

The tingling intensified, and I saw the faded shape of my hands in front of my face. This time there was no pain, just the tingling . . . but the loss of power was leaving me vulnerable.

"What's happening to you?" Arthur asked.

"I'm normal during the hours of sunrise, and sunset," I answered with a shaky voice.

"No worries," Arthur said removing his cloak, and throwing it over my shoulders right as I became fully visible. "Just stay in the tree line as we walk, then we'll wait for your powers to come back before we board the boat.

It was a long walk to the lonely old house; which was a smallish, grey, two story structure. The paint was faded, and the windows were filled with cobwebs. The front porch was crooked. Something about the house wasn't right. Something about it was seriously freaking me out. I wanted to pass it as quickly as possible, but Arthur was taking his sweet time, and moving cautiously.

We were halfway past the house, when a flickering light came on inside. My eyes bulged out so much; I thought they would fall out of my head.

"Arthur," I whispered. "Did you see that? A light just came on."

"Yes," Arthur said. "Ignore it. It's just a candle."

"But that means someone lives there," I said.

"Something lives there," Arthur said. "And we certainly don't want to meet whatever it is."

"I don't understand," I stated.

"Just keep moving," Arthur said.

After we had passed the house, the backdoor creaked slowly open. It was an invitation, but not an invitation we were going to accept. Arthur walked faster, Goliath was right next to him, and I was right off the trail in the brush with Arthur and the horse between me and the house.

The door slammed shut angrily at our refusal to enter.

I jumped in the air with my heart beating a million miles an hour. Arthur pulled his dagger. Goliath reared up in fear.

"Keep moving," Arthur said after making sure nothing was coming out of the house after us.

In a short while my line of trees gave out right as we came to a pebble beach before the lake. A wooden pier about forty feet long stretched into the water. There were no boats, but hanging from one of the posts was a horn.

Arthur looked back towards the house for the billionth time, and then spoke to me.

"Listen, Lance," Arthur said. "We're in a relatively bad place. Can you feel the badness in the air?"

"Shit yeah," I answered.

"We need to be careful," Arthur continued. "We need to stay on our guard, and never take unnecessary chances. I'm not sure what was in that house, but it wasn't good. If we had gone inside, I don't think we would have come out again."

"I understand," I said in a shaky voice.

"Also," Arthur said. "I have a feeling things will only get stranger when I pull the sword out of the stone, and release all the magic."

"Then why do it?" I asked.

"It's the way things are meant to be," Arthur answered. "I don't want to do it, but I need to do it . . . if that makes any sense at all."

"Did Merlin tell you about that house?" I asked.

"No," Arthur answered. "But he gave me some warnings, and I could tell immediately that it was something to avoid."

"So what do we do now?" I asked.

"First we wait for the sun to set," Arthur answered. "Then we call the ferryman."

It wasn't a long wait. As soon as the hour was up, and the sky had gone black, the tingling feeling returned. I told Arthur to go ahead without me while I changed. After all, it wouldn't be hard for me to catch up to him.

He walked onto the pier, pulling Goliath along behind him by his reins. Their steps echoed loudly across the misty lake. Stars were blinking in the night sky, the moon was shining brightly, I could smell rain in the air, and I almost didn't want to follow them.

The Death Reapers were kind of bad, but the old house was horrible, and I was worried about what was coming our way next. We had just entered this new forest. It wasn't as dense after the bridge, but it was a heck of a lot scarier.

In no time at all, my power had returned, interrupting any thoughts of the horrible things waiting for me. I had a mission, and my mission was to protect Arthur.

I followed them soundlessly, moving from post to post without the slightest bit of noise. I crouched five feet from Arthur as he stood next to the edge. The lake had gone still, and a thick layer of mist covered its surface. Lightning began to streak soundlessly across the sky many miles away.

He grabbed the horn, wiped it down, put it to his lips, and blew it loudly. The sound reverberated across the lake. Arthur looked around for me, saw his cloak, put it on, couldn't find me, and shrugged his shoulders."

"You still with me?" Arthur asked.

"I'm here," I answered.

"Think I should blow it again?" Arthur asked.

"That's what she said," I answered.

Arthur started laughing.

"I'll take that as a yes," Arthur said.

"Wait," I said just as Arthur was about to blow the horn again.

"What?"

"Look at the water," I said while pointing with a finger he'd never be able to see.

Arthur searched for just a couple of seconds, and saw what I wanted him to see. Through the mist a shape was slowly appearing. Whatever it was, it was large. We could hear the sound of creaking wood as it grew nearer and nearer.

A giant woman was carved into the front of the ancient boat. She seemed to be in pain. That could have been due to the age of the boat, and its overall derelict condition, but I really didn't think so.

The boat was shaped like a canoe, but the tips of each end rose high into the sky. It had a large box shape in the center that created an indoor cabin. From end to end, it was about the size of a normal house, and almost as wide.

It was headed towards the pier, towards us. At the last possible moment, right when I thought a collision would be unavoidable, it turned slowly but sharply.

"What the fuck?" Arthur exclaimed as the boat came to a stop with its left side facing towards us.

I tried to think of an answer, but before I could, a door not unlike the drawbridge on a castle lowered down and rested upon the pier right in front of Arthur's feet.

"Stay close to me," Arthur whispered, and walked up the drawbridge. I crept up next to Goliath and followed closely behind him. My hand was resting on the hilt of my knife, but I wasn't about to draw it unless I needed to.

In the dim moonlight, shapes began to dart around the corners of my eyes. Right when I thought something was there, I'd turn and . . . nothing.

The shadows began playing tricks on me as well. They'd grow large, and become the figures of men and woman only to vanish as rapidly as they'd come. Arthur had his hand on his dagger once again. Goliath was making noises to show how uncomfortable he was.

The door to the inside cabin opened up behind me. Startled, I jumped straight to the top of its roof, and pulled the knife on my back halfway out of its sheath.

A hooded and cloaked figure glided onto the deck. It slowly and eerily made its way to Arthur and extended its boney, armor encased hand. The shapes and shadows were swirling furiously around us. Arthur stared at the hand for just a moment, and then reached into his cloak. He pulled out a small piece of gold, and dropped it with a clink into the cloaked figure's hand.

The figure examined the gold for a brief moment, and then appeared to bite into it. After the taste test, he looked up towards Arthur.

"The king," The cloaked figure said in a hoarse whisper.

"That's what they say," Arthur answered.

The cloaked figure laughed, a scratchy noise, and slammed its fist into the wall of the inside cabin. Torches all around the boat ignited into flames. The moving shapes and shadows came to an abrupt stop.

They were ghosts.

All of them were slightly blue in color. They were transparent, but you could see their features very clearly. They had the saddest eyes . . . lost eyes. They were dressed in ancient clothes, and robes. Some of them had bruises upon their pale skin. Others had wounds. I didn't know whether to be afraid of them, or feel sorry for them.

Arthur chose the former. I couldn't blame him. The ghosts were crowding around him, reaching out for him, whispering for him.

Arthur took a step back, but it was the cloaked figure that saved him.

"Away with all of you," The cloaked figure growled.

"There are two of us, and a horse," Arthur stated as the cloaked figure looked him over. "Will you take us across the river?"

"You seek to draw the sword?" The cloaked figure asked.

"I mean to try," Arthur answered.

The ghosts on the boat began to chitter and chatter amongst themselves. The cloaked figure turned from Arthur and growled them back to quietness.

"You seek to restore magic to the land?" The cloaked figure asked.

"I guess so," Arthur answered uncertainly.

"This boat is for the lost souls of this lake," The cloaked figure said. "They often prefer the rot of wood, and the light of the torches rather than the dampness of a watery grave."

"Listen," Arthur said with a shake of his head. "I don't understand your situation . . . but if I could help . . . I would . . . I just . . ."

"You will help," The cloaked figure interrupted. "Release the magic into the forests. Bring the land back from the dead, and all will be well for us poor souls."

"I'll do my best," Arthur said uncertainly.

"Then your safety on my vessel is assured," The cloaked figure practically hissed before turning his back, gliding around the large indoor cabin in the center of the ship, towards the rear of the boat, and up a ladder towards the wooden wheel which happened to be on top of the cabin, and directly behind me.

I moved immediately off the platform of the cabin back to Goliath. Arthur saw the motion and grinned.

"Not funny," I said.

"You're not afraid of an army of Death Reapers," Arthur laughed. "But a few ghosts make you piss yourself."

The cloaked figure began shouting out orders to his ghostly crew to raise up the drawbridge when we started hearing the screams.

Human and spirit alike stared towards the shore . . . to the lonely old house that had frightened me as Arthur and I passed it by.

There were Death Reapers and their green fog all around the place. They were pounding on the windows, they were kicking at the doors, and despite their best efforts . . . they weren't getting inside. Well, not all of them at least. Apparently, some of them had already made it inside, and it was their screams we were hearing.

"Ah," exclaimed the cloaked figure. "She caught herself a meal."

"We need to move," Arthur shouted. "Those soldiers are after us."

"Of course they are," The cloaked figure hissed. "They'd like to stop the king before he becomes the king."

More and more soldiers were arriving at the house by the second. Most of them joined their comrades in attacking the old structure, but others noticed our boat in the distance, and began making their way towards us.

"We're going to be in a lot of trouble very soon!" Arthur shouted to the cloaked figure.

The cloaked figure said nothing for a long while. He simply gazed at the approaching Death Reapers.

"There was a time when I'd relish a battle," The cloaked figure finally mumbled. "Truth be told . . . now . . . we spirits are . . . less than we used to be, and matter very little in the grand scheme of things."

"What happens if Arthur pulls the sword, and releases the magic?" I asked.

"Then we will once again . . . matter," The cloaked figure said quietly. "At least in our own small way, but the odds are vastly against you."

"They're getting a whole lot worse by the second," Arthur said.

"We'll do our best," I said. "You've got nothing to lose and everything to gain."

The Death Reapers had arrived at the pier, and began shouting orders to the spirits. I couldn't understand what they were saying because Goliath had started making a lot of noise. The cloaked figure was watching the Death Reapers silently as if carefully considering his next course of action.

Arthur went to the boats railing and looked over the side.

"Lance," Arthur said. "Get ready to jump. We've lost our ride."

"Don't jump into those waters," The cloaked figure growled. "The spirits of this lake are weak, but still strong enough to wrap their clammy limbs around you, and drag you under."

"Fuck!" Arthur shouted as he paced back and forth in frustration.

It was a mistake on his part. The Death Reapers picked him out from the crowd of ghosts immediately upon hearing his shout, but they still weren't approaching. They even looked a bit nervous. I smiled when I realized what it was. They were just as afraid of the ghosts as I was.

"They won't come aboard," The cloaked figure mumbled to himself. How interesting it would be if they boarded my ferry."

"We're at a standstill," Arthur whispered to me. "But it won't last forever. Something's got to give."

He shouldn't have said that. The arrows began to fly as if on cue. We should have hid inside the indoor cabin, but Arthur refused to leave Goliath. It was a miracle we weren't killed in the first barrage.

"You promised to keep us safe!" I shouted up to the cloaked figure. "Are you going back on your word?"

The cloaked figure turned his head right towards me for the first time, one of his arms stretched out an impossible distance until his armored hand grabbed a hold of the fabric of my shirt and pulled me into the air, and back up to the wheel of the boat.

"How dare you," The cloaked figure whispered.

I was terrified. Arthur was running around to the ladder. He was going to try and help me, but what could he do? How do you fight a ghost?

"You promised us!" I shouted.

Flaming arrows were now filling up the nighttime sky, yet they bounced harmlessly off the ancient wood of the ship with no effect.

The cloaked figure's hand shot out and grabbed an arrow headed right towards my face. The flames fizzled out with a soft sizzle as if they had been dipped in water.

"He won't fail," I said to the unknown face behind the hood. "I promise you, he won't fail. I believe in him."

The cloaked figure regarded me silently for a few moments. I didn't like his hooded face so close to me. He smelled of lake water. My shirt was getting damp where his armored hand held me tightly.

"We shall see," The cloaked figure eventually whispered in my ear, and then shouted for his crew to continue our departure just as Arthur reached the top of the ladder.

"Let him go," Arthur demanded slightly out of breath.

"As you wish," The cloaked figure laughed, and released me.

Before Arthur could say another word, the cloaked figure turned his back to my friend, and yanked the wheel hard to the right. The big boat lurched in a mighty heave, and we were on our way right as the green fog of the Death Reapers met the ghostly fog of the river.

A ghost moved up the ladder as I sat there wondering what to do. Arthur moved out of his way, and both of us ducked as low as possible to avoid the flaming arrows still coming towards us.

"See that they are fed," The cloaked figure ordered the silent crew member. "They can use my private quarters for the evening, and let no one attempt to harm them."

The ghostly crew member nodded that he understood, and motioned for Arthur to follow him down the ladder. I went after them, but the cloaked figure put a hand up to delay me.

"Why are you so loyal to him?" The cloaked figure asked. "He's not the king yet. He may never become the king."

"He's my friend," I answered.

"Is that all?"

"He was there for me when no one else was," I answered. "He'll surprise everyone. He only needs a chance."

"Your loyalty is why I protected you," The cloaked figure said. "Without it, I would have let them take you."

"We almost got killed," I said angrily. "What kind of protection was that?"

"You were never in any danger," The cloaked figure answered calmly. "I only wanted to see how he would react in a time of crisis."

"And?"

"He's weak," The cloaked figure answered. "A mere shadow of the man he used to be. The Arthur of old had no fear. Men flocked to stand beside him."

"He lost his wife and son," I said. "Everyone says he hasn't been the same since that happened."

"Keep your loyalty, set yourself as an example, and others may follow. Listen to Merlin as well, the wizard knows things. If he has faith in Arthur, then perhaps the man of old can someday be found once again."

I left the cloaked figure, and went inside the open door of the cabin.

"Is that you," Lance?" Arthur asked after I creaked the floor a bit to make him aware of my presence.

"It's me," I answered.

"The food's not half-bad," Arthur said motioning to the table and the plates of broth, and biscuits."

I grabbed a few biscuits, and went to the rear of the room in order to hide a bit more. The room was quite large with a big bed in one corner, and two cabinets in another. There was a painting of a woman on one wall, a window on the opposite wall, and a mirror on the furthest wall from the door.

"Not much for decorating is he?" I asked to break the quietness.

"I doubt the dead really need a lot of material possessions," Arthur answered.

I watched flaming arrows chase after us in the night through the window until we were so far away the Death Reapers had no choice but to give up. After I finished eating, I leapt to one of the cabinets, and fell asleep. Sometime during the night, Arthur tried put a blanket over me, but missed about half my body.

In the morning, I woke up and much to my surprise I slept right through my power transition period. The sun was up, and I was already camouflaged. I was happy about that. I detested the two hours a day I was human.

Arthur wasn't in the bed.

I started looking for him immediately. It was my job to keep him safe, and I'd slept through the entire night, and morning. I was in quite a state as I ran out of the cabin to the deck of the boat.

There he was.

Arthur was standing at the front of the boat. His foot was upon a crate, and he was staring off in the distance. For the first time ever he looked like a king.

His handsome features, his scruffy chin, his eyes narrowed against the grey sky and the drizzle in the air. I almost dropped to my knees as I approached him. One must bow before the king . . . then he opened his mouth.

"I'm freezing my fucking ass off out here," Arthur said.

✿ ARTHUR ✿

I'd seen more than I'd cared to see. Each situation brought new and even more danger into my life. I didn't want to wake up. I didn't want to crawl out of the lumpy bed of our eerie host, but I had to. I could feel the pull of the sword. I could feel it summoning me, and it was getting stronger and stronger. It knew I was close. How close, I had no idea . . . but I was close.

I let Lance sleep. Poor kid. Despite how smart he was. Despite how much more mature than me he was, he didn't need to be a party to this. I was having serious doubts about letting him continue on. Then I remembered how he'd saved my life. I'd be dead without him.

Dawn came slowly, and the sun shined through a veil of stormy clouds. At the moment there was only a drizzle, but eventually a storm was going to blow through the area.

Our host was suddenly behind me.

"Don't send the boy away," He said. "He'll keep you alive."

"Or I could end up getting him killed," I replied. "What's your name anyway?"

"My name has been lost over the centuries," He said. "You may call me what others call me . . . the Ferryman, for that is my duty."

"Have you seen any sign of the Death Reapers?" I asked.

"An interesting name," The Ferryman hissed. "No, but they're coming. Even now they are on the water chasing you down."

"Anything you can do about that?" I asked.

"Not in the light of day," The Ferryman hissed. "Our powers are even weaker in the day."

"Where'd they even find a boat?" I asked.

"There are other boats on this lake," The Ferryman answered. "Owned by mortals that call this area their home . . . they of course know to stay clear of the water after sunset."

"They might also want to stay clear of that old house as well," I grumbled.

"Only after the sun has set," The Ferryman laughed.

"What's in that house?" I asked.

"Why not enter and find out for yourself?" The Ferryman asked.

"I doubt that's going to happen anytime soon," I answered.

"In that house resides an ancient evil," The Ferryman said after an uncomfortable moment of silence. "Stay clear of it no matter how it tempts you."

"It won't be able to tempt me," I said with a laugh.

"We are near our destination," The Ferryman said in an abrupt subject change. "Stay on the trail. These woods are dangerous, but you'll be safe on the trail."

I nodded in understanding.

I tried to see through the dense mist over the lake, but I couldn't make anything out. A soft creak on the wood of the deck let me know the Ferryman was still behind me. What a creepy dude.

"I'm freezing my fucking ass off out here," I said for lack of anything better to say.

"Aren't you cheery this morning," The voice of Lance answered.

"Ah," I laughed. "Finally got out of bed, huh, little trooper?"

"Sorry," Lance said. "I didn't mean to sleep so late."

"No biggie," I said. "You were tired. No harm in that."

"Next time, wake me up," Lance said. "It's my job to protect you."

"Fair enough," I said. "But you realize at some point, I'm going to be forced to go it alone."

"Why's that?"

"I'm not sure," I answered honestly. "I just know I need to cross the next lake alone."

Lance didn't respond. Maybe he was pissed. I wasn't sure; I couldn't see him to read his facial expressions. I had a feeling he was next to Goliath in the middle of the deck, but unless he was moving, he blended in too perfectly with his surroundings.

He was a bit creepy as well, but I was happy for him. This was the only cure he was going to get in this evil world of red and green fog. I would have taken it as well if I had the same affliction. So what if a tree or wall appeared to suddenly come to life, I could deal with it.

There was something up ahead in the mist.

It was a dark and jagged shape jutting out into the lake.

"What is that?" I asked Lance. "Can you see it?"

"Yes," He answered. "It's a nasty looking pier. It looks like it's been burnt."

The boat slowed as we got closer. I looked up to the wheel, and saw the Ferryman steering the boat. Damn he freaked me out. How could someone be even more intimidating in the light of day than at night?

There were no ghosts in sight. Perhaps they couldn't be seen by mortal eyes in the daylight, or maybe they sank beneath the surface of the water until night fell once again. How was I to know?

The boat turned slowly before coming to a stop in front of the jagged pier. The drawbridge came down again, and suddenly the Ferryman was next to me.

"Remember my words," He said.

I nodded in response, grabbed Goliath by his reins, and made my way off the boat.

"How do I get back?" I asked.

"Summon me once again," The Ferryman answered. "If you have the sword, I'll protect and return you. If you fail, and still return . . . do not call me. I'll kill you."

"Aren't you a dickhead," I said under my breath while stepping onto the burnt pier. I was afraid the blackened wood would wobble or break under Goliath's weight, but the structure was surprisingly sturdy.

I had no idea where Lance had gotten to, but that didn't worry me at all. I looked for the horn with which to once again summon the boat if I made it back, and found it easily enough, right before stepping out onto a small gray sanded beach.

There was once a pine forest before me. All that was left was a dense wall of burnt trees. I knew the cause of it. Excalibur. We were close to area in which Excalibur pierced stone for the second time. The dead forest was the result of an immense shockwave of power.

I hated it.

I hated the destruction of something that was once probably very beautiful. Nothing lived here anymore. Nothing could grow here anymore. The land had been scorched by magic, and I was the cause.

I wanted to leave.

"This place makes me sad," Lance said from the damaged forest as I approached the tree line.

"I know exactly how you feel," I replied.

"We're getting close aren't we?" Lance asked.

"I think so," I answered.

The trail was easy enough to find, it was right in front of the pier. Yet, I held back. I didn't want to enter. There was indeed a sadness to this land. I looked back towards the boat, I could barely see it in the grey early morning mist . . . it also appeared to be sinking beneath the surface of the lake as it traveled away from us.

I entered the forest. The ground was littered with old, blackened branches, but the trail was clear. My boots crunched against the dry ground of the trail as I made my way forward.

"Lance," I called.

"Yes," He answered from the trees to my left.

"Stay on the edge of the trail," I said. "Don't venture into those woods."

"I wasn't planning on it," Lance replied.

Hours later, Goliath nudged my shoulder with his gigantic head. I scratched his ears, and he nudged into me again. He wanted something, but I wasn't sure what. Maybe he was hungry?

Another nudge and a light shove. I was beginning to think he wanted me to hop on his back, and that suited me just fine, my legs and back were getting tired. I grabbed the horn of his saddle . . .

"I wouldn't try that again," Lance said from the trees.

"I think it's what he wants," I said.

"Maybe he only wants you to walk faster," Lance said.

I decided to give it a try. With one hand on the saddle horn, and the other on the back of the saddle, I put a foot in the stirrup and pulled myself up. The damn horse turned and bit me right on the ass.

I screamed, and jumped away. The horse looked at me as if I were the jerk. Lance was laughing, and I wished I could see where the little shit was, so I could peg him with a rock or something.

I was standing there, rubbing my butt when I first heard the howling. It cut right through Lance's laughter, and made Goliath's eyes go wide in fear.

The first note was long, and powerful. It seemed to go on forever. The hairs on the back of my neck stood at attention. It wasn't like any wolf howl I'd ever heard before. When it finally finished, Lance and I waited silently to see what would happen next. We weren't waiting long; the howl was answered from all around us.

"This forest is full of whatever made that howl," Lance said from the trees. "Maybe you should try riding Goliath again."

"I think you're right," I answered while already moving towards the horse.

This time he let me on his back. I breathed a sigh of relief as we galloped off along the trail. My only thought was to create as much distance between the source of those howls and myself as possible. Apparently, the horse and I were once again on the same page.

We moved at a rapid pace, but still a pace that Goliath could maintain. I didn't want him tiring out. I planned on riding him straight to my final destination. The hell with this shit, I wasn't some hero. I was just a normal guy. Maybe in a past life I was some big shot . . . but that was a long, long time ago. That fellow had left the building, and I was sick and tired of dealing with all the weirdness that kept coming my way.

My plan was to run in, cross whatever lake, grab the damn sword, cross the lake again, get back on the damn horse, and haul ass to the pier. After that, I had no idea. It was a disheartening series of thoughts. How was I going to get by all the Death Reapers trying to kill me?

One step at a time.

When Goliath began to show signs of tiring, I slowed him down and walked him. The air was cold, and his back was wet. Could horses catch colds? I didn't know, but I was a little worried about him. Then I remembered that people rode horses all the time in the cold.

"Lance," I called out. "You still with me?"

"I'm here," Lance answered from somewhere above my head.

"You see anything?" I asked.

"Nothing but a sea of black trees," He answered. "But I don't like it."

"Why not?" I asked.

"I don't think we're alone," Lance answered.

"That's ridiculous," I said. "We've gone a long way, haven't heard any more howls, and haven't seen anything."

Lance didn't respond to that . . . the little shit. Those were words I certainly didn't want to hear at the moment . . . because even though I didn't want to admit it, I was feeling the same damn way. Hell, even Goliath was looking a little nervous.

An hour or so later, I started seeing shapes move through the blackened forest around us.

I gently nudged Goliath to move faster with my heels. I say gently, because I had a feeling that if I pissed him off, and he decided to throw me, I'd be dead within seconds.

"Arthur," Lance called out. "There are a lot of them."

"What are they?"

"I can't tell," Lance answered. "They're too fast."

The trail was straight, and I wanted to move, so I gently nudged Goliath again, and he took off like a runaway freight train. Fear spurred him on; I could see the frantic look in his long horse face when I leaned forward in the saddle in an effort to stay on top of him.

I knew the big horse wouldn't be able to keep the pace for a long time, not at this speed but if there was something in this dead forest that could keep up with him . . . they deserved to eat us.

Some uneventful twenty minutes later, my arms and legs were tired from holding on. I could only imagine how Goliath felt, so I slowed him down, and forced him to rest.

"No!" Lance shouted from the trees. "They're right behind you."

I spun my head behind me so fast, I almost gave myself whiplash. I saw a shape on four legs, darting back into the burnt trees. Whatever it was, it had been right behind me . . . and it was immense. Certainly that was no wolf.

Goliath took off again, without any encouragement from me at all. I held on for dear life, wondering what to do. I didn't want the horse to hurt himself, but stopping would probably get both of us killed.

"Arthur get off the horse," Lance called out. "Climb a tree. You'll be safe in the trees."

"I'll also be trapped," I said.

"You're already trapped," Lance said.

"I won't leave the horse," I said.

"Why the heck not?" Lance asked in disbelief.

I didn't bother answering him. I concentrated on riding. I concentrated on keeping my groin from slapping against the hard surface of the saddle. I was a horrible rider. Maybe if I was a better rider, Goliath could have escaped.

I doubted it.

I only had my dagger and my Buck 110. Neither of those items was going to protect me from the large furry monsters hot on my heels. I hated this. I hated the feeling of helplessness. It reminded me of when I lost my father. It reminded me of when I lost my wife and child. It's the worst feeling in the world, and I now I was going to lose once again.

Everyone was right. They might not have said anything, but I could see it in their faces. I was a screw up. They all knew I'd fail. They knew it, and so did I.

My mom believed in me. My grandpa believed in me. I'm pretty sure Wayne believed in me, possibly even Sheriff Tagger . . . that's what hurt the most; I was letting down the very few people that truly had faith in me.

I didn't want this journey. I didn't want this adventure, but it meant something to them, and I couldn't say no. I should have said no. I'd been nothing but a failure since I lost . . . since I lost . . . my wife . . . my poor, poor wife.

Even all these years later it still hurt terribly, as if it had just happened only yesterday. Most days, I fought very hard to not think about her. The pain was too much. I even had to block out the many happy memories, because if I let those come through . . . the pain was soon to follow, like a shotgun blast through the heart.

I noticed the darkening sky . . . Lance.

I called out for him.

No answer.

I called out for him again.

"Keep going!" He shouted from somewhere behind me.

The good news was that the voice came from high up in the trees. Hopefully whatever was chasing me down couldn't climb. The bad news was that I was leaving a kid behind. Then again, Lance wasn't exactly a normal kid these days . . . not that he ever was.

It didn't sit well with me. I hated leaving him, but I had no choice. The howling came again. The wolf-cry meaning that the hunt was almost finished. I saw their shapes keeping pace with me beyond the ugly trees.

They looked like wolves, but they couldn't be wolves. Wolves don't get that big. These things were like three or four times the size of a normal wolf. They couldn't be wolves.

The sky was growing darker and darker, but the attack had not yet come. What were they waiting for? They were easily matching our speed. Were they waiting for the horse to tire out? It would certainly be easier to bring him down if he were exhausted.

As if he were reading my thoughts and agreeing with me, Goliath began to slow down. He'd reached his limits, and the poor horse was breathing way too heavily. I needed to get him some water. A cold drink and some rest would make him feel better.

But before any of that could happen, I had to deal with the creatures chasing us down.

I slid my dagger out of the sheath. Gripping the wooden handle made me feel only slightly better. It wasn't much of a weapon in this situation. I was looking all around us as we moved down the trail. Wondering when the attack would come, and from what direction.

Grunts and growls were coming at me from all sides. The creatures weren't happy that we slowed down. Apparently they were enjoying the chase. Could they tell how exhausted Goliath was? If they could, we were in some serious trouble.

The drizzle that had been annoying me since the early morning finally grew some balls, and became a real rain. I pulled my hood over my head in an effort to keep the rain out of my eyes. I needed my sight. I couldn't let the creatures blind-side me.

Visibility became increasingly more difficult in the rain. The grunts and growls were becoming more hostile. Goliath jerked from left to right in an effort to see our hunters. He whinnied tiredly, but he wasn't ready to give up.

And neither was I.

I shouted out a challenge. The noises stopped. I shouted out another challenge, and Goliath spun in circles waiting for it to be accepted.

Forty feet behind us on the trail, something stepped out of the dead forest. It wasn't a wolf. The beast padded to the middle of the trail, and growled so loudly I felt the shockwaves in my chest. My dagger was going to be remarkably useless.

Goliath issued his own challenge, and reared up on two legs. I damn near fell off as a result, but somehow, in my mad scramble to stay in the saddle, I managed to see light coming from behind me. As soon as Goliath had all four hooves on the ground, I stole another glance, and saw two flames burning brightly farther down the trail.

Could that be people?

Could that be help?

I looked again at the hideous thing that accepted my challenge. It was walking slowly towards us. I took another glance at the torches. They weren't far away. Goliath could make that, I was sure of it.

I yanked hard on his reins, and dug my heels into him roughly. The horse screamed at the indignity, but he turned away from the hideous thing, and charged forward once again.

It wasn't a mighty rush of speed, but it was still fast. I only hoped it would be fast enough. The creature was right behind us. I could hear its snarls, and almost feel its hot, wet breath on the back of my neck.

A slight turn on the trail, and I saw the two flames clearly. They were torches on either side of a great stone gateway that burned brightly despite the rain. The trail went through the open gateway. We'd be there in seconds, but who lit the damn torches? Where were the people? Where was the help we so desperately needed?

They had to be close.

"Hello!" I shouted out. "Is there anybody here?"

No answer.

I could already feel Goliath slowing down. I could even hear his lungs wheezing in protest of the tortures he was being forced to endure.

The sky above us belched out the loudest clap of thunder I'd ever heard, and suddenly the rain became a violent thing. I looked behind to see if it would have an effect on the creature . . . it didn't. He was about five feet behind us, and even worse, he was no longer alone. Four others of his kind had joined him.

"Hello!" I shouted out. "Is anyone here?"

No answer but the sounds of snapping jaws directly behind Goliath's tail.

I screamed out and dug in my heels for the final stretch. Poor Goliath, he was too tired to protest . . . but he did give a final push, and before I knew it, we were through the gate.

Before us was a lake. I couldn't see it until I went through the gate, but there it was, a still lake, at the end of the trail.

Goliath stopped running.

I tried to get him to turn, and confront our attackers . . . he refused. So I jumped off his back with my dagger held high, and made ready to face the hideous creatures so determined to dine upon our bones.

They weren't there.

They didn't cross through the gate with us. Yet, I could see their yellow eyes in amongst the trees of the background. I looked around. A stone wall that went on forever attached to both sides of the gate. We were out of the dead forest, and in a clearing. Well, it wasn't exactly a clearing.

It was a cemetery.

A vast and beautiful cemetery.

This cemetery looked nothing like the last one we encountered. Here the landscape was decorated with high crosses and statues. Knights in armor, frozen in stone for an eternity, full scale horses, and robed saints ... this cemetery had it all. Even the dead forest refused to encroach upon its morbid beauty.

The trail went through the cemetery all the way to a cliff very close to the water's edge. I could see no other paths. Grabbing a hold of Goliath's reins, I led him down the trail. He protested at first, but I stubbornly pulled him along behind me. At the end of the trail was another open gate with torches, and beyond that a flight of wide stone steps that led to a small pebble beach that ran along the water's edge.

Goliath drank greedily.

The rain was still pouring down on us, but we were safe. My cloak offered a little protection from the elements, but my legs were still soaked from the ride. I left Goliath by the water, and walked back to the cemetery as the sky grew darker and darker.

I was waiting for Lance. I needed him to find his way back to me before I continued my journey. I needed to know that he was safe.

I stepped off the trail, and watched as the rain washed away the dirt and grit around the tombstones. More torches lit the area as I walked around. They also burned despite the rain. One minute there would be only shadows, then I'd look away, and when I looked back a torch would be burning brightly.

There was enough light to read the inscriptions on the stone.

I didn't like what I was reading.

"Here lies Everard. He died proudly in the service of our majesty, King Arthur."

"Here rests the body of Sir Randall. A man privileged to fight alongside the mighty King Arthur."

"Here lies Godwin. He fought against the forces of Morgan Le Fay, and was recognized by King Arthur himself."

These were the men that fought for me. This cemetery was the final resting place for all the soldiers of Camelot. How did they get here? Did they follow the sword? Where did they use to reside? Shit, history wasn't even sure an Arthur existed . . . but . . . but . . .

It was too much. Too many lives that proudly served in my army, I couldn't even imagine the kind of man I was back then. I couldn't imagine trying to live up to those expectations.

I walked deeper into the cemetery.

All around me were headstones, and then I saw the crypts. Large buildings of white stone, all of them without doors . . . no, there were doors alright. They were just broken off . . . from the inside.

What the hell?

I went to the closest crypt. I stepped beyond the ruined door at my feet, grabbed a nearby torch, and entered. In the middle of the room stood a knight made of stone. He was clutching a triangular shaped shield.

In front of him was a stone sarcophagus. The sarcophagus was cracked in the middle. Grave robbers? No, it couldn't be. The lid hadn't been moved. I read the inscription on the stone.

"Here lies Sir Galahad, the most noble and loyal of all the Knights of the Round Table."

Son of a bitch. I knew that name. Could it really be him? Could it truly be the resting place of the real Sir Galahad?

I ran back out into the rain. My head was spinning, and I felt faint. I went to the next crypt, stepped over the broken door, and went inside. This one was guarded by a statue as well. The statue however was different in appearance. Instead of a shield, the warrior of stone held a sword. I read the inscription on the broken sarcophagus.

"Here lies Sir Gawain, defender of the poor, Knight of the Round Table, and nephew to King Arthur."

Immediately I thought of Wayne, and smiled. This had to be Wayne, but Wayne wasn't my nephew in this day and age. He was my buddy. Then again, the man stood by me through thick and thin to the point in which I have long considered him family. Could our bond be due to the past blood ties we shared? What a crazy world.

I stepped back out into the rain, at the very edge of the cemetery nearest to the dead forest stood a solitary crypt far away from all the others. I didn't need to go inside that one. Something told me who it belonged to, and I was waiting for him at this very moment.

Opposite the solitary crypt at one end of the cemetery, not far from the trail, and up a steep hill stood the largest by far of the crypts overlooking the lake . . . I needed to see it. I don't know why, I already had an idea of what I would find . . . but I needed to see it for myself.

The rain began to beat down on me even more furiously than before as I made my way up the hill. Lightning flashed across the sky in angry arcs that turned night into day. Thunder boomed and cracked as if gods were fighting just beyond the clouds.

The ground became muddy, and the going got tougher and tougher, but I would not be denied. I pushed and I crawled my way to the massive crypt. So much bigger than all the others, it had patterns carved into its outside walls.

I reached the doorway. The doors on this crypt weren't broken off; they were tied off to remain open. I stepped inside the dark interior, and the massive room sprang to life as a billion torches erupted all throughout the interior.

The walls were painted with scenes of battle, horses, warriors, young lovers, and castles. Above the painted walls were stained glass windows picturing still other scenes that I couldn't decipher from so far away.

At the far back wall was a massive statue of a king sitting on a throne. In one hand and across his lap was a dangerous looking sword. His feet were resting upon a cracked stone sarcophagus. I dusted off the sarcophagus with a gentle hand, and realized I was trembling. The inscription was simple and bold.

"Here lies Arthur, the once and future king."

I gasped out loud, and took a step back. What do I do? What do I say? What do I think? How do I feel? I was standing before my own grave.

The sarcophagus upset me on too many different levels to count. It also made me curious. Part of me wanted to push aside the heavy lid at the crack and take a look at the skeleton beneath it. Another part of me thought of that as some sort of sacrilege. Could I commit a sacrilegious act on my own grave?

I wasn't this man. He was foreign to me. I wasn't great. I was a disappointment at best. Sure, I hadn't always been this way . . . but times change. I drew the short straw. I didn't feel sorry for myself. Nope, that wasn't a part of my personality, but I had my aches and pains, and some aches and pains aren't so easy to ignore.

I missed my wife.

She'd know what to say to me. I was a better person with her in my life. She had the words to make all that was happening, okay. I dropped to my knees before my own grave. How funny it was that I was here before my own grave, but I'd never visited the graves of my wife and child aside from the day they were buried.

I was crying like an idiot when Lance entered the crypt. I knew he was there, because he politely scuffed his feet to announce his presence.

"I'm not a king," I said.

"Not yet you're not," Lance replied softly. "But you will become one. Greatness is in your destiny. You can run and hide as much as you want, but it will find you . . . and you will rise to the occasion."

"I don't . . . I don't . . ."

"Stand strong against the storm Arthur," Lance said from the shadows. "Stand strong against the storm."

His words hit me hard. I was stunned into silence, and then I started laughing. A child was given an adult advice. A child was encouraging me, and his words had more maturity than I could ever muster.

He started laughing with me.

The rain was pouring with a vengeance. Hideous wolf-like demons had us trapped in a cemetery, and a small army of Death Reapers were hot on our heels . . . but we were laughing. I appreciated the sound of his child-like laughter. It made me think of better days . . . stop . . . I had to stop myself. The bad always comes with the good. The bad has the strength to cripple me.

I stood up.

"Thanks for being a pal," I said.

"Thanks for being everything to me," Lance replied.

"So what do you think?" I asked.

"I think it's time," Lance answered. "I'll stay in the cemetery with Goliath."

"You wanna walk with me to the lake?" I asked.

"I'd have it no other way," Lance answered.

On my way to the door, I noticed the other sarcophagus. For a brief second I was confused, and then it hit me. Arthur had a wife.

I didn't bother to look any closer at her sarcophagus, not because of any famous betrayal I might have believed in. I had no faith in any of those stories. I knew Lance too well. Nope, that never crossed my mind at all.

I ignored her sarcophagus because I already had a wife, and I loved her still. No legendary romance from a different time would ever change that.

We left my crypt, and as I walked back down the hill in the fierce rain I couldn't help but take a last look at the Lance's resting place so far away from the others.

"That won't be me this time," Lance said as if he'd noticed where I was looking. "I will never fail you again."

"I don't doubt it for a second, little man," I said.

Before I knew it, I was back on the trail and headed for the gate and stone steps. I could hear Lance moving through the cemetery off to my left. He was making noise on purpose so that I knew he was there. Why did I feel like I was walking to my own execution? What was about to happen? If I found the sword, and freed it from its prison of stone . . . what was going to happen to me? I was nervous.

"You really think this is a good idea?" I shouted over the storm.

"I think it's unavoidable," Lance answered.

Past the gate and down the steps, I searched around at the water's edge. There was no sign of a boat, nor was there a pier with a horn on it.

"What the hell?" I asked while raising my hands in a defeated gesture.

"You're the future king!" Lance shouted against the storm. "Demand that it come. It will obey you."

I stepped to the edge of the lake, mindful that my boots didn't touch the water. I didn't trust the water. There was something in the water.

Somewhere in that lake was an island that I couldn't see due to the storm. I wanted to go there. The pull I felt told me to go there.

"I am Arthur," I shouted out to the angry sky. "I am the once and future king."

I said the words with a conviction that I didn't feel, and afterwards, when nothing happened, I felt rather foolish. I was just an idiot standing in the middle of a storm calling out for a boat.

I saw the outlines of something moving towards me on the lake.

"Lance," I said. "Do you see that?"

"It's a boat," Lance answered.

"Holy shit," I said.

"I didn't think that would actually work," Lance admitted.

"What do I do now?" I asked as the small two-seater boat bumped against the shoreline?

"Get on the boat," Lance said.

I thought about that idea.

"I don't want to," I said.

"Arthur, get on the boat," Lance said.

"Yeah, I don't think so," I said.

"What are you doing?" Lance asked.

"The boat moved by itself," I said.

"It's here to pick you up," Lance said.

"It moved by itself," I said.

"Get on the boat," Lance said.

"You get on the fucking boat," I said. "I don't want to get on the boat."

"Arthur," Lance said. "You don't have a choice."

I hated hearing it, but he was right. I didn't have a choice. I needed the sword if I wanted to go home.

"I hate you right now," I said.

"If I could go for you, I'd do it," Lance said while trying to suppress his laughter.

I got on the stupid little wooden boat, and sat down so that I could see in what direction I was heading. I felt a slight tremble, and the boat slowly moved away from the shoreline. I was far from happy.

I couldn't see anything in the rain. I couldn't see where I was headed, and before long, I could no longer see the shore from which I had departed. I was lost, pulled into the unknown by a force I couldn't understand.

The little boat was filling with water. Shockingly, as ancient as it seemed, I didn't believe it had any leaks. Nope, the water was coming from the sky. The rain was filling the boat. I had no bucket to empty it out. I could only endure the added wetness, and hope that I was safely on the island before the weight of the rain water sank my vessel.

Some twenty or so minutes later, an ugly gash of lightning arced across the sky, and illuminated my world for the briefest of moments. I saw the island. It wasn't far away. I jumped out of my seat, the boat rocked threateningly; I cursed out loud, and sat back down immediately.

No way in hell did I want to fall in that water.

The boat eventually bumped against the soft shore of the island. I carefully got out, and as soon as my feet touched the ground; a sudden burst of light sparked into existence directly in front of me. I shielded my eyes from the initial blaze, and when my vision had recovered sufficiently enough to see once again, I saw two rows of torches spaced about ten feet apart that marked the edges of a trail directly in front of me. Outside the illuminated trail was another burnt forest of pine.

"Arthur"

I looked around in a panic. Nothing to be seen . . . but something called my name. Did I hear it, or was it in my head? I tried to listen, wondering if the voice would come again.

Nothing.

Damn the rain, I couldn't hear a thing.

I trudged down the trail with my head bent low, and my cloak pulled tight against the rain.

"Arthur . . . free me"

I knew it was the sword. I'd heard its voice before, but never so pronounced, never so strong. Sure, it called out to me, but it was always more like a suggestion . . . or a feeling. Now the damn thing was actually speaking to me. Could others hear it? Well, if there were other people around, would they be able to hear it calling me? I didn't think so.

A flash of memory.

It had spoken to me before. When I was a child, it spoke to me. How could I have forgotten that? It called me through the forest, and gave me its name. I was so horribly frightened when that happened. Grandpa Merl came to my rescue. He gave me a home.

"Free me"

"Excalibur!" I shouted.

Perhaps I was a bit insane to be shouting out to a sword, but I didn't feel that way. No, I felt powerful. I felt as if I was headed to another part of me, and when I found that missing part, a new man would be born.

In other words, I was alive with the hint of destiny. The voice didn't scare me like it did when I was a kid. This time, it gave me hope.

Onward I went. The trail was easier to follow than ever with the brightly burning torches marking my way.

Fifteen minutes, twenty minutes . . . how big was this island? I was shivering in the cold, vicious rain. Hopefully, I hadn't given myself pneumonia. Did I feel feverish? No. I felt fucking frozen.

Another gateway appeared soon after I entered a small canyon, and less than a hundred feet beyond the gateway was the edge of vast cliff that rose high above the dead forest on the other side of the island. In the very center of the canyon, right at the edge of the cliff was an impossibly narrow and jagged mountain of black stone that rose over two hundred feet into the air. The trail led to a series of steps carved into the very rock itself. On either side of the steps were brightly burning torches whose light refused to penetrate what lay beyond the final step.

"Arthur"

I had made it. I had arrived. Despite all odds, I was here. I was about to claim Excalibur. I was about to free the sword from the stone. I was suddenly nervous. What if the sword wasn't there? What if it was there and I couldn't pull it from the stone?

Nonsense.

I made my way to the first of the steps at the base of the wicked mountain. The rain was still a fury of pouring water. The steps were slick, and I fell forward onto my hands almost as soon as I began to ascend.

That didn't stop me.

I simply crawled the remainder of the way until I reached the summit. It wasn't easy, and more than a few times I lost my grip and slipped down the wet surface until I managed to reach out and grab something to stop my fall.

At the summit, I marveled as the final four torches burst into flame one after the other, the moment I stepped onto the perfectly squared tile platform that served as Excalibur's resting place. The light made me dizzy as I quickly realized that beyond the other three sides of the platform there was nothing but open air and a long, long drop. The four torches had been placed in the corners of the ten foot square, and they illuminated the stone and its prisoner the sword perfectly.

The imprisoning stone resided in the middle of the platform. It was a dark grey in color unlike the black rock of the mountain, and roughly the size of a large bush or piece of shrubbery in the front of someone's house. There were words carved into it.

"WHOSO PULLETH OUT THIS SWORD OF THIS STONE SHALL BE KING."

I looked from the stone to the sword, curiously taking my time despite the rain. I shivered as I gazed upon the handle ruined by time. The sword was a two-hander, the handle of which seemed at one point to have been wooden and wrapped with some type of metal wire.

Well, the wire didn't look so pretty anymore. It was broken and ravaged in many places. The wood beneath it had been eaten away. It appeared as if it would crumble in my hand if I grasped it too hard.

The pommel and guard were of an unknown material that hadn't fared any better than the handle. Blackened by age, they were nicked and damaged. The guard even looked a bit bent.

Worst of all was the blade . . . or what I could see of the blade. It looked like any old sword that had been dug up after centuries of being buried in the ground, a hunk of iron, misshapen and long past any salvageable stage of rust.

Was this Excalibur?

This couldn't be the great sword of legend. This was a useless relic that belonged in a museum. I was disappointed beyond belief. What a letdown. I couldn't use this thing in a fight. It would break in two if I slapped it against a rock.

I took a step away. I think I had tears in my eyes. How could this be Excalibur? How could this be what Lance, Goliath, and I had struggled for? All our efforts were for nothing.

"Arthur . . . free me"

I didn't know how to react. The only thought coursing through my mind was putting the poor thing out of its misery, but how do you kill something that shouldn't even be alive?

"FREE ME"

I put a foot on the base of the stone, and grabbed the handle with both hands. I took a deep breath, closed my eyes, and pulled. The sword came free easily with a rasp of steel against stone, and then . . . nothing.

Silence.

All around me, nothing but a silence so complete it assaulted my senses in its abruptness. I lost myself . . . I have no idea where. I came to with only the deep sounds of my breathing to keep me company. Long and slow breaths that came and went.

Finally, I opened my eyes.

The sword was in my hands.

I looked at it carefully. The parts of it that were stuck in the stone were just as bad as the parts sticking out. I put my hand on the blade . . . rough; a texture that didn't belong on a blade.

It took me a moment to realize that the rain had stopped as soon as I pulled the blade free. Did that mean something? Was there some importance in pulling free a ruined blade?

Beyond the now empty stone was the vastness of the island and beyond that was the lake. I had almost forgotten I was standing on the very top of a mountain which also happened to be at the edge of a cliff. The view would have been beautiful if the forest was still a living thing. What a shame things ended up the way they did. What would everyone think when I returned home with this useless relic?

The grey clouds above me parted as if by an unseen hand, and a beam of brilliant beam of light shot down upon me from the heavens. I froze as if I had just been caught in a spotlight while burglarizing someone's home. What did it mean? I didn't know, but I had the distinct impression that I was being acknowledged.

Acknowledged?

Approved of?

What the hell?

I felt very inadequate. I felt naked. I didn't want the attention. I only wanted to go home. Geez . . . how the hell was I going to make it home? The odds were certainly stacked up against me.

The ground began to tremble. At first it was only a slight vibration. Then it grew, and grew, and grew. I looked up into that brilliant light as if expecting to find answers, and found . . . nothing.

The stone split in half with an ominous crack, and a massive bolt of blue energy shot out into the sky, following the path of the brilliant light. Somewhere far up into the atmosphere, it slapped against an opposing force with a sound that would have been heard for miles, and spread out across the globe.

The brilliant light vanished.

The ground stopped trembling.

The hairs on my arms were standing on end. Little pebbles scattered all over the platform began to lift up into the air. The broken stone began to gurgle and bubble. Water started pouring out of both halves, only to then cascade off the edge of the platform.

I ran away.

It wasn't easy going back down those slippery stairs, but I took stair after stair as fast as I could possibly move, suffering a multitude of bruises and scrapes along the way. When I finally reached the bottom, I kept on running until I was about a hundred yards away. There I collected my breath and watched as the mountain began to tremble, crack, and eventually collapse upon itself, only to be washed off the edge of the cliff in a froth of rushing water.

What I was witnessing couldn't be the work of Mother Nature. Of that, I was certain. Sure, Mother Nature can be destructive, but this was something else. This was something unnatural. Well if I really stopped to think about it . . . unnatural was rapidly becoming my natural.

Gigantic geysers began spouting out of the earth all along the trail, and a flowing river began instantly forming around me. I was swept off my feet. The sword almost came out of my hand. I crawled away from the water onto wet grass, and watched the river come to life. Wait a second . . . wet grass? This land was dead.

Not anymore, there was grass underneath me. It wasn't long grass by any means, but it was green and alive. I could see that clearly in the light of the torches along the trail that somehow remained unmolested by the river.

The land was coming back to life.

Son of a bitch.

My little two-seater boat drifted along with the current towards the cliff. I ran for it. I couldn't lose that boat; it was my only way off the island. I still didn't want to touch the water of the lake.

I worried for nothing. Before I could reach the boat, it came to the rivers bank of its own accord, despite the flowing water.

I laughed out loud.

Finally something weird happened that would benefit me. Well, if that boat wanted me to hop in once again . . . I was all for it. It had earned my trust.

Something began crawling from the river.

At first I couldn't figure out what it was, but its bent arms and crooked legs resembled the appendages of an insect. It crawled onto the grass, placing itself between me and the boat. I watched as it slowly stood on two legs.

It was a woman.

No . . . it used to be a woman.

The woman part of the creature died a long, long time ago. Standing before me was a dark skeleton, wrapped in black pieces of leather that used to be skin. She wore a long soaking wet dress that clung to her ancient frame in rotted tatters. Her thin hair hung in clumps off what remained of her scalp.

She beckoned me to approach her with a slow movement of her right hand.

I shook my head, no.

She beckoned again.

I shook my head, no . . . again.

She tried to say something to me, and all that came out was a raspy whisper. I grasped the handle of Excalibur tighter, worried about breaking it, and remembered the dagger on my belt. I put my hand on the handle but I didn't draw the blade.

I walked to the skeletal figure. Why the hell was I walking towards the skeletal figure? I should have been running in the opposite direction. Whatever . . . she was between me and my boat, it wasn't like I had a lot of choice in the matter.

When I stood about three feet from her, she slowly reached into the folds of her dress, and brought out a blood red scabbard, with a brilliant golden locket and chape. I accepted the gift reluctantly, all the while marveling that I remembered what the names of the entry point and tip of a scabbard were called.

Why hand me a beautiful scabbard for a ruined sword?

"Thank you," I said.

She bowed her head slightly in acknowledgment of my thanks . . . and I realized who she was. None other than the Lady of the Lake stood before me in all her ruined glory. What had happened to her? All the legends described her as beautiful. I never read anything about her resembling an ancient zombie.

A world without magic.

The Lady of the Lake was a being that existed solely in a world of magic. Merlin used that magic to ensure my resurrection. How terribly she must have suffered.

"I know who you are," I whispered.

She cocked her head to the side, and suddenly I was enveloped in a wave of warmth and love. My problems . . . my pains were gone. Despite her appearance, I sensed her majesty, I sensed her power, I sensed her love; I crammed the sword into the scabbard roughly and dropped to my knees.

"I am so very sorry," I whispered while offering her the sword. "Please, take it . . . find someone else."

She gently reached out and brushed a wet tendril of hair away from my forehead. I started bawling at that point. Yep, I made a real ass of myself. I cried and cried while she gently stroked the top of my head. The embarrassment I felt made me bawl even harder. I'm not a crier, and here I was making an ass out of myself for the second time in the same evening.

She never reached out to accept Excalibur.

"Why won't you take it?" I asked. "Don't you understand what a failure I am?"

She bent at the knees bringing herself level with me, and I could hear the crackles and pops of her joints. She continued to stroke the hair on my head. I didn't cringe at her boney touch. I didn't cringe when she brought her face close to my ear.

"I . . . believe . . . in . . . you," she whispered into my ear in a raspy voice that hadn't been used in probably centuries.

I really started bawling at that point. Oh yeah, it was ridiculous. I cried and cried and cried. That was her presence. That was the power, and awesomeness that rolled off of her in waves. The purity, the love, the kindness . . . what was I to do? I was a slave to her greatness.

When I collected myself, when I stopped my bawling, I looked up and she was gone. I missed her terribly. I missed the feelings she caused inside of me. I missed the way she ignited nerves and synapses with feelings I'd long since thought dead and buried.

I was alone.

I felt foolish.

Excalibur and the scabbard were still in my hand. Why the hell did I make such an ass of myself in front of such a majestic being?

What was I supposed to do now?

The current of the river had calmed down. The geysers of water had stopped bursting from the ground along the trail. The boat was still there . . . waiting for me.

I stood up slowly.

I took a deep breath . . . and smiled. The Lady of the Lake for just a brief moment . . . brought me happiness. That alone was enough to carry me further.

I hoped into the little boat. It shuddered for a brief moment, and slowly pulled away from the shore. I didn't care that the boat moved at a snail's pace as it led me down the flooded trail. It was better than walking because I was seriously exhausted.

I'd seen too much, I'd felt too many emotions . . . a life without pain. What if I could have that life? Would I want it? Yes, I would take it, but that was never going to happen. I would never again be whole.

The torches provided enough light for me to gaze at the pine forest around me. There was green on those long dead trees. Life was coming back to the island at an impossible pace. Flowers were blooming along the banks.

I heard crickets. I saw lightning bugs. The stars twinkled brightly above me in a night sky that seemed anything but menacing.

I leaned back in the boat. Nothing could hurt me on this island. I was confident of that. It was my chance to rest, and take stock of all that had befallen me. I had just met the Lady of the Lake. She came to me. She was real. She believed in me.

Man . . . was she going to be disappointed.

Maybe I dozed off a bit. I'm not sure. I was relaxed; call it the afterglow of meeting a magical being. When I awoke, I was still drifting underneath that beautiful star filled sky. I sat up quickly, and looked around. Where the hell was I? Yes, I was on the lake, but was I headed in the right direction. No problem there. I could see the torches of the cemetery burning in the distance.

The lake still made me nervous.

There was something moving underneath the water. I couldn't necessarily see anything, but I could feel it. Something was waking up, and it wasn't a bunch of ghosts. Shit. Thoughts like that made it worse. I felt like I needed a bigger boat. Was there an extremely large great white shark swimming underneath me?

I wanted off the lake in the very worst way. I kept looking from the water to the shore of the cemetery. It wouldn't be long. The distance was shortening by the second. How the fuck did I speed this boat up?

A small wave made the little boat rock.

Why would there be a small wave in the middle of a lake? There weren't any waves before. The lake was almost perfectly smooth.

Another wave came, this one was a bit bigger, and the boat rocked even more. I yelled at the boat. I demanded that it speed up. I demanded that it get me off the lake immediately.

The boat ignored me.

It was worth a try.

The third wave came, and I realized they weren't waves at all, but the wake of something moving just beneath the surface of the water. What was it? I had no idea, but whatever it was seemed to be circling me.

I was going to be eaten by Bruce the lake shark.

Fuck this.

I grabbed the sword, and started speaking to it.

"This is your damn fault, ya know?" I growled. "Coming after you is going to get me killed. You just wait and see."

The sword didn't answer . . . but I thought . . . nah, I must have been mistaken . . . but for a second there, I felt the sword heat up?

No way.

Stupid sword. Once I pulled it from the rock, it clammed up and became utterly useless. What good was it? Was it supposed to be an inspiration? It was rather ugly to inspire someone. Maybe Grandpa Merl wasn't aware of the condition of the sword.

Part of me wanted to go rob one of the graves for a better weapon. I was sick of only having a dagger. I quickly abandoned that idea. Dishonoring those graves of those people in any way seemed a grievous sin.

I saw fins.

They weren't shark fins, but that wasn't a relief. Nope, they were something else, and I still had no idea what. Sharp spines separated by a greenish membrane. I saw two of them. Was there more than one creature in the water?

I was almost to the shore.

Just a little bit more.

I willed the boat to move faster. Evidently, I possessed no mind powers whatsoever. The boat continued at its nerve-wracking sluggish pace.

The fins came again. This time the creature was closer to the surface, because the fins stood out of the water somewhere close to five feet. I leaned back in the boat. After the fin, I saw the shape of its body glide by, and then I saw the second fin that was slightly smaller than the first move by me.

It wasn't two creatures. It was one very large creature that could easily capsize my boat with a casual flick of its enormous tail. Some twenty feet away from the shore it breached, sending up a spray of water in all directions, and then it was gone.

I didn't see it clearly. There was too much water in the air, and I wasn't facing the right direction. I was too busy staring at the shore, but I thought I saw something. I had to be mistaken.

There was no way I had just seen what I thought I had just seen. There was no way I saw two massive yellow eyes looking at me through the spray of water. That was impossible.

Ten feet away from the shore and I wanted to jump out of the boat and scramble to dry land. I didn't do it though, something inside of me kept telling me not to touch the water.

Eight feet away from the shore, and the biggest wave came and pushed the boat forward.

Five feet away, and something out of a nightmare erupted from the lake and took to the sky on great leathery wings that created so much wind, I was knocked backwards. The spray once again distorted my vision, and then it was gone.

But I knew.

The boat gently bumped onto dry land. I hopped out in a flash. I'm not sure why I hopped out so quickly, my swimming companion had taken to the air, and disappeared. The danger had passed. Perhaps I'd just had enough of the scary lake, and the beasts that lived there.

"Are you okay?" Lance asked from somewhere.

"I'm fine," I answered sarcastically.

"That thing that came out of the water," Lance said. "Was that what I think it was?"

"I'm pretty sure," I answered.

A moment of silence. I'm not sure about Lance, but I was scanning the sky above me. I didn't want to get eaten. I'm sure Lance was doing the same thing, but of course . . . I couldn't see him.

"Is that, Excalibur?" Lance eventually asked, no doubt noticing the sword in my hand.

"Yes," I answered.

"Can I see it?" Lance asked.

"Prepare to be disappointed," I said as I attempted to tug the sword out of the scabbard.

It wasn't easy to remove the sword. The damage done by time had created a misshapen blade that didn't fit very well with the red scabbard.

Finally, it was free. I held it out in the direction of Lance's voice so that he could take a good look.

"What happened to it?" Lance asked after a while.

"Time," I answered. "The sword is ancient. Time itself claimed what many battles could not. Excalibur is ruined."

"How can that be?" Lance asked.

"I have no idea," I answered. "I thought it was a magical blade. I certainly didn't expect to pull this from the stone . . . but I'll tell ya. After I freed Excalibur, I saw something. I think it was the magic being released back into the world.

"I saw that as well," Lance said. "It looked like the best fireworks show I'd ever seen. Do you think Merlin has his magic back?"

"Yes," I answered. "Magic has once again come to this world, but I'm not sure if that's good or bad to tell you the truth."

"After seeing that thing come out of the water," Lance said. "I'm ready to agree with you."

We both laughed at that.

"Well, hopefully my grandpa knows what he's doing," I said.

"He does," Lance said. "I know he does. Your grandpa is Merlin. Merlin knows everything. We need to have faith in him. He won't lead us astray."

I nodded. I wanted to tell Lance about what I had seen. I wanted to tell him about the dead land coming back to life, but I didn't know how. I also wanted to tell him about the Lady of the Lake, and how she made me feel if only for a brief moment. In the end, for whatever reason, I said nothing. My nod remained my only answer.

Goliath wasn't difficult at all to find. His enthusiasm upon seeing me made me a bit nervous. What was in that water? Was my horse drugged? Perhaps he was simply leading me into a false sense of security so he could take another bite out of me.

There were no eyes staring at us through the trees as we reached the end of the graveyard. At the final gate we paused.

"The trees look different," Lance said. "They're coming back to life. I see needles on them."

"Yup," I answered. "I guess magic did that."

"No," Lance said. "You did that. King Arthur is one with the land. Where he walks, nature will flourish."

I crinkled up my face and turned to look at him.

"Did you smoke something while I was gone?" I asked.

"Nope," Lance answered with a laugh. "I think I read that somewhere."

Lance had an amazing memory. It probably bordered somewhere close to photographic. He knew exactly where he read that, he just didn't want to bore me with the details.

"Don't believe everything you read," I said.

"I don't," Lance answered. "But look around you. The closer you get, the greener they become, and the faster they grow."

Wow. I was at a loss for words. Was it truly me? Was I causing this?

"You think Goliath will let me ride him?" I asked.

"No," Lance answered. "But I'd appreciate it if you tried."

I grabbed Goliath by the reins, and looked into his big brown horse eyes. He didn't yank his head away from me. I scratched his nose. He pushed forward for more, and made funny little noises.

"What do you say, big guy?" I asked him quietly. "You wanna give me a break?"

"I dare you," Lance laughed from somewhere on the stone wall.

I went to the side of the horse. I put my left foot in the stirrup. Goliath's head came back to face me. I saw evil in his eyes. A sort of malevolence just waiting to strike . . . of course I chickened out at that point.

"Fuck that," I said, to Lance's laughter.

"Good choice," Lance said.

I walked through the gate, Goliath and Lance followed me. Lance was in the trees. Goliath was behind me. Lance was still giggling. I couldn't blame him. If it was somebody else, I'd be laughing as well.

We heard howling in the distance.

The laughter stopped.

I was worried about that. I mean, I was hoping that we'd seen the last of those hideous beasts, but I wasn't banking on it. What to do? Goliath was scratching at the ground with a hoof nervously . . . but he seemed to want to fight.

That horse had some serious balls.

Me, I didn't want to fight. I had an ancient sword that would break if I used it, and a dagger. Hell no, I didn't want to encounter those things once again. Unfortunately, the only option we had was to move forward and hope for the best.

We decided to walk as long as we could. The more energy we could conserve the better. If they came at us again, then we would run. Hopefully we could get far enough along the trail that Goliath could make it to the end without him gassing out, and without both of us getting eaten. I wasn't worried about Lance. He could get high enough in the trees that he'd be safe.

Forty minutes down the trail, Lance whistled from above me. In response, I moved to the edge of the trail. If I had to, I was going into the forest. I had no other choice.

"Do you see something?" I whispered.

"We're not alone," Lance answered.

"What's out there?" I asked.

"Not sure yet," Lance answered. "But there are a lot of them."

"How far?" I asked.

"About half a mile," Lance answered. "I think they're planning an ambush."

"We'll have to leave . . ."

Twenty-some Death Reapers chose that moment to step out of their hiding places in the forest. They were good. They had spread out enough to keep the green fog that follows them around from building up and becoming noticeable. I never knew they were even there until I was already surrounded.

"Well, well, well," One of the Death Reapers smirked. "Looks like we'll all be heroes, boys."

The other Death Reapers smiled or laughed.

I had Excalibur attached to my belt. A worthless sword, but I wasn't ready to give up. My right hand crept slowly to my dagger until my hand grasped the handle. Goliath reared up right behind me. I thought about jumping on him, and tearing off . . . but the Death Reapers were too close.

I was in for a fight.

A Death Reaper grabbed at me. I pulled the dagger, and rammed it into his sternum before he could blink. Another Death Reaper slashed at my back. The cut was shallow since I was moving, but he managed to open me up.

I twisted under another sword, and slashed at the throat of the Death Reaper that cut me. I was lucky, it was a clumsy slash, but somehow I nailed him.

Two down.

A sword I never even saw coming nailed my dagger right on the guard, and it went flying form my hand. I rolled away. In the corner of my eye, I saw the living forest already attacking my attackers. Lance was with me.

A sword swung in my direction. I fell back out of the way, and it cut only air. I was weaponless. Rough hands grabbed a hold of me. I panicked and dove into a somersault that somehow granted me freedom, but the wickedly rusted blades were all around me.

I was in trouble, and my right hand did what it had been trained to do for some many years. It grabbed the ruined sword still on my belt, and ripped it from its sheath.

The Death Reapers laughed at the sight of the ancient sword.

My grandpa told me not to use the sword. He was very clear about not using the sword . . . but I had no choice. I had no other weapon.

Another sword swung in my direction. I blocked it, all the while fearing Excalibur would break. Metal kissed metal. Excalibur didn't break. Instead, the opposing sword received a nick so large I could see it clearly despite its movement.

I struck out.

My opponent was quick, but I slashed his shoulder deeply. How that was possible, I had no idea. Excalibur had no edge to speak of, but the blood began to flow.

Blue sparks popped around the edge of the blade where it had connected with the Death Reaper. Of course I noticed it, but I had no time to dwell on it because two more were attacking me. I parried. I thrust. Blue sparks continued to pop. One of them overstepped and lost his balance. I opened his throat, and watched him fall out of the corner of my eye as I ran Excalibur straight into the heart of an idiot Death Reaper that charged me out of nowhere.

There was blood all over the blade as I pulled it free. More of those blue sparks started popping out. In the back of my mind, I realized that the blood was causing the sparks. I didn't understand why, but as I opened up the stomach of the Death Reaper whose face I had already slashed, the blue sparks increased to a fury.

A fury that ignited the blade with a blue fire.

Now, if I was shocked that my sword was suddenly on fire, the Death Reapers were completely flabbergasted. They were also frightened.

"It's the great sword!" One of them shouted out before running off into the forest.

"He's found Excalibur!" Another shouted before attempting to tackle me.

"Kill him quickly," Another said.

I had no doubt that the only reason I was still alive was because of all the murdering Lance was doing in the background. As I looked around, I noticed that more and more Death Reapers were joining the battle.

Hell, even Goliath was kicking at the evil bastards.

I severed the head of a Death Reaper trying to tackle me.

"More"

The sword had found a voice once again, and I did my best to listen. Remarkably, I was no longer frightened. I was no longer on the defensive. I was no longer using my skills to stay alive.

No, I was on the attack, and I very much wanted to kill them all.

I slashed, cut, and stabbed while the blue flame grew brighter and brighter. Excalibur was feeding on their blood. I started smiling. The amount of Death Reapers trying to kill me dwindled down enough for me to make my exit.

I went into the forest as fast as I could. They followed, but the trees were thick enough, and had enough foliage on them to allow me to hide despite the bright flames.

Two Death Reapers passed by my hiding place. Two easy swings of my sword, and I cut both of them in half. I also took a large slice out of a gigantic tree with the last swing. I started laughing, as the tree crunched, crackled and finally collapsed in front of me with a thundering sound.

"Release me"

I did as the sword asked, and placed it on the trunk of the fallen tree. Excalibur began to buck up and down. The blue flames spread out over the guard, grip, and pommel. I watched as the sword burned, and when the flames finally died down Excalibur was whole once again.

"My sword," I whispered.

"A part of you"

Truly, Excalibur was a thing of beauty. No mere words can describe the feelings I felt gazing upon the greatest weapon ever created. The blade of the sword was long, and beautiful. It wasn't mirrored or chrome looking, like a cheap movie sword. Not at all, the blade was an icy grey that still managed to cast my reflection back at me. The straight guard was made of gold, and had two serpents etched into it on either side. The two handed grip was wrapped in a silver wire that begged me to pick it up. The pommel was a flat circle of gold.

"Come closer, Arthur"

I did as the sword asked, and picked it back up. Excalibur was almost weightless in my hand. I touched the cold edge of the blade. To my touch it was dull, though it looked insanely sharp. There was an inscription on the blade up towards the guard, 'Take me up. 'I turned the sword over, and found another inscription. This one read, 'Cast me away. '

I had no intention of ever casting Excalibur away, just holding the beautiful sword made me feel alive.

"Behind you"

I spun instantly. The Death Reaper trying to run me through flew right by me, and fell on his face just as three of his buddies stepped out of the blossoming forest and into my line of sight.

"Come on," I encouraged them. "Try."

They tried. What resulted was so easy. I started laughing. I smacked away their swords as if they were being held by children. Then I drew blood, slicing right through the first Death Reapers chain mail as if I were slicing through paper. The blood on Excalibur caused the sword to catch fire once again.

The Death Reaper screamed as I cut him. He screamed even louder when he realized how deep the wound was. I grinned venomously as crimson covered steel in a wave of pain.

A sword flew out towards me. I leaned back out of its way, and struck out at arm holding it. The arm came free. Excalibur was so sharp; the Death Reaper didn't even realize I took his arm until he saw the gushing stump with his own two eyes.

A gave a low power swing at the next attacker, slicing him clean in half right above his hips. The branch directly behind him also came off in a perfectly angled cut. Excalibur was burning brilliantly. Each drop of blood fanned the flames ever so brighter.

The final Death Reaper ran.

"None will survive"

"I couldn't agree more," I sneered as I took off after the bastard.

It wasn't hard to follow him. I simply trailed the wisps of green fog he left on the ground behind him.

I detoured around him when I got close enough.

It was my turn to play games, and I intended to have a good time. Running through the growing forest was easy. I wasn't tired anymore. I felt like I could keep the pace up for an eternity.

"Cut across to your right"

I did as the sword commanded.

"Get ready"

The Death Reaper entered a clearing, and I stepped out before him.

"This dance has only just begun," I said.

Twenty more Death Reapers stepped into the clearing. The bastards were still keeping far apart from each other so that the fog trailing each of them wouldn't merge together and create something dense enough to give away their position.

They had me right where I wanted them.

"Give me everything you've got," I said. "Make the last moments of your life the greatest."

I charged into the midst of them . . . loving every minute of it.

Something moved above me in the trees, right as I received a nasty cut to my left shoulder. I growled at the sting of the wound, and slid Excalibur into the fucker's throat. I turned, and cut. I stabbed, I sliced.

So easy.

It was almost as if they wanted to die.

I was happy to help them.

"Turn"

I did, and avoided a fatal strike. I took both of my attacker's arms in payback. Black spikes rained down from the trees. Death Reapers fell around me before I could cut into them.

"Stop it, Lance!" I shouted out. "They're mine."

I went after more of them. Cutting from one to another, I couldn't miss. I was too fast. I was too deadly. Excalibur made me the perfect killing machine.

More spikes rained down. There were some stars as well, as if added for a bonus effect.

"Lance!" I shouted. "Go away!"

"There're too many of them!" Lance shouted back. "We need to run. More are coming."

"Let them come." I smiled as I killed yet another.

My clothes were splashed with blood. The moans of the dying could be heard from miles away, and still I wanted more. Let them suffer. Let them pay. Let them die for having the arrogance to attack a king.

The spikes continued to rain down. They brought death to Death Reaper after Death Reaper. Lance urged me to leave, over and over again.

"There's still time, Arthur," Lance begged. "Please, let's go."

"Stop your crying, orphan!" I shouted. "I'm sick of you!"

The spikes stopped flying. They did their damage, but I still had more than enough victims to carve into. I took my time. I played with them. I enjoyed myself.

When the last of them fell, I went around plunging my sword into those that continued to draw breath despite their wounds.

I was standing inside a field of death, and I loved it.

"Arthur," Lance whispered in a choked voice from above me. "Arthur, your eyes . . . what's happened to you?"

"Stop your crying!" I shouted back. "I have no time for . . ."

"Kill the boy"

I froze. I couldn't have heard what I just thought I heard.

"Kill the boy"

"No," I said.

"Kill the boy"

"No," I said again.

I looked around me and saw what I had done. I saw the corpses. I saw the damage to the forest all around me. I saw everything, and I couldn't believe what I was seeing. I didn't feel bad for killing the Death Reapers. I didn't feel bad about that at all. Those evil bastards deserved what they got . . . I felt bad about enjoying so much. I felt bad about the vile way in which I spoke to Lance.

"No"

"This isn't me," I said to no one in particular. "This isn't me at all."

"Kill the boy and be free"

"I won't do it," I said.

"Do it now"

"Cast me away," I mumbled as I threw the sword to the ground.

A moment of dizziness came at me like a freight train only to vanish before I could truly become concerned about its appearance. Excalibur burned brightly at my feet. I could feel the pull. I could feel the desire to pick it up.

I walked away.

My left shoulder stung where I had been cut. I looked at it, expecting to see my shoulder coated with fresh blood. The wound wasn't bleeding. I wasn't bleeding anywhere. All the numerous scrapes I'd received were dry as a bone. The cut I'd gotten the other day was no longer seeping.

Regardless, the open cut on my shoulder was pretty bad. I'd need to do something about it. At least stitch it back together. That was going to feel lovely.

I heard a soft thump on the ground behind me.

"Are you okay?" Lance asked.

"Yes," I said. "And I'm sorry about what I said. I don't know where that came from."

"It wasn't you," Lance said. "It was the sword. The sword got inside of you."

"Tell me something I don't know," I said.

"Let me see your eyes," Lance said.

"Why?" I asked as I turned towards the direction of his voice.

"They were red," Lance said at the confused expression on my face. "When you had the sword, your eyes were red."

"Swell," I mumbled.

"What do we do now?" Lance asked.

"I don't know," I answered. "I don't think I should touch that sword anymore."

"You have to," Lance said. "We need Excalibur. Arthur needs Excalibur."

"Fuck that," I growled. "Excalibur is an evil son of a bitch."

"The stories never mentioned anything about Excalibur being evil," Lance said. "They also never mentioned anything about it catching on fire."

"The blood does that," I said. "As soon as blood comes into contact with the blade it ignites."

"It's like a demonic light-saber," Lance said.

"I . . . I . . . oh damn," I stammered, and then started laughing. Lance joined me, but neither of us had a very healthy laugh. It was more like a laugh that spoke volumes on all that we had witnessed. We were tired. Maybe not physically, but our souls were tired.

Excalibur continued to burn angrily on the ground.

"We should head out now," Lance said. "There are more Death Reapers around. They'll be closing in on us."

"Okay," I said, and looked at the burning sword.

"Pick it up," Lance said. "Put it in the scabbard, and don't touch it again."

I hesitated, but I finally did as he asked. The blue flames quenched as the sword slid easily into its home, but I could feel the pull. I could feel the rage. I wanted to unleash again. I felt like a serial killer trying to deny his urges.

"Are you okay?" Lance asked.

"I can manage," I answered. "But it's not easy. This sword packs a punch."

I started walking, as before, the trail came to life before my eyes moments after I started looking for it. I picked up the sword of a fallen Death Reaper as I walked away. I didn't want to be tempted to use Excalibur if we were attacked again.

The forest became darker and darker as the tree's sprouted green. I appreciated that they were coming back to life . . . I didn't appreciate the loss of vision.

"Keep an eye out for movement and green fog," I whispered to Lance who was probably somewhere above me in the tree's.

We walked and walked. I felt like I was in a *Lord of the Rings* movie. Where was my damn horse by the way? I was starting to get a little worried about him.

"Arthur," Lance called out as quietly as he could. "There's something up ahead on the trail. A large mass."

Fear flooded my system, and dumped into my stomach. My legs were jelly as I picked up speed and walked faster. I knew it was going to be Goliath, I just knew it. I was going to lose him right when I was beginning to like him.

"Arthur," Lance called out. "What are you doing? Slow down?"

"It's Goliath," I said. "Isn't it?"

"I can't tell," Lance answered. "It's too far away."

I ran.

Not Goliath. Nothing can happen to Goliath. He was all I had to connect me to . . . stop it. Don't go there. Don't go down that path. Don't think of her.

I saw the big lump in the middle of the trail up ahead. Was it Goliath? Maybe, but I had my doubts. Something about it didn't seem right.

I slowed down, and moved more cautiously. More details came into focus. The lump had hair . . . but it wasn't horse hair. It was longer, shaggier.

I had an idea of what it was.

My hand gripped tighter to the Death Reapers sword. I didn't like the feel of it. It felt wrong. It was also a one-hander . . . I preferred a two-hander.

I was close enough to touch the furry beast, and I did just that. I could feel a heat that told me it hadn't been dead very long. I breathed a sigh of relief. It wasn't Goliath.

I turned to call out to Lance to let him know that it was one of those hideous creatures that chased us earlier, and right as I turned, it came to life and grabbed me by the wrist.

I screamed.

It scared the hell out of me.

I yanked, I twisted, and I turned. Nothing I did made it release its powerful grip. I was so afraid; I didn't even contemplate using the sword in my hand.

The creature turned, and sat in front of me, holding my wrist with those stubby, rough, and warm fingers that were somewhere between a paw, and a human hand. The claws that sprouted from each finger were black and sharp.

Its face was even freakier. It wasn't the face of a wolf . . . or any kind of canine like its body would imply. No, its face had an almost human quality.

A melted version of a man's face sprinkled with short fur, and topped with a hooked nose.

"Stop struggling little king," The creature said. "And tell your friend up in the tree's not to throw his spikes. We wouldn't want to hurt each other would we?"

The creature looked me in the eye, waiting for an answer.

"No," I said. "I don't think that sounds like a good idea."

"Neither do I," The creature said in its deep, deep voice."

"Lance," I called out. "Be cool. I think I'm okay."

"Very good," The creature said while contorting its face into something like a smile, and releasing my wrist.

"What are you?" I asked. "What do you want?"

"We are the Gods of the Forest," The creature said while tapping its long claw on a stone. "We want to ensure your safe passage through the forest."

More of the pack came out of the forest onto the trail. About fifty in total, all of them were large, all of them were hideous. They whuffed and growled at one another as they gathered around me.

"Is it him, Father?" A slightly smaller creature asked.

"It is," The creature before me answered.

"His blood smells special," The smaller one said.

"He has the blood of a king running through his veins," The creature before me said.

"Can I taste it, Father?" The smaller one asked.

The creature before me growled at him furiously, baring fangs that belonged inside a werewolf movie. The smaller one cowed, and backed away as the others pressed in closer to smell me.

"You said you wanted to ensure my safe passage?" I asked.

"We will ensure your safe passage," The creature answered.

"Earlier today you were hunting me," I said.

"Earlier today we were but shallow husks without mind or memory," The creature said. "You freed Excalibur, and released magic back into our world. You freed us. My pack owes you tremendously."

"What's your name?" I asked.

"My name in your language is Father Wolf," The creature said.

"You don't look like any wolf I've ever seen," I said.

"We are the wolves of a different time," Father Wolf said. "Now come, Arthur. You have a destiny to fulfill. Let the pack help you get on your way."

"Where's my horse?" I asked.

"He's at the pier," Father Wolf answered. "He wasn't very comfortable around us."

"He's safe?" I asked.

"Of course he is, little king," Father Wolf said. "Trust me when I say that this pack is now, and always will be, your ally."

❧ DELLIA ❧

I was worried about my son. With everything going on around Mill Ridge, I was worrying about my son. I loved that boy entirely too much.

Most parents probably wondered why I didn't hang my head with shame for having a son like Arthur. They seem to forget the type of man he was before tragedy fell upon him. He was kind, reliable, extremely intelligent, and so very handsome.

Well, he never stopped being handsome, did he?

All those poor girls . . . he handed out broken hearts and broken marriages like they were going out of style. It was no wonder most of the town disliked him so much. All the sleeping around, all the drinking . . . Sheriff Tagger should have fired him thirty times over for all the times he failed to show up to work. The sheriff never did though, he knew who Arthur truly was, and the both of us did our best to keep him moving.

We didn't do the greatest job.

Our hearts were in the right place, but my poor son was just too damaged. The light was gone from his eyes. He was a pale shadow of the man he used to be. The worst of it . . . he didn't seem to care.

My son loves too deeply.

It's not that he's cold. It's not that he only cares about himself. That isn't it at all. He loved his wife and son so greatly, that their loss utterly destroyed him.

So despite his actions during the last bunch of years, I was proud of him. I was proud that he somehow managed to get out of bed every day. I was proud that he hadn't given up, and if he refused to give up . . . how could I ever give up on him.

Sure there were some cringe worthy moments . . . but I believed in him. I believed that the man he used to be would someday come back, and when that day happened, I believed he would shock them all.

That day hadn't happened yet. It would happen soon, but it hadn't happened yet, which is why I was sitting on my front porch fretting about him. If I didn't take the time to worry about him . . . who would?

Obviously there were a few people that cared for him . . . but not enough. Not nearly enough. My son burned way too many bridges for that to be the case, and that made me wonder how the people of this town would ever accept him as a leader. How could they follow someone they didn't even like?

Merlin was unconcerned. Merlin never seemed to worry about the future. He believed that all the pieces would eventually fall into place . . . but he was certainly worried about the immediate. I could see that in his face as he limped up my drive through the slight wisps of green fog that eventually found their way to my home.

His hips were giving him troubles. He mentioned it in passing earlier in the day when I saw him stumble, and Wayne had to catch him. The twisted cane he was using was something new. It seemed as if age were creeping up on him at an alarming rate.

"Before Arthur left, you were moving around like a twenty year old," I said when he reached my porch. "Now you're limping around like an old man that doesn't have a lot of time left."

"Dellia," Merlin said. "You don't want to know. Let's just hope Arthur can free the sword before the attack commences."

"I think I do want to know," I said. "You're all we have against an army that greatly outnumbers us."

"Alright," Merlin said after he made himself comfortable against the railing for the steps. "I'm dying. I won't sugar-coat it. I used the last of my magic to save Arthur. Without that magic, time is catching up to me."

"I see," I said in a calm voice.

"It's not over yet, my dear," Merlin laughed. "If Arthur frees Excalibur . . . well . . . my problems will be over almost as soon as they've begun."

"Your problems?" I asked.

"You never miss a thing," Merlin said. "Someday I'll learn to watch my tongue around you."

"You'll be weak, won't you?" I asked.

"I wouldn't say weak," Merlin answered. "But I certainly won't be the wizard I used to be. In order to grow powerful in magic, one must use magic. The more a wizard uses magic the more powerful he becomes. I unfortunately haven't used much magic over the centuries."

"Because you needed the magic you retained after Arthurs resurrection spell to keep you alive," I said.

"Exactly," Merlin smiled. "Obviously I used a bit of it here and there, but I always made sure to keep a bit for myself."

"I thank you for saving Arthur," I said.

"That would be my sacred duty," Merlin said. "No need to thank me on that."

"How are things going in town?" I asked in an effort to change the subject.

"Sheriff Tagger is organizing our defenses," Merlin answered. "When the Death Reapers break through the barrier of Stronghold Wall, it won't destroy the entire spell. It'll just give them a way in at one particular area. If we can figure out where that area is going to be, we can attempt to swarm them as they rush inside. I've also issued out a great deal of leather and chain mail to the townspeople, in addition to some weapons."

Death Reapers. What an ugly name. I was glad Merlin didn't mention the name to me until after Arthur had left. I'd have never let him go.

"How's Sheriff Tagger doing?" I asked.

"As well as can be expected," Merlin answered. "He's not a young man anymore, but the people of this town love and respect him enough to follow him. If only . . ."

Merlin stared off at something far away, and very slowly a smile crept across his face. I followed his gaze, and failed to find what had captured his attention.

"What are you looking at?" I asked.

"It's what I don't see that impresses me so greatly," Merlin answered.

"What don't you see?" I asked.

"It was raining mightily in the distance," Merlin answered. "The rain stopped very abruptly."

"That's common around here," I said. "You know that."

"Not in that area," Merlin said while limping away down my drive. "Certainly never in that area."

"Are you saying . . . ?"

"Yes," Merlin answered with a laugh.

He really was moving quickly, and by the time I caught up with him I was slightly out of breath.

"Are you sure?" I asked.

"I'm positive, my dear," Merlin said. "Now help me hurry. My damn hips are killing me."

"Where are we going?" I asked.

"The town square," Merlin answered as a powerful beam of light descended from the Heavens, and shone down upon a spot in the area where it had previously been raining.

"Why are we going to the town square?" I asked.

"We need the people to know what we know," Merlin answered with a laugh. "We need them to believe in magic once again. We need them to believe in Arthur."

By the time we reached the town square, every citizen in town had stopped what they were doing and gathered on the streets in front of the Sheriff's Station. It was the large boom of sound that got their attention, but the blue energy streaking all around the sky held it.

"What is it?" Someone asked.

"A rebirth," Merlin answered.

I wasn't looking at the sky. Instead, I cast my gaze around the town square, and looked at the people of Mill Ridge. How many of them would fall before this was over? The torches of our enemy couldn't be seen from the town square, but I knew they were out there just beyond the protection of Stronghold Wall.

The Black Knight and his army of Death Reapers had completely surrounded the town of Mill Ridge.

More and more of them gathered every hour. How they traveled so quickly once they'd found Arthur's location, I had no idea, but death had arrived on our doorstep. All that held them back was a small wall that had been touched by magic many years ago.

Sheriff Tagger came out to meet Merlin.

"Does that mean what I think it means?" Sheriff Tagger asked.

"It does," Merlin answered. "Arthur has reclaimed Excalibur. He has released the magic."

"Listen up, everyone!" Sheriff Tagger called out. "I know many of you are worried, and what I'm about to tell you will be very hard to believe, but you need to know that it's the absolute God's honest truth. There is still hope. This battle has not yet been lost."

Bolts of energy began to strike the ground all around us. Naturally, people began to panic. There were a few shouts, a great jostling as people tried to get indoors, and a loud command for silence.

"There is no reason to fear!" Merlin shouted. "The land is changing. A king has stepped forth from the ashes. All will be well; the time of magic has come again."

The blue energy was ricocheting between the buildings, and breaking the glass windows of the stores. Merlin's speech failed to calm anyone down. The crowd turned frantic as soon as the windows began exploding.

"There was a time," Merlin said apologetically. "When people actually placed great importance upon my words."

"I'm afraid that was a long, long time ago," I said.

"I think it might be best if I just show them who I am," Merlin said.

"How will you do that?" I asked.

"By claiming my fair share," Merlin announced before limping off to stand in the middle of the panicking crowd.

"Everyone!" I shouted out. "Stay calm! Give us one more minute!"

No one was listening. The crowd was out of control, and the blue streaks of energy were everywhere. How nobody had been blasted apart by one of them was far beyond me.

I stifled a scream as a young man looking towards the sky ran headfirst into Merlin, and knocked him down. I tried to run towards him when he didn't get back up, but Sheriff Tagger grabbed me by the arm.

"I'll go, Dellia," Sheriff Tagger yelled over all the screaming. "It's too dangerous. Let me do it."

In moments, I lost both of them in the shuffling crowd. People were running everywhere. I was going to be crushed if I stayed put, so I moved to the nearest tree, and pressed my back up against the rough bark.

I didn't know what to do.

I didn't know how to help.

It was probably because I was the only person not running around that I saw Betsy and Martin first. They came into the town square through a small alley between two stores. They were both shouting something out, but I couldn't hear what they were saying over all the noise.

They were terrified. That I understood from the looks on their faces, but it wasn't the sky that worried them so. No, they hadn't even looked up at the sky, and considering that they were one of the many groups keeping an eye on Stronghold Wall . . .

"Merlin!" I shouted. "They're here! They got through! Sheriff Tagger!"

I burst through the crowd and found the sheriff instantly. Merlin was down, and the back of his head was bloody.

"How many?" Sheriff Tagger asked. "Why wasn't the alarm sounded?"

"I don't know," I answered honestly.

"Stay with Merlin," Sheriff Tagger commanded. "Keep him safe. He's our last hope."

"No," I growled angrily. "That would be my son."

Sheriff Tagger didn't waste time arguing with me. He was off in a flash. People were bumping into me. Someone stepped on Merlin's hand. I placed my body over his. I couldn't allow him to be trampled. It was worth my life to keep him alive. My son needed Merlin more than he needed me. Merlin could guide him. Merlin could prepare Arthur.

The great bell of the church began ringing out just as the bolts of energy stopped raining down upon us. Those bells hadn't been run in decades. The sound was so loud it drowned out all other noise. I looked up to the bell tower in the distance, and I saw Wayne's unmistakable figure pulling mightily on the ropes.

The panicked masses slowed down, and finally stopped.

One after another, they looked up to the bell tower. Wayne was screaming something, but with the distance and my ringing ears, I couldn't make out what he was saying. He began pointing in the direction of the alley Martin and Betsy had come from. I couldn't see what he was pointing at exactly, I was on the ground with Merlin, and too many people were standing all around us blocking my view.

The crowd could see what he was pointing at though, and they certainly didn't like it.

More shouts.

More running.

Somewhere not far away, I could hear a child crying. I wanted to go to the child, but I couldn't leave Merlin.

Merlin . . . poor, poor Merlin. He looked so old and frail beneath me. How could we expect him to save us? What could he possibly do at his advanced age?

Screams.

I heard Sheriff Tagger yelling for everyone to protect the children ... to get them off the street. I heard the sound of metal clanging against metal. I heard the sounds of men dying.

The crowd thinned out a little bit, and between the running legs I could see our enemy flooding into the town square. In small groups they came, and with them the green fog already polluting our town became even denser. They killed everyone they came upon. They surrounded the fighting men, and brought them down with violent hacks and stabs.

Not far away in front of the bakery, I saw the baker's wife get her throat slit as she called out for her husband. He couldn't help her. He was already dead from what appeared to be a thousand puncture wounds.

I shook Merlin gently. I screamed for him to get up. I felt strong hands wrap around my waist. I looked behind me, and saw that it was Wayne.

"He's gone, Dellia," Wayne shouted. "We need to go. They keep getting in, and we can't stop them."

"He's not gone!" I yelled. "He's not gone, we need him."

"I can't protect the both of you," Wayne said as he dragged me away. "Not out in the open."

I saw more horrors as we moved through the town square. More people being murdered, blood was flying through the air only to drench the walls of the stores in red splashes, another child cried out, and I screamed.

I screamed at the ugliness. I screamed at the evilness. I screamed because even though Merlin warned me about what it was like, I couldn't in my modern mind understand. I couldn't comprehend.

"Stop!" commanded a voice with the roar of a god.

Some of the fighting stopped instantly.

"Stop!" Merlin called again in that thunderous voice. Those that didn't heed his warning the first time instantly obeyed.

Wayne quit moving. The axe in his hand was stained red and dripping. I watched as he looked around for the voice, tapped him on the shoulder, and pointed when he couldn't find it.

There on the street was Merlin. Old and bent he was ... but a power came off him in waves nonetheless.

"I am Merlin!" He announced. "This town is under my protection. Keep your miserable lives and leave while you're still able, Death Reapers."

A group of ten charged towards him, right as a final bolt of blue energy blasted from the sky twenty feet behind him. It blew pieces of asphalt forty feet in the air, but Merlin never gave it a glance. His eyes were trained on his would be murderers.

From the smoldering hole in the ground, the bolt of energy emerged, and began to race the Death Reapers to Merlin. The energy carved an angry trough through the street. The Death Reapers screamed out a war cry. I wanted to call out. I wanted to warn Merlin. He was focused on the Death Reapers. He didn't know about the bolt of energy coming at him from behind.

Before I could get my words out, both reached him at exactly the same moment. The result was an explosion of light.

Blinding light.

Everyone was shielding their eyes.

The light moved into the sky. First it was white. Then the white grew darker until it became the blue of the energy bolt. It hovered fifteen feet in the air, and then it shattered in a white hot blaze of sparks.

I shielded my eyes again, and when my vision recovered the light was gone. The ten Death Reapers were nothing more than blackened skeletons. Old Merlin had vanished. In his place was a beautiful boy of about seventeen, naked as the day he was born. His skin soft and pink as if had never been kissed by the sun.

More Death Reapers ran at the boy.

Could it be?

I watched as he brushed a shock of jet black hair off his forehead, and moved his hands in a complicated series of gestures. One by one the invaders closest to him began to burn. Old lampposts bent and twisted in an effort to ensnare others. The deep ponds in the park became great tidal waves that moved through the street catching even more.

It was the break the town needed.

The tide was instantly turned. The men began to join in as soon as they got over the spectacle. I couldn't stop staring at the beautiful naked boy. I marveled at his power. Could it be?

It had to be.

In under thirty minutes, the town was ours once again. The invaders had been defeated. Those that survived scurried back through the small hole they'd made in the wall.

The black-haired boy found me soon after.

"Dellia," He said. "Would you mind finding me some clothes?"

"Are you . . . are you, Merlin?" I stammered.

"Surely I don't look too different," Merlin said in shock. "I only knocked a few years off."

"You knocked a lot more than a few years off," I argued.

Merlin immediately walked to the nearest window, and gazed at his reflection in the glass. All eyes were upon him. Everyone wondered how the old man had changed into a young boy.

"Oh shit," Merlin grumbled. "I certainly went a little overboard didn't I?"

"Well," I said. "Who doesn't want to relive their childhood?"

"Nothing to do about it now," Merlin sighed. "How about some clothes?"

A woman came out of a nearby store with a greasy pair of pants, and a white handmade shirt. Merlin accepted the gifts with a smile, and got dressed before everyone.

"Do I now have everyone's attention?" Merlin asked.

The crowd didn't answer. They didn't need to. Merlin held their rapt attention.

"You've just seen magic," Merlin continued. "Get used to it. This is a new world. A world filled with magic. I am Merlin. I'm sure you've heard the name before. I've come to guide the king. I've come to save the world."

"Who's the king?" Someone asked.

"Why, Arthur, of course," Merlin answered.

"You mean . . . the deputy?" Someone else asked.

"Yes," Merlin answered. "And the enemy is none other than the forces of Morgana. They call themselves Death Reapers and they are currently being led by the Black Knight. Now can someone please explain how they got past Stronghold Wall, and got the drop on us?"

"I can," Wayne said stepping forward. "We had about two hundred people spread out along the wall. We figured by the time they put any real effort into an attack, we'd be able to rally enough fighters to put up some kind of defense."

"Yes," Merlin said. "That sounds like a good enough plan."

"It wasn't," Wayne said. "They didn't make a large scale attack. Instead, they quietly made a small hole under the wall, and sent in many small groups of soldiers. They were on us before we even knew they were there. The main force of them attacked our two hundred defenders, and kept us away from the opening under the wall. We couldn't block them off."

"Which gave their fellow soldiers an easy entrance into the town," Merlin continued. "Well, round one goes to them."

"We've lost a lot of people," Marg Melker shouted from the crowd.

Merlin approached her, and grabbed her hands.

"My poor lady," Merlin said. "I grieve silently for all the lives lost. However, I must focus on the task of saving the rest of us. Do you understand?"

"I do," Marge said.

Merlin gently let go of her hands, and turned to Wayne.

"Where's Sheriff Tagger?" Merlin asked.

"I haven't seen him," Wayne answered.

"Has anyone seen Sheriff Tagger?" Merlin asked.

Everyone looked around, clueless. Some of them began to call out.

"Maybe he went to the wall," Wayne suggested.

"He never made it to the wall!" An angry voice shouted out from behind the crowd.

All of us turned to look. An angry Bedder stalked towards the group, holding the body of Sheriff Tagger. Martin and Betsy were following him.

"Oh no," Merlin said softly. "My old friend. My dear old friend."

Merlin approached Bedder and placed a hand on Sheriff Tagger's forehead. Betsy and Martin were crying. Bedder was seething with rage.

"I was leading the two hundred that were attacked," Bedder growled. "They caught us by surprise, and we still managed to re-group and hold them back until help arrived. Why the hell couldn't anyone take care of the fifty or sixty that got past us? Why wasn't anyone protecting the sheriff?"

Merlin ignored the question, and whispered something into the ear of the fallen sheriff. Bedder grew more agitated at being ignored.

"Do not ignore me!" Bedder shouted.

"I'm not ignoring you," Merlin said calmly while looking up into Bedder's face. "I'm merely saying my farewells to an old friend."

"You chased them off!" Bedder shouted. "I saw your magic! What took you so long to use it?"

"I used my magic as soon as it was available for me to use," Merlin answered calmly. "You must understand, young man. I'm not infallible. I'm also not unbeatable. This is a war. Even if I were at full power, we would lose people."

"Who will lead us now?" Bedder asked. "Sheriff Tagger had the knowhow. He'd served in two wars. He had the experience."

"I'll lead you," Merlin said. "Until Arthur comes back, I've been in more than a couple wars. Now how many men did you lose?"

"Probably around thirty," Bedder answered.

"Find replacements for them," Merlin ordered. "Move all of them closer to the wall, spread them out, and have them walk the perimeter until I say otherwise. Sir Francis has found a weakness. I doubt he'll try the same attack again, so he'll be looking for other places. Let's do our best to be prepared."

"What should the rest of us do?" I asked.

"Pick twenty people, and have them move the bodies off the street," Merlin answered. "The rest of you, at least those that can fight, form up in four groups around the perimeter of the town. Don't approach Stronghold Wall. Stay back and stay loose. If a horn blows, I want the group closest to that area of the wall to move in and defend. The other groups will keep their distance in case our enemy attacks another part of the wall at the same time."

"There are still a lot of people left over," I said.

"Yes," Merlin said. "Those people can get busy providing food, and water to the people doing the fighting. They can also take the children and the old to the high school gymnasium so they'll be far away from the danger."

Merlin walked off alone after that. He headed to the Sheriff's Station, where Bedder had taken the body of Sheriff Tagger. I helped organize, get people moving, and then I went to join him. My goal was to keep busy. I couldn't let myself fall apart. Sheriff Tagger was a dear friend of mine and my late husband. Losing him broke my heart.

As soon as I entered the building, I heard Bedder's voice.

"He was an old man," Bedder said. "He was in no shape to fight."

"I don't disagree," Merlin said. "But who could tell him that?"

There were more angry words from Bedder, and I cleared my throat to interrupt. Both of them looked over towards me.

"I know you're angry," I said to Bedder. "How could you not be angry? He was a lovely man, and a great friend to many of us."

"Ma'am," Bedder said. "I just think . . ."

"I know what you think," I said. "And you're wrong. Sheriff Tagger was a fighter. He wasn't one to let others do that for him. I want you to have those emotions, but I need you to control them. Because right now, there is a large group of people out there that need you. Your leadership got them through the first attack. Go to them. Help them."

Bedder looked like he wanted to argue. Instead, he went to his desk, opened a drawer, and pulled out a small bladed instrument with some leather straps, and a shoulder harness. I averted my eyes as he removed his leather armor, and prosthetic hand.

When all was finished, and the bladed instrument replaced the fake hand, Merlin helped him buckle back up.

"I'll do my best, Ma'am," Bedder said as he walked past me.

"I know you will," I replied.

Merlin and I were alone with Sheriff Tagger's body which was laid out on an empty desk in the back of the room. Bedder had thought to put a sheet over him, and for that I was thankful. Unfortunately, the sheet was white, and the blood of his wounds was already staining it.

I went over to him, and placed my hand gently on his arm over the sheet. He was already growing cold.

"What are we going to do?" I asked.

"They're coming for him," Merlin answered.

"Duh," I said. "They have the town surrounded. Did you think I hadn't noticed that?"

"You misunderstand me Dellia," Merlin said unperturbed. "I'm not talking about the Death Reapers. I'm talking about the forces of Arthur. They're coming for him."

"How do you know that?" I asked.

"I can feel it," Merlin answered. "Now that he has the sword, they will come by the thousands. They will be drawn to him. That is his power. The people love him."

"Have you met my son?" I asked. "Right now he's probably cursing you, me, and this entire town. People don't love him. Most of them don't even like him."

"I like him," Wayne said from the front door. "I've always liked the rowdy prick."

Merlin laughed out loud.

"That's great," I said. "So there are three of us. We should be able to smite down all sorts of trouble with those numbers."

"I agree," Merlin said. "The odds are drastically out of our favor. Wayne, who's the fastest rider in the entire town?"

"That would probably be, Tristan," Wayne answered after a moments consideration. "That kid can ride like the devil."

"Excellent," Merlin said. "Go find him for me please."

Wayne left immediately. Merlin and I both sat next to Sheriff Tagger while we waited for him to return as if our company could ease his drifting soul.

"What are you planning, Merlin?" I finally asked.

"I have no doubts the people will come for him," Merlin said. "I'm simply speeding things up a bit."

In no time at all, Wayne was back with an androgynous, long-haired young man in tow. I knew Tristan very well; it was a small town after all. If I remembered correctly, he was around twenty-one years old. I saved him from a beating once. He was about fourteen or fifteen at the time, and a group of five boys cornered him in the field behind my house for the simple crime of being gay.

I have no tolerance for that kind of nonsense. Two shots in the air with my shotgun proved I was serious, and off they ran for easier pickings. When Arthur came home, and found the poor boy with two black-eyes and a swollen lip sitting at my kitchen table . . . let's just say poor Tristan was never bothered again.

He always waved when either Arthur or I passed by him on the street. He always had a ready smile for us. I liked him.

"You must be Tristan," Merlin said.

"Yes, sir," Tristan answered.

It was clear that the young man was nervous. He was standing before the great, Merlin. No doubt in his eyes. Truly, there wasn't much doubt in anyone's eyes. Everyone saw the magic.

"You're not exactly what I expected," Merlin stated.

"I get that a lot," Tristan said.

"Can you fight?" Merlin asked.

"Yes," Tristan answered.

"Do you have a fast horse?" Merlin asked.

"The fastest horse in the entire town," Tristan answered.

"Very well," Merlin said. "Have Wayne give you a weapon, get on your horse, pick a direction, and ride as if Hell itself were on your heels. Ride until you find them. Tell them that King Arthur has been reborn, and Merlin requires their assistance."

Tristan looked confused.

"Do you really want me to say all that?" Tristan asked.

"Trust me," Merlin said. "It'll work. Tell them to hurry. Camelot is burning."

"How will I get out of Mill Ridge?" Tristan asked.

"Leave that to me," Merlin answered with a smile. "All I want you to worry about is riding fast, because they will most certainly be pursuing you."

"They'll never catch me," Tristan smiled.

"I have no doubt you'll prove elusive," Merlin said. "No go eat and rest up. Tomorrow morning you ride."

Wayne put a big arm around Tristan, and led him out of the station. Merlin looked at me and smiled. Dellia, maybe you should see if you can help some of the injured?

That caught my attention.

"What are you planning?" I asked.

"I've already told you," Merlin answered.

It was incredibly hard to talk to the teenager before me in the same way that I used to speak to the old man. I kept trying to use my motherly powers over him . . . they didn't work. Merlin wasn't a teenager. He was an ancient creature, and nowhere near intimidated by me.

"It seems like you're trying to distract me," I stated.

Merlin laughed.

I didn't.

"Alright," Merlin said. "I want you safe and far from harm's way."

"I'm as safe as anyone else," I said.

"For now," Merlin said. "But I don't want you near me. Eventually the streets will get bloody. There will be a battle. I saw how you handled the minor skirmish earlier. You're not up for this."

"I've been trained," I argued.

"Yes," Merlin agreed. "I made sure of that, but it's not in you to harm another person. You're a strong woman, Dellia. Don't get me wrong, I only think you would be better helping the injured . . . leave the fighting for others."

I wanted to argue. I truly did . . . but he was right. I wasn't a fighter. I stood there like an idiot as the fighting went down all around me. Geez, if it wasn't for Wayne, I might not even be alive. His axe became bloody, and I never even saw him use it.

"You're right," I reluctantly agreed. "I don't have what it takes."

"Now, Dellia," Merlin smiled. "Don't be sad. You're still very useful. Didn't you used to be a nurse once upon a time?"

"Yes, I worked in an emergency room," I answered.

"Can you even begin to imagine how very important that is right now?" Merlin asked.

It was my turn to smile.

"Now a word of warning," Merlin added. "Keep them alive if you can, but understand that you will lose many. Don't hate yourself for it. The forces of Morgana took their lives, not you."

"That's not exactly a great pep talk," I said.

"It's not a pep talk at all," Merlin said. "I'm trying to prepare you. The wounds you will see are unimaginable. Do what you can for them. Ease their pain if it's within your power, but understand we will lose many, many people before this is over. Be ready for it."

"I understand," I said. "I'll do what I can."

"I know you will," Merlin said, and those were the last words we spoke to one another the remainder of the night. There was no need for talking. Both of us simply wanted to sit by our fallen friend, and wait out the deep dark night.

A knock on the door, came in the morning.

Wayne was back. Tristan had his horse, and Wayne brought a few others for the rest of us to ride. Tristan looked nervous. Merlin was asking a lot from him. I worried about whether or not he could accomplish his task.

I would have sent out a bunch of people far and wide in an effort to find help. Merlin was content to send only Tristan. Then again, Merlin was Merlin. Who the hell was I?

All of us rode the horses down Main Street at a leisurely pace. Looking at Tristan, I really wanted to question Merlin, but that was stupid. I had to trust him. He knew things . . . still, I was nervous.

We rode to the edge of town. The large stone entryway of Stronghold Wall got closer and closer. Wayne made small talk with Tristan, as if he didn't have a care in the world. Occasionally, they'd look at Merlin and laugh. Leave it to Wayne to be a smartass.

Death Reapers gathered outside the gate upon our approach. They slapped their rusty swords against the palm of their hands, and smiled.

Merlin glared at them with an open hostility.

"I can't ride through so many," Tristan said. "They'll pull me off my horse."

"That they will," Merlin said. "Unless of course something distracts them."

Merlin raised his arms into the air and twisted his fingers. The dense forest that rose up on each side of the road outside Stronghold wall began to shudder as if a great wind had suddenly picked up . . . but there was no wind.

I watched his face contort, and his fingers mash together. The forest began to churn and weave. Branches began to swing out in deadly arcs.

Wayne cursed aloud.

I was as silent as a church mouse.

"Get ready," Merlin said to Tristan.

Tristan only nodded, and backed his horse up along the road. The forest before us rose and fell, and then it attacked.

Small branches wrapped around our enemies bodies. Roots burst through the ground, and grabbed at their feet. Great limbs swept down, and knocked them to the ground. A great pause came over the forest, as the soldiers ran about in fright . . . the pause can to abrupt end as a great creaking pounded through the air, and the forest closed in around them.

"GO NOW!" Merlin shouted through the strain on his face.

Tristan screamed out, and spurred his horse forward. He charged the living forest, and right before he slammed into the denseness of Merlin's work, the forest righted itself, and moved back to its normal state.

The Death Reapers were no longer there to bar Tristan's way.

There were shouts in the distance. The soldiers that weren't in Merlin's danger zone were closing in, but Tristan was already moving far from harm's way. His horse was fast, but he was being pursued nonetheless.

"They could catch him," I said.

"They won't," Merlin whispered.

"He could fall from his horse," I said.

"He won't," Merlin whispered before he sagged in his saddle and almost slipped off the side.

"Watch yourself, tough guy," Wayne said as he grabbed Merlin by the arm and hoisted upright.

Merlin was sweating profusely. He was also as white as a sheet. Simply put, he didn't look good at all.

"Are you okay?" I asked.

"I'm just tired," Merlin said. "That was a hefty bit of magic I just worked. I think I need a little rest."

"Let's get you back to the station," I said.

We turned our horses and began the long ride back. Wayne kept his hand on Merlin's shoulder in case he fell once again. Unfortunately, Wayne had a wicked little smile on his face and I knew it was simply a matter of time before he made a smartass comment.

"The magic wore you out?" Wayne asked as I shook my head.

"I'm out of practice," Merlin said. "There was a time, when something like what I did back there wouldn't have even made me breathe heavily."

"So . . . your magic is out of shape?" Wayne asked.

Merlin gave him a dirty look, which probably wasn't very easy for him to do given his current state.

"You could say that," Merlin said. "I guess."

"So you have chubby magic?" Wayne asked.

"What?" Merlin asked.

"Your magic is out of shape and chubby," Wayne laughed."

"I dislike you," Merlin said.

Wayne laughed even harder.

I couldn't help but smile myself.

Merlin wasn't laughing. Instead he snapped his fingers, and Wayne's boot caught on fire. Wayne screamed and slapped at his foot, but the flames wouldn't go out. Instead, they appeared to grow.

Only when Wayne fell off his horse due to his frantic struggles, did Merlin laugh. In fact, he laughed mightily. He even began slapping his own leg in his merriment.

"That's not funny!" I shouted.

"I disagree!" Merlin wailed.

"You're going to hurt him," I said.

"No I'm not," Merlin laughed. "Those flames aren't hot."

Wayne stopped thrashing around on the ground, and looked up at Merlin. Merlin kept on laughing. Wayne reached out tentatively towards the flames climbing up his leg. His hand didn't burn. He then looked at Merlin, and started laughing as well.

"You got me," Wayne admitted.

"I did," Merlin laughed.

"Now put it out," Wayne demanded.

"I don't think so," Merlin said.

"Do it," Wayne demanded.

"What's the magic word?" Merlin asked.

"Are you kidding me?" Wayne asked.

"Nope," Merlin answered. "Try again."

And this is how it went all the way back to the Sheriff's Station. Eventually, Merlin did indeed extinguish the non-burning flames from Wayne's leg, but he made sure to have his fun before he did so.

After leaving Merlin at the station, and saying my goodbyes to a still frustrated Wayne, I made my way to the only doctor's office in town. It was located conveniently enough in the town square, rather close to the Sheriff's Station, so I didn't bother to ride.

Upon entering the modest space, I was immediately assaulted by the smell of blood. I looked around. The wounded were everywhere. The corpses of those we lost were laying beside those still clinging to life, those that could still be saved.

I went into action immediately.

I wasn't up on current medicine. My skills came from a long time ago, but that proved to be beneficial. There was only so much modern medicine to go around. I bandaged and wrapped open wounds. I stopped the bleeding.

Dr. Talbert came out of the back room. His white coat was splattered in blood. He looked exhausted.

"Dellia, what are you doing?" He asked.

"I'm helping you," I answered.

"But . . . but," Dr. Talbert stammered.

"Don't worry, I was an ER nurse back when you were still a teenager," I interrupted. "You need the help. Merlin sent me here to do just that."

Dr. Talbert looked at my work, and nodded his consent.

"Very well, then," he said. "We need you in the back."

I was unprepared for what I saw in the back rooms. There were too many dying patients crying for help. I went to them, and whispered in their ears. I did my best to provide as much comfort as I could.

I cried silently, as the first young man died in my arms. I wept harder when a teenage girl followed him. I openly bawled when I lost the first child. After that, I was a bit deadened. Never once did I stop. I did my best. Dr. Talbert did his best. We saved as many as we could.

Lives were being lost and saved, one after another. My world became a whirlwind, and all the while I worried about Arthur. Where was my son? Was he safe? Was he making his way back to us?

❧ GWEN ❧

My father was dying. I had just gotten the news. The great man had been struck down in our latest battle. The tears hadn't come yet. I was still in shock.

I was two valleys away from the actual battle. I was safe and sound. My father always made sure I was safe and sound. He protected me. He loved me. He fought wars for me.

Why wasn't I crying?

The soldier that gave me the news refused to look me in the eyes. He was devastated. He hated telling me something like this. I put my hand on his shoulder in an effort to comfort him.

"Will you get me a horse?" I asked.

"Of course," he answered.

My thoughts drifted back to the beginning. Not the beginning of the wars mind you . . . I was thinking about the beginnings of my life. I was a runaway. Not in the literal sense, I was eighteen when I left, but I was still a runaway. I ran from my pain. I ran from my father.

My mom died when I was seventeen. It truly broke me . . . no . . . not just me; her death broke up my family. Well, that's not right either. I broke up our family. I did that. I was so devastated by her death, that it changed me as a person.

Before I lost her, I was a straight A student. I kept out of trouble. I was the apple of my parents' eyes. I succeeded in everything I did. Their pride in me drove me to greater and greater accomplishments.

I was so happy.

And then . . .

Nothing.

I was an empty shell. I hated myself. Nothing made me happy. So I abandoned school. I tried drugs and alcohol, and that worked for me. It filled the hole inside my soul.

My military father of course tried his best to get me back on the straight and narrow. All of his efforts were in vain. I rebelled against him. I took my anger out on him. I took my sorrow out on him.

He loved me, and I hated him for loving me. I didn't deserve love . . . and then I was gone. On my eighteenth birthday, just a short while before graduation, I vanished. I ran far away. I disappeared without a trace.

I ended up in Southern California. I probably should have died. I probably should have overdosed . . . but by some miracle, I didn't. Blame that one on my looks. I was a beauty. I say that without arrogance. My looks always embarrassed me.

Men came out of the woodwork to take care of me. They provided for me. They bought me expensive things. They kept me drunk and high.

What kind of men did this for me?

The worst kind imaginable. I was self destructive, after all. I chose the drug dealers and high class criminals. I gave them what they wanted, and they gave me what I wanted.

I moved up and up the ladder. In no time at all, I was dating millionaires. I was living in their posh apartments. I laughed at their crimes. What did I care? When someone hates themselves, they aren't too quick to judge the actions of others.

And then the red fog came.

Southern California was one of the first places to get hit in the United States. The cities began to riot. Los Angeles became a battle zone. The military eventually tried to come in and establish the peace. It didn't work out to well. The citizens fought too hard against them.

People were being murdered in the streets. The man I was living with was executed by an underling that wanted to take over his territory. I watched him bleed to death in the living room, but I was too far gone to help. Not that I would have. He was a terrible man.

The riots got worse and worse.

The military was everywhere. Guns no longer worked, so they used clubs and plastic riot shields. More and more people died. Los Angeles would not be tamed.

When the green fog came, we were so busy fighting each other we barely noticed. Well, we noticed when the enemy came. The dead-looking soldiers with their silver eyes, and wet hair. Their blades were rusty, but oh so sharp.

They came in large numbers, and slaughtered military and rioters alike. Nothing could stop them. I hid amongst the other survivors. We scavenged food. They helped me when my body went through the terrible withdrawals. That was the first group I came upon. I'll always remember them.

One night the dead-looking soldiers came and hacked them all to pieces. Man, woman, and child fell to their blades. I never screamed. Instead, I ran. I ran for all I was worth.

After that, I hooked up with a few other groups. It wasn't hard to be accepted. Not with my looks. Men always wanted me around. No matter how hungry I became, I was still beautiful.

All of them died.

They were butchered. I saw it happen so many times, I lost count.

Eventually, the main force of the dead-looking soldiers moved on, but they left a large enough group to mop up anyone that was left behind.

I had to be careful. I had to hide. Staying in the shadows was my rule. Avoiding daylight was my religion. I never hooked up with another group of survivors. It was too dangerous. They were always discovered. I kept to myself. I scavenged what I could. Many nights I simply went hungry.

Eventually, I returned to my old penthouse.

I don't know why I went there. I guess it was a lack of options. The net was tightening around me. The dead-looking soldiers were aware of my existence. They were hunting me down. I don't think they wanted to kill me. I think they wanted other things.

In the end, after almost a week without food, I left the safety of my penthouse during the bright light of day. I needed something to eat.

It was a mistake.

I was discovered almost instantly. I ran, and they chased. Through the trash strewn lobby I headed back up the stairs. My hope was to lose them in the complicated labyrinth of my six story apartment building, but they were too close behind me . . . too hot on my heels. Stairway after stairway I ran, and they grew closer and closer.

They were laughing as I slammed the door of my penthouse behind me, but it was a heavy and reinforced door. Their laughter soon turned to curses as their green fog crept through the cracks and entered my home. Sadly, I knew the door wouldn't hold forever. It wasn't designed for the kind of abuse they were attacking it with.

Eventually, my pursuers would break through. Eventually, they would capture me. In a panic, I ran to the kitchen and grabbed the biggest and sharpest knife I could find. I refused to give in without a fight.

The onslaught on the door continued . . . and then it stopped abruptly. The dead-looking soldiers ran off towards what I can only describe as a commotion coming from many floors below me. I could hear their pounding feet as they retreated from my door.

Soon afterwards, I could hear the sounds of a battle. If I had to guess, the fight was coming from the lobby. Who would be fool enough to attack such a fearsome evil?

The sounds of clanging metal, and the screams of the dying ended rather quickly. I strained my ears to pick up new sounds. Would I be left alone? Would they come after me now that their attackers were vanquished?

I was breathing heavily. My heart was pounding in my chest. It was hard to hear over those noises, but I tried my best. What would my fate be? Would I die now, or would I be spared?

I heard footsteps outside my apartment. Doors were being kicked down. Men were shouting that rooms were clear. They were coming back. My fate was decided.

There were no tears in my eyes. I was beyond terrified, but there were no tears in my eyes. I was not going to be their prize. I refused to be raped and abused. I was going to die. When they got through the door, I would fight until they had no choice but to kill me.

Fuck it.

There was a polite knock on my door.

What the hell?

That was unexpected. Of course I ignored it, and then the knock came again. I heard a voice outside the door, but so advanced was my fright . . . it didn't register. Did I just hear my name being called?

No.

The dead-looking soldiers didn't know my name. They only knew that I was beautiful. My imagination was playing tricks on me. I gripped the kitchen knife so hard it hurt my hand, and I prayed that it would be over quickly.

The pounding began on the door once again. I watched as it shuddered in the door frame. I didn't hide. I stood at the end of the hallway. I would meet my attackers with a fury. I wouldn't run and hide.

The door rattled and shook. The pounding was horrendous. I gritted my teeth and stood my ground. I wasn't thinking at that point. I was beyond thinking. My days had come to an end. I became emotionless. Let the tide surge against me. Let it roll over and consume me. My days were misery. Death would be a release.

The door burst open.

I held my ground.

But, it wasn't a dead-looking soldier that came forward through the broken frame. It was . . . no, it couldn't be . . . it was . . . it was my father.

My daddy.

General Findabair, himself.

No. My eyes were playing tricks on me. It couldn't be him. He no longer existed in my world. I left him so very long ago.

I made a noise. It came from my throat. It was ugly, more like a moan and very unlike a word.

"My baby girl," my father said. "I've traveled so far to find you."

I screamed.

I screamed at the cruel trick, and I held my knife before me in as threatening a gesture as I could manage.

"No," my father said patiently. "I'm here now. I'll make it all better. I'll take care of you. There's no more reason to fear."

"You're not my father!" I screamed.

"I am," he said. "Did you really think I wouldn't come for you? I've been traveling since the red fog came. I'm here. It's me."

I shook the kitchen knife at him, but he stepped forward anyway. He moved my weapon out of the way, and wrapped me in his arms.

That's when I really lost it.

I'm a pretty tough girl. I've had to be, but there's something about being wrapped up in your father's arms. . . you feel so . . . so . . . safe. You feel protected.

I sobbed like a baby.

I sobbed for all that I had to endure. I sobbed for the life I had chosen. Worst of all . . . I sobbed for leaving my father. I sobbed because I took my anger over my mother's death out on the one person that loved me unconditionally.

My legs gave out. My father held me up, and I cried even harder.

My daddy.

My daddy was here.

My daddy found me.

Eventually, he gently lowered me to the ground, but he never let go. No, he absolutely never let go of me. Throughout the remainder of the day I cried, and he held me tightly, whispering affirmations of his love.

There were others, but none of them disturbed us. I could hear them in the background. They paced outside my broken door.

My father wasn't alone. He'd brought an army with him. He'd gathered them as he made his way to his only daughter. At first it was just him. Like he said, he set out to save me the moment the red fog began to sweep across the land. It turns out that he always knew where I was. He was waiting for the day that I either needed him, or the day that I wanted to come home.

Along the way, he helped people. That was his way. He was a leader. Those that needed aid were given aid, and in turn . . . they followed him.

When the green fog came, he took his followers and fought back. Things didn't go his way at first, my father lost many battles to the dead-looking soldiers, but he was no quitter. The people needed him, and he'd studied long and hard the ways of war. He was no stranger to the history. In no time at all, he adapted to the ways of warfare in this strange new world.

From the defeated, he took swords, shields, and chain mail. Training began in earnest. They travelled, they trained, they saved, and they fought. That was the way of things. My father was a beacon of hope in a world filled with . . . evil.

Of course people followed him. How could they not? Their towns were ravaged. Their relatives were slain, but General Findabair stood tall and proud. His army grew stronger and stronger. The battles he fought were bigger and bigger. From state to state he traveled and slew the dead-looking soldiers.

He was a hero.

He was a legend.

He was my father, and he did it all for . . . me. I cried even harder when he told me his tale. How could I have been so horrible to him? How could I have run away? What wrongs had he ever committed against me?

"Shush, my pretty girl," he whispered in my ear. "I'm here now. You're here now. That's all that matters. We're together at last."

I loved my daddy. He was the kindest, most gentle man I'd ever known . . . but he was also something else. He was a fierce general, and he gave no quarter to our enemy. Later, much, much later, he told me what his plans were.

Death Reapers, that's what the dead-looking soldiers called themselves, and my father wanted to eradicate them all. He wanted to wipe them from the face of the earth. My father had seen evil in all its forms, but nothing compared to the vileness of what currently roamed our planet.

His travels had given him a purpose, and his purpose was just.

"Take me with you," I begged.

"Of course, my love," he answered. "I'd have it no other way."

And that was the beginning.

After securing Southern California, our massive group of survivors moved forward. From state to state we traveled. Sometimes we stayed in a place for an evening. Sometimes we stayed for a month. All the while, we gathered more and more people to our cause.

Some of them came because they had no other place to go. Some of them came because they understood the need to fight back. They understood that if we failed . . . the world would fall.

The battles were violent. They were bloody. We lost people, but our enemy lost even more. We struck them down everywhere we found them. My father outsmarted the best of them. The battles were often won before they ever began.

I started to train. I had no interest in the sword. That wasn't my specialty at all. No, my interest was in the bow. There were things that I could do with a bow that amazed my instructors, but my father never allowed me anywhere near the many battles.

I was far away and protected at all times. I would ask why, and his only response was that if he ever fell, the people would need me to take his place.

The people.

The survivors.

The lucky ones.

They loved me dearly, all of them. They took care of me . . . well, they sort of babied me. When my father went out to fight, I was never truly alone. They stood by me. They whispered words of encouragement in my ear. They patted me on the back.

What would I do without them?

They were my world, and my father was my sun, but I kept all but my father at a distance. Time and loss had frozen my heart, and no one but my father had a pick sharp enough to pierce it.

"Let me fight," I told my father. Let me stand with the other archers. "Let me help."

"To what end?" my father would ask.

"I can be beneficial," I said.

"I have no doubt of that," my father would respond. "But someday, we may lose. If both of us fall, these people that we protect will have no one to lead them."

His reasoning was sound. I hated it, but it was sound, and now he'd fallen. Now he was dying. My father was dying. The great man that came to my rescue was dying, and I was nothing more than an orphan.

I rode over the hills and through the trails. I rode as fast as I could. I needed to be there for the end. I needed to tell him . . . what? I don't know. I needed to tell him, how very much I loved him. I needed to tell him what his love meant to me.

I needed to tell him how sorry I was for all that I put him through.

I rode past the dead and dying. Men parted for me as I approached. All of them lowered their heads. The green fog was already fading from the field of battle. My father wasn't hard to find. He was surrounded by his men. The closest to him were the doctors. They were arguing amongst one another. My father had been covered with a blanket, probably, an effort to keep me from seeing his wounds, but I could see the blood staining through the cloth . . . too much blood.

I dismounted my horse and ran to his side. His face was too pale. His eyelids fluttered. He seemed so weak. I'd never seen him look weak before.

"I'm here, Daddy," I declared. "I'm here. I won't let you go."

"Now that my dear would be an incredible achievement," my father said.

"Don't you leave me, Daddy," I said. "Don't you dare leave me."

"My time is over," my father said. "Your time is just beginning."

"I don't want a time without you," I said. "We've spent too much time apart."

"You can do this," my father said. "Lead them. Love them, be the great woman you were meant to be."

"Daddy," I sobbed. "How can I do that without you?"

"Because you are strong, my love," my father said. "You are so very, very strong. Now promise me that you'll protect them. Promise me that you'll continue the fight."

"Don't make me promise, Daddy!" I screamed. "Don't force me to let you go!"

"Sweetheart," my father whispered. "My time is at an end. Sorrow cannot stop things. You must learn to accept loss . . . don't let your heart be your downfall. Be strong my beautiful daughter. Make me proud."

And then, my father was gone.

"I promise, Daddy," I said to his still form. "I'll protect all of them, and many more. I'll lead them. I'll win this war. I won't quit until everyone is safe. I'll make you proud."

I held onto my father for a long time. I can't even remember how long, but eventually his soldiers gently pulled me away. I don't remember the ride back to my tent, but I remember the funeral.

It took place right after sunset. We always had our funerals shortly after the battles. Our enemies collected the bodies, and we would have none of that. Our dead would be honored. Our dead would be released, body and soul.

A pretty girl named Tara came over to me. She stood by my side through the entire event. When the fires were lit, and I turned away, she was the one that kept everyone away from me.

I was loved. I knew that. Thousands of people were there for me . . . but I was all alone. I no longer had family. I vowed to keep my heart frozen. I vowed to never love again. The pain when I lost a loved one was too great. I cried myself asleep that night. I hated myself that night. For all the horrible things I put my father through, I hated myself.

The morning came and went. I felt no better. There was chaos in the camp. I ignored it. Of course they were scared, they'd lost their leader. I was scared.

Tara came and brought food that I never ate. She was worried. Everyone was worried about me. I heard arguments late at night. I didn't care. I couldn't get out of bed. Death was something that I just couldn't handle. Death was my weakness.

Five days after my father died, Tara told me what had been going on in the camp.

"Their leaving," she said. "Half the soldiers are leaving. The entire camp is in an uproar. I'll stay with you until the end, but our forces are being cut in half. We will not be able to protect ourselves if the Death Reapers come . . . and they will come."

I didn't answer her. I didn't have the words. Instead, I turned over and gave her my back. I fell into a deep sleep. Sleep was better than reality. Sleep was as close to death as I could get. Sleep provided a break from the pain of my broken heart. My dreams allowed me to soar amongst the clouds.

That night, my dreams were different.

I saw my father.

He was wearing his armor. There was a great puncture in the middle of his chest. There were blood stains on the chain mail around the puncture.

"Gwen," he called. "Is that you?"

"Yes, Daddy," I answered. "I miss you so much. Please don't ever leave me again. Please don't make me face this world alone. I don't have the strength. You overestimated me. I'm not strong enough. I'm too weak. They won't follow me."

"Oh my baby girl," my father whispered in my ear as he wrapped his arms around me. "Don't you fear. You'll find your way. You are more than strong enough. You are brave beyond words. You'll find your way . . . your time has come. Make me proud."

"Daddy," I cried. "I don't know how."

"Take all the love trapped inside your heart," my father said. "And let it go. Make the people you protect your new family. Let them see how much you care. They will return all that you give them. Love them, and they will fill your heart in return."

"I can't, Daddy," I said. "It hurts too much when I lose them."

"Find a way my beautiful daughter," my father said. "Find a way."

He held me for a long time. I felt the strength in his arms, and when I looked at him, his wounds were healed, and he seemed like a much younger man.

"I need to leave you," he said.

"No," I said.

He laughed softly at that.

"Someday we'll be reunited," he said. "But until then, I have another task for you."

"What task?" I asked.

"Find the reborn king," my father said. "He is hope. He is salvation . . . he needs you by his side, and trust me when I say this . . . you need him. Your paths are intertwined. Your destinies are one. The reborn king can right the wrongs. The reborn king can cleanse the land, but he's lost his way. Find him. Be patient with him. Help him find his way back. Believe in him."

"I don't know what you're talking about, Daddy," I said with my voice sounding more and more like a little girl. "I don't know who he is."

I held onto him as tightly as I could, but he was pulling away, and in pulling away he was becoming fainter and fainter. I could barely see him, but I heard his final words.

"Find the reborn king."

I awoke with a start.

Tara was there.

They're leaving," she said. "I told you about it, but you didn't listen. Maybe you can't listen, but our days are at an end. Too many of our warriors are leaving, and their taking a lot of the civilians with them. I wish you'd talk to me. I wish you'd tell me what to do."

I sat up in bed.

"I need a quick bath," I said.

A half an hour later I was clean, and ready to go. The most trying part of my life was only a few moments away.

I exited my tent wearing the leather armor of an archer. I had my bow in my left hand. As I marched towards our deserters, a crowd began to follow me.

All of them sensed a bit of destiny. I sensed a bit of destiny.

The crowd got larger and larger as I made my way towards the deserters. I could hear them talking amongst each other. I kept a slow but steady pace. I didn't want to leave them behind. I needed them behind me. I needed them to witness my best efforts.

If I failed . . . well, then I failed. There's no shame in that, but I'd try my hardest. These people deserved my best effort. I meant to give them just that. They wanted a leader . . . I would give them a leader they could be proud of. I'd never be able to fill my father's shoes, but they'd never doubt how hard I tried.

At the far edge of camp, I came upon the deserters. All of them were packing horses, and wagons. I took a long hard look. Somehow, I hadn't been able to grasp just how many were leaving me.

"Who's in charge here?" I asked.

None of them answered. None of them met my gaze.

"Please tell me," I said. "Who's in charge?"

All of them stopped their packing, and sort of looked at their shuffling feet. They were ashamed, and that made me sad. They shouldn't have been ashamed. I abandoned them in my grief. It wasn't the first time I'd made that mistake. They were only doing what they felt was best for them.

"Who's in charge here?" I asked for the third time.

"I guess that would be me," a man named Reynolds answered.

"Reynolds, where are you going?" I asked.

"We're going back to Southern California," Reynolds answered.

"What will you do there?" I asked.

"We'll establish a community," Reynolds answered. "We'll live our lives."

"You'll die," I said. "Eventually, our enemy will come for you."

"Maybe they won't," Reynolds said. "They already touched down on that area. There's no reason for them to come back."

"Your being there will give them a reason," I said.

"We have fighters," Reynolds said.

"Yes," I said. "And a braver bunch of men I've never encountered, but they aren't enough. Our enemy outnumbers us. They will kill the men, claim their bodies, rape the women, and do God knows what with the children."

"You can't know that," Reynolds said.

"I do know that," I said. "As far as I can tell, as far as I can see . . . we are all that protects this world. If we lose you, and the people that follow you, all is lost."

"Don't put that on me," Reynolds said. "I'm tired of fighting. I'm tired of killing, and watching my friends die."

"That is your weakness," I said. "That is also your strength. You care, and you should. You care because you are human. You are capable of love. Our enemy isn't. They will fight until we kill every last one of them. They never grow tired of the violence. They never get sad, and they'll root you out, and fall upon you like a plague."

"What would you have me do?" Reynolds asked. "What would you have all of us do?"

"Fight for me," I said calmly. "Fight with me."

"You plan on taking your father's place?" Reynolds asked.

"I plan on making him proud," I answered.

"You think you're up to that?" Reynolds asked.

"I mean to give it my best shot," I answered.

Reynolds was on the fence. He meant well, but he wasn't sure if following me was the right thing to do. I couldn't blame him.

"Hear me now!" I shouted out to everyone. "I am my father's daughter!" I mean to carry on where he left off. I'm asking all of you to follow me. I'm asking for your support. I'm asking you to have faith in me. We are all that stands between our enemy and total domination. We must keep fighting. We must make a stand. Your children and loved ones deserve to grow up safely, and that will never happen until this war is won."

The crowd began to clap, and murmur their agreement. Reynolds still looked undecided. I watched him look from face to face. He wasn't a bad man. He was simply a tired man. He was a man that had seen enough violence. He was a man that wanted to get away while he still could. Unfortunately for him, he was a man I needed. He had a skill and knowledge for warfare that I did not yet possess.

"Reynolds," I said. "Don't leave me. Don't leave us. We need you. We need your expertise to make this world safe once again. We need your help. We need your guidance."

I watched as his shoulders fell. I watched as he rubbed his brow, and ran his fingers through his grey-streaked black hair. I watched as those same fingers tugged on the long grey streaked beard hanging from his chin and cheeks.

He drew his sword, and the camp grew deathly quiet.

He met my gaze, and that simple act in itself was impressive. I wasn't used to that kind of boldness. He walked over until he was standing directly in front of me.

"You are truly your father's daughter," Reynolds said.

"I won't fail you," I said to him, and then I spoke to the crowd. "I won't fail any of you! I'll fight alongside you, and I'll never quit. Together we can reclaim this world! Together we are invincible!"

That was the moment. The unforgettable moment. Reynolds thrust his sword into the ground before me and fell to his knees.

"Forgive me," Reynolds said. "I swear, from now until the day I die . . . I'll serve you faithfully. I'll guide you when you seek my advice. I'll protect you when our enemy knocks upon your door. I'll never let you down."

The crowd joined him. Every last man, woman, and child fell to their knees.

"Stand, my friend," I said. "You embarrass me. I'm not worthy of such kindness. I'm an orphan, like many of those gathered here right now. Stand up and join me in the sun."

Reynolds stood . . . but something happened. I felt the hand of fate in the air. I felt it in my soul. Things were changing. I only prayed I'd be strong enough.

The months flew by after that fateful day.

Battle after battle was fought. I won them all. I outsmarted our enemy, and our soldiers outfought them. My people celebrated our victories. Our numbers grew and grew until we were ten thousand strong. In camp, life was good. We had food. We had weapons. My people were as happy as they could be.

Tara waited on me hand and foot. Reynolds rarely left my side. To tell the truth, their attention was a bit embarrassing, but normally I was so tired at the end of the day that I lacked the strength to argue.

I fought with the men.

That in itself wasn't too abnormal. Many of the women from our camp fought in the battles. Some of them used swords. Some were partial to spears. Others, like myself, used a bow. Unlike everyone else however, I used my bow from horseback. I rode out with the other horsemen, and while they used relied on their swords, I brought down twice as many enemies with my bow.

And then one day, a great beam of light parted the clouds and shone down upon a spot many days away from our camp. Where once it was dark, now it was light. The people of my camp gathered around to watch the wondrous sight. The rain in that area had stopped right before the light pierced the clouds. There was no reason for the abnormality . . . it simply was.

There was a bit of panic when the gigantic blue lightning bolt burst from the ground, and shot up into the atmosphere only to rebound across the earth. Many of my people thought it was a bad omen somewhere along the same lines as the fog, but I somehow knew that wasn't the case. I somehow knew that the bright light and the blue energy was something good.

Three days later a rider approached the borders of our latest camp. That in itself wasn't unusual. People joined us all the time, but this rider was being pursued by a small battalion of Death Reapers.

"Let the rider cross into our borders," I said. "Let our enemy follow him, and when both of them are deeply in our net, close it upon them."

My men jumped to obey my commands. Inside my tent, Tara helped me strap on my leather armor.

"We need better armor," I mumbled as she pulled tightly on my straps.

"We have more than enough chain mail," Tara said.

"No, we need plate," I said. "I've seen it occasionally. Even a few of our men wear bits and pieces of it, but we need to be more self sufficient. We need to make our own weapons. We need a blacksmith."

"I'm sure someone in the camp can handle that," Tara said. "But don't have those worries now. You need to keep your mind on the task ahead of you."

I smiled at her worry, and punched her in the arm playfully. Tara squealed and ran. Reynolds was waiting for me outside the tent. I had matters to attend to.

"Our men are attacking as we speak," Reynolds said.

"Then lets join them immediately," I said.

Our horses were close by. The ride to the battleground took us over an old overgrown road. I briefly marveled at how the forest was reclaiming the area. In another couple more years, the road would be gone. My duty was to make sure my people didn't join it in the afterlife.

Reynolds wasn't wrong. The second we rounded the last hill, we came upon a raging battle amidst a green fog. My men had encircled our enemy. It wasn't a tough battle, but it was violent. For once we had them grossly outnumbered . . . still, the situation had me wondering. So many riders after a lone young man, why?

My bow sang as I brought down Death Reaper after Death Reaper. My horse was running so fast, I barely heard the creak of the bow, but I felt its strength. I felt its power. I rode in circles around the battle. I took impossible shots, and all of them hit their mark.

I saw the young man that was being pursued break away from the clashing soldiers. Four of the Death Reapers rode after him. He was in danger, but there were too many of my own soldiers in need of help, and that prevented me from going to his aid immediately.

As I fired arrow after arrow, I kept an eye on the young man. He rode out a short distance, and leapt off his horse. To my surprise, he unsheathed two Japanese-styled blades from his back, and faced his attackers.

One after another, he killed them all. His movements were a series of twirls and slashes . . . almost like a dance.

"Where did you learn to fight like that?" I asked as I finally approached him.

"Nowhere," he answered. "It just makes sense to me."

"What's your name?" I asked.

"I'm Tristan," he said with wide eyes and a serious voice. "And you would be the most beautiful woman I've ever laid eyes on."

"What?" I asked with a laugh.

"Excuse my bluntness," Tristan said. "Where did you come from?"

"Far away from here," I answered.

Behind me, the battle was over. We'd not lost a single man. All that was left to my soldiers was the unenviable task of putting the Death Reapers that still clung to life out of their misery.

"What's your name?" Tristan asked.

"Gwen," I answered, and to my shock, Tristan dropped to one knee.

"I have a message for you," Tristan said. "King Arthur has been reborn, and Camelot is burning."

A reborn king.

I suddenly felt faint.

My dream. My father ... he told me to find the reborn king. The reborn king was hope, and salvation. I saw stars before my eyes. Suddenly Reynolds was there, and grasping my arm to keep me steady in my saddle.

"Who sent you?" I asked.

"Merlin sent me," Tristan answered.

I was glad to have Reynolds's hand on my arm.

"You don't say?" I asked.

"Believe me milady," Tristan said. "I know it sounds crazy, but I've seen things."

I considered his words. I'd seen some things as well. I knew deep in my heart that when my father spoke to me, it wasn't simply a dream. It was more than that ... much, much more.

"Why do you take a knee before me?" I asked.

"Because I know who you are," Tristan said. "You are Guinevere. I cannot be mistaken. You may not know it yet, but I know it, and I'm at your service."

There it was ... the kiss of destiny ... why couldn't I laugh at his words? Why did they have a not so subtle ring of truth about them? Was I truly ... ? I couldn't be, could I?

"I think the young man has been in the sun too long," Reynolds said.

I didn't answer. I couldn't stop staring at Tristan, but in truth I barely even saw him. My mind was elsewhere. I had visions I couldn't focus on, fleeting images that were gone before I could lock them down. A past that wasn't mine.

"Milady?" Reynolds asked with a touch of concern.

"I'm fine, my friend," I said, noticing the way he'd just addressed me. "This young man is need of our help. See that he's given water, and a place to rest. Tonight we'll have diner in my tent. Would that be okay with you, Tristan?"

"Yes, Milady," Tristan answered. "But I must remind you. Time is of the essence. My town is under siege."

"You can tell me all about it at diner," I said.

"I'll have Izzy take care of him," Reynolds said. "He can keep him entertained until diner."

"Very well," I said before riding off.

I needed a moment to collect my thoughts.

When I got back to my tent I was flushed and flustered. A reborn king, Tristan spoke of a reborn king. He mentioned Arthur. He called me Guinevere. What the hell was going on?

Before I knew it, Tara was pulling off my leather armor.

"It's too humid," Tara said. "You don't look good. You look as if you're going to pass out. What happened out there?"

"Destiny," I mumbled. "I think my destiny has found me at last."

Tara stopped, and I squeezed her hand in an effort to reassure her that I was okay.

"Talk to me," Tara said as she knelt in front of my chair.

I told her everything. I told her of the dream. I told her of Tristan. I held nothing back.

"Tristan is one of the Knights of the Round Table," Tara said.

I groaned.

"Is he?" I asked.

"Haven't you ever head or Tristan and Isolde?" Tara asked.

The two names together rang a bell. I shuddered.

"I've heard of them," I answered. "I think they made a movie out of it or something. I probably saw it."

"Where is Tristan now?" Tara asked.

"He's being taken care of," I answered. "He seemed a bit dehydrated. Reynolds was going to have Izzy see to his needs. Later tonight, we'll have diner here."

Tara didn't hear that last part.

"Do you realize what you just set in motion?" Tara asked.

"What?" I asked in return.

"Tristan and Izzy," Tara said. "Do you know Izzy?"

"I've seen him around," I answered. "I haven't talked to him very much."

"Well congratulations anyway," Tara said. "You and Reynolds just sent an epic love story into motion."

"Huh?" I asked.

"Tristan is Isolde," Tara said. "Tristan and Izzy."

"Don't be ridiculous," I said. "They're both . . . oh . . . *Oh* . . . I get it. Do you think?"

"Yes," Tara said. "But even more amazing is who you are."

"That's unbelievable," I said. "It can't be true."

"I believe it," Tara said. "There's something about you. You're different. You're meant for great things. I believe it completely. All of it adds up."

"I'm not sure that's what I wanted to hear," I said.

"Of course not," Tara said. "You don't want to be great. You want to be a normal everyday girl, but fate has other plans for you. You'll be great whether you like it or not. Heck, you're already well on your way."

"I don't know what to do," I said.

"Find out all you can about Arthur," Tara said. "That's the key. See if he really is our salvation."

"My father said he lost his way," I said.

"And what better person than you to help him find it," Tara said. "I'll start preparing diner now. Can I get you anything before hand?"

"Whiskey would be great," I said. "Do we still have any?"

"We do indeed," Tara answered before running off to find the bottle.

I spent the rest of the day sipping whiskey. I'm not sure why. I've never been partial to whiskey before. I was more of a wine type of girl, but whiskey suddenly appealed to me greatly.

After the sun had set, and the table was prepared my guests arrived, and sat with me at the table. I was at the head. Tristan was on my right hand side. Reynolds was at the opposite end, and Izzy was on my left.

Throughout Tara's wonderful meal, I kept catching Tristan and Izzy smiling at each other. I smiled at their antics. I tried not to. I didn't want to embarrass them, but I couldn't help myself. Love was in the air, and love was something to be cherished in this day and age. Love was something to fight for.

After the meal came more whiskey. My head was buzzing, so I only took a small glass. The others however, filled their glasses.

"Tell me about the reborn king," I said to Tristan.

"Arthur," Tristan said. "I know him pretty well. He's always been good to me."

"You're holding something back," Reynolds said. "I can tell it by the way you hesitate when you speak of him."

"Make no mistake," Tristan said. "Merlin is the man in charge. Arthur used to be something special. He used to be . . . incredible, but he's lost too much. His wife and son . . . after they died, well, Arthur changed . . . he didn't handle their deaths very well."

He didn't handle their deaths very well. Who did that remind me of? I had a brief flash of regret as I pictured all that I'd put my poor father through.

"Tell me more," I said in a quiet voice.

"He's a good man," Tristan said. "He's just lost his way a bit. I don't know what else to say. I'm a bit player in a much bigger game. All I know is that the enemy is at our gates, and they're trying desperately to get in. All that stands in their way is Merlin and a bit of old magic. We need help."

"And help is what you'll receive," I said. "Have no fear my friend. We'll march to Camelot's aid first thing tomorrow morning."

"Thank you, Milady," Tristan said. "Thank you so much."

"It's what we do," I answered with a forced smile.

After that, small talk was exchanged. More information was shared in addition to a few laughs, and eventually everyone set out to get a bit of sleep. A curious thing happened as Tristan was about to leave my tent.

"My town," Tristan said. "It's not truly called Camelot. I live in the town of Mill Ridge, but Merlin told me to say Camelot. I'm not sure why."

"Perhaps when you have a Merlin," I said. "A name change on the town is in order."

"How can I argue with that logic," Tristan said.

Tristan still stood at the doorway of my tent.

"What's wrong?" I asked.

"I'm very sorry," Tristan said. "I just can't help wondering what will happen when Guinevere meets Arthur."

"I see," I said.

"Be patient with him," Tristan said. "He'll push you to your limits, but there's a good man hiding inside of him."

Tristan didn't wait for me to reply. He simply left without another word. I don't think he realized what thoughts were left dancing inside my mind after his words.

First, he held a deep loyalty to the man. Such a loyalty wasn't something I could ignore. The second thought he left me with was the same exact thing he was wondering. What would happen when I met, Arthur.

I will never break my vow. I will never love again. I loathed the very idea. To lose a loved one was terrible. It was earth shattering, and life ending. When I lost my mother, I died inside. When I lost my father . . . I . . . when I lost him . . . I . . .

I ran from my tent. I ran past the guards at the edge of our camp. I ran all the way up a green hill, and sat on its far edge. The stars were bright enough to read by. The night was cool. The tears came forward. I cried and cried, and all the while I wondered if their truly was a person out there destined to love me.

Well, I didn't want his love. I wouldn't accept his love. Let no man pierce the ice of my heart. Let me never again feel the sorrow of a lost love.

I was afraid.

My destiny was upon me.

I was standing at the edge of an abyss, and I had no one to catch me.

I heard footsteps on the soft grass behind me.

I didn't turn. I knew who it was.

"Milady," Reynolds said. "You shouldn't be outside of the camp. It's not safe."

"I'm sorry," I said. "I had a momentary lapse in judgment. Please go back, I'll be right behind you."

"Why do you refuse to look at me?" Reynolds asked.

"Reynolds," I said. "Go back. I'll be along shortly."

"I'll not leave your side," Reynolds said stubbornly.

"I need to be alone right now," I said. "Please . . ."

"Never," Reynolds said. "I can see your tears. Tell me what's wrong. I'll make it right."

"I lost my father," I said too abruptly.

"You did," Reynolds said. "And perhaps you never truly mourned him. This is nothing to be ashamed of. You have every right to shed your tears. Your father was a great man, and he loved you greatly."

"I'm a leader," I said. "I should control my emotions."

"Yes," Reynolds said. "But you're also a human being. A living breathing human being and you have a right to be sad. We've all lost someone. Yet, all of us were given a chance to properly mourn. You were thrust into leadership before you'd dealt with your pain. The burden of that guilt lies upon me. I forced your hand. Forgive me?"

"There is nothing to forgive," I said. "You did what you felt best in the absence of leadership. I should thank you. You came back to me. You came back to an inexperienced girl, and supported her."

"I would have it no other way," Reynolds said. "But something tells me that you weep for other reasons as well."

"I do," I said.

"I'm here for you, milady," Reynolds said.

Finally, I turned to him. Tears were in my eyes. A lump was in my throat, I was embarrassed, but I needed someone. Perhaps a battle-hardened warrior wasn't the best person to bare my soul to . . . but he cared for me. He wanted to help.

"I've never loved anyone but my mother and father," I announced. "I care for the welfare of others, I truly do, but I keep them at a distance. In this world, at this time, people die. I can't handle death. I love too deeply. Death is my ruin. Death is my downfall."

Reynolds came up behind me, dropped to his knees, and wrapped me in his chain mailed arms. The gesture was too much. I lost it. Reynolds had never so much as shaken my hand before.

"Your burden is beautiful," He said. "Your burden tells me that I made the right decision. The love will come to you. It's already coming to you. I could see that the minute your father found you. Love isn't something you can hide from. It isn't something you can run from. It will find you. It will always find you."

Was that the truth of it?

Was love finding me?

Was the ice melting?

Yes.

I was weakening. I knew it. I cared too much for the people following me. They were my everything, but now, with that odd touch of destiny in the air, I was frightened. Tristan's words echoed in my soul.

What would happen when I met Arthur?

Nothing! I made a vow to never love again, and that icy vow was my armor. Let me be strong. Let me hold it together. Never show weakness. Care for them. Protect them, but never let a single person shine too brightly.

"What do I do?" I asked.

"Do what you've been doing," Reynolds answered as he gently released me. "You are your father's daughter. The path you choose will be the right one. I shall wait for you at the bottom of the hill."

"Reynolds," I whispered right before he disappeared from view.
"Yes, Milady?"
"Why did you bow to me that long ago morning?" I asked.
Reynolds smiled.
"How could I not, Milady," Reynolds said.

♣ MERLIN ♣

Where was Arthur? He should have been back. Obviously he claimed the sword, but where was he? Each evening, more and more of the Death Reapers arrived. They were drawn to Mill Ridge. They wanted Mill Ridge.

Very soon the attack would come.

Every few hours, small groups of them would force their way under the fence just as they did on the evening Arthur drew the sword from the stone. The townspeople would fight them off, but damage was always done. Sir Francis was whittling away at our numbers by sacrificing his pawns.

I didn't have an answer to his method of attack. He sent just enough soldiers to cause damage, but not enough to get jammed up at their point of entry. We killed all of them, but they always managed to claim a few lives on our side as well.

I dreaded the sound of a blowing horn. I knew a blowing horn meant we had a breach in our defenses. It meant we were under attack. The entire town dreaded the sound of the church bell. That sound was now reserved for a worst case scenario. It meant that we were losing. It told all of our defenders to retreat from their posts, and head to the town square in a last attempt to hold our ground.

There was no chance of retreating. Our enemies were too numerous. Stronghold Wall was thoroughly surrounded. We'd run straight into their net.

Where was Arthur?

We needed him to claim his rightful place. We needed him to lead. Only his military genius would be enough to win this battle. Was he up to the challenge? If he were here, would he accept his role, and do what must be done? I had my doubts about that.

Reinforcements were on their way. I knew it in my heart. That was simply the way things were. They would flock to Arthur regardless of whether he was ready for his responsibilities or not. Now, who Tristan would find first . . . of that I had no clue, I had an idea, but I certainly didn't know for sure. There were knights out there waiting to take their place next to him, but there was someone else as well.

She would be beautiful beyond all words. Her loyalty and faithfulness would be without question. Her strength and determination would be immeasurable. All of that, however would pale next to her heart. Her heart was the reason people loved her.

She would come for him. She'd be drawn to him above all others. Oceans would be ponds to her. Miles would be meaningless. Theirs was the greatest love ever to have been lived. She would be drawn to him beyond reason. They were a single soul destined to be reunited.

She was hope.

With her, I would re-ignite the spark within Arthur. I would bring him back to the man he used to be. Only Guinevere could make him love again.

Speaking of love, Dellia was worrying me. She worked non-stop in an effort to help the injured and dying. The woman was exhausted, but she refused to quit. Perhaps I had made a mistake when suggesting she help the doctor.

Worst of all, I could see the worry in her eyes. I would sacrifice all of the magic in my body to remove that worry. Arthur and Dellia were family to me, and aside from Wayne, they were the only bit of family I had left in this entire world. Sure, they weren't family by blood, but they were family in my heart, and in a life as long as mine . . . well, they greatly mattered to me.

What could I tell her?

Arthur wasn't dead. Of that, I was certain. I would feel it if he were dead, just as I could feel the sadness in his heart. Perhaps he was captured? No, Sir Francis was here for Arthur, if his soldiers had already captured him, there wouldn't be so many Death Reapers closing in around us. There was one more option I hadn't wanted to consider.

Excalibur.

What if the sword had gotten to him? I should have given him a better warning. Arthur was new to this new world. He might have used the sword.

He might have been overwhelmed by the sword. I should have drilled it into him. Do not use that blade. Excalibur has grown resentful.

The sound of a horn.

I exhaled a deep breath of air from my young lungs, and stepped away from Sheriff Tagger's desk. My magic was needed.

Wayne was riding up for me just as I exited the Sheriff's Station. He threw out a big arm as he rode by. I caught it, and swung up behind him on the horse.

"Where is the breach?" I asked.

"Past the farms, at the entrance of the town," Wayne answered.

"Then we must hurry," I said.

Wayne rode fast, and I held onto him tightly in an effort to keep from being thrown off the horse. I was tired. My strength wasn't the greatest. Secretly, I worried about my magic. I had been pushing myself rather hard. Would I be strong enough to help our defenders when they really needed my help?

The sound of the horse's hooves against the road was almost soothing. The bouncing around was not. In all my years, I had never owned a horse. I preferred walking to riding. The forest was my friend. The fields my ally, I rarely rushed anywhere. Then again, never before had I been placed in such a dire situation.

Arthur was always there. Arthur always had a plan. Yes, I advised him. I taught him to be a great king, but he certainly never needed my aid in the matters of warfare. I only helped whenever I could.

The shops blew by us. The open fields that were full of crops followed next. Soon, we came to the stone entryway of Stronghold Wall. This was the only entrance into the town of Mill Ridge. Wayne directed his horse to the left, and ran alongside the wall. The horn was still sounding off.

I saw the battle in the distance. The reinforcements that stood in waiting were moving in as we arrived. Our enemy had already left their mark. Many of our men were lying on the ground. Wayne pulled his short battle axes from their sheaths on his back, and entered the battle.

I slipped off the back of his horse, and summoned my power.

Dirt and rocks flew towards the breach underneath the wall. I pelted and covered those that were still trying to enter. I pushed my magic to its limits. Small tornadoes of rock and dirt attacked the breach, and eventually closed the hole.

A lone Death Reaper ran towards me with his sword held high. I was tired, but I had no choice. I needed to defend myself. Wayne beat me to it. He ran his horse behind my attacker and cleaved his skull in half.

"Stay by me!" I shouted to Wayne. "I'll need your protection."

"What about everyone else?" Wayne asked.

"Don't argue!" I shouted. "That's what I'm working on."

I closed my eyes and summoned fire. A great ball of it manifested between my open palms. Fire was a spell never meant to be a weapon. It was meant to be used for survival purposes, but it lent itself well towards destruction.

When the orb was big enough, I sent it on its way. From enemy to enemy it flew. Its touch brought pain and death. I weaved it in and out of the combatants. I controlled it until I could control it no longer, and then I let it dissolve. That wasn't a problem. The damage had already been done. I took too many of them down. The remainder was easily swarmed.

"Very good," I said as the last of them fell and the green fog faded away. "I think I'll go back to the station and have a rest."

"That chubby magic getting you all tuckered out?" Wayne asked.

"If it wasn't," I said. "I'd have the horse ride you back into town."

"Moody teenagers crack me up," Wayne laughed.

We rode off as a few members of the reinforcements took care of the wounded and the dead. The dead must be burned, or else their bodies would soon become our enemies.

"This is getting bad," Wayne said as soon as we came to Main Street.

"I agree," I said.

"I've seen a lot of shit go down," Wayne said. "So I'm pretty much convinced that you know what you're talking about."

"Do you have a question somewhere in all those words, numb-nuts?" I asked.

Wayne laughed a bit at my tired response. My youth was catching up to me, regardless; it felt good to insult him.

"I do have a question," Wayne said after a bit. "Do you still think help will be arriving?"

"Yes," I answered honestly. "Help will be arriving, but we must hold out until that moment."

"That won't be easy at this pace," Wayne said. "What about Arthur?"

"Arthur will be arriving as well," I said. "But that doesn't mean he'll save the day. I have a feeling that finding the Arthur of old will take time."

"You really think he can save us?" Wayne asked.

"Yes," I replied.

Another horn blew in the distance.

"Uh oh," Wayne said.

"Let's go," I said.

"I'm going," Wayne said as he spurred his horse into action. "But it's awfully soon after the last attack."

"It certainly is," I said without adding anything else to the conversation. I was too worried for a long conversation.

Past the farmland we rode, and then Wayne took a detour through the fields. Crops brushed against our legs as his horse plowed onwards. There was a black smoke filling up the sky coming from the direction in which we were headed. Wayne must have noticed it, but he never said a word.

When the fields finally ended, the houses began. It was a pretty neighborhood. The people of this town cared about Mill Ridge. The yards were clipped and the shrubs were trimmed.

Wayne's horse tore chunks out of the first lawn we rode over. From there, we hit a street, rode to an intersection, hung a left before moving across more lawns, and eventually ended up behind the last row of homes closest to Stronghold Wall.

The battle was raging.

To my right, and separate from the battle was a small group of Death Reapers. Instead of fighting, they were setting fire to the houses. It was a common tactic designed to lower morale. In the future, I had plans for this town, but the future was not upon us. The townspeople would be devastated by the loss of their homes.

I told Wayne to help with the battle, and I hopped off the horse. There were only five arsonists. They shouldn't be too much trouble, and they were far enough away from the battle to keep me from worrying about being struck down from behind.

I ran towards them until I was about twenty feet away. They had just broken a window and were preparing to toss in a torch. I balled my right fist, and enveloped it with my left hand. The flame on his torch sputtered out instantly.

The Death Reapers had no idea I was behind them. As they sought to reignite their torch, I twisted and contorted my fingers. I imagined the roots of the nearby trees bursting through the ground and attacking them.

I pushed with my will to make my imagination a reality. The tree roots responded. One after another, the invaders became entangled. They screamed out in fear and hacked away at the roots, but the plant life was strong and healthy. Their screams turned from fear and entered the realm of pain as the roots climbed up their chests and began to squeeze the life out of them.

In the distance, I heard another horn blow from an entirely new direction.

Wayne was already riding towards me. There was blood all over his twin axes, and grey shirt. Why wasn't he wearing any armor?

"Did you hear that?" Wayne asked.

"I did," I answered while looking for the breach in the wall.

"We need to close the breach," Wayne said. "And then we need to go help the other group of defenders."

"I can't close that breach," I said after finding the large hole under the fence. "They've made it too large this time, and too many of them are coming through."

"Then what the hell do we do?" Wayne asked.

I looked around frantically. What was I looking for? I had no idea. An answer? An idea? I found nothing but the chaos of battle, and the lonesome sounds of the wounded and dying. The green fog was becoming thicker and thicker.

Reinforcements were arriving. I could see them rounding the corner of a house not far away, but their numbers were small. Meanwhile, more and more Death Reapers were pouring through the breach and digging away at its edges in an effort to enlarge the hole even further.

"I'm so sorry," I muttered. "I have failed everyone."

"What are you talking about?"

"I was supposed to protect this town," I said. "I've failed. My magic simply isn't powerful enough. I've failed. I've never failed at anything before."

"Grandpa Merl," Wayne said in an effort to grab my attention.

I ignored him. My attention wasn't his to grab. I was watching the townspeople clash against our enemy. I was watching the sparks fly from the clanging swords. I was watching shields become battered and eventually discarded. I was watching men fall. I was watching men die. I was watching the Death Reapers advance.

"Grandpa Merl!" Wayne shouted.

Somewhere in the back of my mind I heard him, but I couldn't respond. I was watching the end, and all I could do was wonder why our reinforcements had not yet arrived.

"Merlin!" Wayne shouted, and this time I heard him.

He called me Merlin. I turned to him and smiled.

"I hear you," I said. "We need to hurry."

"What are we doing?" Wayne asked as I climbed up behind him.

Another horn sounded off in the distance.

Another breach in the wall.

I took it in. I reflected upon it briefly. I couldn't save the town, but there was still hope for the people.

"Ride as fast as you can," I said with urgency. "Head towards the churches bell tower."

Without another word, Wayne gave heels to his horse. The horse bucked up, and ran forward as I shouted out a command for everyone to retreat.

Before we turned the corner, and I lost sight of the green fog and battle, I heard the men and women defending that area of Stronghold Wall begin to shout out my order of retreat.

I breathed a sigh of relief.

Wayne took us to the nearest road, and thundered down the empty street. Small groups of Death Reapers came at us, but they were spread too thin to be a bother. Wayne even rode down a few of the ones too stupid to get out of his way.

Mill Ridge was being overrun.

More houses were burning.

Sir Francis wanted to wipe this town from the face of the earth, and he sought to do so with fire and steel.

Another horn blew in the distance.

I needed to hurry. Our defenders would fight valiantly until the bitter end. After all they were defending their homes, and their very right to live . . . but they would lose. They would die. I had a better solution. Well, it wasn't really better, but it would give us more time, and time was something we sorely needed.

I couldn't doubt myself.

The sword was drawn.

The people would come.

They had to come.

We hit Main Street and turned left.

"Faster," I said. "Faster. Lives depend on us."

"I'm going as fast as I can," Wayne said.

That's when I started to whisper to the horse in a language only animals could understand. I explained my need. I explained my urgency.

The horse understood. The horse heard my words, and ran faster than he'd ever run before. Wayne was shocked at the new burst of speed. He gripped the reins tighter and braced himself. I in turn gripped Wayne tighter around his midsection.

In no time at all, we entered the town square and reached the bell tower of the church.

"Ring the bell!" I shouted. "Ring the bell!"

I saw a young teenager's head poke out of one of the open air slots. He looked at me, and I shouted again. With a nod he vanished from view.

The bell rang out a second later.

It rang and rang and rang. I ran back to the entrance of the town square. The Main Street was empty. My heart was pounding in my chest. Where were the people? Was I too late? I cursed myself for freezing at the worst of moments. I was no longer used to battle. It had been such a long time, and my magic was weak.

I hated myself, and I watched the empty street. Let them come. Let them survive. There was still hope . . . if only they'd come.

With the bell ringing loudly behind me, I waited for a response. Wayne soon stood next to me. He had his weapons in his hands.

"This can't be the end," I said. "It just can't be. There so much left to do."

"They'll come," Wayne said. "Give them a moment. They'll come."

The moment stretched on and on. I could sense Wayne's impatience. He was about to ride out in search of answers when the first of our people made their way to Main Street. We saw them in the distance. They ran as fast as they could.

At first it was a group of three coming from the same battle Wayne and I had just retreated from. More followed them. Some were limping. Some were being aided by others. From the other side of the road came even more.

A few minutes later, they came from all directions, and even behind us through the alley. All in all, it took close to a half an hour before all of our people were safely inside the town square.

Dellia and a few others including the doctor were working furiously on the wounded. Some were passing out food and water. Bedder was organizing able bodied men and women to guard the two entrances of the town square. He also began placing archers on the tops of the shops that outlined the square.

Our defenses were being set up rapidly. That was good, but it wouldn't be enough. Our forces were untrained and tired. Too many had been lost before the bell sounded out. The entrance on Main Street was over two car lengths wide, with tall shops on either side. We wouldn't be able to stop their charge when they chose to push their way in.

"There's a lot of smoke out there," Wayne said.

"They're burning more homes," I said.

"Pretty soon we won't have a town to defend," Wayne said.

"The homes and the shops are inconsequential," I said. "What matters is the land. The land is sacred. The land is Camelot. The homes and shops are weak in this new world."

"Tell that to the people that are losing everything," Wayne said.

"I'll do better than that," I said. "I'll replace their homes. I'll make them safe. I'll raise a new town from the ashes of what was lost."

"How are you gonna manage all that?" Wayne asked.

"I will resurrect Camelot," I said.

"You mean the actual Camelot?" Wayne asked. "You're going to build it here?"

"No," I answered while looking towards Wayne's former auto shop. "I won't be building anything. Magic will pull it from the ground."

"Geez," Wayne said. "Can you really do that?"

"Yes," I answered. "Not yet, but soon."

"Until then," Wayne said. "We defend the land inside Stronghold Wall."

"Exactly," I said. "Now tell me, do you still have automobiles in your shop over there?"

"Yeah," Wayne answered. "I have about ten. Five of them were restorations. The other five were oil changes. After the red fog, there wasn't much reason to finish any of them up since they'll never run again."

I snapped my fingers, and the chain around the garage doors burst apart, as the door flew open. After that, I made a grabbing motion with my right hand and pulled my arm back.

The first car came towards us on screeching tires. I pushed it past us and used it to block almost half the entry way into Town Square. Another car came after that. I used it to fill the other side.

When the third car came, Wayne threw a fit.

"Hey," Wayne said. "What the hell? That one's a restoration. I could make good money on that?"

"Yes," I said. "In a world where cars no longer run, I can bet a lot of people will be lining up to take it off your hands."

"Yeah but . . . ," Wayne attempted to say.

"Wayne, do I make this look easy?" I said as I lifted the car into the air and slammed it on top of the other two."

"Sort of," Wayne said.

"Well, it isn't," I said. "So shut up."

To his credit, he kept his mouth quiet as I pilled all the cars on top of one another, and blocked the entryway.

A crowd had begun to gather as cars began levitating in the air. I couldn't blame them. It wasn't exactly like they were used to magic. Even Bedder was watching closely.

"How powerful are you?" Bedder asked after I was finished.

"Not very," I answered.

"Will you be able to help when the fighting starts?" Bedder asked.

"I need to rest," I said. "I've exhausted myself, but yes . . . I will help when the fighting starts."

"Will you be beneficial?" Bedder asked.

"C'mon, dude," Wayne said. "Don't be a dick. He's done more than anyone else has to protect this place."

"Truly you haven't spent enough time fighting if that's what you believe," Bedder said.

"How about I kick your . . ." Wayne tried to say before I cut him off.

"Stop it," I said. "The both of you . . . stop it. Our enemy is outside this square. They have already breached our territory, and soon the fighting will begin in earnest. Now, to answer your question, I'm weak. My magic will grow stronger as the days pass, and I use it more. Right now, it's not that beneficial . . . not in the grand scheme of things. I'll rest up as much as I can. I'll do my best to be fresh when the fighting starts."

"Why aren't they attacking?" Bedder asked.

"There's no need to attack us right now," I said. "Sir Francis has us exactly where he wants us. He's tightening his noose as we speak. First he will move the bulk of his army inside Stronghold Wall. After that, he'll continue his attempts to demoralize the people by burning their homes and crops. The attack will come afterwards. "

"The burnings already commenced," Wayne said. "When can we expect the attack?"

"There's no telling," I said. "Some wait weeks, even months. They try to starve out the people. Others are impatient and attack as soon as possible."

"What will Sir Francis choose?" Wayne asked.

"He'll probably attack by this evening," I said. "That will give him enough time to move his troops inside the wall. He won't mind sacrificing the lives of some of his men to breach what little defenses we have."

"Do you still think help is headed our way?" Wayne asked.

"Yes," I answered.

"That makes you a fool, Merlin," Bedder said. "There will be no help. Tonight there will be only death and destruction."

"If you have a way out of this," Wayne said. "We're all ears."

"Sadly, I do not," Bedder said. "Therefore, I will fight. It's all I can do, and it won't be enough."

I walked away. I had no words of comfort. I myself doubted whether or not help would arrive in time. Bedder wasn't a pleasant man, but he had a point. If things didn't align perfectly . . . we were all in serious trouble.

I felt Arthur's presence.

I stopped immediately, and sent out my senses.

Yes, I was positive. I could feel Arthur's presence. He would be arriving sometime tonight.

I smiled. No, I laughed out loud. Arthur was coming home.

Before I had even managed to compose myself, I ran to Dellia. With all the exuberance of the teenager I resembled, I told her that Arthur would be coming.

"How can you be sure?" Dellia asked.

"Because I'm Merlin," I answered.

"Give me a straight answer," Dellia demanded.

"I can't," I said. "I don't know how I know . . . I just know."

"What about reinforcements?" Dellia asked.

"I don't know," I answered. "But I hold fast to my belief that they'll arrive in time."

"We should have sent more people," Dellia said.

"Tristan will be enough," I said.

"How can you be sure?" Dellia asked. "What if my son is coming home to a deathtrap?"

"Tristan has succeeded," I said. "He's bringing help."

"Who's he bringing?" Dellia asked. "How many?"

"I have ideas," I said. "But I have no definitive answers."

"You think it's her don't you?" Dellia asked. "You think she's coming for him?"

"It makes sense," I answered. "She will be drawn to him above all others. She will need to be by his side, but make no mistake . . . others are coming as well. It's always darkest before the dawn, my dear. Tonight will be long and full of nightmares, but tomorrow will be a new day."

The rain came.

One second before, and the sky was clear and blue. Now the rain was falling from white clouds that were rapidly turning grey. It wasn't a downpour, but it wasn't a sprinkle either. I didn't mind it at all. The day had grown hot, and the rain was refreshing.

Hours later, the rain grew angry, and developed slight chill as the little bit of sun still left in the grey sky descended behind the mountains on the horizon. Everyone in Town Square watched the scene quietly.

We were as prepared as we were ever going to be for the attack. Our defenders were rested and fed. Doctor Talbert and Dellia were preparing to help the wounded. Blades were sharpened, and arrows were handed out to our archers on the rooftops.

I watched the burning homes from atop the roof of the Sheriff's Station. I watched as the light of the fires illuminated the green fog, and the great army gathering inside of it.

"Merlin," Wayne said as he slid over the roof, and stood behind me. "You should wear something more than a t-shirt. Maybe get out of the rain for a bit."

"I don't catch colds," I answered.

"It's still pretty miserable out here," Wayne said.

"I want to see when it happens," I said.

"When they attack you mean?" Wayne asked.

"Yes," I answered.

"It's not like they're going to sneak up on us," Wayne said. "All the archers are keeping an eye on them."

"The archers aren't properly trained," I said. "None of these people are properly trained."

"Not for war, no," Wayne said. "But folks in this town are hunters. The archers on those rooftops grew up with a bow in their hands. They won't miss."

"I have no doubt they'll do their best," I said.

"I sent a few more people to help out Dellia and Doctor Talbert," Wayne said. "That gives us a medical staff of five."

"Do they have the necessary skills?" I asked.

"The skill level ranges," Wayne answered. "But they're the best we have."

I scanned the distance. I watched the forces of Morgana moving into position. I looked beyond them out into the dark horizon, and I saw . . . nothing. Our reinforcements were nowhere near us. The battle would start without them.

We were in trouble.

Finally, a small group of about one hundred of our enemy began to march forward down Main Street with lanterns held high above their hands.

"It's beginning," I said solemnly.

"Let's go then," Wayne said.

The two of us left the rooftop of the Sheriff's Station, and walked over to the three story building on the left side of the blockade of cars. We entered through the front door, walked past all the farming equipment for sale, found the stairway, and took it to the rooftop.

There were five archers waiting there for us. All of them looked nervous. Two of them served in the military at some point in their lives, and handled things slightly better . . . but no one appreciated the odds we were about to face as the night progressed.

"We're the first line of defense," I told everybody. "Don't worry if they get past you, and make it over the cars. We have archers in the park waiting to pick them off."

"Why are they carrying lanterns," A man asked.

"They want us to know they're coming," I answered. "They seek to scare us . . . and distract us."

"Distract us from what?" A woman asked.

"I'm not sure yet," I answered. "But we have more archers spread out along the buildings in the Town Square. They won't catch us unawares."

"It's hard to see anything with all the rain in my eyes," someone else said.

"Pull your hood farther over your head," I said.

Fire and green fog moved towards us on Main Street. I wiped my damp hair away from my eyes and glared. They were close enough for me to use my magic, but I wanted to conserve my strength.

When they entered the range of the archers I saw all of them notching their arrows. I looked across the barricade of piled cars at the building across from us. The seven archers there were notching their arrows as well.

"Not yet," I said. "Wait until they charge."

"How stupid are they?" Wayne asked. "They have no shields, and they're holding lanterns. Why the hell are they making themselves such easy targets?"

"I've already answered that question, numb-nuts," I said. "Pay attention when I talk. I say some really important shit sometimes."

Suddenly, all the lanterns dropped to the wet street and our attackers charged.

"I can't see them anymore!" Someone shouted.

"Where are they?" Someone else demanded.

I looked to the sky. The night was so black I could barely see the clouds. The rain washed against my face, and I began to whisper and twist my fingers.

It was an old spell. So old that I'd almost forgotten it, but it was a neat little trick I often used when I was younger and people hadn't yet heard my name. It let them know I had power.

After I cast the spell, I waited a brief moment. I ignored the worrying archers. I paid no attention to our attackers when they began to yell at us through the darkness. I simply waited.

A massive arc of lightning slashed and cracked across the sky. Those around me jumped in fright. The sky had been quiet until that very moment.

I brought the lightning and thunder.

I smiled as I looked below us at the charging Death Reapers. The lightning lit them up almost perfectly. I chuckled at my cleverness and our archers began to fire upon them with arrows.

Blackness.

"Wait for the lightning!" I called out.

Another arc cut across the black sky and illuminated the land mere moments after the first. Our enemy was still charging and screaming, but already nine of their number had been dropped.

More arrows were flying. The sounds of twanging bow strings competed and lost against the deafening sound of the rolling thunder. I watched another group of figures fall.

It wasn't enough.

When the lightning flashed a third time, they were already climbing the barricade of cars. Our archers fired down upon them without fear of being attacked because the pile of cars didn't reach the tops of the two buildings on either side.

"Keep firing!" I shouted. "Let nothing stop you!"

They did as I asked. As the rain pounded us and our enemy flooded towards us, the archers did their job.

"They're coming!" Someone shouted from farther down the Town Square. I couldn't exactly tell from where, but they seemed to be on the roof of the shop across from the Sheriff's Station.

That one worried me. The buildings that lined the square weren't nearly as tall as the two at the entrance on Main Street. Some of them were only one story.

"I need help!" That same someone shouted out.

"Merlin," Wayne said. "Should we go?"

I didn't answer at first. I was looking below me at the attackers that managed to make it over my barrier of cars. I watched them charge and try to spread out only to fall dead as more archers hiding inside the park picked them off one after another.

"Merlin!" Wayne shouted.

"Yes," I answered. "Let's go."

Together we ran back inside the building, charged down the three flights of stairs and exited onto the street. From there, we ran forward, cutting through the park, passing the hidden archers, and ending up on the street in front of all the shops that bordered the Town Square across from the Sheriff's Station.

"Who needs help?" I shouted out.

There was no answer.

"Who needs help?" Wayne shouted out in his louder, more obnoxious voice.

"Here!" A woman shouted back to us.

We ran into another shop. This one happened to be two stories tall. We took the stairs three at a time. We exited to the roof, and found four archers firing away under a flash of lightning.

Wayne and I ran to their side. He pulled his twin axes and chopped at the grappling hooks already thrown onto the edge of the roof. I looked out into a sea of houses that hadn't yet been burned to the ground. When the lightning flashed again, I saw the forces of Morgana charging at us. They ran between the homes in a random pattern, but eventually they all had to cross a wide empty street in order to reach the back of the wall of shops.

That was where the four archers were picking them off.

Sadly, we were grossly outnumbered, the rain was fierce, the land was dark, and the lightning wasn't flashing nearly enough. More and more grappling hooks flew to the rooftops. Wayne did his best to cut them away, but he wasn't able to reach the other roofs.

I ran to the edge over looking Town Square.

"Send a few fighters with swords to the top of every roof!" I shouted. "Send them now!"

The situation was infuriating. I hadn't planned on any rooftop attacks. I was frustrated and pissed. How the hell could I predict what Sir Francis would send our way? His army grossly outnumbered ours. All we could hope for would be to find the strength to deal with whatever came forward.

I watched groups of men and women wielding swords emerge from the park where they had been waiting behind the archers. A few Death Reapers had already made it over the roofs and were dropping down into the Town Square when they were confronted by our fighters.

Small fights began to break out on the streets. The archers were alternating between shooting down the advancing enemy and cutting through the grappling hooks that ended up on their rooftop.

Things were looking bleak, and they only grew bleaker still when the archers all the way across the Town Square also began to call for help. We were being attacked on three sides, and our archers were spread out too thinly to keep the Death Reapers out.

Then Bedder began shouting orders from below me on the street. Our fighters rallied together, defeated those who had already breeched our walls, and spread out amongst all the shops in the great square to defend the rooftops. That left only archers in the park, but it was a necessary decision.

When our fighters reached the rooftops, more fights broke out as they sought to protect the archers. They were outnumbered as well, but they fought with a passion. They fought for their friends. They fought for their lives.

Inside another thirty minutes, the rooftops were ours once again. Yet, the Death Reapers were far from finished. They soon began coming at us from all directions. Our archers would pick off as many as they could, and our fighters would attack any that made it to the roof.

Our system was working . . . barely, but it was working. Because despite their numbers, they still had to scale the brick walls of the shops, and we were able to strike them down almost instantly once an arm or head appeared. We were also able to cut their ropes, and watch them fall to the ground only to get picked off by an archer.

I allowed myself a small smile.

That's when the flaming arrows flew through the night, and put a real damper on my good mood. They would land on the rooftops, and create a small fire that seemed untouchable by the rain. After enough fires broke out, and we were all illuminated enough to make easy targets came the arrows untouched by flame.

Both archers and fighters began cry out in pain after being struck by arrows. I called for help, and help came. They moved the wounded off the rooftops in cloth stretchers with poles, and ran them to Dr. Talbert, Dellia and the others.

Shields were placed in front of the archers, but the shields were an inconvenience as they attempted to fire their bows, and with the exception of a few pipes, and possibly an old air conditioner box, cover was in short supply on the rooftops.

An arrow flew at me, and I plucked it from the air and cast it aside angrily. More and more Death Reapers charged against our walls. An arrow flew towards Wayne as he was furiously hacking against a rope and grappling hook that had been thrown over the edge of our rooftop.

I snatched it mere inches from his face.

"Son of a bitch," Wayne said. "I never even saw it until you grabbed it."

"That's because you're not as cool as me," I muttered.

I turned away and looked out over the scene. We were losing. Inch by inch our enemy got closer and closer. They inflicted more and more damage. We wouldn't survive the night at the pace we were going.

We needed to fall back to the park. From the edges of the forest our archers could inflict damage. When they enemy came into the forest, our fighters could strike them down, but before we retreated to the park, we needed to move the wounded out of the doctors' office. Otherwise they would be sitting ducks just waiting for an enemy soldier to walk in and begin hacking them to pieces.

I went to the side of the roof, and called Dellia's name once, twice, on the third call she ran out of the doctors' office and entered the street.

"Merlin!" She called back to me. "I'm here."

"Move the injured to the park!" I shouted.

"I can't do that," Dellia replied. "Some of them are in too bad a shape."

"Dellia," I said as calmly as I could. "We don't have a choice. We need to get off the rooftops."

Dellia nodded in understanding, and ran back inside.

People were looking at me. They wanted off the rooftops. Staying up here meant death, but I needed them to stay just a little bit longer.

"Be brave!" I shouted. "We must move our wounded first. Be brave just a little bit longer."

They did as I asked. Against all odds, the people stayed. I could only guess as to what their thoughts were, but they stayed and they fought, and some of them died.

I watched as homemade stretcher after homemade stretcher was carried into the park. Too many of us were wounded; too many of us were dying on the rooftops.

I decided it was time to act.

I walked to the edge of the shop, and focused my will. I whispered a few words to add to the spell I had already cast. Then I pushed my mind deep into the angry sky overhead, and took control.

The largest lightning bolt yet seared through the sky, and I alone directed its course. As it battered forth, I reached out my arms, and clenched my hands. Instead of cracking across the sky, I brought it to the street and introduced it to the advancing Death Reapers.

Enemy after enemy was burnt to a cinder . . . electrified on the spot, as the bolt arced along the street below us.

For a moment, the battle ceased entirely, and smoke from the corpses drifted to the heavens despite the pounding rain.

Another lightning bolt broke out from the clouds, I claimed it as well. This bolt I sent to the homes. In a wave of destruction, I used the bolt to tear down all of our enemies' cover. I wanted to leave them with nothing but terror. How dare they use our own homes against us? How dare they hide in the same places we raised our children?

The lightning bolt would burst through an outside wall, scatter inside, igniting everything in its path, only to emerge from another wall and enter another house. I hated doing it. I hated causing all the damage I was causing, but it needed to be done.

One after another, the homes began to collapse upon themselves. The attackers inside of them were crushed instantly. I kept on. I gave them no refuge. Let them attack us in the open. Let them show their bravery.

"Merlin!" Wayne shouted against the booming thunder after what seemed like hours. "It's done. The wounded have all been moved. Let's go!"

I released the sky from my grip, and fell to the ground.

Wayne was lifting me as I looked around.

Most of the rooftops on our side of the town square were empty. Only a few of our fighters remained. I had done my job. Now I needed to regain my strength.

I was in and out as Wayne impatiently broke through the rooftop door. Brief flashes of a dark stairway greeted me whenever I opened my eyes. It was a momentary break from the rain . . . a welcome break. Another broken door and we reintroduced ourselves to the rain. I could hear his boots pounding on the street. Then came the scent of the park. The forest smelled clean and refreshing.

"Put him here," someone said. "Keep him out of the rain."

Wayne set me down gently, and moved away.

I heard the sound of rain hitting leaves and branches. Occasionally, a drop would break through the natural barrier, and land on my neck.

I tried to speak, but only moaned.

Somewhere in the back of my cloudy mind I told myself that I'd really overdone it. The self-chastising should have been funny, but I lacked the energy to laugh.

I slept for awhile.

The sound of Bedder's voice awakened me. He was organizing. He was leading. Good for him, these people needed a leader, but he seemed to enjoy it a little bit too much. The man made me uncomfortable. I wasn't sure if I trusted him or not.

The sound of twanging bow strings informed me that the Death Reapers were flooding into the town square. Were they attacking from all sides now? They certainly had the manpower for that sort of thing.

I tried to open my eyes.

They fought valiantly against me, but eventually succumbed to my will. The first person I saw was Betsy, the deputy. She had been injured. Dellia was trying to stop her bleeding while Martin, the other deputy, was holding her hand.

I had forgotten all about those two. They stuck by Bedder during the battles, which kept them on the opposite side of the town from me. I had originally wanted to spread the deputies out, but neither of them was of significant leadership quality despite, their loyalty.

I sat up as the screams of dying men echoed throughout the park. Betsy was dying. I could tell that from the moment I had a better angle on her wounds. Dellia was screaming at her to hold on as tried frantically to staunch the flow of blood pouring from a stab wound under her arm.

The poor girl was in an extreme amount of pain, and she tried her best to be brave even though she knew her time was at an end.

"Dellia," I said.

"Shut up, Merlin," she answered.

"Let her go," I said. "You can't save her, and you're causing her undue pain."

"I can save her," Dellia said.

"You can't," I said.

Poor Martin cast his gaze between the two of us as we argued. At that moment I realized what he himself may not have even known. Martin was in love with Betsy.

Betsy turned her head towards me as Dellia worked even harder. I saw the pain and fear in her eyes and my heart shattered into a thousand pieces. Next she turned her head towards Dellia, and placed her small, pale hand upon Dellia's arm.

"No more," Betsy said in a quiet voice.

Dellia stopped.

"I can do it," Dellia said. "I can stop the bleeding."

"No more," Betsy repeated.

"I can . . . I can," Dellia stammered. "I can't . . . give up on you."

Betsy died.

I felt her soul exit her body and leave our world. Martin fell over her lifeless body and cried. Dellia fell backwards from her knee's, and silently watched him mourn. There was a look of pure anguish etched across her features.

I stood up. It wasn't easy, my legs were still shaky and my head swam, but I managed the task. The first thing I did was walk over to Martin, and whisper in his ear. He stopped crying, looked me in the face, smiled the saddest smile I've ever seen, and held tightly to Betsy's hand.

"Dellia," I said while offering her my hand. "Let me help you stand."

Reluctantly, she took my hand and I helped her to her feet.

All around us were the wounded. Tarps had been hoisted into the trees while I slept, in an effort to keep the rain off of the injured. Our improvised medical staff was doing their very best to help everyone, but their simply wasn't enough help to go around.

"Do you remember what I told you?" I asked Dellia.

She looked at me with eyes full of tears, and studied my face. I knew what she was searching for. She was attempting to find humanity in my youthful features. What she didn't know, was that I had seen death in all its many forms. I had seen it so many times, I simply accepted it, but that certainly didn't mean I was unaffected. I was never unaffected. I was merely useful.

"Do you remember what I told you?" I repeated.

"Yes," Dellia whispered.

"Tell me," I said.

"Keep them alive if I can," Dellia said. "Don't hate myself if I can't. The forces of Morgana took their lives, not me."

"Now look around you," I said.

Dellia looked around at all the wounded, crying out for help. Hopelessness took the place of anguish on her features.

"They need you," I said. "All of them . . . they need you."

"There's so many," Dellia whispered.

"And you won't be able to save them all," I said. "But you'll save as many as you can."

She pulled her hand from me and slowly walked away. At first it seemed as if she was aimless and lost, but a wounded teenager reached out for her as she passed by, and Dellia dove into action.

The twanging sound of bowstrings gave way to the sounds of metal against metal. We were losing ground, and our enemy was taking it swiftly.

I made my way to the sound of the battle ever curious as to why I only heard it coming from one direction.

The green fog was everywhere as I moved through the trees. Down at my feet I saw the still twitching body of one of our attackers. I moved by him hoping that I'd see more.

A sword swung at my neck, I grabbed a hold of the blade stopping it immediately, pulled it forward, twisted it out of the Death Reaper's hand, and then hacked him to death with his own weapon. Fortunately for me, I didn't cut very easily.

Other Death Reapers swarmed at me through the trees. I twisted their necks, stole their swords, and killed them all. My body was tired. My magic had been overused. I needed to get physical even though I detested physical combat.

One after another I brought them down around me, and as I did so, I pushed my way forward. Where were my people? Had they already been defeated?

I had almost reached Main Street when I finally found everyone. We were in luck; the Death Reapers that had attacked me were the ones that somehow managed to slip by the line of citizens that fought so hard to keep them from gaining entry into the forest of the park.

I stayed behind them, and picked off any others that got through our defenses. Many of the archers had been slain. Those that were still among the living were firing their bows quickly and at close range.

There would be no giving up. The idea of surrendering never crossed their minds. Surrendering meant death. Our enemy had no mercy.

I bumped into Bedder.

His sword was dripping blood.

Wayne was right behind him.

"Why are they only attacking on this side of the park?" I asked as the three of us hacked and slashed.

"I have no clue," Wayne answered. "But it's better for us. We'd all be dead already if they surrounded the park."

"Let's give them a show of power," I said. "Make them think twice about entering the park."

"What do you have in mind?" Bedder asked.

I looked around. Some of our people had shields. Some of them did not, but many of the fallen Death Reapers carried shields, and their corpses were ripe for the picking.

"Pick up shields!" I shouted. "Back away and pick up shields!"

It took time for all of our fighters to grab a shield, but eventually they'd all complied, especially after Wayne marched up and down the line shouting the command.

"Archers!" I shouted. "Fall behind the shields, and stay close."

That took much less time. The archers didn't want to be on the front line. They shouldn't have even been anywhere near the front line.

When all of them were ready, I gave another command.

"Push forward!" I shouted.

At first only a few of them gained ground, but the others kept trying. Soon they were pushing, heaving, stabbing, and moving the invaders away from the park.

This was good. I wanted to see the street. It was too odd that we hadn't been surrounded. What was coming?

Five minutes of pushing and the invaders were out. I had no belief that we'd be able to keep them out long, however, in no time at all; they'd rally their forces and push back. We'd only gotten as far as we'd gotten because we'd caught them by surprise.

There was nothing unusual on Main Street with the exception of Morgana's forces climbing down the walls of the shops like an army of ants.

What was I missing?

I looked to my left. There was the entrance to the Town Square, and the barrier of cars. Some of the archers were still at their posts on top of the buildings on either side . . . the others had probably been killed.

That's when I saw a small group of Death Reapers enter their buildings. I tried to shout out a warning, but the archers couldn't hear me over the cracking thunder. What was so important about this street and those buildings?

Something was coming.

Sir Francis wanted the street cleared, and he wanted the two buildings cleared of archers. I felt the panic rise up in my gut. I saw the danger zone, and I could do nothing to prevent it.

Should I pull everyone back into the park? No, that wouldn't work. We had wounded in the park. No other options presented themselves, so I decided to make our final stand right where we were standing.

I kept looking towards the archers on the two buildings as I fought. That's the only reason I saw them waving their arms frantically. I never heard them, but I saw them. I tried once again to shout out a warning. They never heard me, and I almost took a sword in my gut for the effort.

Shortly after my final warning shout, the Death Reapers that invaded the buildings made their way to the roof top, and massacred the archers.

"Something's coming," I said to Wayne and Bedder.

"What?" Wayne asked.

"I don't know," I admitted. "But it's going to be bad."

Seconds later, everyone heard the loud boom. It echoed throughout the land. We could hear it between the thunder cracks. Heads turned to the barrier of cars. I yelled at them to focus their energies on the enemies in front of us.

Again came the boom. The barrier of cars shook. The top car fell off the pile and landed on the street in a sound that was completely lost beneath a crack of thunder, but all of us felt the vibrations.

I knew what was happening.

The Death Reapers we were currently fighting were only here to weaken us and pave the way for the real attack, and the real attack was now beating upon our door. Knowing what was happening, and having a solution are regrettably two different things.

"Keep fighting!" I shouted. "Give them everything you have!"

"What the hell is that?" Bedder asked.

"The end," I said.

"How is your magic?" Bedder asked.

"I'm running on empty," I said. "Controlling the lightning took too much out of me.

"We can concentrate our archers on whatever comes through that barrier," Wayne added in a stroke of intelligence I didn't know he possessed.

"Good idea," I said. "See that it gets done."

Another boom vibrated across the earth. I thought I heard it over the thunder, but I couldn't be sure. My heart was hammering inside my chest. I wiped my bangs from my eyes wondering if the wetness on my forehead was sweat or rain . . . probably it was a mixture of both.

Where were my reinforcements? How could she not come? She should have been the first to arrive? Where was Arthur? Could even he make a difference in this lopsided battle?

How could I have been so wrong?

Another boom, this one everyone heard, and the barrier of cars collapsed as the skull faced battering ram pushed its way through.

There were small fires burning in the skull's eyes, giving it an appearance of a monster straight from the pits of Hell. But it was made of wood and stone, and pushed forward on wheels powered by Death Reapers.

The cacophony of noise from the falling cars was buried under another crack of thunder. The skull head was withdrawn.

Moments later, hundreds of Death Reapers began to flood into the town square. Luckily for us, our archers were there to meet them. They fell by the dozens as lightning lit up the land. I even conjured a tiny bit of magic to light the street lamps so the archers would easily be able to find their targets.

The simple act of lighting the oil streetlamps almost made me pass out. If it wasn't for Wayne, I'd have gotten killed. Why couldn't someone else come to my aid in my time of need? If we survived the night, which was extremely doubtful, Wayne would be hell to live with.

As it was, I merely watched stupidly as he hacked away at any Death Reaper foolish enough to get near me. I had to give it to him, the man could fight. He twirled and struck, ducked low, and came up high. Many of the invaders lost their lives due to his twirling battle axes.

The Death Reapers flooding into the square that happened to make it past our archers joined together with those we were pushing against. Their added numbers made us lose ground rapidly. Our fighters started to fall. Everything was coming to an abrupt end . . . and then, Sir Francis, the Black Knight himself, rode his mighty white steed into the town square.

The Death Reapers came to an abrupt stop. Our fighters didn't push the issue. They were tired and injured. They welcomed the break. They needed the break.

Sir Francis rode his evil steed down the empty street. His soldiers backed away from him as if he alone commanded the road. I looked to Wayne. I looked to Bedder. Both of them were at a loss.

I walked to the middle of the street, and stood in front of him and his stupid horse.

"Merlin," Sir Francis hissed, realizing it was me immediately.

"Francis," I replied.

"Where is he?" Sir Francis asked.

"Where is who?" I asked in return.

"Don't play the idiot with me," Sir Francis growled. "My men tell me that he may not be here? Is that true? Where is Arthur? Where is the future king?"

I should have known something was up. I really should have, but I was tired. I was so damn tired. My magic was weak, I hadn't slept, and I was exhausted. That's why it didn't register when everyone including all the Death Reapers turned and looked behind me.

So what happened really took me by surprise.

"I'm here!" Arthur said in a loud voice from behind me.

I turned just like everyone else, and saw him ride slowly up the street atop the great horse, Goliath. He was drenched to the bone, but still looked regal and handsome. Goliath was making loud noises at Sir Francis's white steed as he walked forward. I recognized the sounds as a challenge. Sir Francis's steed, though smaller responded with his own angry noises.

Excalibur hung from Goliaths saddle. It was beautiful to behold. Even more shocking . . . Arthur had the scabbard as well.

"I've been waiting for you," Sir Francis said. "Have you prepared yourself?"

"Come and find out?" Arthur said as he approached.

Arthur held a different sword in his right hand. He was challenging the greatest warrior in the land, and he doing it without Excalibur.

Sir Francis drew his sword as Arthur approached him. Arthur brought his low and to the side. The horses bit at each other, and eventually Sir Francis's steed began to back away. Goliath was backing him down, establishing his dominance and superiority.

Sir Francis twirled his blade. I saw his legs move in an effort to spur his horse forward, and I ran to Arthur's side. I lacked power, but Sir Francis didn't know that, so I ignited my hands and curled my lip.

Sir Francis wasn't impressed, I could sense his urge to attack . . . but the greatest shock of all came when Sir Francis froze solid, and looked past Arthur and myself before turning to see how many of his Death Reapers were there to support him.

"This isn't over," Sir Francis growled before abruptly yanking his horse to the side, and galloping out of the town square. His fellow invaders immediately followed him, and I stood there like an idiot wondering why.

Until I realized that something else had crept up behind me, and turned around once more.

The Gods of the Forest were slinking down Main Street behind Arthur. Their lips were curled back baring their teeth. They were ready for battle. They wanted a fight. They craved the blood.

I smiled at the greatest of them all.

He smiled back as the last of the Death Reapers retreated through the entry way, and rushed towards me. Wayne tried to stand in front of me in an effort to block his path, but I gently patted him aside. Father Wolf came at me, stood on his hind legs, and embraced me.

"My old friend," I said. "I can't tell you how very happy I am to see you in this day and age."

"The future king released us," Father Wolf said.

"Yes," I said. "He's released magic back into the land."

"He needed our help," Father Wolf said. "Too many Death Reapers were running him down. So I gave him our protection."

"You did well, my friend," I said. "I thank you for your aid."

"Perhaps we should now..." Father Wolf said before I tuned him out entirely.

Something had just occurred to me.

Excalibur.

The great sword.

It was beautiful.

It must have tasted blood. Only blood could have restored the sword, and that meant Arthur had used the magic blade. I walked abruptly away from Father Wolf, and the fifty or so gathering Gods of the Forest. I moved closer to Arthur. He was dismounting Goliath, and our surviving fighters and archers were gathering around him.

This was Arthur's moment to shine. The people were ready to be led. Of course, Arthur fucked it up.

"I need a drink," Arthur said. "Where's Shakey?"

"I'm here!" Shakey called out from the back of the crowd. "What can I get you?"

"Whiskey," Arthur said as he followed Shakey into the tavern not twenty feet from where they were standing, leaving the crowd speechless and me embarrassed.

"He's not quite the king you were hoping for," Father Wolf stated.

"No," I said. "He isn't, but I have hopes for his future."

"That young man is damaged," Father Wolf said. "Before you thrust greatness upon him, you must first heal what has been broken."

"I expect that to happen sooner rather than later," I smiled.

Father Wolf was shocked.

"Does she come this way?" He asked.

"How could she not?" I answered.

Father Wolf smiled, and it was a frightening sight.

"I must look upon her again," Father Wolf said. "A beauty such as hers is not often seen."

"Stay as long as you'd like," I said. "But have a care as to who you eat."

Father Wolf laughed at my joke, but I didn't. The Gods of the Forest were not the most stable of allies. They also weren't gods in the strictest sense, but they did protect the forest, and in days long forgotten, men would worship them, and pay them proper homage before crossing into their territory.

The townspeople stood around looking confused and muttering to themselves. A few of them were eyeing our new allies warily.

"There will be another assault!" I shouted. "We've only set them back momentarily. Grab food, and rest awhile. Put some guards on top of the buildings so we aren't taken by surprise."

I set off after Arthur, and Wayne followed closely behind.

As I stepped into Shakey's tavern, my senses were assaulted by the smell of blood. Three of our wounded enemies had crawled in the large barroom and bled to death. Shakey was lighting lanterns, and keeping himself busy as Arthur drank alone at his bar.

"Arthur," I said. "We need to talk."

Arthur looked over towards, and as he did so, I caught a flash of movement out of the corner of my eye. Lancelot was also in the tavern. Good for him.

"Be a good kid, and fetch Sheriff Tagger for me," Arthur said.

"I can't do that," I said.

"I don't care how busy he is," Arthur added. "Just go get him."

"Sheriff Tagger is dead," Wayne said. "So is Betsy."

Arthur looked towards the two of us without expression, before turning back to his drink and downing it in one gulp.

"Why don't you find my grandpa and my mother then," Arthur said. "This is a battle we aren't going to win. I wanna get the fuck out of here."

"Arthur," I said. "I need you to listen."

Arthur turned to us once more. This time there was real concern in his features.

"My mother?" Arthur asked.

"She's fine," Wayne answered impatiently. "So is your grandpa."

Arthur's look of worry turned rapidly to disgust at having been worried.

"Then go get them," Arthur said. "What the hell, Wayne. You scared the shit out of me."

"Arthur listen to me," I tried again.

"Listen kid!" Arthur yelled before gaining control over his emotions. "Just shut up, and do what I say. I don't want to have a chat. I don't want to get to know you. I just want to see my mom and my grandpa."

"He is your grandpa," Wayne blurted out.

Arthur, on the verge of going into another rant, halted abruptly. He looked me over from head to toe, and shook his head in disbelief.

"Is that you?" Arthur asked.

"Yes," I answered.

"You look like a nerdy teenager," Arthur said.

"I overdid things a bit," I said. "I'll grow out of it . . . eventually."

"It'll be hard to call you Grandpa Merl from now on," Arthur said.

"Feel free to call me Merlin," I said.

Shakey poured Arthur another drink, and I waited patiently as he sipped and shook his head.

"We need to leave," Arthur said eventually.

"We'll never get past our enemy," I said. "There are too many of them, and too many of us are wounded."

"We'll all die if we stay here," Arthur said. "We need to cut our losses, and make a run for it. I made it through them to get in here. It wouldn't be too hard to sneak out a small group."

"You would abandon the people of your town?" I asked.

"What the hell have they ever done for me? Arthur asked. "Wayne, you could bring your family. The Gods of the Forest will keep us safe long enough for us to escape."

"Arthur," Wayne said. "You have no idea how many people we've already lost, and everyone else will die without us."

"Everyone will die with you," Arthur retorted. "The Death Reapers are animals. They kill everything they can kill, and there's way too many of them to fight, but we can lose them in the forest."

"Death Reapers?" I asked. "You spoke to them?"

"Not really," Arthur said. "One of them just had a big mouth after I nailed him."

"Nice," Wayne said.

"Shut up, Wayne," I grumbled. "Now Arthur, listen to me. This town needs you. They need you to be king. You can't simply run away."

"Watch me," Arthur said. "I'm not playing this game anymore. Do you know how many times I almost got killed going after that stupid sword? This isn't my fight. The people here don't care about me. I intend to take what's mine, and leave. If you two want to stay . . . well, I can't stop you, but I'm getting my mom out of here."

"Your mother won't leave," I said.

"The hell she won't!" Arthur shouted.

"And you're wrong," I said. "This is indeed your fight. The Death Reapers are here because of you. It's you they want."

Arthur considered my words.

"Tough shit," He said after a bit. "I don't give a rat's ass about this town or the people in it. Have you even looked outside the town square? This place is burning to the ground. That fire burns despite the rain. Come morning, the only thing left will be this stupid bar."

"Hey," Shakey said.

"Sorry, Shakey," Arthur said. "But you hear what I'm saying don't you? There's nothing left to defend. We need to run."

"It's not about defending anymore," Shakey said. "This is about survival. We can't make a run for it. Too many of us would be cut down. Too many wounded would be left behind. I know this town hasn't exactly been good to you since your wife died, but you haven't exactly been good to this town. It's a new world, Arthur. It's time to let go of the past, and do the right thing. I'm staying. These people need everyone they can get."

"Help is coming," Wayne said. "Merlin believes that. He sent out Tristan. Before things get too bad, we'll have reinforcements."

"You sent out one person?" Arthur asked.

"That's all we'll need," I said.

"Fuck that," Arthur said. "I'm leaving. I'm taking my mom. I'm not dying in this town for anyone."

"Arthur," came a voice from behind me.

Everyone turned to see Dellia standing in the doorway. Her eyes were full of tears at seeing her son alive and in one piece after all the recent death she'd seen. Martin was standing directly behind her. The usual smile that marked his features was gone forever.

Arthur got off his bar stool, and crossed the room to hug his mother. She cried out loud and brushed his wet hair away from his face.

"My boy," Dellia cried. "My sweet and beautiful boy, I was so worried. Where have you been?"

"Fighting," Arthur answered. "The Death Reapers were after me from almost the beginning. It was hell, but I made it back, and now we need to leave."

"But . . ." Dellia said.

"No buts," Arthur said. "We're leaving. A small group of us can make it out of here. It won't be a problem."

Dellia looked confused, so I came to her rescue.

"Arthur doesn't want to fight," I said. "He wants us to cut our losses and make a run for it. He's used the sword."

"You used, Excalibur?" Dellia asked.

"It was either that or die," Arthur said. "But don't worry; Merlin can have his stupid sword. I won't be touching it again."

"Why's that?" I asked.

"It has an ill effect on me," Arthur said while glaring daggers at me. "I brought it back for you, and now I don't want it anywhere near me. You'll find it on Goliath's saddle."

"No he won't," Wayne said.

"Well, that's where I left it," Arthur said.

"Then I guess it followed you," Wayne said in the same angry tone. "Look by the doorframe."

Sure enough, Excalibur had appeared next to Arthur. Arthur of course, didn't take that revelation very well at all. He backed away instantly, and headed back to his bar stool.

"Shakey," Arthur said. "Pour me another, would ya?"

"Sure thing," Shakey said becoming very nervous.

Without a doubt there was a slight chill in the air accompanying Excalibur's abrupt appearance.

"Did one of you bring the sword in here?" Arthur asked after downing another drink, and tapping his glass for a refill."

"We did not," I answered.

"So the sword is going to follow me around?" Arthur asked.

"Yes," I answered. "It's your sword. It will be there for you until the day you die."

"I don't want it," Arthur complained.

"That hardly matters," I said. "Excalibur wants you."

"What's the big deal?" Wayne asked before picking up the sword, and attempting to pull it from its sheath.

"Don't do that," I told Wayne. "That sword isn't meant to be drawn by you. It won't take kindly to your clumsy . . ."

Wayne screamed out and dropped Excalibur to the floor. He was waving his injured hand back and forth in an attempt to air out the injury. I could see the scorch mark on his leather glove.

"What the fuck?" Wayne asked. "It got all hot, and burned my freakin hand."

"It's not your sword," I said. "No one touches Excalibur but Arthur."

Arthur himself wasn't paying any attention to me. He was staring at the fallen sword which was standing straight up in the air, almost as if it were balancing on its tip.

"That's not exactly normal behavior from a sword," Shakey added to the discussion.

"It's possessed or something," Arthur said. "It speaks to me. It makes me act differently. I don't want it."

"Then it will follow you until you do want it," I said. "Excalibur has been twisted by time and separation, but you can still master the blade . . . you simply have to have the willpower."

"Good luck with that," Arthur said before downing another drink. "Mom, we need to go. This town is dead, and what's left of its inhabitants are dying. We need to leave."

"Why can't I get through to you?" I asked. "You are so much more than this."

"Lower your expectations," Arthur responded with a sneer.

"*They're coming!*"

All of us turned to the doorway. Everyone but Arthur and Lancelot ran out of the tavern. Bedder was organizing those of us still able to fight. I ran to his side.

"What's going on?" I asked.

Bedder looked to me, and turned his head in the direction of the entrance to the town square.

"It's all of them," Bedder said. "The whole fucking army . . . The Black Knight isn't taking any chances this time. We're all fucked."

My heart sank inside my chest.

Help had not arrived.

The end was so very near.

"How far away?" I asked.

"They're less than a mile out on Main Street," Bedder said.

The Gods of the Forest began to surround us.

"We owe your moody king," Father Wolf growled. "What can we do?"

"After they come through," I said. "Attack from the sides, weaken their resolve."

"The king won't be fighting?" Father Wolf asked noticing that Arthur had not left the tavern.

"No," I answered. "He'll be running. Dellia, Wayne . . . you will also stick next to Arthur."

"Wait a second," Wayne complained. "I'm needed here. I can fight."

"That's why you will be sticking next to Arthur," I said. "The world needs Arthur; it doesn't need the inhabitants of this town."

There it was . . . the truth. The looks everyone gave me told me their opinions. Too bad for everyone, that their opinions simply didn't matter. I wasn't only fighting for the town. I was fighting for the future of this world.

❧   GWEN   ❧

We travelled as fast as we could, which wasn't very fast with a group the size of ours. Tristan became quite agitated whenever we stopped moving.

Earlier on he wanted to leave our noncombatants behind and move forward with only the soldiers. His idea was sound, but I couldn't leave my people so far away from me. If something was to happen, and I was too far away . . . I'd never forgive myself.

I must admit though . . . he was making me nervous. The hope of the future was in my grasp. The one man that could end this Hell on earth, and it was taking too long to reach him. The journey was difficult, and we didn't have nearly enough horses or wagons for everyone.

Normally, all that wasn't much of a problem, we took our time when we travelled. It worked out well for us. Why hurry towards yet another battle? Let the people relax, and take their time. They'd need as much rest as possible for the future, because the future was always cold and violent.

Before the last leg of our journey, after we'd finally found a spot in which to safely deposit our noncombatants. We erected a temporary camp not far too from the town of Mill Ridge in a secluded area. It was the best option we were going to get in a crazy world.

My soldiers prepared for battle. They armed themselves, fed, and sharpened their swords. They also kissed their loved ones goodbye. We were riding into a situation we didn't fully understand. We were going to the aid of town under siege, based off the words of a young man I didn't know.

It felt right.

I knew it in my heart. Tristan was on the level. This wasn't a trick, this was destiny. I was nervous, of course I was nervous . . . but that didn't mean I would fail in my task.

Merlin, and the reborn king . . . I'd be there for them. If they could save this world, I'd follow them both.

We ran into trouble not long after leaving our noncombatants. It wasn't much, a few minor skirmishes, nothing to brag about really . . . but small groups of Death Reapers, no more than a hundred or so all together headed in the same direction we were headed.

Something was definitely going on.

Father, grant me the strength to aid Merlin and the reborn king. Allow me to be brave in battle. Allow me to lead my soldiers to victory. Help me do my part.

Those words circled inside my head over and over. Why was I so nervous? It wasn't the battle. I had seen many battles. It had to be Merlin and Arthur, something about meeting the two of them worried my terribly.

In the late-afternoon, the rains came.

Most of us were prepared for the rains. This area of the country rained all the time. We bundled up as best we could in an effort to keep dry. Tristan was without a cloak, I watched as Izzy shared his, and the two of them rode side by side.

With the last light of day, the rain grew in intensity. It pounded against us; as if it meant to keep us away . . . we pushed forward even harder. My army was strong, but I still had my worries. Even the best of them would get tired eventually. Mile after mile chipped away at our strength.

I was about to call for an hour long break when Tristan finally announced that we'd reached the end of our journey.

"Where's the town?" I asked.

"You'll see it as soon as we get around that last hill," Tristan answered and spurred his horse.

I followed him, Reynolds followed me, and the three of us rounded the hill and looked down into the beautiful valley below us. In the dark of night, the fires of the town stood out like beacons. Somehow, the flames raged despite the rain.

Camelot was indeed burning.

"No," Tristan whispered. "We're too late. I . . . I failed."

"What's that square area with the taller buildings?" Reynolds asked.

"That's just the town square," Tristan answered as Izzy slipped a comforting arm around him.

"Then we're not too late," Reynolds said. "It looks like the citizens have made that area their last refuge. I can see our enemy marching upon them as we speak."

I looked to where Reynolds was pointing, and though I couldn't make out individual shapes at our distance, I could still see a faintly glowing line of what were probably lanterns. It was a long, long line. The Death Reapers marched slowly, in no hurry. Their prey was trapped, and would be easily overcome.

"We need to close the distance," I said.

"They outnumber us greatly," Reynolds said.

"Ride and talk," I said and spurred my horse foreword.

Urgency spurred us onward. We had an impressive amount of horsemen, but most of my forces travelled by foot. It's a credit to them that despite their weariness, they rushed to the defense of those that needed defending.

"Those on horseback can arrive first," Reynolds said.

"Go on," I said.

"We divide our horses," Reynolds continued. "We put half our riders on the left side, and the other half on the right side of the marching Death Reapers. We then wait until a decent portion of them enter the town square before we attack. That way it'll be difficult for them to turn around and come back at us . . ."

"Because the people of Mill Ridge will be attacking all the Death Reapers that entered the town square," I interrupted, already liking the idea.

"Exactly," Reynolds said. "The townspeople attack them from the front. We attack the flanks, and our foot soldiers will move up directly behind them, and attack from the rear."

"They'll be caught by surprise twice," I smiled. "I think it'll work. Good job. We can bring them down before most of them know we're even among them."

Reynolds called a halt, and everyone came to a stop. After that he went over the plan. The horsemen would ride ahead, but would not attack until those on foot had arrived. The only worry I had with the plan was how long it would take the foot soldiers to arrive, but one look at all their determined faces told me that they'd be moving as fast as their legs could carry them.

Brief moments later, and we were riding hard towards the town of Mill Ridge.

Through the pounding rain, we made our way. We didn't slow down, and we certainly never stopped. We needed to be in position before the others attacked. Time was of the essence.

As we reached the outskirts of the town, we rode past a low stone wall, through an odd looking gate. Tristan had told us about that. He said it was called Stronghold Wall. He also said it was full of magic and kept the enemy from entering the town.

I guess the Death Reapers figured out a way around it.

I could see a light blue shimmer emanating from Stronghold Wall. The shimmer danced at the edges of my vision, and caused a strange tingle throughout my body as I rode through the gate.

The town may not have been large with inhabitants, but it was certainly large enough in acreage. Flat farmlands that offered no cover whatsoever spread out for miles, and if it weren't for the rain and the night our plan would have failed from the get go.

Because, even though the main portion of the Death Reapers forces were marching towards the town square, there were others of their kind about, guarding shabby little soldier camps in the fields. If they were there, there were probably others doing patrols.

We had to be stealthy.

Tristan drew a quick map in the mud, and Reynolds put the tip of his sword in the area he thought best to make our attack. I agreed with him, and our forces divided. As always, Reynolds stayed by my side. Tristan and Izzy led the other group.

The battle in the town square began as we were discussing our positions. We could hear the shouting, and yelling even from a distance. They were the normal sounds of battle, and I was used to hearing them. I was even used to hearing the screams and moans of the injured and dying. The roars and growls were something new entirely. Those sounds sent shivers up my spine.

Tristan was in a state as he left to make his way to his attack point. He wanted to rush in and help. It must have been horrible to hear those noises, and not be able to act, but acting now would be fruitless. Acting now would inflict only a momentary inconvenience to such a massive force. We needed to wait.

I led the way towards our attack point. I kept close to Stronghold Wall. Most of the little camps in the fields were near the road, so we were pretty far away. We could hear them though; they were laughing, and celebrating their eventual victory.

Eventually we came to the burning homes. There were some problems when we reached that area. Whether or not they were actual patrols, I couldn't say. To me they seemed like looters, but they were still dangerous. If they gave out a warning, we could have countless numbers of them attack us.

Reynolds and I rode about fifty or so yards ahead of the rest of my horsemen. When we encountered these looters, we'd watch them from a distance for awhile, making sure of their exact numbers.

They were normally in groups of three, but sometimes they had a wounded straggler tagging along with them. It didn't really matter, they weren't in large enough groups to stop us, and we picked them off from a distance with our bows.

In one area, I saw a large hole that had been dug under the fence.

"Do you think this is how they got in?" I asked.

"It must be," Reynolds answered. "The people here didn't have enough guards to cover the area. A good number of Death Reapers could gain access before they were ever discovered."

All around us were corpses. Some were Death Reapers. Others were the townspeople.

My heart sank.

"How many have been lost?" I asked. "How many are now holding back the tide that threatens to engulf them."

"We'll do everything we can, Milady," Reynolds said.

"Such horrible losses," I said. "If only we had gotten here sooner."

"Our moment will arrive very soon," Reynolds said.

Not far away, in a house that had been as of yet untouched by the fires, there was a gathering. Reynolds and I left our horses behind, and quietly made our way to one of the front windows. Inside was a group of twenty Death Reapers. They had found themselves a fully stocked bar, and were enjoying a brief respite from the rain.

They had trampled mud all over the once pristine looking carpet. They had broken shelves, and smashed holes in the walls. Their destructiveness caused my heart to blacken . . . especially when I saw a broken child's toy lying at the far end of the room.

Had the child and his parents been able to make it to the town square? Or were they already dead inside a backroom somewhere in the house.

215

"Gather ten of our men," I said. "Make sure they all have daggers. The long swords of our enemy will work against them in such tight quarters."

Reynolds reluctantly left me at the window, and went to gather the men. I sat at the side of the house behind a bush as I waited for him. I could hear the Death Reapers talking inside. They were talking about Arthur, and Merlin. From what I could hear, Arthur might not even be in the town. Their leader had sent forces after him . . . apparently it was a rather large force since the original group failed to return.

In no time at all, my soldiers had arrived. I sent six of them around the back, and I walked in through the front door. At first our enemies were startled at the intrusion. A lone girl stood before them in leather armor.

I watched as they clumsily rose to their feet. I glared as they drunkenly reached for their weapons.

"Wait a moment," one of them said. "Take a look at her. She's a beauty."

"That she is," another added. "I'll go first."

"The hell you will," another joined in. "You went first the last . . ."

I pulled an arrow from the quiver on my back, and notched it to my bow, but I didn't pull the string. I waited. I wanted to see their reaction.

Smiles and looks of excited anticipation fell away immediately. They were worried and wondering if they could rush me before I brought one of them down. At this distance, I could bring at least three of them down before they reached me, but they had no way of knowing that.

"Come on, beauty," one of them said. "Don't be that way."

"Surely we aren't so bad as death," another added.

"I'll be gentle," another joined in. "As long as you drop the bow."

"Come and take it from me," I said as I drew back the arrow, let it fly, and pierced the throat of the Death Reaper that told me to drop my bow.

The drunken fools went into action then, and I surprised myself by bringing not three but four of them down. Well, actually I cheated a bit. I had to kick the final Death Reaper backwards in order to create enough space to shoot the arrow that pierced his heart.

After that, my men rushed in behind me, and the others burst through the back door. I was right, the Death Reapers swords worked against them in the close confines of the house. The fight was over in seconds.

"That was foolish," Reynolds said. "What if they had an archer as well?"

"I would have shot him first," I said. "Now we need to get into position. I'm not sure how long the people of this town can hold out."

It turned out, that the townspeople were giving their attackers a pretty rough time. The enemy forces were pushing their way into the town square, but very, very slowly.

"Tight spaces," Reynolds said after we reached our position and watched the battle. "The entrance is only two car lengths wide, the vastness of their army will eventually overcome the townspeople, but for now . . . they're slowed down."

That's when I first saw the Black Knight.

He was an immense man on an equally immense and evil looking white horse. Even from a distance, I could hear him screaming at his soldiers. He ordered them to push harder. A death from the enemy would be far more merciful than a death from Morgana.

Tristan had told us what he knew about Morgana and the Black Knight. It wasn't much, but their names were familiar. He left out how frightening the Black Knight was . . . no words could describe the terror he caused. He was truly a living nightmare.

"Maybe we should send some arrows his way," Reynolds said. "I'd hate to be the one standing before that beast on a battlefield."

"Arrows might piss him off," I said.

"True," Reynolds said. "He's gonna be a bitch to bring down. That's for sure."

"I'll leave it to you," I said.

"How kind of you," Reynolds laughed. "It'll probably take thirty of us. Did you get a good look at his horse?"

"Yes," I answered. "That animal looks possessed."

"Well," Reynolds said. "I guess it'll go down just as easily as its rider after we put a few arrows in it."

We were quiet for a moment, both of us trying to see what we could of the battle. Neither of us could see much of anything though, the buildings and angle blocked our view. Behind us, both horses and riders waited impatiently.

"Do you think Tristan and the rest of our men are in position?" I asked after a bit.

"Yes," Reynolds answered without hesitation.

"You seem pretty convinced," I said.

"They would rather die than let you down," Reynolds said.

I sighed, and sat back against the side of the shop we were all hiding behind, and watched the massive army surge and press, yet gain no distance on the townspeople.

Something happened.

I'm not sure what it was, but the resistance began to weaken.

The Death Reapers began to move forward.

I jumped to my feet.

"Be calm," Reynolds said while gently grabbing my arm.

"Those people will be massacred if they can't stop them at the entrance," I argued.

"There's nothing we can do until the bulk of our army arrives," Reynolds said.

"They'll be here any minute," I said.

"I agree," Reynolds said. "But we need to wait until that moment."

"It may be too late," I said.

Reynolds blew out a lungful of air, and kicked a stone on the ground as he began to pace. Normally I listened to his advice. This wasn't going to be one of those times, and he knew it. He didn't like it, but he knew it.

Reynolds stopped his pacing and motioned for one of our men to bring up our horses.

"Alright, Milady," Reynolds said. "But you don't lead the charge."

"What?" I asked.

"You aren't great with a sword," Reynolds said. "Our enemy will close upon us rapidly. You'll be of more use on the outside with your arrows."

"I'll also be safer," I grumbled.

"An added bonus, Milady," Reynolds said. "I won't lead this charge if it endangers you needlessly. Out of all of us, you need to survive the most. I'm sure our men will agree."

I glared daggers into his soul, but his soul was immune to my temper tantrums. I had no choice but to agree knowing full well that if anything went wrong, I'd charge in anyway.

"Do what needs to be done," I said. "But do it quickly."

Both Reynolds and I mounted our horses. I watched as he drew his sword, and then listened to the endless sounds of steel sliding against leather as close to a hundred men and women all drew their weapons as well.

I raised my arm high in the air, and when I brought it down again . . . we were off.

There was an excitement coursing through my veins. It's hard to describe this particular brand of excitement because it only happens to me when I'm charging into battle with an army behind me.

It makes me feel powerful. It makes me feel invincible. The odds were stacked against us, but I wasn't worried. I knew the rest of my army would come. I also knew that Tristan and the other half of my horsemen would join in the minute we made contact with the enemy.

No doubts.

Our horses thundered down the old road. Shops flew by us, and our enemy grew closer and closer. With the exception of hooves on pavement, no sound was made.

Less than a block away, the great marching army of our enemy finally noticed our charge. They tapped at one another and shouted, but it was too late. They didn't have enough time to organize a defensive.

I screamed out a battle cry.

Reynolds joined me.

All of our men joined me, and the battle was on.

Our horses crashed against them, and their riders cut and slashed. We were a great sea of horse flesh and chain mail that wouldn't be denied. I veered off to the left at the last possible second, and shot out as many arrows as I could before circling back to make another run.

In the distance and on the opposite side of the road I saw the great knight in his black armor. He was charging his white horse towards our men. I felt my eyes narrow as I watched him, and I felt my heels tap against my steed, as I started riding in his direction.

I weaved in and out of my own horsemen, and when I was past their charge, I rode along the right-hand side of the marching Death Reapers.

They tried to grab me. They tried to cut at my horse and my legs, but by the time they realized I was there . . . I was already gone.

When the Black Knight was in range, I shot an arrow at him. My aim was true, but his armor was too tough. The arrow clanged harmlessly off in the distance.

I got his attention though. The Black Knight came to a sudden stop, and turned his head in my direction. I couldn't see his eyes, but I could feel his penetrating stare.

When I got closer, I also slowed to a stop, and we sized one another up. I suddenly felt very alone, and I was thankful that his massive army was between the two of us.

I managed to fire off one more arrow before a group of the Death Reapers broke free from their ranks and pursued me.

It was the first time since my father found me that I was happy to be retreating. The way that knight stared at me . . . it was like he knew me, and that sounds pretty ridiculous considering I couldn't see his face.

I rode back down the side of the road to where my horsemen were fighting. I fired off arrows whenever I saw one of them get into trouble. I did my best to keep the swarm of the enemy off of them. There were other archers on horseback as well, but they didn't ride and shoot like me. Instead, they stationed their horses away from the fighting and shot down what they could.

The number of Death Reapers we were facing was staggering. Up close and personal, they were fearsome and vicious. The green fog and glowing lanterns added to an already a horrible scene.

Tristan and the rest of my horsemen charged into the chaos.

I heard my men cheer as they joined the fight. Now there were also archers on the other side of the road. All of us would do our best to keep the fighters safe, but the battle was a great serpent that undulated and swirled. Targets were hard to find, and all too soon, the battle left the road. The fighting men and horses pushed against the shops on one side, and the un-burnt homes on the other.

The great marching army of Death Reapers was no longer marching. On that point we had already succeeded. Instead of continuing their push into the town square, almost half of our enemies might was forced to contend with the attacks on their flanks.

My riders were skilled; they kept constantly on the move. To stop for only a brief moment meant certain death. Our enemy could surround them in a second.

I looked for the Black Knight, and couldn't find him. For that at least, I was grateful . . . and then I saw the first of my men go down. I heard his horse scream out, as it suffered a multitude of strikes. I saw the animal rear up in defiance, and then nothing.

The horse and rider vanished underneath a great mob of red flashing blades.

Immediately afterwards, I saw another horse and rider go down. The element of surprise that caused us to look so impressive was gone. The Black Knight had his army back under control.

Without so much as a hint, the tide began to turn, and we began to lose.

I stowed my bow, and pulled the long sword that hung from my saddle. I wasn't good with a blade, but I was an excellent rider.

Gripping the sword in one hand, I charged into the swarming mob. My enemy fell beneath my trampling horse. Those that came to the right and left of me were fatally hacked by great sweeping swings that stung my wrist and echoed up my arm.

It was a stupid mistake.

Within moments, I felt their hands on my legs. I felt them pulling me down. Before the severity of my situation could even register, I was slammed hard on the pavement.

My sword was still in my hand. I swung it clumsily in an effort to create some distance, but rough hands grabbed at my arm. I felt a great wrenching on my wrist, and my sword was taken away.

I was held down. A dagger was raised above my heart, I noticed that the rusty blade was dripping with the blood of my men. I looked to the face of the man holding the weapon. He was smiling through his crooked and broken teeth.

"Do it!" I screamed.

His face went suddenly slack. Then his head rolled away from his shoulders and bounced off my belly. The cold hands holding my arms and legs were instantly gone. I stood up, and saw that Tristan was on foot, and battling them mightily.

"Gwen!" Reynolds shouted from not far away.

"I'm here!" I answered.

Tristan was a sight to see. The way he twirled his two blades, the way he cut through the impossible numbers . . . and then Reynolds was next to him, and the two of them were keeping me safe.

I saw my sword and crawled over in its direction. The weapon hadn't been flung very far, and soon it was in my hand, and I was back on my feet. Somewhere beyond the press of men, the green fog, the rain, and the shouting I heard a horse scream.

I tried my best to aid Reynolds and Tristan, but every time I stepped forward to swing at the Death Reapers, one of them would push me away.

"Let me help!" I demanded.

"Then stay alive," Reynolds said.

Soon we were surrounded. Reynolds and Tristan stood spaced out on either side of me, but the press of the mob forced them to slowly back up into me. It wasn't long before I could feel their chain mail scraping roughly against my arms.

A massive surge collided against both friend and foe. A collective push that knocked me off my feet onto the wet street, when I got back up I heard the cheers. I saw Reynolds laughing. I saw Tristan smiling.

The rain had stopped, and my foot soldiers had arrived.

They must have been tired. They must have been, but they cut and slashed their way through the heart of the battle, and joined us in the center.

I saw my horse across the street. By some miracle it was still alive.

"Go," Reynolds said after realizing what I was staring at. "Go now, you'll be safer on the horse."

I ran as fast as I could. I splashed through red stained puddles. A Death Reaper reached out for me as I ran, and I slid through the mud underneath his outstretched arms. He continued to chase after me. I could feel his sword cutting through the air as he swung at my legs.

He was gaining, and without a better option, I aimed the tip of the sword behind me, and placed the hilt under my left arm.

Then I dropped to my knees.

The momentum of my pursuer caused him to run himself through on my blade, and slam into me. I sprawled out on the ground, as the Death Reaper screamed in pain.

My forehead had hit a rock, and I could feel the blood flowing down my face from a cut right above my hairline. My vision was swimming. Sound vanished. I grabbed at the wound, fearing it was much worse than it actually was.

The bleeding was minor, but the pain was a living hell. That's when I noticed that the green fog wasn't as dense as it had been.

I climbed to my feet, swooned and fell back into the mud once again. My horse wasn't too far away. I willed it to come to me. If I could only get into the saddle, I could get back in the fight. The horse was unimpressed with my mental attempt at summoning it to my side.

I tried again. I don't know why, it just sort of felt like the right thing to do. My body instantly relaxed, my hands clenched and un-clenched in the mud, a tingling began at the base of my skull, and the horse shook its head, before walking towards to me.

As the tingling vanished, I lost what little energy I had left. My head dropped into the mud, it was all I could do just to turn my head a bit to breathe. I felt the horse nuzzle against my ear, and I tried to rise. I brief chill gripped my heart and I worried that I might have given myself a concussion, but not even that gave me the energy to rise.

My eyes closed. The sounds of the battle raging all around me became quieter and quieter. The last thing I noticed before passing out was that my horse was standing over me as if she meant to guard my defenseless body.

Time went by. I drifted on a cloud. The deepest sleep I'd ever experienced had overtaken me. Voices were calling my name. I recognized some of those voices. Slowly, I opened one eye.

My horse was still standing guard, but upon noticing that I was awake, she snorted once and wandered off a bit in search of some grass to eat.

The green fog was gone for the most part. Only wisps of it were left floating in the air. Bodies were being taken away on stretchers. The wounded were being tended to.

I missed the battle.

I was ashamed of myself.

My head hurt like a bitch.

The world seemed to have trouble stabilizing. I heard someone . . . maybe Reynolds call out my name. I wanted to answer, but I lacked the strength. I strained my entire body trying to remove myself from the sucking mud . . . no success.

A slim teenager appeared out of nowhere. He had black hair and was wearing only a t-shirt and a pair of jeans. He was talking to my horse.

"Where is she, sweet lady?" The teenager asked the horse as he placed his forehead against hers. "She's not far away is she? You can trust me. I'm her friend. I promise you."

The teenager turned his head in my direction.

"Are you sure?" He asked the horse.

I tried to raise my arm so that he could see me in the mud, but it was no use. I was too tired, and though my mind was relatively active, my body had not yet decided to join the party.

I tried my voice, and was shocked to hear the weak sound that came forth. Not far away I could hear still hear voices calling out my name.

The teenager moved closer to me. I managed to wiggle my fingers, and was positive that I caught his attention.

"There you are, Milady," he said as he knelt down next to me in the mud. "We've been looking . . . well, well, well . . . this is definitely unexpected."

I looked up at him. He was a handsome young man . . . slightly nerdy, but still handsome. I watched silently as he flicked his fingers and somehow made his hand glow blue. He then moved his glowing hand over my heart.

Tiny lightning bolts shot out of his hand, pierced my heart, and just like that . . . I once again had energy.

"What the fuck?" I asked.

The teenager laughed.

"What happened to me?" I asked.

"You used magic," the teenager said. "A fair bit of it as well. That horse of yours would have defended you with its life."

"I did what?" I asked.

"You used magic," the teenager answered. "It's always pretty tiring the first time. I think I slept for a week after I cast my first spell, but that was a long time ago. Forgive me; I didn't expect you to have the . . . talent. I'm a little caught off guard."

"Who are you?" I asked.

"I'm Merlin," the teenager answered. "And you are Guinevere."

"So I've heard," I replied. "Tristan asked me to help your town."

"Well," Merlin mused. "Wonders never cease. I'm shocked that Tristan was able to make the connection."

"Where's the Black Knight?" I asked.

"He's retreated along with his remaining Death Reapers," Merlin answered.

"We should fortify the town," I said. "They'll come back eventually. Perhaps it would be better to chase them down, and bring the fight to them."

"I think you should relax a bit," Merlin said. "You've been injured, and you also used magic. Fighting should be the furthest thing from your mind right now."

Reynolds, Tristan and a small band of my men ran up as I was climbing to me feet. My fingertips moved a lock of hair from my forehead, and brushed against the head wound causing me to wince.

"Is that you, Milady?" Reynolds asked.

"Am I that hard to recognize?" I asked.

"You're covered head to toe in mud," Tristan said.

I looked myself over as best I could.

"So it would seem," I said.

"Merlin," Reynolds said. "Can you do anything for her?"

"Certainly," Merlin said with an evil little smile.

He twisted his fingers together, and a small rain cloud manifested from thin air right above my head. I was almost impressed until the cloud started to rain, washing the mud away from my skin and clothes with ice cold water. After that I was just irritated.

"Now there's the beauty I remember," Merlin laughed.

"Merlin!" A voice shouted out from somewhere above us.

Merlin's laughter stopped immediately.

"Where is he?" Merlin asked.

"He's at the gymnasium," the voice answered. "He's been wounded. I had to leave him when I saw how many there were."

Merlin's face changed into something rather scary.

"Grab your horses," Merlin ordered everyone. "This isn't over yet."

✤ WAYNE ✤

The end was near.

The final bell had been rung. The Death Reapers were coming . . . all of them. There would be no escape, only a battle. I worried about my wife and children. I worried about all the children. So far they were all safe. The high school had not been touched, but how long would it be after the last of our defenses fell before our enemy went looking for all the folks that couldn't fight?

To make matters worse, Merlin didn't want me to help in the battle. He wanted me to babysit Arthur.

"Wait a second," I tried to argue. "I'm needed here. I can fight."

"That's why you will be sticking next to Arthur," Merlin countered. "The world needs Arthur; it doesn't need the inhabitants of this town."

I let Merlin's words sink in, and then decided that I hated them. Arthur may be some kind of hero, but he wasn't exactly ready to step up to the plate yet. I had a wife and kids. To me, they were just as important as Arthur.

I opened my mouth to argue.

"Wayne," Merlin interrupted before I could form a single syllable. "Your wife and children will have no future if Arthur falls . . . and Dellia, I know you don't want to abandon those under your care, but Arthur won't leave without you. You must go."

"It's not that I don't trust you Merlin," I said. "But I'm sorry . . . I won't run without my wife and children."

Merlin's face darkened . . . before lightening abruptly as an idea formed in his mind.

"Take Arthur," Merlin said. "Gather your family, and keep all of them safe. Lancelot will accompany you. You'll find him extremely helpful."

That one caught me off guard. Nobody had seen Lance since the beginning of this nightmare. I looked all over for him, but when that kid wanted to hide . . . nobody was going to find him.

"Nobody can find Lance," I said.

"I sent him after Arthur," Merlin said.

"You didn't," Dellia complained. "Merlin, how could you? He's just a boy."

"We all have our parts to play," Merlin said. "Now go. Get Arthur out of here."

"But what about Lance?" Dellia asked. "I haven't seen him. Are you sure he made it back?"

"He's been right next to Arthur this entire time," Merlin said. "Now enough questions . . . get going."

Dellia gently grabbed me by the arm, and led me back inside the tavern. Arthur was pretty drunk at this point. Hopefully he wouldn't be useless in a fight, because Arthur was incredible with a sword.

"Alright Arthur," I said. "You win."

"Yay," Arthur laughed. "What'd I win?"

"We're leaving," I said.

Arthur looked at me.

"We're leaving town?" He asked suspiciously.

"Yes," I answered.

"I'm not leaving without my mom," Arthur said.

"I'm leaving as well," Dellia said.

Arthur smiled, downed the last of his drink, and stood up clumsily from the stool.

"It's about time," Arthur said. "Let's get the hell out of here."

"That's the plan," I said. "But first we need to grab my family."

Arthur considered my family his family. He gave no arguments whatsoever. He merely asked where they were, and nodded his head in agreement when I told him.

"What about my . . . geez . . . I can't even call that kid my grandpa anymore," Arthur said. "What about Merlin? Is he coming?"

"No," Dellia answered. "Merlin will be leading the battle."

Arthur looked extremely unhappy at that bit of news, but he expected it. I watched as he opened his mouth to say something, thought better of it, opened it again, and shook his head.

"Fuck it," Arthur finally uttered. "Let's get out of this town."

"What about you, Shakey?" I asked as we headed to the door.

"You folks go on without me," Shakey said. "I was born in this town. I don't plan on ever leaving."

Arthur and I nodded to him, and stepped out into the rain. I heard a soft rustling sound come out the door immediately after me. I turned to look thinking Shakey had changed his mind, but he wasn't there. I saw a blur of movement going up the wall to my side.

"They're getting closer," Merlin said. "Don't use the horses. You'll need to sneak out of town. If they see you leave, they'll chase you to the ends of the earth. Now go!"

None of us had to be told twice, we raced down the street as our remaining townspeople readied themselves at the entrance of the town square. Arthur kept looking back to his Grandfather. He hated leaving him, but he certainly didn't hate leaving Mill Ridge.

Rounding the corner, we came upon Bedder who was making his way towards the entrance. Bedder sneered at Arthur. Arthur ignored Bedder.

"I told Merlin not to have faith in you," Bedder said.

"Looks like you were right," Arthur said.

I was truly shocked when Arthur didn't take a swing at the man. Maybe it was the small pitchfork on his left arm that replaced his prosthetic hand. I doubted it though, Arthur wasn't a coward. He just wasn't invested in the town or the people living here.

We ran to the small alleyway. Dellia was already getting tired. The poor woman hadn't slept, and probably hadn't eaten. Arthur placed his arm around her shoulders.

"Maybe we should take some horses," Arthur said.

"Merlin said not to," Dellia said.

"Mom," Arthur argued. "Merlin isn't going to survive this battle. Nobody here is going to survive this battle."

"Son," Dellia smiled. "Never bet against Merlin. I've known him a long time. He's never led me astray. Have faith in him."

"Let's go," I interrupted as we passed a couple of guards and entered the alley.

Again, I saw a blur of movement through the rain. Something seemed to be climbing down the wall. I froze, but whenever I looked for it, I lost it.

"What's wrong?" Arthur asked.

"I keep seeing something," I said.

"A movement?" Arthur asked.

"Yes," I answered. "But as soon as I see it . . . it's gone again."

"You'll get used to it," Arthur said. "Let's keep moving."

I had one thought . . . Lance. I didn't say anything, there wasn't time, but I had suspicions. Merlin mentioned Lance earlier. He said something about him being with us ever since Arthur came back . . . but I never saw him. Could it be?

Outside the alley, the land was open and wide. Flat farmland was all we saw. The Death Reapers wouldn't be able to catch us unawares in this area, but a few miles off to the right, and the farmland gave way to the forest. The forest made me nervous.

"To bad you don't want that sword," I mentioned to Arthur as we made our way towards the forest with wide, ever-alert eyes.

"You don't want to know what that sword did to me," Arthur said.

"To bad it didn't make you a badass," I laughed quietly. "You've always been a bit of a pussy."

"You have no idea," Arthur said with the strangest look on his face.

"Do you think the Black Knight could pick it up?" I asked.

"No," Arthur answered.

"Why not?" I said. "He's all armored up."

"Because the sword is following me," Arthur said. "It's waiting until I'm weak. When I'm weak, it'll call to me."

"It's following you?" I asked. "Have you seen it outside the tavern?"

"Yes," Arthur said.

"Where?" I asked.

"It was in the alleyway," Arthur answered.

"Shut up," I said with a laugh.

"It's not funny," Arthur said sluggishly.

"It's kinda funny," I argued.

He responded by slapping me upside the head, and I heard a giggle from somewhere out in the empty field. My hand went instinctively to one of the battle axes on my back.

"Don't worry about it," Arthur said.

"Yeah . . . I'm gonna worry about it," I said.

"It's just Lance," Arthur said.

"Why can't I see him?" I asked.

"Merlin gave him a potion," Arthur answered.

"So he's invisible now?" I asked.

"Sort of, but not really," Arthur answered.

"What the fuck?" I asked a little too loudly.

"Would both of you be quiet!" Dellia growled. "Do you realize what's happening here? Wayne . . . you know full and well that sword is going to follow Arthur. Merlin said that much back at the tavern. As far as Lance goes, you leave that boy alone. All that matters is that he's happy."

"Is he happy?" I asked.

"Yes," Arthur answered solemnly.

"Wayne?" Dellia continued. "Please."

"Yes, Ma'am," I answered.

"Let's just focus on getting to your wife and kids," Dellia said. "I'm sure they're worried sick about you."

I hugged Dellia right then and there. Her words were comforting. Soon I'd be with them. That thought alone put a song in my heart. Arthur wasn't really capable of comforting words nowadays. They seemed to make him uncomfortable.

He watched the exchange between his mother and me with only a slight interest. When the hug ended, Arthur put his hand upon my shoulder.

"You ready?" He asked, studiously.

"Yeah," I answered.

"Then let's keep moving," Arthur said.

The rest of the walk was in silence. At the edge of the forest, Arthur took a knee and tried his best to peer down a trail that had existed long before the two of us were ever born.

"I can't see anything," Arthur said.

"Neither can I," I said.

"Lance," Arthur called out quietly. "Give it a look."

There was a rustle of grass, and a branch high above me suddenly swayed as if from a stiff breeze. We waited. . .

Finally, I saw movement on another branch, and heard the soft thud of feet hitting the ground not far from me.

I still couldn't see Lance.

"There were a couple small groups," Lance said from somewhere off to my left.

"Can we go around them?" I asked.

"No need," Lance answered.

"We can't fight them," I said. "If they raise an alarm of some type, we'll never make it to the high school."

Arthur looked over at me.

"What?" I asked.

"Lance took care of them for us," Arthur said.

I thought about it.

"Wait . . . what?" I asked. "He didn't . . . did he?"

"Yes," Arthur answered. "The trail is clear. Lance, you stay up high, move ahead, and keep a look out. I don't want any Death Reapers sneaking up on us in the dark. Wait for us at the edge of the forest."

A blur of movement, and Lance was gone. I think. Who the hell can really say when you can't even see the kid? Regardless, we were able to enter the forest and follow the trail. The thick foliage even provided some much appreciated cover from the rain.

Almost immediately, we came upon two bodies. One of them was sliced up horribly. The other had his neck cut so deeply that his head was barely attached.

"Lance did this?" Dellia asked.

"Yes," Arthur said.

"That sweet little boy," Dellia said. "Why would Merlin turn him into . . . into . . . well, I don't know what he is anymore."

"Merlin freed him, Mom," Arthur said. "Lance wouldn't have lasted very long without that potion, not with his condition."

Ahead of us, leaning against a tree was Excalibur. The gold and silver in the handle glowed in the moonlight. I still wanted to grab it. I wasn't stupid enough to try it again, but I wanted to.

"There's your buddy," I told Arthur.

"I see it," Arthur shrugged.

"Maybe you should at least carry it," I said. "You can put it on your belt."

"I'm not going near that thing," Arthur said. "There's something very wrong about it."

We came upon more bodies. Lance was turning out to be very good at killing Death Reapers. An invisible assassin . . . I'd have never guessed it. Dellia was right, Lance was a sweet kid. It bothered me that he was forced to commit the violent acts necessary to keep all of us safe and undetected.

When we came to the edge of the forest, the three of us knelt down behind some bushes and trees and surveyed the area. Nothing could be seen but a thin strip of grass separating the forest from the nearby homes. There was no green fog in the immediate area, but that didn't tell us what was beyond the first grouping of homes.

"I can take a look around the houses," Lance volunteered from somewhere over our heads causing both me and Dellia to jump.

"Alright," Arthur said. "Make it quick and stay on the rooftops of the homes."

We waited what about ten minutes. Once I thought I saw someone peek out from behind a house four blocks away. I tried to show Arthur, but by the time he looked the figure I'd seen was gone.

"The area is thick with Death Reapers," Lance said from above causing me and Dellia to jump once again.

I looked upwards in the trees, but I couldn't find the slightest sign of him. I noticed that Dellia was also looking, but Arthur hadn't even bothered.

"Are they still in small groups?" Arthur asked.

"Yes," Lance answered. "Lots and lots of small groups."

"Well," Arthur said. "We've got a problem then."

"All it'll take is for one single Death Reaper to spot us and we're going to get swarmed," I said.

"What if we stay close to the houses?" Arthur asked. "With all the rain; maybe if we stay in the shadows . . . we'll be okay."

"There's also a lot of shrubs and bushes to hide behind," I added.

"No use still talking about it," Arthur said. "Lance, you take the high road. Do your best to let us know if we're about to run into trouble."

"Okay," Lance said.

I heard a soft rustling, and after waiting a moment, Arthur stepped out of the forest in a crouch. Dellia followed him closely, and I took up the rear.

From the direction of the town square, I heard the first sounds of battle. Both Arthur and Dellia heard them as well, and stopped in their tracks.

"That's blade on blade noise," I said. "That means we must be low on archers. Otherwise the archers would have taken some shots first and tried to pick some of them off before things went hand-to-hand."

Arthur nodded and shook his head. I understood his thought process. He thought their final stand was idiotic, and even though he wasn't fond of most of his fellow townspeople, he probably felt more than a little bad that they were all sacrificing their lives.

"Maybe help will arrive," Dellia said to no one in particular.

"I just wish that Merlin would have come with us," Arthur said.

"Merlin can handle himself," I added. "I wouldn't worry about him too much."

"I know a good place," Arthur said. "It's where I found the sword. The Gods of the Forest live there. Anyway, it'll be a safe place to hide."

"I think it's best to keep on the move and try to shake them off our trail at first," I said. "The Death Reapers aren't likely to stop searching for you until they have a body. Without our horses, they'll have a speed advantage."

"That might be a good idea," Arthur said. "We may even need to split up,"

"You can stop yourself right there, son," Dellia interrupted. "I'm not losing you, not even for a second."

"Mom," Arthur said. "It's the best thing for everybody. Me being around will put all of us in danger."

"There's danger everywhere," Dellia argued. "Morgana seeks to imprison the world. Merlin's told me all about her. No place will be safe while she's around. She must be defeated."

"Dellia's right," I said. "There's really no reason for you to leave. We'll all be in danger no matter what you do."

"We'll talk about it later," Arthur said as we reached the first house and quietly made our way to the bushes in the front yard.

Farther down the road we saw a group of three Death Reapers moving across the street. We waited a bit, and three more of them crossed the road not two houses away from us.

"This is going to be a bitch," I grumbled.

"Looks that way," Arthur agreed before moving to the next yard.

The new yard had a large stone fountain with an angel statue in the center. The three of us crouched behind it, and waited nervously as Arthur scanned the area.

"It's clear for two more houses," Lance whispered causing me to jump out of my skin yet again.

"You need to stop scaring me ya little shit," I growled.

He was standing on top of the fountain. If he hadn't said something, I'd never have known he was there. As it was, I finally got a look at him. Or more accurately, I knew where he was; because truth be told, I couldn't tell what was him and what was statue. The camouflage was that perfect. His skin blended into the gray stone flawlessly.

233

He caught me looking at him, and shifted quickly, moving more of his body behind the statue. Out of respect for the kid, I stopped prying.

"Let's go," Arthur whispered after watching the exchange.

Two more houses and we found ourselves crouched down behind a large tree. There were two groups of Death Reapers arguing with each other in the next yard. We were about to backtrack, when we noticed a third group approaching us from the rear.

"There're six in front," I whispered. "And now there's three more behind us."

"We'll need to fight," Arthur said. "The Death Reapers behind us are headed in this direction."

"Okay," I agreed. "Let's hit the three behind us first."

"No," Arthur argued. "Let's use the element of surprise on the six. We'll drop more that way."

I agreed, and watched silently as Arthur shifted the ugly sword he'd been carrying to his right hand. I wondered if he was still as good as he used to be with a blade. It had certainly been a few years since those days of practicing in his back yard under the tutelage of all those masters.

Arthur ran at the Death Reapers, and I followed closely behind him. The man was fast; I had trouble keeping up with him. When he reached the group, he had already cut two of them down before the others even knew he was there.

I swung both my axes, and in seconds we'd killed all of them, but their green fog hadn't even begun to fade before we were once again in the middle of the fight as the three Death Reapers headed our way from behind rushed to join their comrades.

Arthur was a thing to behold. He'd lost nothing from his youth. The Death Reapers couldn't keep up with him. He twirled and lunged. He ducked and sidestepped. Their blades whistled through the air only inches from his face, but they couldn't touch him.

I killed the Death Reaper I was fighting with a hack to his lower right ribs and followed that up by dropping my other axe on top of his head. After looking up, I couldn't help but watch Arthur take on the other two. People can master all sorts of different things. Arthur was a master of the blade.

In moments, he skewered one Death Reaper, and before his victim could fall, Arthur spun him around impaling the final Death Reaper as he charged forward hoping to stab Arthur while his attention was focused elsewhere.

I watched silently as Arthur pushed both twitching bodies off his sword.

"Wow," I said. "You haven't lost your touch."

"This isn't a game," Arthur snapped. "You should have given me some backup after you took out the other one."

"It didn't look like you needed any help," I said stupidly.

"It doesn't matter what it looks like," Arthur said. "They were trying to kill me. All it takes is one stab or a cut, and it's finished. Do you get that?"

"I do," I said. "I'm sorry. It won't happen again."

Arthur looked around, saw that the coast was clear, walked over to me and placed his hand on my shoulder. I was all but hanging my head in shame.

"I know it won't," Arthur consoled. "Just be aware . . . a second is all it takes. One split second, and the fight is over. It's not a situation you want to watch play out. If we get the chance to tip the odds in our favor . . . take it."

"Are you boys okay?" Dellia asked as she came out of hiding and approached us.

"We're good," I answered.

"Where's Lance?" Dellia asked and I realized for the first time that he hadn't joined in on the fight.

"If he's not here," Arthur said. "He's otherwise engaged keeping us safe. It's nothing to worry about; he'll be along when he can."

Without another word Arthur had set off again. The way was clear block after block. After awhile, I began to wonder why things were going so easy. Something wasn't right, but I wasn't sure what it was.

The answer came a few blocks away from the high school.

We were crouching low, and keeping to the shadows. Everything was going perfectly, and then . . .

"Arthur!" Lance called out from a rooftop above us. "Run!"

To his credit, Arthur didn't panic.

"Where?" Arthur asked.

"Down the street, and to the left," Lance answered.

Arthur reached back, grabbed his mother's hand and took off as fast as she could go. I ran just a little bit behind them. However, I saw no danger. Whatever had spooked Lance was unknown to me. I kept looking behind us as we ran . . . but I couldn't see anything.

We rounded the last house on the street, and hooked a left. I gave one last look behind us, and that's when I saw what had Lance so spooked. It stopped me dead in my tracks.

The Death Reapers were pursuing us. All of them had grouped together in a great mob, and they were searching for us in an organized way. I could see the green fog swirling around them despite the rain.

"How?" I asked.

"The bodies," Lance said from somewhere nearby. "We should have hid the bodies."

There were too many of them to fight. From the brief glance I had, there seemed to be about forty of them. We had to run . . . but where? We were close to the high school, but we couldn't go there. That would lead them right to all the children and the folks that couldn't fight.

"What do we do?" I asked.

"We need to lead them in the opposite direction," Arthur said. "Or we can just keep a good enough distance, grab your kids and get the fuck out of here before they show up and pin us down in the school."

"What about all the other people in the school?" I asked not even bothering to hide the shock in my voice.

"We tell them to run," Arthur said. "Or maybe they can barricade themselves in the basement or something after we leave."

"Arthur," Dellia said. "That's horrible. You should be ashamed of yourself. There are children in that high school."

"They're not my children," Arthur said. "And they should have been evacuated a long time ago. You two need to wake up and realize what I've been telling you. This town is dead. Merlin should have made a run for it. He didn't. The four of us can't save everyone, and I'm not going to die trying."

"We'll lead them in the opposite direction," I said. "It's the least we can do."

"Fine," Arthur said obviously wishing I hadn't chosen that option. "We need to get their attention. I guess I'll do that part."

"No you won't," I said. "I'm supposed to keep you safe. So I'll do it myself."

This time it was me walking away without another word. I truly didn't get Arthur. He wasn't a coward, but he adamantly refused to play the part of the hero. He only wanted his mother to be safe, and he wanted far away from the battle. Why wouldn't he step up? He was an incredible fighter. What was his problem?

Not far away the sounds of the battle intensified, and though it tore at my heart not to run back and aid the people I spent my entire life with, I followed Merlin's orders.

Sort of.

Merlin probably never would have let the group of us lead a group of forty Death Reapers on a wild goose chase ... but Merlin wasn't here, and despite how desperately I wanted to get to my wife and kids, there was no way I was gonna lead the Death Reapers straight to all the people hiding out in the high school.

So I walked out to the middle of the street, waved my arms around, and screamed out a bunch of obscenities. The Death Reapers saw me immediately, and all of them rushed towards me in a great shouting mob.

I ran for all I was worth.

Arthur had Dellia by the hand and was practically dragging her behind him. She was slowing us down. As we turned on to another street, I realized how rapidly the Death Reapers were gaining on us. We needed a plan. As tough as Dellia was, she couldn't handle this kind of pace.

We were in trouble.

Arthur let go of Dellia's hand and charged ahead as if he could read my mind. He headed towards a house on the left, and hit the front door with his shoulder at full speed. I grabbed Dellia and followed after him as quickly as we could.

It was the shittiest idea I'd ever heard of, and the idea of getting trapped inside a house truly did not appeal to me. . . but what else could I do except follow him?

"Arthur!" I shouted. "We'll be trapped in here."

"Not really," Arthur said. "I have an idea. Go upstairs, and head to the back bedroom. Then climb down the tree outside the window."

There was a way out. That's all I needed to hear. I grabbed Dellia, and ran up the stairs.

"What about Arthur?" Dellia asked.

I looked over my shoulder. Arthur was closing the front door, and piling furniture in front of it since the lock was now broken off.

"He'll be right behind us," I said.

Dellia put her brakes on at the top of the stairs.

"Arthur is the important one," Dellia said. "And he's the one endangering himself?"

Shit.

She had a point.

Down the hallway, I could hear the sound of breaking glass followed by Lance's voice calling us out.

"I'll help him," I told Dellia. "Now go to the window."

"No!" Dellia growled. "I won't leave my son."

Shit.

The damn woman was as stubborn as ever.

I ran back down the stairs. My breathing was excruciatingly loud in my ears. I saw Excalibur in the corner of the front room, just waiting for Arthur to pick it up. Its red leather scabbard was the color of blood in the low light. I ignored the sword, and grabbed the other end of a large wooden hutch Arthur was dragging towards the front door.

We barely had the piece of furniture in place when we felt and heard the first slam. We pushed hard, trying to wedge it in behind the small couches Arthur had already gathered.

The second slam on the front door knocked it right out of our hands. The third slam shattered the flimsy wood of the door and after that; the Death Reapers were piling inside.

At least they were trying to pile inside.

Arthur and I disagreed with their decisions. We hacked and stabbed at them through the furniture. Blood and pieces of wood were flying everywhere . . . but little by little Arthur and I were being forced backwards.

"Fuck it," Arthur said. "Let them come in."

I watched as Arthur backed away, and kicked odds and ends to the side of the room so that he'd have more space in which to fight. Nope, he definitely wasn't a coward, but I wasn't ready to let them in just yet. I chopped at limbs, and stabbed at faces. I did my best to keep them away, but after all the fighting and running . . . I was getting tired. The only thing that kept me going was my family . . . and the fear of death. Let's not forget the fear of death.

A halberd, which is a sort of axe head on a long wooden pole, was thrust at my body. I managed to dodge away at the last second, but another halberd was thrust out at my new position.

More halberds came after that, and I could no longer hold the door. A group of Death Reapers rushed inside. They were filthy, and smelled like wet dogs and urine. The rain water dripped off their chain mail onto the floor. Their tunics were so muddy, I could no longer see their menacing emblems . . . but I could still see their silver eyes, beneath their soggy hair.

They rushed past me towards Arthur. Their halberds were a bad idea inside the house. The low ceilings and tight spaces made them more of a hindrance than a useful weapon.

Arthur side-stepped the first lunge, and chopped down on one of his attackers hands. He twirled after that, and another Death Reaper fell to the floor disemboweled. He was so fast; I completely missed the killing blow. Also, I was a bit distracted. Now that the halberds were no longer stabbing at me, I once again resumed my job of keeping the mob out of the house.

I was still very tired, but I had a bit of a second wind, and I fought like hell. Despite my attempts, every now and then a couple of them would rush past me. I didn't try to stop them once they were in the door. If I tried, I'd have gotten stabbed in the back for my efforts.

I let Arthur handle those fellas.

I tried my best to keep my eye on him. The most I could do was throw out quick glances in his direction. I liked what I saw. The room behind me was filling up with bodies. After he killed them, Arthur kicked their corpses to the sides of the room in order to maintain his killing room floor.

I heard a thump on the stairway to my side.

"More of them are coming!" Lance shouted from the stairs.

All I could see from my quick glance was Dellia, and what was possibly a blur against the wall next to her. Dellia had a worried look on her face, and I was wishing I had Lance's abilities when I heard Arthur cry out behind me.

I turned quickly around.

Arthur had been stabbed.

I wanted to go to him. I couldn't. I was the only thing holding back the tide. How could that have happened? Arthur was so damn skilled. I moved to the side to hide behind the wall of the house while I continued to hack away.

Arthur was bleeding from his left side, right below his ribs. I'm not sure what organs resided in that area, but judging by the amount of blood . . . they seemed pretty important. I watched as he staggered, and blocked another slash from the Death Reaper bearing down on him.

A group of three slipped by me, and rushed after Arthur.

I hacked even harder. I kicked and shoved the sofa back into place trying to slow the Death Reapers down. I stole another glance. Arthur stumbled and fell. His chest was heaving. I could only imagine how tired he was. He didn't look exactly well rested when he came home. How long has it been since he'd slept?

More Death Reapers slipped inside the house. My thrusts were getting slower and slower, but I refused to give up. I was going to go down swinging. I'd die fighting for my friends and family. Why did Dellia have to be here? Poor Dellia, let her live. Whatever gods existed in this new and violent world . . . deliver her from this evil.

Someone rushed down the stairs, and ran into the front room.

"No!" Dellia screamed out in a voice I'd never heard from her.

I turned, and saw Arthur's mother pick up a fallen sword, and charge selflessly into battle to defend her only son.

"You can't have him!" Dellia screamed as she blocked Arthur's death blow. "You can't have my son!"

I watched as she took on the Death Reapers all by herself.

She twirled and lunged. She stabbed and slashed. One by one they fell beneath her wrath. The woman had skill. At some point in her life she'd been trained . . . and trained well.

I stole glimpses as much as I could.

I watched Arthur crawl across the room. He wasn't moving very fast, but he was moving. He was also trying to shout out something to Dellia, but either no words were coming or I just couldn't hear what he was saying due to noise.

Tears were flowing down my face. I was screaming and bawling. Not because I was afraid. I was past being afraid. I was crying because for the first time in my entire life I finally saw and understood the depth of a mother's love . . . and it was beautiful.

My mother was a drunk. I spent most of my childhood with Arthur, Dellia, and Merlin. Dellia accepted me readily and always made me feel welcome. She bought me clothes, and fed me. When I was a teenager, she gave me money for dates and lunch . . . I loved her like a mother, and in turn she loved me like a son.

I couldn't stand seeing the pain and fear in her eyes. I couldn't stand knowing that sooner rather than later . . . she would fall next to her son.

Arthur.

I was supposed to protect Arthur.

He made it across the room. He was reaching out for Excalibur. The sword leapt from the wall, and fell into his hand.

Nothing.

Arthur was too injured. He lacked the strength to stand. The Death Reapers were trying to get to him. Dellia was all that was standing in their way.

No.

No.

No.

This will not be the end. I will not witness their death. They were my family. I owed both of them so very much.

I screamed out my rage. I screamed out my despair, and with that perfect picture of a mother's love firmly set in my mind, I charged into the great mob of Death Reapers.

It was a foolish thing to do. It shouldn't have worked, but it did. I stopped the tide, and scared the shit out of them. I swung my axes like a madman. My third wind had arrived. I was charged and ready to go.

The Death Reapers backed away.

Some of them ran halfway down the street before meeting up with their reinforcements and doubling back to continue the attack. Others weren't so fortunate. My twin axes bit deeply. The crunch of bone and the inevitable arterial spray made my evening.

Not far away from where I was standing, I saw some of them drop to their deaths without anyone touching them. Others followed afterwards. Those that tried to surround me died before they could close the distance.

Small black spikes were sticking up from their backs and necks.

Lance was providing backup.

"Go back to Arthur and Dellia!" I shouted. "They need your help!"

"You go back to them!" Lance shouted in return. "I can do more good here!"

I hated leaving him, but by the looks of things he was right. I was only going to get myself killed. Lance could retreat at a moment's notice.

I ran back inside the house. Two Death Reapers tried to follow me. They were slashed down by a shadow that couldn't truly be seen.

The fight inside the house was still raging. Three of her attackers were all that were left standing, but they were backing Dellia into a corner.

I had to act fast.

I threw one of my battle axes across the room. The blade bit deeply into the back of my intended target. It crunched through rib bones, and struck his heart.

The other two were so shocked by my sudden and dangerous appearance, they turned towards me without thought, forgetting about Dellia entirely. It was a mistake on their part.

Dellia stabbed the closest one through his neck, and before she managed to free her sword, I ran forward, and buried my axe deep into the final Death Reapers sternum.

The battle in the house was over.

Dellia ran to Arthur's side. She was pulling at his clothes, looking for the wound.

"It's not bleeding!" Dellia exclaimed. "I see the wound, but there's no blood."

"It's the sword," Arthur said weakly. "There's something about the sword that stops my wounds from bleeding. It also seems to numb the pain. Help me to my feet."

I went to Arthur, took his hand, and pulled him up. He wavered a bit, but he stood.

"Strap the sword onto your belt," I said.

"Good idea," Arthur replied.

"Can you move?" I asked. "We need to move."

"I can move," Arthur answered.

"How'd you know about this place?" I asked.

"You mean the tree by the window?" Arthur asked.

"Yes," I answered.

"The girl that lives here is married," Arthur said. "I had to run out when her husband came home."

"I should have known," I laughed.

"Let's go," Dellia said and ushered both of us towards the stairs.

As it turns out, Arthur was a bit weak from the blood loss, but with whatever painkillers Excalibur provided, he able to move surprisingly well, and that was a good thing.

Once inside the upstairs bedroom with the broken window, and the nearby tree, I closed the flimsy door, and pushed the bed, cabinet and dresser in front of it. It wouldn't hold them back very long . . . but hopefully it would hold them back long enough for us to become scarce.

By Dellia's orders, Arthur was the first out the window. Dellia was next, and just as it was my turn, I heard pounding on the door.

I grabbed the branch of the tree, attempted to climb down, slipped, and landed on my ass next to Arthur and Dellia.

"Let's go," Arthur said. "We'll move through the backyards. They'll have to guess which direction we took."

We moved quickly, no longer worrying about running into Death Reapers since they were all back at Arthur's ... hell ... I don't know what to call her. Anyway, they were all back at the nice lady that cheated on her husband's house.

As luck would have it, after breaking into the bedroom, the mob of Death Reapers chose the wrong direction in which to pursue us. I can't say I blame them. The rain was fierce, and the night was dark. It'd be impossible to follow our tracks.

Arthur came to an abrupt stop.

"Lance?" Arthur asked. "Where's Lance?"

"He was holding back the Death Reapers," I answered solemnly.

Arthur started heading back towards the house, I tried to grab a hold of him, but he smacked my hand away roughly with the new Death Reaper sword he managed to pick up as we headed to the stairs.

"Arthur," I said. "You can't."

"The hell I can't," Arthur said. "He's my friend, and there's too many of them for him to handle alone."

Dellia looked from Arthur, back to me. She didn't know what to do, but I could see that the idea of leaving Lance behind was killing her as well.

"Arthur," I called out as quietly as I could. "We'll be killed if we go back there. Please don't make me chase after you."

"I'm not dead," Lance laughed from a tree above me. "Not even close."

Arthur didn't say a word. He just ran back towards the high school, though there was a slight smile on his face as he passed Lance's tree.

We crossed the open soccer fields leading up to the school. The grass here was still short because the kids continued to use the fields in the mornings and evenings ... until the green fog came of course.

We ran alongside the school, until we came to a lonely door way in the back only a couple football fields away from Stronghold Wall. The metal door was locked.

"Use Excalibur," I said to Arthur.

"Go fuck yourself," Arthur replied. "I can hear the damn thing whispering in my ear already."

The anticipation of getting to my kids and Wendy was overwhelming. My beautiful wife, I missed her so very much. All I could picture was her loving arms wrapping around my waist as I kissed her soft hair.

"I'll break it down," I said with conviction.

"How about we knock first?" Dellia asked.

I stood back as Dellia gave a few gentle raps on the door. They were loud enough to echo around the high school, but not loud enough to echo back into the neighborhood we'd just vacated.

There was no answer.

Dellia knocked again.

"Fuck this shit," I said. "I'm gonna break it down."

"Shush," Dellia said. "I hear footsteps."

"Who is it?" A familiar voice asked.

I rushed to the door.

"Wendy," I said with tears in my eyes. "It's me baby, open the door"

Wendy did as I asked. The feeling of her arms around my waist was pure ecstasy. I loved her. I loved her with my entire being.

"We don't have time for this," Arthur grumbled. "Let's get your kids and go."

"Yes," I said and pulled away from my wife.

Wendy's eyes went wide in fear.

"How bad is it?" Wendy asked.

"The worst," I answered.

I saw the tears forming in her eyes.

"We need to grab the kids and go," I said.

"What about everybody else?" Wendy asked.

"Sweetheart," I said. "We barely made it here ourselves."

Wendy placed a hand over her mouth, and I watched the tears cascade down her face. The decisions we were forced to make were horrible. I made them on behalf of Merlin's word, and for the safety of my family.

Wendy would listen to me. She'd know my decisions didn't come lightly.

She led us inside the high school. In the dark hallways, I saw her wipe at her eyes. Arthur was leaning against the outside wall as we were hugging. It took him a bit to move himself forward when we went inside. His skin was a very pale sickly color. I was worried about him, but his injury would have to wait. We needed to move. Eventually, the mob of Death Reapers would catch up to us.

"What do we tell everyone?" Wendy asked.

"We'll tell them the situation," I said. "They can run as well. Or maybe some of them will choose to stay and hide."

"But they can't come with us?" Wendy asked.

"Not if you want to survive," Arthur said rather brusquely.

Dellia kept trying to check Arthur's wound as we walked. I could hear them bickering softly behind me. Arthur wanted to be left alone.

We went down a flight of stairs, and into an even darker hallway. The double metal doors that blocked off every fifty feet of hallway on this level were all wide open. I saw posters on the walls from before the red fog. I saw trophies and classrooms. At the end of the hallway beyond another set of double metal doors, was a final flight of stairs. This one led to the basement level, and before us was a large, rectangular open area where students used to serve food and drinks back when Arthur and I attended this school.

Against the far wall of the large rectangle were three metal doors. Beyond those doors was the gymnasium. Wendy knocked on the center door twice. She was answered by five knocks, and gave a final four knocks in return.

The door opened.

We went inside quickly.

Torches burned along the plain cement walls of the gymnasium. It cast the large room in a soft glow, and showed us all the worried faces huddled together. They were young and old. Male and female . . . and there were many.

I heard Arthur take a sharp intake of air.

His face had gotten even paler, and his eyes darted around the room. Back and forth, back and forth, now and then freezing before moving on once again . . . I couldn't figure out what was catching his attention.

Sonny Larson's, ten year old son came forward and asked if we'd seen his mother and father. I told him we hadn't. I lacked the heart to tell the boy that both his parents had been killed.

I looked at Arthur as the boy walked away. He was aghast.

"Who's that kid?" Arthur asked after he caught me staring at him.

"That's Sonny Larson's kid," I answered. "You remember him, right? He went to school with us."

"Yeah, I remember Sonny," Arthur said. "He's dead isn't he?"

"Yes," I answered honestly. "Sonny and his wife died early on."

Arthur's eye's turned red, and I finally understood. It was the children. The room was filled with children. Arthur hadn't even known there were this many children in the entire town. He stayed away from people and worked nights. He didn't go to social gatherings. He went to bars.

Since the death of his wife and child, he avoided the town. The people he had to deal with on a regular basis were the troublemakers, and drunks. Most of them disliked Arthur, and Arthur disliked most of them . . . how decadent Mill Ridge must have seemed. No wonder he didn't care about abandoning the people. His world was so very small. How could I not have noticed what he was doing to himself?

In this room, in addition to the children, were the innocents. The women and elderly that couldn't fight . . . these weren't people that Arthur was used to dealing with. He harbored no ill will towards any of them. He probably didn't even know most of them lived in the same town.

His eyes were still darting around the room. No doubt some of the faces were familiar to him. No doubt they brought him back to better times, times when we were younger and had the whole world ahead of us. Most of all he watched the children with their mothers. They were the most innocent of all. Love untouched, untainted by the evil flooding around the town. He was thinking about his lost son. He was thinking about his lost wife. He was thinking about all that he'd lost, and he was hating himself for wanting to abandon these good people.

Tears were coursing down his face.

"We can't leave them," Arthur said.

Dellia came forward to put her arm around his shoulders, and Arthur backed away as if her touch would burn him to a cinder.

A thought suddenly came to me. Merlin's face when he told us to gather my family! Merlin had expected this reaction. He'd been counting on it. He knew the children and their mothers would touch some part of Arthur that hadn't been touched in a long, long time.

Well played Merlin. Well played.

"Arthur?" I asked.

"I won't leave them," Arthur stated flatly without even looking at me.

I heard raised voices behind me. Apparently, Wendy was telling the town elders how bad things were outside the high school. A panic began to spread across the gymnasium. I went to stand beside my wife.

The questions were coming rapidly. One after another.

"Is my husband alive?"

"Have you seen my daddy?"

"How much time do we have?"

"What should we do?"

On and on the questions came, I answered what I could. Sobs began to echo out as wives and parents learned of their husbands' and children's deaths.

"It'd be best if we went our separate ways," I told them, hating myself. "We'll all stand a better chance if we go our separate ways."

"What if I'm too old to run?"

"Who'll take all the children?"

"Can we come with you?"

"How can you do this to us?"

"I'm sorry," I said. "I'm so very sorry. I have to think of my own family."

"Where's Arthur?" A familiar voice asked from somewhere in the crowd. "I saw him come in. I knew him since he was a child. He'd never abandon us."

It didn't take long for the crowd to find Arthur. He was in the far corner, as far away from the light of the torches as he could get. Old Man Cranky-Pants stepped out from the crowd, and walked over to him. The crowd followed behind him. Their worried faces hopeful at last.

Old Man Cranky-Pants, a name given to the meanest son-of-a-bitch to have ever lived in Mill Ridge. It was a name I came up with when I was a kid, after being chased from his backyard pond more times than I can count. Old Man Cranky-Pants didn't like kids. I'm not sure he liked anyone . . . but he liked Arthur.

Once a week, young Arthur marched up to his front door, and politely asked if we could swim in his pond. Each and every time, Old Man Cranky-Pants yelled and screamed at him until Arthur was forced to jump off the man's porch and run for his life.

Two years into Arthur's attempts to gain access to the forbidden pond, Old Man Cranky-Pants had a stroke. He was in the hospital for about a month, and to be perfectly honest most people didn't think he was going to make it. The old bastard hung on though, and imagine his shock when he came home to find out that Arthur had been mowing his lawn regularly.

After that, Old Man Cranky-Pants had a soft spot for Arthur, and the forbidden pond was no longer forbidden.

"Arthur," Old Man Cranky-Pants said. "Are you leaving without us?"

Arthur looked the old man straight in the face, and considered his words for only a brief moment.

"No," Arthur said in a soft voice. "I'm not."

"Welcome back, son," Old Man Cranky-Pants said. "We've missed you."

Arthur nodded, and the wheels began to churn. Wendy and I went over to him immediately. On the way we passed Dellia, and though she was terribly worried, we could see the pride in her son etched on her face.

"Do you have a plan?" I asked Arthur.

"We can't run," Arthur said. "We also can't fight them. There's too many. All we can do is barricade ourselves in here and hope that Merlin knows what he's talking about."

"That's not the greatest plan," I said.

"It's all we have," Arthur said.

"Wendy," Arthur said. "The hallways on the second floor are filled with double metal doors. Do you have the keys for all of them?"

"It's a universal key," Wendy answered.

"Who's got some shine?" Arthur asked the crowd around us.

Nobody answered him.

"Come on," Arthur said. "I can smell it in the air."

It took awhile, because the old-times don't like to hand over their moonshine, but eventually we had a small pile of jugs and mason jars lined up by the door.

After that, Arthur was explaining his plan and putting everybody to work when we heard a soft voice called to us from behind a set of nearby wooden bleachers.

"Arthur," Lance said. "I can sneak behind the Death Reapers and pick them off."

"No," Arthur said. "The hallways are too confined. It's too dangerous. I want you in the gymnasium in case they make their way through the barriers."

"No," Lance said. "I'll stay by you."

Arthur shrugged his shoulders knowing that he wasn't going to win the argument. After that, Arthur told everyone to arm themselves. We'd do everything we could to discourage them, but if the Death Reapers made it to the gymnasium . . . we'd have to fight.

"Are you sure they'll even come?" Wendy asked.

"They were already searching houses when we hit the area," I answered. "Sooner or later they'll get here . . . probably sooner now that they know we're in the area."

In no time at all, I had a canvas bag of moonshine over my shoulder, an unlit torch in my hand, and I was kissing my wife and children goodbye while Dellia hugged Arthur tightly and told him to be careful.

Arthur was moving pretty slowly with his hand over his wounded side as we made our way back through the door we'd all entered through. I was worried about him.

"Are you going to be okay?" I asked as we reached the top of the staircase and Arthur placed some Mason jars of moonshine along with a ceramic jug a few steps down.

"I don't have much of a choice," Arthur answered. "I'm in this fight despite the injury."

"Will you be able to run?" I asked.

"I better hope so," Arthur answered.

"Do you think . . . ," I tried to ask before Arthur interrupted me.

"Wayne," Arthur said. "You can't do this alone."

"Okay," I relented. "It was worth a try."

"I appreciate that," Arthur said.

"If we get out of this," I said. "I'm dipping into that moonshine."

"I've already been dipping into it," Arthur smiled. "This shit will knock down an elephant."

We laughed quietly, and continued to the back door of the high school, hiding jars and jugs and we moved. Outside the door, the rain was pouring just as fiercely as it had been. Both of us were still dressed in sopping wet clothes but we'd gotten used to the bone chilling cold.

"You see anything?" I asked Arthur.

"Nope," Arthur answered.

"You hear anything?" I asked.

"Just the rain," Arthur answered. "And the battle at the town square."

The wait was the worst thing about the entire situation. The anticipation was killing me. Would help come like Merlin believed? Would the Death Reapers find us before help arrived? Would we lose the battle, and have the entire massive army of Death Reapers come charging into the school hell-bent on killing the elderly, children and doing God knows what with the women?

I couldn't let my family be taken.

That thought had been on my mind since the beginning. I couldn't let my family be taken. If push came to shove . . . I'd take care of them. I had to, but the very thought of it broke my heart into a thousand pieces.

Time went by slowly.

The rain stopped abruptly and right as I was finally starting to relax a bit, Arthur gently closed the metal door and turned the lock above the knob.

"Light the torch," Arthur said.

Quickly, I did as he asked. The hallway around us was suddenly washed in a soft yellow glow.

"How many?" I asked.

"Enough," Arthur answered.

"Maybe they'll pass us by," I said.

"Maybe," Arthur said.

Time crawled to a standstill. The next few minutes felt like decades, and then the inevitable came to pass. The doorknob moved, and the door rattled on its hinges.

Arthur motioned for quiet by placing a finger to his lips. The two of us back-tracked down the hallway. In the light of the torch, I could see Arthur's face. He was sweating profusely.

Something hard hit the door.

Arthur pulled out a mason jar. A cloth was stuffed into the puncture at the top of the tin lid. I brought the torch close to the cloth, and Arthur motioned me away.

"Wait till they're inside," Arthur said.

Another loud bang as something slammed against the door. It shattered the quiet of the dark hallway.

"C'mon you fuckers," I growled.

Three times did the trick, the door blasted off its hinges, and two Death Reapers tumbled to the floor in its wake. Arthur held up a finger as I brought the torch closer.

"Wait," Arthur said.

The soaking wet Death Reapers rose to their feet slowly. The water dripped off of their bodies and created a puddle on the floor. The green fog began to pollute their end of the hallway. One of them wore a small helmet with a nose-guard. He had large stitches around an abnormal looking chin.

They took slow steps forward, and behind them like a scary scene from a horror movie came the rest of their fellows. They looked as if they'd manifested out of the rain. Their silver eyes glinted in the torch light.

"Now what are you lads up to?" The helmeted Death Reaper asked?

"Come and find out," Arthur said in a strange voice.

"I think we will," The helmeted Death Reaper replied.

The group of them came closer and closer. It was maddening that they moved so slowly. Why the hell couldn't they just rush us and get it over with.

Arthur waited patiently. I could hear his ragged breathing next to me, but I couldn't take my eyes off the advancing Death Reapers.

"Now," Arthur said.

I lit the cloth on fire. Arthur watched it burn for a moment and threw the burning Mason jar at the helmeted Death Reaper. The glass shattered against his chest. The flames followed the moonshine and our enemy began to scream out in fear and pain.

I reached into the canvas bag and grabbed the final large ceramic jug that I'd been carrying. I heaved it through the air, and it crashed at their feet sending highly flammable liquid all over the place.

Arthur and I didn't stick around. We rounded the corner and hit the staircase. After making it to the next level down, we moved to the first set metal doors, I grabbed at our first cache of moonshine, and started pouring it all over the floor right in front of the door.

"You're wasting it," Arthur said in that strange voice.

"No it'll go up," I argued.

"It'll catch, but it won't be that impressive," Arthur said. "You need to . . . need to . . ."

"What'd you say?" I asked.

No answer. I looked for him beyond the metal doors, and found him on his hands and knees. He was blinking his eyes rapidly as if there was something wrong with his vision.

"Arthur!" I shouted and dove to the ground next to him. In a split second, I had my arm wrapped around him, and was getting ready to carry him back to the gymnasium.

"No," Arthur said weakly. "Don't worry about me; just get ready to throw the next Mason jar."

Reluctantly, I let him go, and readied the moonshine.

The Death Reapers came soon after that. They were moving a bit faster now as they came down the hallway after us but they still weren't running full out.

I stood just beyond the doors, and let them see me. Again, the dumbasses came forward. I lit the Mason jar, and hurled it towards them. I didn't score a direct hit, but the flames began to spread nonetheless.

Without waiting to see how much damage I was able to cause, I slammed the metal doors closed, and locked them up tightly. The seams between the doors and the frames glowed from the flames just beyond.

I scooped up Arthur with one arm and held out the torch in front of us as we slowly made our way to our next destination. It was tough keeping him moving, and I could already hear the Death Reapers pounding on the doors I'd just locked.

I wanted to throw the torch down, pick him up, and haul ass . . . but I needed the torch. I wouldn't have time to light another one.

"Wayne," Arthur said.

"What?" I asked.

"Let me go," Arthur said. "They're depending on you. Let me go."

"No," I said.

"Wayne," Arthur said. "You're my brother. I need you to live. I need you to protect my mom. I need you to look after Lance."

"We are brothers," I said. "And that's why I'll never leave you, not in this lifetime not in the next."

He kept quiet after that, and did his best to keep one foot in front of the other. At the next set of metal doors where we'd hidden our next cache of moonshine he became unresponsive. I checked his pulse, he had one but it didn't seem exceptionally strong.

I readied my moonshine weapons, and watched as the Death Reapers broke through their metal barrier, and charged towards me. I smiled at how they paused near the two sets of metal doors between me and them. I smiled harder as they approached my area, and I stepped out with another bottle of burning moonshine.

They did their best to take cover, but the flames spread far and wide along the hallway. The ceramic jug came next before I slammed and locked the doors.

I threw Arthur over my shoulder, and ran to the stairway.

Once past the doors, I didn't wait. I locked them shut behind me, and kicked over the moonshine Arthur had placed on the stairs. The liquid splashed all over the place, and it scared the shit out of me to run through it . . . but I need to get to the basement level. I needed to get Arthur to his mother.

As soon as I was off the staircase, I threw my torch behind me. I heard the whoosh, and I felt the heat on my back and neck as I started calling out for Dellia.

A door opened up.

People came forward and helped me carry Arthur inside the gymnasium. Dellia was suddenly there. She was cutting open his shirt and going to work the wound that still refused to bleed.

From behind me, I heard pounding and screams from the top of the stairs. I wanted to close and lock the door to the gymnasium behind me, but I didn't know if Lance had made it to the room or not.

"Lance!" I shouted out the door. "Are you there? Where are you?"

I hadn't had time to think about him before, but I certainly noticed his absence. Did he end up staying in the gymnasium after all? Where was he?

I called and called his name. He never answered, and as the green fog began to descend the stairway, and fill up the large room before the gymnasium, I reluctantly closed and locked the door.

There was a flurry of movement after that as people pushed and shoved their way to the door. A barricade was being erected. Would it be enough? I didn't think so, but it gave them something to do.

I looked for Arthur, Dellia had moved him somewhere . . . I didn't know where. Why didn't he let her look after him sooner?

Damn it.

I contemplated finding a seat and just waiting things out. I was ready to give up. All hope was lost. I was tired. We'd given it our best shot, but what did we really hope to accomplish? There were too many of them. We never stood a chance.

Time moved slowly onwards. Never once did I dare to hope. The Death Reapers would come. The day had not been saved. When the fire burned down enough . . .

Fists began to slam against the doors of the Gymnasium. People around me began panicking and darting about in aimless patterns that I couldn't understand.

That's when I saw my wife.

She had a sword in her hand, and she was standing in front of one of the doors with a group of elderly men and women.

I looked among the chaos, and eventually located my kids. They were looking right at me. My kids. I was a father, and my kids were relying on me.

I reached over both shoulders and pulled free my twin battle axes. I wasn't a leader, but I was a fighter . . . and I was getting pretty damn good all things considered. I would not go down without a fight.

I stepped between the doors and the people.

"Get ready!" I shouted as I paced back and forth. "Show no mercy. Kill anything that comes through these doors. Kill them before they kill you."

The Death Reapers began to scream at us through the metal barrier.

I wanted to offer more words of encouragement, but the tone . . . the shrillness of their screams was distracting me.

I stopped talking. I stopped pacing, and turned towards the doors. I couldn't figure out why they sounded so odd. I went to one of the doors, and placed my ear against the surface. My wife shouted for me to get away, but I ignored her.

Everyone got real quiet.

I heard growls coming from behind the metal. I heard the sounds of swords clanging together, and I heard Merlin shouting orders.

I smiled, and turned around.

Anxious faces looked towards me with breathless anticipation. I smiled even bigger.

"What's going on?" Someone asked.

"The reinforcements have arrived," I answered.

❧ LANCE ❧

I had to get help.

I recognized my limitations, and I recognized the amount of Death Reapers entering the school was too great to overcome.

In order to protect Arthur, I must first abandon him.

As the last of the Death Reapers entered the school, I slipped out the empty door. The cool night embraced my body. If felt like a reviving bath next to the humid halls of a school I could never attend.

It was time to move.

My original plan was to stay behind the Death Reapers and pick them quietly off, one after another. There were just too many of them. We hadn't counted on that. I know Arthur didn't want me in the fight, but Arthur had to learn that I wasn't a child he needed to protect. I was the protector.

So, I chose to ignore him. I do that sometimes.

Now my plan was scrapped, and a new one had formed. It wasn't very hero-like, but it was a necessity.

I moved as fast as I could. I covered the open ground of the school in seconds. I avoided Main Street. I didn't want to get bogged down amongst the enemy. Instead, I ran to the nearby homes, and leapt to their rooftops.

From there, I traveled even faster. I leapt from house to house; sometimes I even used backyard trees. I was really moving.

At the end of the line, I climbed up the tallest tree in a split second and freefell across the street dividing the homes from the rear of the shops bordering the town square. I landed on the edge of a tall building.

I moved across the rooftop, and took a look at the battle zone. Groups of Death Reapers had broken through. There was fighting everywhere. An arrow whizzed by my ear, and I had to crouch even lower than I was already crouched.

I was positive it was just an errant shot that almost claimed me as its target, but I wasn't about to take chances. From left to right I searched for Merlin. Merlin could send help to Arthur. I couldn't find him. The chaos was too frenzied. Too many people were running. The forest of the park blocked some of my view.

I heard the sound of cutting air.

It happened so fast, I didn't even have time to turn around. The blow landed hard on the middle of my back.

I fell from the roof.

I'm not sure how my attacker knew I was there. I'm guessing he heard my footsteps, and possibly saw a brief movement in the air that was gone as soon as it was seen. I have no idea what he hit me with, but I wasn't cut open. It felt more like blunt trauma.

A lone Death Reaper hiding on the rooftops, just waiting for someone to come along . . . just my luck. Well, it wouldn't have been so bad had I not landed so terribly on the street right next to the curb of the sidewalk. The street was my undoing.

The street hurt.

I was groggy, and I didn't want to move. How the heck was I still alive after falling off a four story building? Still, I was hurt. I didn't know how badly.

I couldn't seem to catch my breath.

"Where are you, little demon?" A scratchy voice asked from behind me. "Just move a wee bit more so I can bash in your brains."

No thank you.

I froze solid. I didn't even turn my head as the Death Reaper came out of the shop and began looking for me on the sidewalk. He held a bat in his hand. An empty scabbard bounced against his hip. The idiot must have lost his sword.

I could get up, and rush towards the forest, but I wasn't sure I could move fast enough. I wasn't sure I could do anything fast, not even grab the knives on my back. The Death Reaper was too ready for me, too ready to pounce.

A small green fog drifted around his feet. How did I not see the fog when I landed on the roof? I should have cleared the area before I started looking for Merlin. Under normal circumstances I could have easily killed this guy.

"Come now, little demon," The Death Reaper taunted. "I know you're here somewhere, I heard you hit the street. Didn't sound very pretty . . . I bet you hurt yourself. Let me make everything better."

He was standing directly over me.

He was prodding the ground with the bat.

Just a little more to the left and he'd find me.

I heard footsteps.

I could almost feel their vibrations against my body as they drew nearer and nearer. If the Death Reaper had back-up coming, I was done for. No. The Death Reaper screamed out a curse word, and I heard bodies collide.

I turned.

It was Martin, the deputy. He had a sword in his hand, and he was fighting the Death Reaper. I pushed myself off the street. I still had my strength, and my breath had come back into my lungs, but my arm hung at an awkward angle and radiated pain throughout my body.

I screamed out when I tried to move it.

The Death Reaper heard me.

He looked in my direction. Martin tried to take advantage of the distraction, but the Death Reaper was too experienced. His bat collided with Martin's sword hand, and the sword fell to the sidewalk.

I used my uninjured arm, and began pulling one of my knives, but before it cleared its sheath, the bat met Martins forehead, and instantly changed the shape of the man's skull. I screamed out, and the Death Reaper whirled towards me.

"Did I just bash a friend of yours, little demon?" The Death Reaper asked happily.

"I'll kill you for that," I said.

"Such a young voice," the Death Reaper smiled.

He charged me, and I ran. My knife never cleared its sheath. The odds of winning the fight were against me. The area was too open. It'd be too easy to spot my movements. My camouflage wasn't perfect. There were holes if you knew what to look for.

The forest of the park was too far away, instead of heading there, I ran into the open door of the shop I had just fallen from.

The Death Reaper was right behind me.

257

This shop happened to be a grocery store. The owner's pretty daughter was a year older than me. I did my best to hide between the racks of canned goods, and vegetables. The Death Reaper made a mess of things looking for me.

"I'll find you sooner or later!" The Death Reaper shouted. "I know your tricks. All I have to do is look for the odd shape. That's it; pretty simple . . . I'll stab every shape that doesn't belong."

That wasn't so easy in the dark room, but the Death Reaper was as good as his word. He stabbed out and slashed everything that looked suspicious to him.

I was embarrassing myself.

Arthur was stabbed through the gut, and he still fought. I had a dislocated shoulder, and I was hiding like a frightened child.

I am a child.

The heck with that, I have a duty. I have a job. I could hide because I was in pain, or I could act like the knight I was supposed to be.

I decided to act.

Silently I moved from my hiding place. Silently I drew my knife from the sheath on my back. The steel made a slight rasping sound as it cleared the leather. The Death Reaper didn't hear the noise, but I did. I found the noise comforting.

I moved quietly between the racks. I could hear his boots against the tile floor. I knew where he was even though I couldn't see him.

I had two choices, I could take him from behind or I could take him from the front. I chose to face my hunter. I wanted to see the surprise in his eyes. I wanted to be malicious. He made me afraid, and I wanted to repay him.

I moved for the interception.

Once I was in position, I crouched low. As he rounded the rack I was crouched behind, I stood up quickly, slashed him across the groin, and moved a few steps away.

I looked into his face.

At first he was confused. He saw my movement, he felt my touch . . . but the pain hadn't registered.

"I see you," the Death Reaper said.

"Not for long," I said.

The Death Reaper took a step towards me as he brought up his sword. The skin around the cut I'd made ripped open as he moved and a great splash of blood and intestines fell to his feet.

His legs gave out, but his arm thrashed wildly and caught a hold of the nearest rack of grocery supplies. For a brief moment, he held himself upright, looked in my direction, smiled, and yanked the heavy rack down on top of me.

I fell to the floor of the grocery store, and couldn't move. I watched as the Death Reaper, still holding his sword, crawled towards me.

I pushed against the metal rack pinning me to the floor. I pushed despite the pain in my shoulder. It heard the metal of the rack grind against the rack behind me, then I heard a loud screech, and the weight on my chest doubled.

I now had two grocery store racks on top of me.

I thought about Arthur as the Death Reaper continued to crawl towards me. He jabbed with his sword, but he wasn't near enough. He crawled a bit more, jabbed again, crawled a bit more, and right before he would have stabbed me in the face . . . he died.

"Hah!" I shouted out.

I was still trapped.

I couldn't move. I couldn't get the leverage to push. My shoulder still radiated pain throughout my body.

"Oh," I whispered.

I tried squirming out from underneath the two racks. No luck there, something heavy was blocking me.

The clock was ticking. I didn't expect any of this. Arthur needed me. All those people needed me. I was stuck. I tried this. I tried that. Nothing seemed to work. I wanted to cry. I was so frustrated, I wanted to cry.

Instead, I focused on popping my shoulder back into the socket. I only had a few inches of room on that particular shoulder, but I was very strong. Pulling my wounded shoulder back as far as it would go . . . I slammed it into the rack on top of me.

Pain exploded inside of me, and I groaned loudly . . . but I did it again. I did it again and again. I slammed my shoulder until I felt the pop.

I did it.

I was exhausted.

Time passed slowly. I had no idea of how much, because I had no way of telling time. I alternated between intense struggles to free myself and brief rests to gather my strength. It was during one of my brief rests when I heard the softest of footsteps.

"Who's there?" A girl's voice asked.

It wasn't another Death Reaper.

"I am," I answered.

"Who're you?" The girl asked.

"I'm Lancelot?" I answered.

"You're who?" The girl asked right before she stepped into my field of vision, and I recognized her immediately as the grocery store owner's pretty daughter.

"I'm Lance," I said.

"I'm Cindy," Cindy said. "You're that boy that lives with Arthur, aren't you?"

"Yes," I answered.

"I don't like that man," Cindy said. "He dated my sister, and made her cry."

"He does that to a lot of girls," I replied.

"I guess so," Cindy said. "Hey, why can't I see you?"

"I'm tricky like that," I answered.

"Well you should be in there somewhere," Cindy said as she began peering past the debris that had fallen from the racks.

"Don't look for me, please," I said.

"Why not?" Cindy asked.

"I have problems with people looking at me," I answered honestly.

"I heard something about that," Cindy said.

"I'm also kind of magical," I said. "I blend into things . . . I dunno how to explain it."

"Wow," Cindy said. "I wish I could do that."

"No you don't," I said. "You're too pretty to hide."

Cindy giggled.

"Can you help me get free?" I asked.

"Of course," Cindy said. "It shouldn't be too hard. I'll just remove some of these cans and boxes."

Cindy went to work, and in no time at all she had the reduced the weight on top of me by almost half. I only needed a little more.

"Hey," Cindy said. "I can see you . . . well, kind of. I see your outline when you move. You're the same color as the floor and the shadows."

"Don't look, Cindy," I said. "Please?"

"Okay," Cindy said while turning her head away and going back to work on sliding boxes and lifting cans out of the way.

After a bit, I pushed against the racks. They lifted, and while Cindy had her back towards me, I bolted out of my temporary prison.

"Where'd you go?" Cindy asked upon hearing the noise of my escape, and failing to see me behind another rack.

"You did it," I said. "I'm free. I have to leave now, but don't leave your shop until someone you recognize comes to get you."

"Can we talk again?" Cindy said. "I think you're kind of neat."

I smiled under my mask.

"Yes," I answered as I ran for the door.

"Meet me in front of the church tomorrow night!" Cindy shouted behind me.

I ran past the sidewalk, across the street, and into the park. The battle was over, and by the looks of things, no major event had happened. The Black Knight's forces were simply beaten and forced to retreat. It must have been rather anti-climactic.

I took to the trees once I was inside the park. I saw wounded people everywhere, but I didn't see Merlin. Outside the park, the people of the town were running back and forth. I could hear them calling out the names of their loved ones.

Above all others, I heard one name in particular. A name I'd never before heard in Mill Ridge. People were calling for her over and over. I followed the calls, I was fairly certain I'd find Merlin looking for her as well.

Taking to the rooftops, and this time surveying my surroundings until I was certain I was safe, I ran quickly . . . at the far edge, I leapt into the sky, and ran down Main Street on the side of the road.

There were horses everywhere and bodies as well. I tried not to look at the bodies. I was afraid to see someone familiar, but despite my efforts, I still caught brief glances of their faces. They were unknown to me, and that made sense . . . reinforcements had obviously arrived. That would explain all the horses . . . geez, that would explain how we managed to win the battle.

Perhaps things weren't so anti-climactic after all.

I felt the panic rise up in my chest.

Was I too late to save Arthur?

Up ahead I saw a small raincloud form ten feet from the ground; I crossed the street and ran in that direction. Crossing the street made me nervous . . . the soldiers there occasionally noticed a blur of movement.

Once across, I leapt to the top of the closest shop, and made my way to the cloud. In no time at all, I saw Merlin, breathed a sigh of relief, and then caught myself. Arthur still wasn't safe.

"Merlin!" I shouted down at them as soon as I got close enough. Merlin was laughing before I called his name. Upon hearing my voice he became scary serious.

"Where is he?" Merlin asked.

"He's at the gymnasium," I answered. "He's been wounded. I had to leave them when I saw how many Death Reapers there were."

"Grab your horses," Merlin said to the people around him. "This isn't over yet."

I didn't wait for them, I was too panicked. Instead, I stayed on the rooftops, and made my way back to the high school gymnasium by way of the direct route.

Behind me, I could hear Merlin's voice telling people to hurry. I heard people shouting in return, and calling for horses. I heard the Gods of the Forest begin to howl.

Who was that girl underneath the raincloud?

I'd never seen anyone so absolutely beautiful in my entire life.

Could it be? Was she?

It had to be. Hers was the name people were calling . . . Gwen. It had to be her. Only Guinevere had a right to be that pretty.

How would Arthur react?

Arthur . . . I ran even faster. I ran and leapt until my heart felt as if it would burst inside my chest. As fast as I moved, the Gods of the Forest were even faster. I watched as ten of them ran through the streets below me. I tried to keep up, but I couldn't.

More Death Reapers had gathered by the back door of the high school. The Gods of the Forest fell upon them immediately. The sounds they made as their teeth tore through chain mail will haunt me to the end of my days.

I landed among them with no fear.

"Lead the way, Lancelot," Father Wolf said.

I rushed inside the dark hallway, pulling my knives from my back as I did so. I leap down the stairs, and noticed all the scorch marks from the fires. There were also burnt Death Reapers, but not nearly enough. Too many had made it to the gymnasium floor.

I heard the sounds of pounding metal from below. We'd made it in time. The Death Reapers hadn't broken through. Arthur and Wayne should be safely locked up inside the gymnasium.

"They're in the room at the end of this staircase," I whispered down to Father Wolf from the ceiling as he halted underneath me. "They're trapped."

Father Wolf smiled up at me. I couldn't hide from the Gods of the Forest . . . but strangely, they never seemed to bother me. I was okay with animals; they didn't set me off like people did.

I watched as the Gods of the Forest crept slowly down the stairs, and followed them. To my shock, there were even more Death Reapers banging upon the metal doors than I had expected, enough so that I was worried about my furry friends.

Could they handle so many?

The Gods of the Forest were tough, but there were probably at least two hundred Death Reapers between them and the gymnasium. The Death Reapers were also beginning to notice they had company.

If the Gods of the Forest were concerned about the number of enemy soldiers before them, they didn't show it. They charged straight into them with reckless abandon. Very quickly, they were lost in the thick of battle.

The blood however, wasn't lost. I could see it spray out and wash down upon the Death Reapers. Some of them were screaming. Others were still banging on the metal doors, but now they banged for a different reason.

I leapt to the ceiling, and crawled over the small army. From there I hurled my spikes and stars with deadly accuracy. I brought down enemy after enemy . . . but their numbers were too great, I heard a wolfish howl of pain, but I couldn't see what had happened in all the swirling bodies.

Another wolfish howl of pain echoed in my ears, I gritted my teeth and threw more spikes and stars. I wasn't doing enough . . . the great sprays of blood were no longer splashing out.

The Gods of the Forest were losing.

That's when Merlin and his new friends arrived. They charged down the stairs and flooded into the room. They hacked and stabbed. The Death Reapers screamed in pain. They begged for mercy . . . but mercy was not given.

I saw Father Wolf leap out of the struggling mass with a severed arm clenched in his jaws. He pounced over to a different section of the room, and the blood began to spray anew.

Merlin was at the edge of the room, using his magic to make a metal pipe, high on the wall turn into a serpent that struck repeatedly at the Death Reapers.

They tried to battle the metal serpent, but their blades couldn't puncture its skin. In turn, the pipe-snake's great fangs were coated in a deadly poison that bubbled the skin and melted the bones of any Death Reaper unfortunate enough to have been struck.

The beautiful woman was also in the thick of things. Guinevere . . . she was firing arrow after arrow. Her aim was incredible, and a thick man with grey and black in his hair and beard stood next to her striking down any Death Reaper foolish enough to try and attack her.

And then it was over.

The battle must have only lasted a few minutes.

It felt like a lifetime.

I watched silently as Merlin twisted his hands causing the metal doors of the gymnasium to fly open. The wizard didn't wait for anyone to let him in, he ran inside shouting.

"Where's Arthur?" Merlin demanded. "Where is he?"

I could only see a glimpse of the inside of the gymnasium from where I was clutching to the ceiling. I thought for a second that I might have seen Wayne, but I couldn't be sure, and if it was Wayne . . . where was Arthur? Why was Merlin still calling for him?

I looked towards Guinevere, and found her on the outskirts of the crowd, still next to her angry looking protector. She had the strangest look on her face as she watched the drama unfold.

Minutes ticked by on a clock that wasn't there.

The crowd of soldiers opened up, a floating bed sheet powered by magic, and pushed by Wayne came out of the room. Arthur was lying unconscious on top of it. Dellia was walking next to the impossibly stiff sheet holding Arthur's hand. I waited impatiently on the ceiling as the gymnasium emptied behind them. I dropped to the floor as the great room I was in cleared of soldiers.

I found a corner . . . and cried.

I thought I was alone.

I wasn't.

"What troubles you so terribly, young Lancelot?" Merlin asked in my general direction.

He must have come back for me.

"I failed him," I said. "I tried my hardest, but I failed."

"You failed no one," Merlin smiled. "Because of you, Arthur and all those people will live through the night."

"But Arthur . . ." I stammered. "He wasn't moving. He looked so pale."

"He was injured," Merlin said. "But he'll pull through. We just need to get his organs stitched up and sealed off. He has magic on his side after all."

"The sword," I said.

"No," Merlin said. "The scabbard is what protects Arthur. The scabbard is magical as well. It keeps the wearer from bleeding. Well, that is the legend at least. In reality, it does a bit more. It also keeps the organs functioning, and deadens the pain . . . to an extent."

"You're sure he'll be okay?" I asked.

"I'm positive," Merlin said. "You brought him help when help was needed. He wouldn't have held out much longer. You saved him."

I smiled under my mask.

"Where are they taking him?" I asked.

"They're taking him to the Sheriff's Station," Merlin answered. "They'll need to open him up in order to fix him up. He's in for a lot of pain tonight. I don't envy him, but tomorrow will be a new day."

I jumped to my feet.

"Going somewhere?" Merlin asked as he looked around the room.

"My job isn't over," I said. "While Arthur lives, I'll watch over him and protect him with my life."

"I'm very proud of you," Merlin said with a smile. "I have no doubt of your continued success."

In seconds, I had caught up with the mob of people. I moved past them quickly from above, all the while scanning for any signs of danger. When I reached Arthur, I noticed that he was talking quietly to his mother who still held his hand.

As we entered the town square, great cheers rang out from all those that stayed behind. The Gods of the Forest were nowhere to be seen. I knew they had been wounded . . . some of them might have even died. I watched them leave the basement of the high school, but they must have left before I caught up with everyone.

The celebration continued as alcohol was passed around and people were reunited with their friends and families. Despite the many lost lives, people were happy to be alive, and the newcomers mixed freely with what was left of the township.

Arthur would have loved the party.

I stayed outside the Sheriff's Station, and peered through the windows. Arthur was transferred to the large desk at the edge of the main room, and Dr. Talbert was summoned. When the doctor arrived, he was floored. The poor man just couldn't understand how Arthur wasn't bleeding out on the table. Merlin eventually arrived with flushed cheeks, and a drink in his hand. He explained about the scabbard, and forbid anyone to touch it.

The scabbard must stay on Arthur's side.

I watched as they cut him open and stitched whatever organs had been damaged. Everything was going great until Arthur woke up. He screamed his lungs out, but Dellia, Wayne and Merlin held him down so the doctor could work.

The celebrations outside continued despite Arthur's screams.

After they stitched up his insides, they cauterized the outside of the wound. Arthur screamed even louder than before. This time, the celebrations quieted down a bit . . . at least until Wayne came out, asked for a drink, and told everybody that Arthur would be okay.

Most of the partiers were the newcomers, and even though Arthur was a complete stranger to them they cheered at the news. Turning my attention back to the window, I saw Dr. Talbert pack up his supplies, and leave the Sheriff's Station after giving a few instructions to Dellia.

Arthur was quiet. I hopped to another window, and realized that he was sleeping . . . either that or he'd passed out. Dellia wanted to stay by his side, but I could hear Merlin urging her to go and aid the doctor. Arthur would be fine, but there were others that needed her skills.

Many of the people from the high school left the celebrations all around the town square, politely poked their heads inside the Sheriff's Station and asked about Arthur. Merlin would tell them that he'd be fine, and they'd smile and leave.

None of the fighting men from Mill Ridge came to check on him.

Shortly before dawn Guinevere stepped from the shadows of the forest and faced the Sheriff's Station. I could see the worry etched all over her beautiful face. She'd never met Arthur, but she seemed almost drawn to him. She stood in the shadows for the longest time. The leather armor had been replaced by a flowing white dress. It'd be easy to mistake her for an actress if it weren't for the dark red, hooded cloak she was wearing to fight the chill. The cloak made her appear otherworldly, like a princess out of a story book.

All she needed was someone to pull back the hood, and kiss her upon the lips. Would she go to Arthur? Would she steal a kiss if she did go to Arthur? I wanted her to go to him. I wanted her to love and care about him.

Guinevere took a step forward.

I held my breath.

She took another step ... and Wayne came wobbling down the street with a bottle of liquor in his hand, singing at the top of his lungs. Guinevere vanished back into the forest as if she'd only been a dream.

"Don't you have a family to go home to?" I asked angrily as Wayne approached the Sheriff's Station.

My voice startled him so badly he almost dropped his liquor bottle.

"Damn, kid," Wayne growled. "Why the hell do you keep doing that to me?"

"You make it easy for me," I said, laughing despite myself.

"Well," Wayne said slowly due to his inebriation. "The wife and kids are celebrating like everyone else. I just wanted to check on my buddy. Why are you here?"

"I protect Arthur," I said.

Wayne considered my words.

"You know ...," Wayne said. "You really saved our necks out there. Arthur is lucky to have you by his side. Hell, we're all lucky to have you around."

Wayne looked drunkenly around for me, but never once got close to my actual location. I didn't help matters by moving around either.

"Thank you," I said.

"Is he awake?" Wayne asked.

"Not yet," I answered.

"Well," Wayne grumbled. "I'll drop him off a bottle anyway. He'll appreciate it when he wakes up. I imagine he's gonna be sore as a mother fucker. Excuse my language."

Wayne went inside, and accidentally slammed the door against the opposite wall. Merlin came out of the back room, and before the door closed ... I saw a suit of shining armor. Why did Merlin have a suit of armor in the backroom of the Sheriff's Station?

"Wayne," Merlin said. "Be quiet ... he's still asleep."

"Sorry," Wayne said in his loud booming voice. "I can't help being mighty."

Wayne laughed heartily and Merlin, who had been drinking himself, joined with him.

"Hey," Wayne said. "You're not old enough to drink."

Merlin laughed even harder.

"I can drink you under the table," Merlin said.

"Bring it on, nerd!" Wayne shouted.

"Shush," Merlin said. "We need to be quiet."

"Too late," Arthur said from his make-shift bed."

"Day-um, boy!" Wayne shouted. "You look like hell. No, you look worse than hell. You look like my ex-wife."

"You don't have an ex-wife," Arthur laughed.

"Oh," Wayne said.

"Hand over the bottle," Arthur said.

"Gladly," Wayne said walking over and handing Arthur the bottle.

"Dellia is going to have a fit," Merlin said with an evil laugh. "I'm going to tell her."

"Why would you tell her?" Wayne asked.

"So I can watch her yell at you," Merlin laughed.

"I have a lot of catching up to do," Arthur said before taking a chug.

The bottle was passed back and forth. Eventually, Arthur removed the belted sword and scabbard from his waist and tossed it to the side of the room so he could sit up, and drink easier. Merlin cringed at that one, but kept his mouth shut.

When the bottle was finished, another one mysteriously appeared. I felt the now familiar tingle against my body as the dawn grew closer and closer.

Very soon I'd have to leave.

The smells of cooking food and merry laughter flooded the town square. Children were playing just a little ways down the street. The new day was going to be a good one. I was anxious to see all the new people when they weren't covered in blood and mud.

An alarm horn sounded off in the distance.

Bedder and some other soldiers ran to the Sheriff's Station. Merlin and Wayne met them at the front door.

I glanced to the horizon . . . I had only a brief amount of time before the change.

"They're robbing the graveyard outside of town," Bedder announced to Merlin.

"Why would they do that?" Wayne asked.

"They steal corpses," Merlin answered. "Morgana uses the bodies of the recently deceased."

"That's where she gets her soldiers," Bedder said.

"Yes, Merlin said. "The bodies are just empty vessels that Morgana fills with the ruined souls of her vast army. Serving Morgana is an eternity of slavery."

"There are no recently deceased bodies in that graveyard," Bedder said. "And it's outside the town. We should just let them waste their time."

None of them noticed Arthur's face. The weary smile was gone, and a cold fury burned behind his gray eyes.

"How many are there?" Merlin asked.

"Roughly a hundred," Bedder answered. "Certainly not the entire army . . . but Sir Francis is there. He's over-seeing things."

"It's probably a trap," Merlin said. "That's the only thing that makes sense."

"Let them have the graveyard," Wayne said. "It's not like they can hurt anything. How'd you even find out about it?"

"Gwen has patrols outside of town," Bedder answered. "I have patrols inside of town. Her people relayed the information. They're ready to attack."

"No," Merlin said. "There's been enough fighting for the time being. A graveyard isn't worth the risk."

"My wife and child are in that graveyard," Arthur said in a low and dangerous voice.

The room became silent.

"Arthur," Merlin said. "We can't just . . ."

"My wife and child are in that graveyard," Arthur repeated.

Wayne was silent for once.

"You'd have us risk our people's lives . . . for corpses?" Bedder asked.

I honestly believe that if Arthur had been standing next to Bedder, he'd have killed him. That was how fierce his gaze was as he slowly turned in Bedder's direction.

"Coward," Arthur said.

"Says the man that ran," Bedder retorted.

"Hey now," Wayne interrupted. "You weren't with us. Arthur is no coward."

"So you say," Bedder said.

"Arthur," Merlin said. "I'm sorry. We can't risk it."

"I thought I was the king," Arthur said.

"It's not that simple," Merlin said.

"And good luck finding people to follow you," Bedder added. "Not after the way you behaved in this town."

Arthur's upper lip came up in a silent snarl.

"Gentlemen," Merlin said. "Let's take this conversation elsewhere. Arthur needs his rest, and this conversation is only distressing him."

"Merlin!" Arthur shouted as Merlin quickly shuffled the group out of the Sheriff's Station. "Damn you, Merlin!"

"I'm sorry, Arthur," Merlin said. "Try and get some rest. I'll check on you as soon as I can."

Nobody noticed but me. How could they? Arthur was in a rage, and Merlin was the last one out the door, but I saw Merlin's fingers wiggle . . . I saw the door to the back room slowly drift open.

Arthur swung his feet out of the bed.

He was muttering under his breath.

I looked to the horizon, and saw the first rays of the sun peeking out over the hills. My body was already changing . . . but I couldn't let Arthur do what I knew he was about to do.

I quickly ran around the building, dove through the front door, crossed the room, and threw myself in the small closet. Inside the closet it was dark and cool. It was the perfect place to wait out the hour of my humanity.

"Lance," Arthur said. "Is that you?"

"Yes," I answered through the closet door.

"You shouldn't be here right now," Arthur said.

I cracked the door slightly, and looked around the room as my body changed. Arthur wasn't even looking in my direction. His gaze was focused on the armor waiting just behind the open door.

"Arthur," I said. "You can't do this. You've been wounded, and you'll be outnumbered."

"That's my wife and child out there," Arthur growled as he shifted his gaze to the sword.

The sword.

Excalibur was ready. The blade was standing straight up, just waiting for Arthur to grab a hold of it.

"Be strong," I said. "Something's not right here. I think Merlin might have planned this."

"He wants a king," Arthur said as he stood up. "I'll give him a king . . . one that's covered in rivers of blood."

"That's not you talking," I pleaded. "That's Excalibur. The sword has been waiting for a moment like this."

Arthur entered the back room, and vanished from view. I called to him. I pleaded with him, but he was past the point of talking and my words fell upon deaf ears.

Long moments later, it wasn't Arthur that stepped out of the back room. Before me, was a figure of legend. Before me was a powerful knight whose sole purpose in life was battle. I could do nothing but watch as the knight strode powerfully towards Excalibur, and claimed it as his own. In the back of my mind, I could almost hear the sword sing out triumphantly.

I screamed out to Arthur. I tried to bring him back. I screamed, and screamed, and screamed . . . but Arthur was gone.

I couldn't go to him.

I couldn't defend him.

I was merely a child trapped in a closet, waiting for the first hour of dawn to pass him by. I cried, and pounded against the wooden door. Why couldn't he have waited for me? Why couldn't all this have happened an hour later?

If destiny truly wanted Arthur to play his part in this war . . . this wasn't the way to do it. The person that just left the Sheriff's Station was no king. He was a monster with blood red eyes.

❧ ARTHUR ❧

"We should just let them waste their time."

"It's not like they can hurt anything."

"A graveyard isn't worth the risk."

Their words echoed around inside my head after they left. My poor innocent wife and son, how could they not understand? How could they not realize what was happening? I couldn't allow this to continue.

My wife needed me.

My son needed me.

Excalibur was calling me.

You are the son of the dragon

I couldn't ignore the blade.

You are the great king

I couldn't take it. Its words penetrated every ounce of my being. It promised me victory. It promised me revenge. It made me powerful.

Let no enemy withstand your wrath

Lance was in the room. He was talking to me. I was talking to him, but it wasn't really me . . . not anymore.

Don your armor

Yes, the armor. The shining armor. I could see my reflection against its smooth surface. The armor would protect my body. A knight should have protection. A king should shine.

I didn't remember standing up or crossing the room, but there I was, standing before the armor in nothing but my underwear. The helmet was a menacing work of art, shaped like a dragon's head. It was like no medieval helmet I'd ever seen before.

I placed it on my head and my vision blurred. I closed my eyes, and when I opened them again, I was covered in armor with only vague memories of straps being pulled and buckled as if by invisible hands.

Enchanted

The sword knew. The sword would not abandon me. The sword was a part of me. The armor was enchanted. That was fine, I barely felt its weight, and my vision was almost perfect through the eye slits of the helmet. Hanging off my left shoulder was a red cape. In the center of the cape was a white circle with a red dragon.

This had been my armor in a past life.

I went back to the main room. Lance had gone temporarily quiet.

Take me up

Yes, I wanted the sword. I wanted to feel the silver wired grip in my armored hands.

Take me up

Excalibur was waiting for me. A surge of power entered my body at the first touch, I smiled underneath my helmet.

Never cast me away

Lance screamed for me as I exited the Sheriff's Station. I wish that I could say a part of me cared. I wish that I could say a part of me resisted Excalibur, but that would be a lie.

The sky was an eerie gray as the sun fought against the dark clouds of another gathering storm. Goliath was there waiting for me. How he'd known to come was beyond me and I didn't question his showing up. It felt too natural. Even the armor covering a large portion of his massive body felt natural. This is what was meant to happen all along. Why had I been so foolish in resisting?

A blood covered king

Yes, I'd show all of them how to deal with our enemies.

Goliath scratched at the ground, and made loud angry noises that seemed amplified coming from underneath the spiked plate mail on top of his head. His eyes were wide with fury as if he also sensed that my dead wife was about to be violated with putrid and evil magic.

"Are you ready?" I asked.

Goliath bucked up and beat his front hooves against an angry sky. Thunder boomed out, and lightning began to flash. I smiled once again.

People were shouting in the distance. I ignored them, and mounted my great and majestic steed. I believe Wayne and some others may have even rushed forward in an attempt to grab at the reins, but they were all too easily pushed aside as Goliath bucked up again and charged forward.

We trotted quickly down the street. People gathered on the sidewalks, but kept out of our way. As we reached the exit to the town square, we broke into a gallop just as the rain began to fall from the sky.

Hooves pounded against the asphalt of Main Street, and rain ticked off my armor in little pings of sound. Did I have thoughts? I must have, but it was hard to focus past the rage. Did I have a plan? Certainly not . . . I didn't need a plan, my enemy was weak. Their numbers meant nothing to me.

Out of Mill Ridge we rode. I knew shortcuts through the forest. Apparently, so did Goliath. I barely had to guide him at all. He was as hungry for battle as I was. The trails twisted and winded. The mud was thick and dangerous.

Goliath would not be stopped. Thick, furry bodies ran beside me through the forest not five feet away from the path.

Time flew by. Riding the great horse became natural, ducking under low hanging branches, and leaping over fallen tree's second nature.

At the end of the forest, through the trees . . . I saw them. I saw the Death Reapers. Some were standing guard. Others were digging. The cemetery was filled with their green fog, and they had a great wagon on which to pile corpses standing by. It was halfway filled with the defenders of Mill Ridge. In the distance, over a mile away was another wagon traveling to an unknown destination for hideous purposes.

Even in defeat they profited from our loss.

They must have gathered up our fallen even as they were forced to retreat. I'd make them pay. I'd make them suffer.

Goliath and I broke through the forest at a dead run, and entered the grass filled field before the cemetery. The yellow grass turned green as I passed. The Death Reapers took notice of my approach and those of them that had horses rode out to meet me.

I drew Excalibur from the scabbard at my hip. When had I strapped on the sword? I twirled it in my hand as I rushed to meet my enemy. Excalibur screamed with joy.

I met the first five Death Reapers in a crush of chain mail against plate. Our swords sang out, and our horses twirled. Excalibur drew blood, and the blade ignited.

Five riders fell from their horses, and Excalibur was blazing in blue flame.

"It's him!" The Death Reapers screamed. "It's Arthur!"

They hesitated.

I didn't.

I struck them down one after another. My sword was always in motion. Limbs flew, and shields were severed. Nothing stopped Excalibur.

To the left

I blocked a swing from an axe just in time. Then I threw a punch with my armored fist, and knocked the Death Reaper from his horse. Goliath spun, kicked out, and dropped another horse and rider.

After that, we plowed into the thick of them.

Merlin was correct. I had wandered into a trap. Sir Francis had another couple hundred Death Reapers hiding in the cemetery, and a large portion of them rode out to meet me. Did he really think I could be stopped?

Goliath pushed through and crushed more bodies beneath his great weight. Excalibur struck them down one after another. Swords and axes clanged against our armor, but they never pierced our skin.

The Death Reapers barely slowed us down, and those not killed in our passing soon fell to the Gods of the Forest who'd been following me since I left Mill Ridge. They were hungry for battle. They enjoyed the kill.

Would it be enough?

I had no idea. There was a pretty big chance that the numbers would overwhelm us sooner or later . . . but not before I killed Sir Francis.

Suddenly I was through the majority of them and at the entrance to the graveyard. Sir Francis, the Black Knight was waiting for me in a swirl of green fog. His sword was drawn, and he held it over his shoulder without a care in the world.

I was going to enjoy this.

Be careful

I entered the cemetery, and Sir Francis moved deeper inside. He was leading me somewhere, and I had a pretty good idea as to where. Behind me, I could hear the screams and growls of battle.

None of the Death Reapers still inside the cemetery came at me, but there were a lot of them, and they glared as I passed them by in search of their leader.

It didn't take long to find him either.

He stood waiting for me in a large square clearing by a pond. His sword was still over his shoulder. All around us were tombstones. Some of the Death Reapers were gathering to watch. I dismounted and entered the clearing.

I suppose I could have charged Sir Francis down, but I didn't want to do that. I wanted to show him that I was the better man. I was cold and calculating. I knew how to win a fight, and I held my rage in check. I wanted to beat him before I took his life. I wanted him to know he was about to die. How dare he enter these hallowed grounds.

"I knew you would come," Sir Francis said. "What better way to draw you out than going after your wife and child."

"You made a mistake," I said.

"That remains to be seen," Sir Francis said.

The day did its best to brighten, but the storm clouds cast a gray hue over everything. The soft rain made a continuous hissing sound as droplets sizzled against Excalibur's burning blade.

Take him

I walked forward, and tested the waters. Sir Francis snapped into action, and side-stepped out of my way. He moved unbelievable fast for such a large man. He circled behind me, and I turned to meet his attack but it never came.

"Is that the best you can do?" Sir Francis asked.

"Not even close," I answered.

"Show me your skills," Sir Francis demanded. "Give me a challenge."

"I intend to do more than that," I said.

Stop talking

I jabbed forward. Sir Francis struck out not at my body, but my blade. The power of his strike caused my arms to fly high in the air. I stepped backwards quickly and evaded his next move, which was a slice at my midsection.

"You move fast for a man in armor," Sir Francis said.

"I'm faster than you," I said.

"Never," Sir Francis said as he swung his blade at my head.

I blocked, countered and missed. This set off a series of strikes and counter strikes as the two of us moved all around the square.

He was a great swordsman.

The sounds of our swords connecting echoed throughout the cemetery. When we broke apart, each of us twirled our weapons in a show of skill meant to intimidate our adversary, and then we came at each other again.

He was prideful, and his pride was getting the best of him. He couldn't kill me. I was a far cry from the man he had so recently tried to murder.

I wasn't afraid of him.

Back and forth we went. He'd attack, and I'd counter. Neither of us were gaining ground, and neither of us were losing it either.

I made a mistake.

I stepped in too close, and Sir Francis was able to use his size and strength advantage against me. His grip on my right wrist was crushing. I yanked my arm away in response not expecting him to release me at the last moment.

I lost my balance, and before I could recover he swung his sword under my chin making my helmet fly from my head. I rolled out of the way as he attempted to finish me off with a downward stab that ended up piercing the ground instead of my flesh.

He'd opened my chin. I could feel the burn of the wound despite the lack of blood. That was unfortunate. Sir Francis gained some confidence, and attacked with a renewed fury.

He realized immediately that I'd never fought anyone with his size and strength, and he set about using both to keep me unbalanced.

It was all I could do to keep his swinging weapon away from me. I could no longer strike back; I could only defend as he rained down blow after blow with all his vast strength. His Death Reapers were cheering merrily, but they just didn't get it.

Sir Francis had all the advantages, but those advantages chip away at a person's stamina. I was more than happy to help him tire himself out, but I had to give credit where credit was due . . . he had more stamina than I had anticipated.

After what seemed an eternity, Sir Francis began to wheeze inside his helmet.

"Don't get tired, Sir Francis," I said. "I'll kill you if you do."

My taunts only served to enrage him. Sir Francis lifted his blade high in the air, took a step forward, and brought his blade down in an arc. I blocked it easily, sidestepped, came around behind him, and slashed deeply right behind his knee.

The Black Knight screamed out his rage, and I took a few steps away from him in case he decided to charge.

"Do you think your taunts and your pathetic strikes can bring me down?" Sir Frances shouted.

"I think I'm better than you," I said simply. "Sooner or later . . . you'll fall."

Both of us came at each other.

Sir Francis had lost a step or two, and he was limping badly on his injured leg. However, he was still a skilled opponent, and any skilled opponent that has spent years mastering his craft was always dangerous.

I didn't become overconfident. I kept my fury in check, and I relied on my skill. He struck out, and I blocked. I struck out, and Sir Francis blocked. Sometimes we sliced open air, and had to back quickly away before the other could take advantage.

My strikes were getting stronger and stronger. Sir Francis was slowing down. I appreciated that.

"It's coming, Sir Francis," I said. "Can you feel it?"

"Shut up and fight," Sir Francis said.

I cut him again. This time it was on the inside of his left arm. He pulled back just a little too slowly . . . and paid for it dearly.

That's when the Death Reapers that had been watching us fight decided to get involved. They charged in, and very suddenly I was the one in danger.

I swung and backed away in an effort to keep my enemies in front of me. It was difficult, there were a lot of them, but Excalibur helped. The warnings the sword gave me kept me alive. Those warnings were like eyes in the back of my head.

I twirled and danced at the head of the pin. One wrong move on my part, and I was a dead man. Worst of all, Sir Francis hadn't stopped his attempts on my life, and he was now free to swing away at me with wild abandon. I was in trouble. Sooner or later the hammer would drop.

I needed to kill the bastard before that happened.

She's coming

That one caught me off guard.

The sword was normally pretty helpful, but that wasn't helpful . . . that was downright distracting.

Who was coming?

I moved the fight among the tombstones, and Sir Francis and his Death Reapers followed me willingly. The tall headstones made it more difficult for them to surround me. They tried, but I managed to kill any of them that stepped out too far away from the group.

Sir Francis was a different story. Apparently he'd found his second wind, and decided to give up on the wild swings. Crossing swords with him was no longer quick. It was an elongated exchange that I couldn't afford with all the Death Reapers coming at me.

She's coming

Something was obviously bothering Excalibur, but if I didn't know who, "she" was . . . what could I do about it?

The Death Reapers got closer and closer. One of them managed to smack a mace against my ribcage, and the instant pain on my side told me that he'd broken some ribs. It was my turn to wheeze, and I did it proudly.

I pushed towards Sir Francis, it was now or never. A Death Reaper came from the side, and slashed me at the elbow. His blow was hard enough to cut through my armor, and it was a combination of impact, and cutting damage that caused my arm to go numb.

No.

No.

The word kept repeating in my head. I had failed. I had my chance, and I blew it. This was the second time I'd failed my family.

Without choice, I backed away. The Death Reapers surrounded me in a loose circle. I tried to place my back against a relatively tall tombstone, but I was blocked immediately.

She's coming

They all rushed me at the same time. I blocked and twirled. All their attacks dented and bounced off my armor except for a slight cut on the base of my neck. I struck out, overextended myself in an amateur move, and somehow lost my balance.

It should have been the end of me.

But I wasn't alone.

The Gods of the Forest leapt into the fray, and behind them came the armored knights. Their attack was ferocious and without mercy. It was the distraction I needed, and I rolled away from the center of the melee.

I came to a stop right before the edge of a four foot grassy hill. I stood up slowly and weakly. My legs trembled and the grass was wet. I lost my balance, and slid down the little hill, stopping only after my back collided with a short and stubby tombstone. Placing a hand on that tombstone, I used it to find my feet just in the nick of time. A Death Reaper had followed me, and I barely managed to avoid his dangerous downward swing.

Excalibur was still in my hand.

The rage still thundered in my heart . . . it was time to let it loose.

I was wounded but my wounds weren't incapacitating. I still had my great skill, and that skill coupled with all my rage gave me energy.

I smacked away the Death Reaper's next swing, and brought Excalibur right through his midsection . . . all the way through.

I ran back up the slippery slope, and immediately engaged another Death Reaper. He fared no better, and his head rolled down the hill in my wake.

I slashed and hacked, forcing my way to the front of the battle which had spread out amongst the graveyard. Sir Francis was fifty yards ahead of me, and I was rapidly closing in on him.

She's coming

I screamed out as I charged forward. Great gouts of blood sprayed into the air all around me. The knights that came to my aid began to notice my path of destruction. Despite their best intentions, they started to fall back away from me.

They feared me.

They feared my animosity.

They feared my deadliness.

Soon I was standing at the head of all of them. The Death Reapers recognized me as the biggest threat, and concentrated on bringing me down.

They were wasting their time. Merlin had arrived, and using his magic, he cleared a path for me all the way to Sir Francis. Death Reapers screamed as the ground below their feet burst as if from an explosion. Limbs flew in all directions, bodies landed all around me.

Those not blown up by Merlin met Excalibur.

She's coming

The Black Knight had moved away from his men. He'd gone to a place he never should have violated. The oak tree still provided shade over the two tombstones just like it had on the day of their funeral. The grass was green and becoming greener still as I approached. A bench was nearby. I'd never sat on it.

The piles of dirt of either side told me a story. Closer inspection brought tears to my eyes, and a great guttural scream to my throat.

"Do I have your attention?" Sir Francis asked from only ten feet away.

Yes, he did.

I charged, and swung low. Sir Francis blocked, but I was already in motion before he could recover. Excalibur cleaved deeply into his left arm, and Sir Francis screamed.

Maybe I smiled. Maybe I didn't . . . but I attacked. I came at him with a viciousness and carelessness that I would have considered ill advised at any other time. Back and forth we went. Some of my swings were wild and my sword sliced through tombstones. Sir Francis's attacks were feeble, easily swatted away as if they merely annoyed me.

In my rage, I was a different fighter. Sir Francis was unable to adapt. He stumbled, and I nailed him again across his back. Excalibur opened his rusty armor like a hot knife through butter. I could see the red begin to flow.

She's coming

Sir Francis threw handful of grass and dirt at my face, my reaction gave him the time he needed to get back to his feet. Out of the corner of my eye, I saw the Gods of the Forest, and all the knights gathering behind us. The battle was finished. Sir Francis would not escape.

I charged him greedily. He was mine. I didn't want anyone to interfere. Sir Francis barely dodged a killing blow. I came at him again. I was relentless. I wanted his death. I yearned for his death. My skill was forgotten. Excalibur was a club, and I used the great weapon to beat down my enemy.

I got closer and closer. I pushed harder and harder, anxious to steal his life before anyone tried to help me. Sir Francis began to beg and plead. He asked for quarter. No quarter was given. I just kept hammering him down.

She's coming

Sir Francis fell to his knee. With a great scream I moved to take his head, and as I swung he went into action.

I'd fallen into his trap.

He'd used my rage against me. He allowed me to make mistakes in an effort to draw me in close and as soon as my guard was completely down, and all my skill forgotten . . . he struck.

Stupid man.

He spun out of the way, came up behind me, and drew back for a blow that would surely pierce my heart. He never realized my swing wasn't truly meant to take his head. I expected him to move. I knew he was playing me for a fool.

In a great arc I swung Excalibur in a swirling pattern, and then twisted completely around before the arc reached its crescendo. The Black Knight's sword arm was severed at the elbow.

Sir Francis . . . the Black Knight was a great swordsman. I was a master.

I paced in front of him while he stumbled in agony clutching his gushing stump, and screaming inside his helmet. I waited for him to regain his composure, and when he did . . . I took his left leg above the knee.

I listened to him scream some more. It was the sweetest music I'd ever heard.

She's coming

"Where are they?" I asked.

"They're gone!" Sir Francis screamed. "When next you see them, they will be polluted by the darkest magic you can imagine!"

I watched the rain mix with his blood. For some reason, I was mesmerized by the sight of the two liquids meeting, and the small puddles forming around his stumps.

"Where are they?" I asked in a calm voice I no longer recognized as my own.

"To you," Sir Francis whispered. "They are lost forever."

I took his head with a roar and an explosion of violence. I watched as the helmet rolled away, and the head of the Black Knight fell out of its metal encasement.

His brown hair was long, filthy, and covered in lice. Maggots festered in the great gash between his right eye and left cheekbone. It was the wound that surely stole the life from the body's original inhabitant. His mouth was forever frozen in a grimace of pain, showing his rotted teeth.

How terribly he must have suffered . . . and for that, I was glad.

She's coming

My rage wasn't satiated. Something inside of me must have broken. I found no solace in my enemy's death. Old wounds had been opened. Future scars began to fester.

I snapped.

I swung my magical sword at the tombstones around me. They cleaved into pieces. I swung at the wet grass around me; great swathes of dirt flew into the air. I screamed. Over and over again I screamed out to an audience that didn't dare interfere.

The battle was won. The outcome decided. We were triumphant, but I found no solace. I found no comfort. My wife and child. My poor, poor wife and child . . . taken from me, stolen from me. Defiled. Lost once again.

I screamed out my rage.

I went to their graves. I had to see them again as if I were wrong; as if I were mistaken the first time I saw them empty.

They were still empty.

Wayne approached me and put his hand upon my shoulder. I recognized him through his armor before he even took off his helmet.

"Arthur," Wayne said. "I'm sorry. I'm so very sorry."

"Take your hand off of me," I said.

"Wait a second, buddy," Wayne said. "I know it's tough. I know you're hurting . . . but let's think about this for a second."

I smacked him away, and watched as he fell to the ground.

"You have no idea!" I shouted.

Bedder was next. He did his best to restrain me, and ended up unconscious on the ground. More of them came after that. All of them fell beneath the weight of my anger.

"None of you have any idea!" I shouted to the crowd behind me. "You don't understand!"

I turned from them. I faced the empty graves.

"Where are they?" I shouted. "Where are they?"

Arthur

She's here

I dropped to my knees. I screamed out my sorrow and rage. Why this? Why them? How could anyone be so cruel?

Vengeance.

That's what I wanted. I wanted to track them down. I wanted them to suffer. I wanted all the Death Reapers to suffer. I would find them. I would hurt them . . . I would . . .

Silence.

Peace.

A stillness all around me.

A presence behind me.

It was foreign and familiar all at the same time.

I stood and turned, and there she was.

A red cloak covered her, keeping her warm despite the rain, but I could still see her face despite the hood. I could see the short dark blonde hair. She was beautiful. No, she was breathtaking. Her blue eyes were the color of the sea after a storm. I could swim in those eyes for an eternity.

My world suddenly came to a standstill.

I had never seen her before in my life, but my heart and soul recognized her immediately. She was all that I ever wanted. She was all that I ever needed. She was life. She was the future. She was an end to the pain. She was an end to the empty nights.

She had no words, but I could see the sorrow in her face as she looked at me. I could see the blame. She hated herself for not finding me sooner. Tears were coming from those gorgeous eyes. I wanted to pick her up. I wanted to take her someplace safe, and tell her that everything would be okay.

I didn't.

Instead, I swam in those eyes. I dreamed of a better place, I dreamed of a place in which only she and I existed.

Her soul spoke to me, and my soul answered. Together, they talked about finding each other again. They talked about how difficult things had been. They spoke of losses and pain. They cried and offered solace to one another.

Finally, when I could no longer handle the waves of emotion rolling between us, the connection was broken. My heart was beating inside my chest. Her hand came up as if to caress my face.

"Stay away from me," I said before walking away.

❧ GWEN ❧

Who was he?

Why was I drawn to him?

I already knew the answer.

I caught glimpses of him as they pulled him away from the gymnasium. He was injured, but he'd survive. Of course he'd survive. Destiny was upon the both of us. I wanted to view him with an almost scientific detachment . . . but something was drawing me in closer.

Something had a hold of my soul.

Forget destiny . . . this was different. This was something unexplainable, something I'd never felt before.

I didn't like it one bit.

Celebrations broke out inside the town square as soon as we arrived. We'd been victorious. I wanted to join them. I tried to join them. Even those that had lost loved ones came out . . . but something distracted me.

I changed out of my armor into a white dress covered by a red cloak that kept the chill away from my bones. I joined the festivities. I joined the celebration of life, but something was nagging at me. A pull, that's the only way I know in which to describe the feeling.

I felt a pull.

When no one was looking, I slipped into the woods. I had never been in this town before, but I was guided by an unseen hand. Before I knew it, I was at the edge of the forest and staring at the Sheriff's Station.

I wanted to go to him. I wanted to see him. I almost did . . . but then the big guy appeared. He had to be a friend, a very close friend. He was singing loudly and horribly. I watched as he headed towards the Sheriff's Station, and then I regained control over myself and slipped back into the woods.

My heart hammered as I made my way back to my people. I felt as if I were losing something precious. It was hard to walk away.

Reynolds met me in the forest.

"Where've you been?" Reynolds asked.

"I went for a walk," I said.

"You shouldn't be alone," Reynolds said.

"I'm fine," I said. "Thank you for worrying about me, but I'm fine."

"Then come, Milady," Reynolds said. "There's wine a plenty. We've saved the day. It's time to celebrate."

"Just one glass," I said. "I need to be alone. I . . . have . . . oh, I'm just being stupid."

Reynolds looked at me with concern in his eyes.

"I think I understand," Reynolds said with a smile.

"Then you know more than I do," I grumbled.

I was given a house to sleep in, and I took full advantage of the kind offer after sending out patrols and making other arrangements. The sun was just about to rise as I climbed the stairs looking for a nice comfortable bed. I yawned loudly, and heard a horn sound out in the distance.

No time for rest.

I ran back down the steps and out the front door of the house. Reynolds was riding up as I mounted my horse.

"What is it?" I asked.

"The Black Knight and his Death Reapers are still in the area," Reynolds answered. "They're raiding a cemetery."

"Does Merlin know?" I asked.

"A man named Bedder and some others just went to inform him," Reynolds answered.

Would Merlin want to continue the attack? Under normal circumstances it'd probably be a good idea, but everyone was tired, and I'd already sent out half my forces to retrieve the people that we'd left behind.

I thought over the situation, and made up my mind. It wasn't going to be a popular decision, but it was the best option.

"I'd like to attack," I said.

"Milady?" Reynolds asked.

"Our people will be traveling through this area," I said. "I don't want Death Reapers roaming the forests. I'm thinking of their safety."

"Then we should meet with Merlin," Reynolds said. "I'm sure he'll be able to help."

The ride to the town square was interrupted by more rain, and a knight on horseback. Everyone made way for him as he galloped down Main Street in his shining armor. His red cape flew out behind him.

I knew who he was instantly.

I was a witness to something . . . incredible.

"We must hurry," I told Reynolds.

"Why?" Reynolds asked.

"Our king has gone off to war," I answered.

The town square was a buzz of activity. Some of the people that lived in the town weren't interested in helping Arthur. Others were all for it. I volunteered myself and my men. Merlin told me to stay behind, but he'd take my men.

"Now is not the time to be sexist," I scolded. "Where my men go, I go."

Merlin stopped barking orders for a brief moment and looked at me.

"You have no idea how important you are," Merlin said. "If anything happens to you . . . hope is lost. You'll stay behind. You'll stay safe."

"You forget yourself, Merlin," I said. "I take orders from no one. Do you want my help or not?"

Merlin gave me a dirty look. It would have been humorous coming from a normal teenager, but you could see the age and wisdom behind his eyes, and that gave the look gravity.

"Suit yourself," Merlin said. "But I have no proper armor for you."

"None of my soldiers have proper armor," I said. "I'm used to . . ."

Merlin wasn't listening. Instead, he punched his fists right into the street. He reached down up to his elbows, felt around, and heaved as if he were pulling something heavy from the ground.

Up and down the street, the pavement began to crack and break apart. People ran to the sidewalks as if the earth were caving in under our feet. Merlin ignored them all, and kept pulling.

Shining suits of armor erupted from the ground.

"Find the one that belongs to you!" Merlin shouted. "You are the future knights of Camelot. Prepare yourselves for combat."

"There aren't enough for everyone," I said.

"Not everyone can be a knight," Merlin said. "The others are foot soldiers, and we have more than enough chain mail for them."

"How are you going to decide who gets what?" I asked.

"I'm deciding nothing," Merlin answered. "Old positions are being returned. The armor will choose the knight. They've been enchanted."

His words were true. My men went to the armor as if it belonged to them. They'd walk around until they found the suit that seemed to want them, and begin buckling it on.

The armor seemed to help them whenever they got confused.

Merlin whistled, and saddled horses came forward in search of riders. I watched in awe, totally caught up in the magic of what was going on all around me. When I finally came back to my senses, I turned and saw Reynolds pulling an armored glove over his hand.

"You too?" I asked.

"It's mine, Milady," Reynolds smiled. "I remember this armor. I remember the pride I felt wearing it. I was meant for this."

Merlin came over to us.

"We'll ride hard," Merlin said. "The distance isn't great. We'll have to leave those without armor and a horse behind. The Gods of the Forest are already following him."

The Gods of the Forest frightened me. They were the first magical creatures I'd ever encountered after the Death Reapers. They weren't pretty. They were downright ugly, but without them the town of Mill Ridge would never have withstood the forces of the Black Knight long enough for me and mine to arrive.

They were on the side of the good guys.

When everyone was armored and mounted up, Merlin sent them off. It was a sight to see. Forty armored knights charging down a broken road in their shining armor as the rain fell and the thunder boomed out around them. I held back to take in the visual. Merlin came up beside me. Both of us were sitting on our horses.

"It's like a scene from a movie," I said.

"No," Merlin said. "It's our future."

A pretty older woman came running towards us.

"My son!" She cried. "Merlin what happened?"

"We'll bring him back, Dellia," Merlin said.

"He's injured," Dellia continued. "How can he possibly . . . Oh my God . . . are you . . . can it be?"

She was looking right at me. Was I frightening her? It didn't appear so, but the shocked look on her face as she stared at me was alarming.

"Dellia," Merlin said calmly. "This is Gwen. Her and her people have come to help us."

"Yes," Dellia said collecting herself.

"If you'll excuse us," Merlin said. "Arthur is in need of our assistance."

We rode hard after that, easily catching up to our knights which mostly consisted of my men. Merlin led the charge. He knew where to go and he knew the quickest way to get there.

The paths in the woods we took were a luxuriant green. The type of green I'd never seen before. A part of me wondered if Arthur had caused this. The closer we got to him, the faster the knights rode.

Before I knew it, we had broken through the forest, and entered an open field of green. Ahead of us, the Gods of the Forest were tearing into a large group of Death Reapers. As one, our knights drew their swords, spurred their horses and charged into the green fog.

"Stay back, my Queen," Merlin said as he pulled back and rode next to me. "Let the knights do their duty."

I smiled at Merlin, and spurred my horse.

I charged to the side of the advancing knights. When I'd passed the lot of them, I cut to the right and rode in front. I was not a meek woman that needed to be protected. I was an archer. I was a warrior.

I would lead my men into battle.

I pulled free my bow. I notched an arrow, and I let it fly. My aim was true. I pierced the throat of a Death Reaper, and watched him fall. After that, I let more arrows fly. My aim was without fail, but before I knew it the fighting became too close for comfort.

Death Reapers were grabbing at my legs as I spurred my horse and urged her away from direct confrontations. I wanted to ride up and down the sides of the battle. I wanted to pick my shots, and help my knights.

Reynolds was next to me.

He swung and claimed lives. He was incredible with a blade. Before I knew it, I was free. I shot more arrows. I took more of them down, and made them pay. The Gods of the Forest did their job as well. Steel slapped against steel, and teeth and nails raked through chain mail.

In moments, the battle was over, and we headed into the graveyard.

Merlin dismounted from his horse at the gates. The green fog was thicker in the cemetery; we couldn't see how many Death Reapers we were about to face . . . but none of us considered stopping.

The Gods of the Forest gathered around Merlin, and he whispered into the largest animal's ear. The knights dismounted from their horses, and joined him as he entered the sacred ground of the cemetery.

I waited at the gates as my knights filed inside; making sure that nothing came at us from behind. Before I could regain my position in front another battle broke out. From what I could see from the back, there was a large number of Death Reapers attacking Arthur, but before they could strike their fatal blow . . . we arrived.

Chaos.

Things happened too fast. We had no time to plan. I had no time to properly lead, but the armor was solid. Only five of my men fell to the ground before the battle was over.

I shot arrows when I could, but without armor and no horse . . . I couldn't push my way to the front lines.

The Gods of the Forest spread out. The knights spread out. Reynolds was by my side once again as we rushed forward.

I saw Arthur clearly for the very first time.

He was alive!

My heart skipped a beat!

I watched him butcher the Black Knight.

I watched him take apart an unbeatable warrior.

After that, he lost his mind.

He swung out against his friend. He swung out against the man named Bedder. Others tried to restrain him, and they fell to the side as well.

Arthur screamed out his rage and frustration. He yelled at the gathered knights, he fell to his knees in front of the empty graves.

A moment of calm.

I stepped forward. Reynolds tried to stop me. He didn't want me anywhere near the crazed man, but Merlin appeared in front of us.

"Let her go," Merlin whispered.

To my surprise, Reynolds did as he asked. The rain was still coming down, and I raised my hood as I stepped away from the crowd.

Not a word was spoken. The only sounds heard were the rain drops hitting the grass, and the many horses whinnying in the distance.

The world went into slow motion.

He stood and turned as I approached.

Handsome wouldn't be enough to describe him. Up close, he was beyond handsome with his grey eyes, and reddish-blonde hair. I took him in. I absorbed him. His whiskers were on the verge of becoming a beard. He was in pain, but he fought on despite his injuries.

I knew him.

I'd never before seen his face, but I knew him. Beyond the handsome exterior, I saw the sadness, and it broke my heart. I understood him. I knew what he needed . . . but I hesitated. If I offered what he needed, I myself would be in danger.

And then it happened.

I gasped out loud as our very souls broke free and joined together. They spoke novels to one another. They understood one another. Our souls were prepared to wait. They were prepared to be patient.

I once again knew the unbridled joy I'd known as a little girl. I knew the happiness I'd known before I'd lost my mother. I understood what this world could become. I understood what my future could become.

I tried to touch his gorgeous face.

And he roughly broke the connection.

"Stay away from me," Arthur said as he walked away.

I watched him go.

Handsome to a fault, strong beyond words . . . but I saw the pain in his eyes. I listened to his soul. Arthur was damaged. Arthur was broken . . . but the spark was still inside of him. It merely needed to be ignited.

I collapsed to my knees on the wet grass, and cried loudly. I didn't care who saw me. The pain I'd witnessed was more than I could bear. Reynolds wrapped his arm around me, not understanding what had happened but worried nonetheless.

"Father Wolf!" Arthur shouted as he walked away. "I need you."

The largest of the Gods of the Forest moved by me, and Merlin stopped him.

"Do what needs to be done," Merlin said.

"Are you asking me to do what I think you're asking me to do?" Father Wolf asked.

"I'm telling you that Arthur won't recover from this day until what he's lost has been given peace once again."

Father Wolf went to Arthur, and two of them began to argue. I couldn't hear the entire conversation, but I understood that Arthur was sending them out to recover the bodies of his wife and child. Father Wolf was willing, but he wanted the pack to go alone. Arthur would only slow him down.

Merlin had to get involved, and once he did, the matter was quickly settled. The Gods of the Forest took off in pursuit of the corpse-stealing Death Reapers.

Arthur paced back and forth in the rain, while the rest of us erected up small tents in which to wait things out.

"Milady," Reynolds said. "Perhaps we should get you out of this weather. You need your rest. Let me take you back to Mill Ridge."

"I want to see what happens," I said distantly.

The Gods of the Forest came back six hours later. Behind them, they pulled a carriage with two caskets, one for an adult and one for a child. Arthur ran immediately to the caskets. His touch was gentle as he placed his hand on first one and then the other.

"Everyone can leave now," Arthur said.

The knights began to gather up their supplies. I came forward from my tent to argue. It wouldn't be safe to leave him all alone in a cemetery.

Merlin came forward and kept me from speaking out.

"Look to the trees," Merlin said and pointed. "Arthur will be protected."

I saw a flicker of movement where Merlin was pointing. Something was alive in there.

"What is it?" I asked.

"His name is Lancelot," Merlin said.

"Will he be enough?" I asked.

"The Gods of the Forest will stay behind as well," Merlin answered.

Reluctantly, I left.

It wasn't until the next day that Arthur returned to Mill Ridge. I watched him slowly ride down Main Street from the high bedroom window of my borrowed home. He looked tired, and empty. How could he not? He'd just buried his wife and child for the second time.

My heart went out to him.

"Will you be staying?" Merlin asked from the doorway, startling me.

"Yes," I answered. "I'm following a dream."

"Very good," Merlin said. "He'll need you."

"I don't think I can help him," I said turning back to the window in order to catch a final glimpse of Arthur meeting up with his mother and his friend Wayne, before the trio vanished behind a group of shops in the distance.

"You already have," Merlin said. "It was your presence that released him from the grip of Excalibur. Just the sight of you brought him back."

"Then he told me to stay away from him," I said.

"Be patient with him," Merlin said causing me to turn around and face him once again. "He needs help finding his way back."

"I've heard those words before," I said.

Merlin only smiled.

"My father spoke them to me after he died," I continued.

"The magic inside of you can occasionally bridge the gap between life and death," Merlin said. "You have great power. Very soon we must begin your training. Two wizards are better than one."

❧ EPILOGUE: ❧

TEN DAYS LATER,

MERLIN

The boy was angry. No, that was an understatement . . . the boy was in a rage. I'd need to be guarded. I'd need to be prepared in case one of his lethal spikes flew towards me.

I didn't think that would truly happen, but it paid to be prepared.

"You set him up," Lancelot growled from a dark corner of the Sheriff's Station which was rapidly becoming my home. "You knew how he'd react. You knew the Death Reapers would go after the graves."

I let him rant. I let him rave. He'd been doing it for the last hour. The same meaning colored in different phrases and mixed with various and colorful curse words that he wasn't quite used to using despite spending so much time with Arthur.

"Can I speak?" I asked.

Nothing.

"I'll take that as a yes," I said. "I knew the Death Reapers would do something. I knew they'd strike out at him."

"He could have died!" Lancelot shouted.

"Yes," I admitted. "That's why I made sure his armor was at the ready. That's why I made sure that Goliath was at the ready. I cannot control Arthur. Arthur is a king, and I am merely an advisor. I do what I can to keep him safe . . . but occasionally; he will take matters into his own hands.

"I wasn't there for him," Lancelot said. "The sun was coming up. I wasn't there for him."

"I know," I said. "Even you have your limitations, but all has ended well enough. We won the day. The Black Knight has been defeated. Arthur has become a hero. The Gods of the Forest recovered the bodies of his wife and child. Why are you still so upset?"

"What place do I have?" Lancelot asked.

"You are Arthur's protector," I answered. "While you live, he will live."

"I'm not enough," Lancelot said.

"You're the best we have," I said. "Listen to me very carefully. This war isn't over, and Arthur still hasn't claimed his rightful place. He'll need you. He'll stumble and fall. Keep him safe as best you can, and always understand . . . I make choices for the betterment of this world. I think not of the individual. I think only of humanity itself."

"So you don't think of Arthur?" Lancelot asked.

"In the very depths of my heart . . . I love him dearly," I said. "But the world is what I seek to save, not the individual. That's why you're here. You can think about Arthur. You can keep him safe, and that leaves me free to think of the world."

"Someday," Lancelot said. "You and I may become enemies."

"No," I said. "That will never come to pass. I'll anger you. I'll distance Arthur . . . but I'll never be an enemy."

A flutter of movement, and Lancelot was gone. I would have wondered what had taken him so long to confront me, but I already knew he had a girlfriend. Word gets around quickly in a small town.

To be young and in love was an amazing thing. A beautiful thing . . . and love would save us all. Love would be the force that conquered Morgana. Love would destroy her. No evil could stand before love, and that was Arthur's greatest weakness. He loved too greatly. Love could bring him to his knees. He refused to accept his destiny, he refused to play his part, because that would require him to love once again, and if Arthur loved again . . . he could also lose once again.

I heard movement outside my home.

Guinevere had finally come to call upon me. Her lessons were about to begin. She was our salvation just as much as Arthur was. She would bring hope to all of us. Poor Guinevere . . . she had only the vaguest notion of what her life would soon become. She was destined to be the love of Arthur's life. She was destined to become a queen. But before any of that came to pass . . . she must first learn how to use her abilities.

The forces of Morgana would someday return.

For now however, the trying times were over. We were tested and bruised, but we overcame and persevered. Now we were preparing ourselves for the future. Guinevere's people fit in perfectly. Mill Ridge was no longer called Mill Ridge . . . This area; this town was now known only as Camelot.

I alone understood what the future would hold.

Our darkest times were not yet beyond us.

Unimaginable horrors were headed our way.

A king would claim his throne.

A love would defy all odds.

Welcome to the Camelot Wars.

This is only the beginning!

ABOUT THE AUTHOR

MICHAEL CLARY was raised in El Paso, Texas. He is the author of The Guardian Interviews (The Guardian, The Regulators, and Broken). He is an occasional practitioner of Mixed Martial Arts, and collects bladed weapons of various types. Before he wrote novels, he wrote and directed Independent films. Currently, Michael is living in Temescal Valley, California with his wife, family, and three Pit Bulls. You can follow him at www.michaelclaryauthor.com

CPSIA information can be obtained at www.ICGtesting.com
Printed in the USA
BVOW02s2204130815

413341BV00001B/2/P